MARK OF THE HUNTRESS

LISA CASSIDY

Tate House

National Library of Australia Cataloguing-in-Publication entry

Creator: Cassidy, Lisa, 2021 - author.

Title: Mark of the Huntress

ISBN: 978-1-922533-04-3

Subjects: Young Adult fantasy

Series: Heir to the Darkmage

First published 2021 by Tate House

Cover artwork and design by Jeff Brown Graphics

PROLOGUE

A'ndreas,

        Attached is the information you wanted. There really wasn't much recovered back then, just burned scraps, but I asked one of the Hub's clerks to summarise the remnants for you, as per below. It's from a journal, apparently, so there's probably a little more dramatic licence taken than you'd like.

    Next time please chase down your own research. I already have too many things demanding my attention when I travel to Carhall, I don't have time to spend in dusty archives doing favours for you.

    Regards,

    Councillor Rawlin Duneskal

    Mage Council representative to Karonan

SUMMARY OF BURNED REMAINS.

    We take them as babies.

    Small infants handed over to us by willing—and sometimes not so willing—parents to stern-faced soldiers. They are transported—

    ...

    We place each new infant in a wooden crib in a room filled with rows of identical wooden cribs. Nurses make sure the babies are fed and changed when they need to be. During the day, they are removed from the cribs and left there to roll, crawl, or toddle about the room. They are taken outside for an hour or two of sunshine and fresh air each afternoon.

...

Any physical or other kind of affection is strongly discouraged. The children are never kissed or hugged. Never spoken to outside the bare necessities of issuing instructions. When—

...

...are able to walk un-aided, they are removed from the first room and placed in another. This one with narrow beds and windows. They are given names, then, so they can respond when being individually called upon. We never—

...

—when their training started. The children are woken an hour before dawn by a loud bell and a firm instruction to get up and dress. They return to their beds an hour before midnight. The long day in between is filled with learning. Affection of any sort continues to be discouraged. Any nurse or minder seen violating this rule is instantly—

...

At sixteen years of age, those that have survived the many tests and trials along the way—we find by this age usually only half of the children remain— are considered ready. They are dressed and equipped and sent away to fulfil their purpose.

...

When he was still alive, he occasionally visited, that eerily remote expression of his taking in the rectangular room and the tiny children within it. Assessing. Thinking. No doubt working them into his plans.

After his death, we kept taking the babies. Kept planning, preparing.

,,,

We have been discovered! The recent disaster has doomed us. Such ability to... was not supposed to be possible. I do not think—

End of summary of burned remains.

CHAPTER 1

Lira moved quick-footed through the dark library. Lonely books and rolls of parchment sat neatly stacked side by side on endless rows of shelves that towered above her. The air was still. The silence was heavy with a sense of emptiness, abandonment.

Exactly as it had been that night.

Only this time the air wasn't so cold that her breath frosted in front of her face and there was no terrifying rattling sound echoing through the darkness, like chains being dragged inexorably across the floor.

Lira paused anyway when she reached the edge of the study atrium near the main library entrance, years of living on the dangerous streets of a port city having trained her to always study an open space before entering it. The tables were draped in silvery moonlight from windows high above. Some of the chairs were askew, and scraps of forgotten parchment lay scattered under a centre table. An initiate had left their brown robe hanging off the back of one chair.

It was as she'd expected. Lira had waited until it was nearer dawn than midnight before venturing down the side stairwell from her dormitory level, wanting to be sure the earlier party to welcome back the kidnapped students had finished. Tired initiates and apprentices would seek their beds, not the library.

Her staff hung loose but ready from her left hand. The nightmare of the past few weeks might be over, but she'd never walk into this library unarmed ever again.

Confident the area was clear, Lira set off across the atrium, weaving quickly between tables and chairs, wanting to reach the cover of the shadowy stacks on the opposite side as soon as possible. She did her best to ignore the sharp tug of pain in her left calf and the echoing ache in her right side. Finn A'ndreas and his apprentice healers had done a good job on her multiple injuries, but everything still felt sore when she pushed herself. The stairs down into the library had caused multiple registers of complaint from her still-healing body.

Once she reached the opposite side, her shoulders relaxed, and she slowed her pace, all senses alert for anything that would warn her that she wasn't alone. But even on a regular day, nobody came to the library this late, including its master, Finn A'ndreas.

Success tonight was vital.

Her position within Underground, a secretive rebel group run by the Shadowcouncil, wavered on a precarious edge. They'd claimed to have kidnapped her along with the other apprentices to maintain her cover with the Mage Council... but Lira still couldn't shake the look of triumph on Lucinda's face when Lira had been strapped to that table to be experimented on. It was seared into her memory.

They'd wanted something else from her. And even though she'd been returned alive to Temari Hall along with the others, Lira hadn't made the mistake of thinking her position within the group was as secure as it had been. She had openly flouted Lucinda in her efforts to survive her kidnapping, and the Shadowcouncil member wasn't the type to forgive or forget disloyalty.

The only way Lira could think to regain their trust was to complete the task they'd set her before her kidnapping—stealing a letter that Councillor Rawlin Duneskal had written to A'ndreas. If she could get her hands on that, then she could present it to Greyson, the local

Underground cell leader, as proof of her contrition and ongoing loyalty to the group.

Of course, she was gambling on the fact that Underground didn't have good enough access to Temari Hall to have accomplished the task in her absence. But Lira was accustomed to gambling with bad odds.

And *if* she was successful, she could not only continue spying on Underground for the Mage Council, but more actively help the council destroy them.

Lucinda would burn for what she'd done to Lira.

And if Lira earned the trust and respect of the council in the process, even better. It would only make achieving her ultimate goal that much easier. A seat on the council. All of them seeing *her* rather than her grandfather.

The door to A'ndreas' office was closed and locked, but that was no trouble for a telekinetic mage who'd learned to pick locks far trickier than this one by the age of eight. Lira slipped inside and closed the door behind her.

She waited the few moments it took for her eyes to adjust to the dim interior—but even then she could only just make out the piles of parchment and books stacked haphazardly on the desk. It was too dark to make out what any of them were.

Reluctantly, she summoned just enough of her magic to bathe her hands in a violet glow, then began methodically going through what was on the desk. She didn't want to touch anything she didn't have to. As chaotic as it looked, Finn A'ndreas was a very clever man, and she doubted he didn't have some system for managing everything in here. Or a way of noticing if it were different than how he'd left it.

One scrawled note near the centre of his desk caught her eye—her name was written on it, along with the students who had been kidnapped with her. It looked as if he'd been musing on the reasons they'd been taken, or maybe just trying to figure out what had happened to them by putting his thoughts to words. Next to Haler's name, he'd scrawled a '*why*' with lots of question marks after it. But what made Lira freeze was what was written beside her name.

'*Who is her father? Is he connected?*'

Lira had no idea who her father was, only that he'd been someone her mother knew during the time she'd lived in Karonan, and that he'd had no interest in being a parent. Lira didn't even know if he'd been aware the mother of his child was the Darkmage's daughter.

Lira doubted it. Her mother had been so secretive about her identity. And surely her father would have taken more interest if he'd known he'd fathered an heir to Shakar Astor? Especially if he was involved with Shakar's old network. No, A'ndreas was on the wrong track. Which didn't help her at all.

A faint creak outside—just one of the shelves settling—broke Lira from her daze. Getting lost in A'ndreas' musings about her father wasn't what she was here for. Her father had never been a factor in Lira's life and that wasn't going to change. Ignoring the parchment, she continued with her search.

Frustration began to affect her focus as time passed and she had no luck. The violet glow from her magic was bright enough that anyone passing through the dark library would notice it glimmering through the narrow space under A'ndreas' office door, and even though the chances of that were small, there was only one mage at Temari Hall who wielded magic of that colour.

Nothing on the desk looked like correspondence—it was mostly student homework, research material, and A'ndreas' musings on various things. The man liked to write a lot of random notes.

Trying to ignore the impatience rising in her chest, she moved her search from the desk to the shelves behind it, forcing herself to slow enough to run her gaze thoroughly and methodically over everything.

Just as she'd decided she was going to have to start physically rifling through the things on his desk and shelves, her searching gaze caught several pages of stacked parchment sticking out from inside a book... and the wax seal on one edge looked familiar. When she gently tugged it out, the full seal of the Mage Council was revealed—the leaping flames of a bonfire.

Glancing behind her to ensure she was still alone, Lira carefully opened the book, took out the parchment, and placed the book back. She searched through the pages, heart leaping in triumph when she saw Councillor Duneskal's scrawled signature at the bottom of one of the pages.

This had to be the letter the Shadowcouncil was looking for.

Although... the contents didn't seem particularly interesting or important. Duneskal complaining about doing a favour for A'ndreas by collecting the remains of some old journal from the archives in Carhall. Lira let out a breath. Maybe Underground had just been testing her ability to access A'ndreas.

To be sure, she made quick work of searching over the remaining shelves. But she couldn't see anything else that looked like a letter, and she didn't have the time to physically search every document in the room.

It was risky to take the letter with her—A'ndreas would notice it missing sooner rather than later—but she didn't have time to linger and copy it all out. She'd been in here too long already. She would just have to hope he put the missing letter down to his untidiness.

After carefully folding the parchment and tucking it inside her robe, Lira let go of the trickle of magic she'd been using and stood still until her eyes adjusted back to the dim light. Then she eased the office door open and stared out into the dark row of stacks beyond to make sure they were empty. Assured of that, she slipped out and closed it behind her, using a touch of magic to re-engage the lock.

Just as the lock clicked into place, *something* made her hesitate. A whisper of noise... no, not even that... more like the faint ripple of another presence in the darkness. Lira froze into complete stillness, like she would have had she felt the same thing on the streets of Dirinan in the early hours of the morning.

Nothing moved. No sounds disturbed the silent library. But the space felt different than it had when she'd been in A'ndreas' office, heavier, an edge of *otherness* to it. It wasn't the fear or cold inspired by a razak, but something more familiar. Something human.

Someone else had come into the library while Lira was searching the office. A smile of anticipation wanted to curl over her face, sparked by the little shiver in the pit of her stomach, but she held it off and kept her focus instead.

Lira started moving, keeping to the shadows. She wasn't afraid of whoever it was. She was well able to take care of herself, and the darkness was her favourite hunting ground, but she'd rather not be seen. Best that nobody know she'd been in the library tonight. Especially if A'ndreas did notice the missing letter.

And as boring as its contents seemed, the letter tucked in her robe was her ticket back into Underground. Relief loosened her shoulders at the thought of that as she made her way back across the study atrium —ensuring it was empty before breaking cover.

Moving faster once she was back in the dark stacks on the other side, Lira read the presence of someone else just as she headed around a high bookshelf and into the walkway leading to the side stairwell entrance. She slowed, drawing on her magic at the same time her left hand reached for her staff.

"Truce?" The Darkhand stepped out of the shadows, hands in the air.

Lira stopped dead. The sight of Ahrin Vensis was an emotional fist to the gut of combined longing, despair, grief, and fury... the fury directed at herself, for feeling any of those other things. They were a mirage. A useless pit of emotion that served no good purpose because there was no point to them.

Because Ahrin Vensis felt nothing for Lira.

Worse, she was Lira's enemy now.

"What do you want?" she asked, pleased that her voice came out flat and uninterested. At least now she knew what had tripped her instincts earlier. A shiver of foreboding rippled through her, similar to the one she'd felt earlier when she'd spotted Ahrin in initiate robes at the party. What was the Darkhand doing at Temari Hall?

Ahrin took a step forward, everything about her relaxed, at ease. "I admit to curiosity as to what you're doing in here at this hour."

"You can't be half as curious as I am as to why you're here," Lira countered.

A little half-smile was all she got in response.

"You're really not going to tell me?" Lira snapped. "Are you here to spy on me, kill me? Kidnap more students? Murder everyone in their sleep without breaking a sweat?"

"Did you just pay me a compliment?" Ahrin's smile widened.

Lira said nothing, merely held the girl's gaze, not letting that smile get through her guard. Ahrin was masterful at faking emotion—from charming rogue, brisk businesswoman, seductress, to ruthless killer. She wore the guises as perfectly as she wore her long coats, a tool she deployed to get whatever she wanted. But none of them were real. The only time Lira ever thought Ahrin was her true self was when she killed or fought. Then... well, those times she was at her most dangerous, but also most genuine.

Ahrin shrugged when Lira didn't respond, voice turning businesslike. "My purpose with regards to you is entirely dependent on whether you're still loyal to Underground."

"And if I'm not, you're going to kill me?" She lifted an eyebrow. "Here in the middle of the Temari Hall library."

In an instant, Ahrin was inches away from her, so close Lira could see the flat, killing look in Ahrin's eyes, feel her warm breath on the skin of her cheek. So close she could have cut Lira's throat already if that had been her intention. "You know I can. And would."

"But not tonight, I take it?" Lira lifted an eyebrow, refusing to back down in any way. Standing in the dark, so close to death, the thrill stirred in the base of her belly. It offered to warm her, make her brave and unstoppable.

"Control it, Lira, don't let it control you." Ahrin's voice was cold, as if she could see exactly what was going on inside Lira. "You're playing with fire and you won't come out the winner if you step wrong."

"I don't take orders from you any longer," Lira murmured, shifting even closer, demonstrating her lack of fear. "And I like fire."

"I warned you not to get in my way."

She had. And she'd meant it. And still Lira wasn't scared. She smiled a little, the edges of her mouth curling up even though deep down she knew Ahrin was stronger and could kill her in a blink. "And I warned you not to get in mine."

"Then it seems we're at a stalemate." Ahrin's eyes glittered dangerously. "Not for long, Lira Astor."

Lira held her gaze a moment longer, then shrugged. "I'm going to bed." She walked around Ahrin, deliberately leaving her back exposed to the other girl. "Enjoy the empty library. It's peaceful this time of night."

No attack came, and Lira found herself almost disappointed by that. When she glanced back a few steps later, the Darkhand had vanished into the shadows of the library. Her gaze narrowed—what *had* Ahrin been doing in here tonight?

In case Ahrin had feinted before circling back to follow her, Lira veered away from her planned route and went for the main library entrance instead. The study atrium was just as empty—no sign of Ahrin anywhere—as Lira crossed it and walked down toward the main doors. Part of her noticed that the bloodstains where Fari's dead friend had lain sprawled that night had been scrubbed clean away.

Lira pushed through the left door, only to freeze when it was halfway open, shock whispering through her. The bloodied corpse of one of the school's guard dogs lay sprawled on the floor just beyond the doors, mere steps away. It was barely recognisable, deep slashing wounds tearing open several areas of its body where it lay in a widening pool of blood.

The kill was fresh.

The air was cold, but normal winter cold. No rattle broke the silence. And if a razak had killed the dog, there wouldn't be so much blood.

This was something, or *someone,* else.

Lira drew her staff as she thought back to the prickling of her instincts when leaving A'ndreas' office. She'd assumed Ahrin had tripped them, and maybe Ahrin had done this... no, the Darkhand was a trained killer, not a sadist. She killed for a purpose, not for pleasure, and she killed efficiently. This dog had been torn apart.

A quick glance around revealed an empty corridor and stairwell. The instincts that had roused earlier were dormant now, suggesting whatever had done it was gone. Uneasiness flickered through her, but she dismissed it after only a brief hesitation. Her focus had to be on winning her way back into Underground, not getting caught so close to the library at this hour.

With quick strides, Lira circled the corpse and headed straight up the stairs. Someone would find the dog in the morning and the Temari

Hall masters could deal with it. She had the letter she needed. Anything else wasn't her problem.

Even so, the bloody sight lingered in her dreams as she slept that night, refusing to be completely banished.

Instinct warned her she should ignore it at her peril.

CHAPTER 2

The raucous hum of breakfast time at Temari spilled out of the dining hall as Lira approached. The clinking of cutlery and plates, the laughter and student chatter, the scrape of chairs, it all raked like claws over her senses. Her eyes were gritty and her head pounded faintly. She hadn't slept well.

Again.

It hit her once more when she stepped inside, as it had each of the three mornings since she'd been released from the healing rooms; the sharp dissonance of normal life after what had happened. The school routine continued as it always had, seemingly untouched, at least for the students.

But less than a month earlier, the Shadowcouncil had managed to breach the walls of the academy, kill several guards—not to mention a mage master and a Taliath student—and kidnap seven students without anyone noticing a thing. Or being able to find them. The brazen return of all but two of the students in the middle of a busy day of lessons had only reinforced how dangerously unprepared the Mage Council was for the genuine threat Underground so clearly posed.

When she paid attention, though, it was clear life at the school wasn't completely untouched. Even before the kidnapped students had been returned, the numbers of guards at the gated entry to the school had been doubled and now included at least one, usually two, Taliath warriors or trainees. No Underground member wielding illusion magic would get past a Taliath—and that was the current theory for how Lira and the others had been returned without anyone noticing.

And while the students seemed determined to behave as if everything was all right again, the masters were tense, watchful, clearly doing their best to hide their unease at the deeply worrying implications of what had happened.

If only they knew that the Darkhand of the Shadowcouncil was now a student at the school. Four days since being released from the healing ward and Lira had yet to figure out where to start with that problem.

Her recent lack of sleep *could* be explained by all of that, of course. Or by her thoughts continuing to linger uneasily on wondering who or what had torn apart a vicious guard dog and left it displayed outside the library like a trophy three nights earlier. When she'd risen the next morning, she'd waited for the news of what had happened to move through the student body like lightning.

But it hadn't.

By the following day, she'd realised that one of the masters must have discovered the corpse and removed all traces before any of the students saw it. Which meant Lira couldn't ask about it, because she couldn't let anyone know she'd seen it.

It wasn't only that information that was being kept hidden. Dead guard dogs aside, none of the masters had kept her informed about what was happening in response to their kidnapping.

Anger simmered as she waited for food, keeping her attention determinedly on the line of initiates and apprentices being served breakfast ahead of her. Part of her wanted to scan the room to look for... she cut herself off. No. Even though she felt exposed, self-conscious. Ahrin might be there somewhere, watching Lira, studying everything about her. She kept her shoulders straight, expression forbidding, and looked only ahead. If Ahrin was watching, she'd see nothing of Lira's anger or unease.

Once she had her tray of steaming oatmeal and juice, she walked her usual route around all the inner tables to one on the right side of the room, along the wall, as far as it was possible to get from all the populated tables.

As she walked, she kept an ear out for what the morning chatter was about. Once again, none of what she heard mentioned a guard dog's corpse being found, and the atmosphere was too cheerful for what she'd expect if the students knew about it.

Weary and annoyed, she placed her tray down harder than she'd intended, the too-loud clattering noise setting off a throbbing headache. She sat carefully, her stiffening muscles protesting now that she was no longer exerting herself. The hour she'd just spent out in the training yards hadn't been kind on her still-healing shoulder, ribs, and leg. Waiting for them to heal properly wasn't an option, however, not when Underground could come for her again at any time.

The safety she'd once felt inside the walls of Temari Hall had very soundly proved to be a dangerous illusion.

She needed to get the letter she'd stolen to Greyson. If the masters at Temari wouldn't tell her anything, she'd seek information from Underground instead. And Tarrick and Dawn had given her permission to try and re-join the group.

Normally the thought of how dangerous her mission was would set her heart beating faster and send anticipation sparking through her veins. But now uneasiness roiled through her stomach instead, killing any appetite that might have come from her physical workout.

Lucinda had been so desperate to get Lira on that experiment table... And Lira had allowed herself to be manipulated into it, to—

She forced herself to take a steadying breath and bury those thoughts. If she managed to convince Greyson to accept her back, she had to be strong again, *stronger*, ready for whatever came next. She couldn't afford any weakness.

First, she needed to get back in. Greyson usually left messages in an agreed hiding spot to notify her of upcoming meeting times, but she'd checked since her return and there had been nothing. If he didn't reach out soon, she was going to have to figure out some other way to track him down.

The easiest option, of course, would be to go to Ahrin.

But Ahrin Vensis was the Shadowcouncil's blade, their right hand. More, she was dangerous, not to be trusted, and had a way of getting past all Lira's guards without even trying. She had no desire to tangle further with Ahrin until she was on better footing with the Shadowcouncil. Best to pretend she didn't exist.

As always, the thought of the Darkhand sent Lira into emotional freefall. Fury, betrayal, delight, longing, grief, regret... all of it lodged together in a tight ball in her chest that made one bitter mix.

Enough. Lira took a deep breath, pushed all thoughts from her mind, and focused on her breakfast. The scent of cinnamon wafted up from the mostly untouched oatmeal before her and her appetite roused in response. She spooned up a mouthful and ate hungrily, the tasty food quickly starting to make her feel better.

The clatter of another tray being dropped onto the table sent a thrum of instinctive readiness through her, and she started, violet light flaring around her hands. She blinked at the sight of Fari Dirsk dropping into the seat opposite hers.

Not Ahrin was all she could think for a moment, unsure whether she was relieved or bitterly disappointed. "What are you doing?" Lira snapped, angry at both the interruption and her own confused response to it.

Fari looked up from her oatmeal, an eyebrow lifting at the flash of violet light from Lira's hands. "Eating breakfast. What are you doing?"

"Yes, but why are you doing it *here?*"

"I'm aware that you are different from the rest of us, Lira, but generally when one goes through a scary and life-threatening experience with another person, it's custom to check in, see how they're doing." Fari peered at her. "You doing okay?"

Lira stifled a smile despite herself. At some point during the nightmare of recent weeks, Fari's perky cheerfulness had stopped being irritating. But before she could muster a response, Fari was talking again. "Your nose has healed crooked. I told you to let me fix it."

"If I had it would probably be even more crooked," Lira muttered. "But I'm fine, and you look fine, so you can go away and leave me alone now. We're all checked in."

"That's rude, Spider." Fari spooned up her oatmeal, chewed and swallowed. "Have you been to see Lorin yet?"

"How's his leg?" The words were out before Lira could stop them, and she cursed herself for showing a shred of concern. These people were not her friends. She shouldn't care about Lorin or his injured leg.

Unbidden, her memories brought back that dark hall. Razak everywhere. Tarion, Garan, Lorin. All of them staying with her. Fighting to the end. Not running away, not leaving her alone.

They might not be friends. But they weren't meaningless, not strangers, not anymore. She filed that acknowledgement away with all the other things she couldn't yet figure out how to tackle. The list was growing alarmingly large.

Fari's cheerful expression darkened. "I take it that's a no?" She sighed. "It's pretty bad. The healers are still working on it. Master A'ndreas saved the leg, but..."

"What?"

"I'm sure it will be fine." Fari avoided Lira's gaze and spooned up another mouthful of oatmeal.

Lira hesitated. "Have you heard anything about Athira?"

"Nope." Fari scowled. "We're too lowly. Or young. Or helpless, I guess, to be told things by the grownups."

So it wasn't just Lira that had been ignored. That was something.

"Morning ladies." Garan Egalion appeared, dropping his tray onto the table with an even louder clatter than Fari had before favouring them both with his charming grin. When neither Lira nor Fari swooned, the grin was downgraded to a friendly smile. "Why are we sitting all the way over here?"

"Because she's got no friends." Fari jabbed her spoon in Lira's direction.

"Which is exactly how I like it, so if you could leave me alone, that would be great." Lira didn't try to hide her exasperation. She wasn't in the mood for other people, even if these ones were making some confusing attempt to behave as if Lira wasn't a complete outcast at Temari Hall and that they'd never, *ever,* spoken to each other at break-fast—or any other time of day—before. "I'm trying to eat."

"All right." Garan lifted his hands in mock surrender before picking up his tray. "Never let it be said that I stayed where I wasn't wanted. Love the new look on you, Lira, the nose is just the perfect shade of crooked. See you in class later."

She scowled at him. He winked, flashed that smile again, then strolled off, whistling under his breath.

"Do you think he's worked out that I like girls yet?" Fari asked. "Pretty much everyone in Temari Hall knows it, so why he persists with the flirting, I really don't know. Something tells me he's not your type either, Spider."

Ahrin's face floated into Lira's head. She pushed it firmly back out, her scowl deepening. Then she ate another mouthful of her food. Silence persisted, but Lira refused to break it.

"Your glaring is giving me indigestion, so I'm going to go too." Fari eventually stood and picked up her tray and spoon. "Catch you later. Oh, and by the way, you can call me Ari."

Lira opened her mouth but Fari was already gone, weaving after Garan through the tables to go and sit at another one in the centre of the large space. The students there greeted her with smiles and laughs and uneasy looks in Lira's direction.

Her eyes lingered on those full tables, but her thoughts were far away. Discouraging Garan and Fari from sitting with her was part instinct—a survival mechanism learned years ago for keeping people at a distance—and part memory of Lucinda claiming to have eyes on Lira inside the walls of Temari Hall.

She had to assume the Underground spy was still at the school, and even if not, their Darkhand was. Which meant she had to keep the others at arm's length. Best not to have the spies reporting anything unusual or changed about Lira.

But watching them laughing, so at ease in each other's presence... it made something inside her tighten with sadness. She'd always dismissed them as indulged, soft, and utterly unaware of the realities of the world outside their bubble. Which was still true. But now she couldn't help but wonder what it would be like to belong to that group? To be accepted and wanted? To share those laughs?

She sighed, her appetite fading again. It was stupid to wonder. It would never happen, not for Lira. The Magor-lier's agreement to let her try and regain access to Underground only confirmed it. He and Dawn A'ndreas were so worried about Underground that they were willing to risk Lira's life to bring it down.

She'd bet all the gold in the world they wouldn't take that risk with Fari or Garan or Tarion.

The Mage Council wasn't Underground, but they wouldn't necessarily treat Lira any differently in their desire to achieve their goals. The council's goal to protect the collective might be more noble than that of Underground, but it made no difference to their willingness to use her.

And she had no desire to sacrifice herself for either side. She wanted Underground dead and buried and was willing to do whatever it took to achieve that—irrespective of what the council wanted.

Before she could stop herself, Lira scanned the room for the first time since sitting down, looking for Ahrin's dark hair and tall frame. The distraction of knowing she was at Temari Hall was as uncontrollable as it was infuriating, even though Lira had done everything she could to avoid her since the night she'd run into her in the empty library.

Lira stood, dumped her tray on the pile of other used trays, then left the dining hall with quick strides.

Where she promptly collided with Ahrin just outside the main doors.

Ahrin recovered her balance with unnerving grace and raked Lira from head to toe in a single look. "You normally pay better attention to your surroundings."

"Ahrin." She had to fight hard to keep her voice cool, unruffled, when her heart thudded painfully in her chest. Damn.

"Lira," she mocked, smiling that wicked smile of hers. The brown initiate robe looked as good on her as everything else always did, despite the fact it hung like an oversized potato sack on everyone else. "You've been avoiding me."

"Doesn't that give you a hint?" Lira walked away, hoping that would be the end of it.

Instead, Ahrin turned and fell into step with her. "Prickly Lira is alive and well, I see. I'm pleased, I thought she was lost forever."

Lira's mouth thinned. "Why are you here?"

"I was going to get some breakfast. It's a thing you do in the mornings," she said. "The meals here are so much better than what we used to eat back in Dirinan. In the early days, at least. It got better towards the end, didn't it? Remember that time we stole the sack of chocolate powder from that factory in—"

"Don't play stupid, I know you're far from it." Lira stopped dead and turned to face Ahrin after a quick glance around to make sure nobody was paying them any attention. They were halfway between the tower and the dining hall, snow covering the ground around them. The area was momentarily empty. Even so, she kept her voice low.

"I've been instructed not to tell you why I'm here. Keep pushing and I'll take issue." Threat shivered in Ahrin's voice.

Lira didn't doubt her. It didn't scare her like it should, though. She warned herself not to underestimate Ahrin. "Yes, I'm fully aware of how loyal you are to Underground. I'm loyal too, in case you'd forgotten. To their *purpose,* anyway. We're on the same side."

"Lucinda would argue that your behaviour recently puts the lie to that statement."

"Well, I could mount a strong argument that Underground's behaviour towards me—the kidnapping, torturing, experimenting— puts the lie to their insistence that they value me."

Lira had already decided she wasn't going to beg or plead her way back into the group. That wasn't her, and they'd see through it in seconds, Ahrin in particular. She would play to her strengths instead, the cool arrogance she'd inherited from her grandfather—use it to leverage how badly they needed her to achieve their goals. That and the letter.

"Torturing?" Ahrin lifted an eyebrow. "Isn't that a little dramatic?"

"What would you call being hunted down by razak in the dark? Strapped to a table so tightly you couldn't move while your magic was slowly drained away?" Lira demanded. "Or being manipulated into handing yourself over to be tested on without knowing the true purpose of the experiment?"

Ahrin's face hardened, and she stepped closer. "That was *your* choice."

"You manipulated me into it and we both know it." Lira let those words sit for a moment, then waved a hand and moved on. "I want the Mage Council gone. I want what my grandfather wanted. I hope Underground can achieve it," she said steadily, lying just as comfortably as she told the truth. There was no room for being squeamish about dishonesty in the world Lira lived in. "But that doesn't mean I'm going to allow them to treat me like garbage, like a mindless follower. I want respect, Ahrin. They need *me*, not the other way around. I will be *their* leader, and yours, one day."

Ahrin stared at her for a long moment, then shrugged. "Good."

Lira huffed a breath. "That's it?" Scepticism filled her voice.

Ahrin shrugged. "Even if I had any doubts, you haven't told anyone here who I am. That proves your loyalty."

"So you made me go through all that for no reason?"

The ghost of a grin crossed Ahrin's face. "I do like it when you get all high and mighty."

Lira shook her head and turned away. Making Ahrin believe her was no mean feat... but any pride in succeeding was drowned out by a flicker of unease. She should have reported Ahrin's presence to Dawn and Tarrick the moment she'd seen her.

But if she'd done that, they would have acted instantly against the Darkhand to protect their precious school and its students, and Lira's cover would have been completely blown—and with it any remaining chance, however slim, of talking her way back in to Underground.

Lira wasn't willing to let that chance go. Not for the council, not for anything. It was a dangerous gamble. If they found out Lira had hidden Ahrin's presence from them... she had never fooled herself into believing that just because Dawn A'ndreas seemed to trust her, that the rest of the council would. She was Shakar's granddaughter, after all. It would only take a single mistake by Lira to send that unease, that wariness they felt, into outright distrust and fear. And that didn't fit with Lira's ultimate plan. She needed them to respect her, want her, trust her, so she could make them forget Shakar had ever existed.

Finally, then, it would all be over and she could just be Lira.

She turned back to Ahrin, bolstered by the thought of that.

"They're telling me nothing here. Is the group getting much heat from the council search?"

"Nothing serious." Scorn edged Ahrin's voice. "At least not yet. What did you tell them?"

"As little as I could get away with." Lira shrugged. "If you need me to feed them anything specific, say the word. In the meantime, I need you to get me into Greyson's next meeting so I can make nice."

"And if I don't?" Ahrin arched an eyebrow at her high-handed tone.

"I have leverage over you too, remember," Lira said softly. "What would Lucinda do if I told her you tried to help me escape back at that place?"

"Are you threatening me?" Ahrin sounded amused, rather than annoyed.

"If I need to."

Ahrin's mouth quirked. "She'd believe me over you any day, so go ahead and do your worst."

Lira nodded, bitter realisation sinking through her. "Your complete lack of concern only confirms you weren't really helping me escape. It was another manipulation, I'm guessing, and a clever one to make me think you're on my side. Especially since Lucinda was obviously planning to return all of us anyway."

"On the contrary," Ahrin said coolly. "I simply don't allow myself to be leveraged, as you know very well."

Her tone warned Lira to back off, that not doing so might result in the sudden loss of an important limb, but Lira pushed back. "If you're here to spy on me—"

"I'm not," Ahrin said, the threat in her voice vanishing as quickly as it had come. "I'm your ally, Lira, remember that."

"Sure, an ally who willingly handed me over to get experimented on because she was being a good soldier following Lucinda's orders." Lira snorted, waving off the denial she could see forming in Ahrin's expression. "Where is Athira?"

"I can't tell you that because I don't know."

Lira studied Ahrin's face, trying to determine whether she was telling her the truth. There had been only sincerity in her voice and

Lira couldn't think of any reason she'd lie about this. But Ahrin was a master liar.

"I've been patient this morning because I know you have a lot of questions, but never talk about any of this here again, understand?" Ahrin spoke softly. "Discussing it means the information is in our surface thoughts and any telepath in the area could read it."

"I—"

"Don't tell me about your excellent mental shielding, because we both know surface thoughts can still slip out, especially around a strong telepath. I'm not willing to risk that."

Lira scowled. She was right. But it was also a perfect excuse for not giving her a straight answer on anything. Lira's frustration seethed. Ahrin was always so damned clever.

"I can't promise anything, but I'll ensure Greyson is aware that you're back at Temari," Ahrin continued. Again, she sounded sincere, though it was impossible to be certain. "He may have orders from the Shadowcouncil. If he does, I won't get in the way of that."

It was a warning, and Lira took it as such. "I don't need your protection. If he's been ordered to kill me, I can deal with that on my own. Besides, Lucinda doesn't want me dead. She'd never have sent me back here alive if she did."

A cool smile played at Ahrin's mouth. "That may be so. But you'll need more than words and arrogance to regain their trust, Lira."

"I'm not an idiot," she said. "And if you get in my way, I'll tell them about you helping me."

Ahrin didn't seem to hear her. Her gaze had shifted to the dining hall; the sounds were audible from where they stood, cheerful students enjoying their breakfast. "I was wrong, wasn't I?"

"What?" Lira snapped, exasperated.

"I accused you of coming here and forgetting all about us, but I was wrong. You're not one of them. If you were, you wouldn't sit on your own in there every day." Ahrin's gaze finally turned back to her, dark and curious. "I noticed."

"You're half right." Lira took a step back. "You don't know anything about me anymore, Ahrin, as much as you pretend to. It's been two and a half years since you walked out on all of us."

22

"You counted the time too, huh?" Ahrin asked softly.

"Don't." The word came out cold, harsh. "Don't pretend to care, that you *ever* cared. I know what you are. You manipulate and you lie to get what you want. I won't be fooled by it again."

She walked away before Ahrin could say anything more.

THE ACHE of resentment roused by her conversation with Ahrin lingered strongly enough by nightfall that Lira went to her room and angrily scrawled out a letter to Dawn telling her about the Darkhand's presence at Temari, using the code they'd previously agreed on.

The only address she had for Dawn was in Alistriem, and sending it via anyone else was too dangerous, so if Rionn's lord-mage was in Carhall with the council it might be some time before she received it. Still, Lira scribbled furiously, quill scratching over the parchment.

By the time she'd finished, her wrist was aching and a more rational train of thought was beginning to prevail. If she got this letter, Dawn would act instantly against Ahrin; her son and nephew were still at the school, after all, and her concern for them would trump everything else.

And Ahrin being arrested by the council and removed from Temari would completely blow Lira's cover with Underground. Chewing on her lip, Lira stared at the words, torn.

Unbidden, those final moments on the stairs floated back into her mind. Ahrin had tried to help her escape, urged her to flee and save herself while the razak had been distracted with the others. She'd claimed to care about Lira.

Lira sank forward in the chair, pressing a palm to aching eyes. As much as she wanted to—and she did, more than she was willing to admit to herself—she couldn't believe a word Ahrin said. Even if she *had* sounded so sincere.

There had been an ulterior motive to her actions, there always was when it came to Ahrin, but for the first time, forcing herself to be objective, Lira wondered if maybe that motive wasn't one Underground shared.

Her gaze narrowed. She should have considered that already...

would have if she wasn't so compromised when it came to the Dark-hand. Lira understood Ahrin far better than Underground ever could. Ahrin's ambitions were mercenary. There was no way she cared two coppers for the Shadowcouncil's belief in the superiority of mages, or the rank and file's desire for better conditions. She would only have joined the group for what they could give her in terms of wealth and power.

Lira could use that.

A little smile spread over her face as an idea sparked. Ahrin claimed to be Lira's ally... well, Lira could put that to the test. What if she stopped avoiding Ahrin and instead worked to win her trust, *used* her to get greater access to Underground? Make Ahrin *her* right hand, rather than the Shadowcouncil's.

If Lira brought the Darkhand to the Mage Council's side... well, that would all but ensure Underground's destruction. The Darkhand's depth of knowledge on the group and its operations had to be unparalleled. Certainly it was enough for the Mage Council's significant resources to wipe them off the map in a single blow.

Lira tapped a finger against the parchment, weighing up the plan. It would be a dangerous game to play, one that Ahrin was a master at. If Lira lost she'd be out of Underground—if not dead at their hand—and in severe trouble with the Mage Council. Taking a gamble like this, continuing to keep Ahrin's presence a secret, would undoubtedly lose Dawn's trust if she found out. Worse, it would give the council real reason to be suspicious of Lira. She might even be expelled from Temari Hall and lose her chance to become a full warrior mage.

But Lira had learned from Ahrin for years. And she didn't owe the Mage Council anything.

If she played the game and won... she'd have everything she wanted.

The thrill uncurled in her stomach, and she let it spread through her, heady and seductive. She didn't try to push it away or keep it in the box she'd buried it in since first arriving at Temari. It was too late for that. She wasn't going to win this without the edge it gave her, the fearlessness.

Lira folded the letter and placed it at the bottom of her drawer.

She would beat Ahrin this time.

CHAPTER 3

L ira woke with the sound of angry rattling echoing through her
senses.

Sweat slicked her skin, her body so hot it felt like her
blood was boiling in her veins. She froze in her bed, heart thudding in
terror, trying to work out whether the rattling she'd heard was from a
nightmare or reality.

Her room was dark, minimal light trickling through the cracks
between the drawn curtains across her window. The bedding around
her was soaked through with sweat, as if someone had dumped a pail
of water on her as she slept.

Not again.

Gritting her teeth against the panic threatening to rise up and
crush her whole, she forced herself to push off the sodden sheets and
swing her legs over the side of the bed, rather than curling up and
hiding under the covers like she desperately wanted to.

Then she sat at the edge of the mattress, fingers curling into the
fabric, body beginning to shiver as the cold air touched her damp skin.
For a long moment she sat there, breathing too quickly, unable to
move, senses straining to read the darkness for any threats.

Eventually, using every shred of resolve she possessed, she forced herself to stand up; a quick, jerky movement. Then, to keep moving. Every part of her wanted to throw her clothes on as quickly as she could and run from the room, but she forced herself to slowly pull on breeches, then shirt and robe, still listening for any unusual sounds outside.

Everything was quiet, though. Her heart continued to thud anyway, echoes of the rattling still in her head. She was reaching for one of her boots when the first call of a bird chirped outside. Abruptly her shoulders relaxed and her heartbeat began to slow. She sank back down to the bed, head hanging in sheer relief.

She was fine.

She was in Temari Hall, it was approaching dawn, and the nightmare was over. Even so, Lira stood at her door afterwards, fingers wrapped white-knuckled around its handle for several long moments before she could force herself to open it and step outside.

As she did, the panic started to fade and reason returned, with it coming mortification and fury, both directed at herself.

This was her new reality since the day she'd been released from the healing ward. Every night she went to bed desperately hoping it would end the following morning. And every day she woke to it happening again.

During daylight hours she was fine, normal, the old Lira. But once she fell asleep at night... they'd drugged her so many times that going to sleep was now a terrifying affair. Every time she woke she was back there. In that room, or strapped to the table, or back to that first night when they'd taken her with razak hunting her through the dark library.

It was unbearable. Crushing. Mortifying. And she couldn't stop it.

She *hated* it. Hated it with everything inside her. She'd never forgive Underground for doing this to her, taking away her strength and confidence and replacing it with fear. For stripping away the self-assurance she'd learned in Dirinan and sending her plunging back inside that terrified young girl who'd waited in the dark for a mother who would never come home.

More than anything in the world, she wanted to leave that girl behind, forgotten, as if she'd never existed. Lira took a steadying breath. She could do it again, just like in Dirinan. She just had to destroy Underground. And then she'd be fine.

Sucking in another long breath, she closed the door behind her. Started walking. Felt the final remnants of terror fade when she passed another third year apprentice up early and heading for the bathing room. Relaxed entirely as she reached the front entrance and saw the open doors and two apprentices and two Taliath on guard. All were at ease, chatting idly to one another.

Turning away, she headed through the ground floor corridors then out the back entrance of the tower, crossing frosty gardens to the southwestern wall of the school grounds. It was still curfew, so nobody was going to let her through the front school gates, but she'd already solved that problem.

The area of the outer wall she headed for was out of sight of any of the nearby buildings, and only someone on the higher floors of the tower would be able to see her scramble up the tree near it—a gamble she took that this was unlikely so early in the morning.

Once she reached the right branch, she balanced carefully, focusing her mind and summoning her magic. It was too far to make a normal jump across to the top of the wall, but none of those charged with designing the security of the grounds when building it had had the imagination to envision a telekinetic mage using their magic on themselves. Either that, or they'd just been more focused on keeping threats out than students in.

Taking a breath, she jumped, simultaneously using magic to throw herself toward the top of the wall. Her balance teetered precariously as she landed, and she fell to her knees, bracing herself with flattened palms. Still clumsy. But better than the last time she'd done it. Pleased enough with that, she swung her legs over and dropped down the other side, using another touch of magic to slow her fall.

For a moment she stood in the ankle-deep snow, soaking in the quiet of the morning and the still air around her. The always-there tightness in her chest loosened.

She set off at a swift jog along the lake shore. After a while her left calf began aching, soon joined by the throbbing of her newly-healed ribs, but she ignored the pain and pushed on. By the time she'd headed several miles west along the shore, then circled back through the quiet forest, she was confident nobody was following her. Cutting back towards the shore, she found the fallen log in a small clearing where one of Greyson's people left messages to let her know of upcoming meetings.

The narrow space inside it was still empty.

Stifling frustration, Lira left quickly. By now curfew had lifted, and the risk was higher that someone would see her leaping to the top of the school wall and down the other side, but she did it as quickly as possible, chest heaving and muscles trembling by the time she regained the cover of the trees.

The sun was edging over the horizon, casting everything in a golden glow as Lira made straight for the outdoor sparring courts. Her breathing was fast, body sore, but after a week of this she was already feeling stronger. Better. Soon she'd have that edge back. Except... the thought of her nightmare earlier caused that confidence to waver, the tightness in her chest closing like a vice, but she took a deep breath and did her best to push the doubts from her mind.

The courts were empty at such an early hour, and she had the area to herself as she collected a bow and quiver of arrows from the weapons' storage shed and set up one of the targets.

Normally only the Taliath students used these weapons during their combat training. Mages continued to be taught the use of staffs— familiarity with other weapons wasn't considered necessary. But recent events had taught Lira the foolishness in that. Her staff had been practically useless against razak, and she fully intended to be better equipped next time she faced one of those monsters.

In the hush of early dawn, she settled into a rhythm of loosing arrow after arrow at the target until her aim improved enough that she could hit inside the inner three rings on two out of three shots. She ignored the ache from her frozen hands and the sting of newly-earned blisters on her fingers turning bloody. She pushed away the soreness in her right shoulder that still hadn't fully healed, the ache in her bruised ribs whenever she drew the bow back all the way. And she kept going, arrow after arrow.

Pain didn't matter. Growing stronger, better able to survive, *that* was what mattered. After a while the pain faded into the rhythm of shooting and the world narrowed to her steady breaths, the thump of an arrowhead into a target, the creak of her bow as she drew it.

When she was satisfied with her progress, she collected the arrows, bow, and targets, and neatly stored them away. She'd just closed the door on the weapons' storage shed when the school's bell began ringing.

It took her a moment to process the sound, and then her hand reached for her staff without thinking.

Situated right at the top of the tower, the Temari bell was only used for two purposes; to signal danger or imminent attack on the school, or urgently summon the students together.

It took another second for Lira to dig through her memory for the lesson where initiates were taught the two different ring patterns, and then she let go of her staff, allowing it to drop back into its holster. This one was summoning the students.

The bell continued tolling, a deep, ominous, sound, as Lira made her way from the sparring courts through the gardens around the tower. Students were already pouring out of the front doors and onto the pebbled drive and lawn surrounding the large weeping tree in the centre of the drive. Lira weaved her way through the crowd to the top of the main steps—figuring if she wanted to be able to see what was going on, she needed higher ground.

Curious chatter filled the morning, sleepy students quickly waking in the cold air and the surprise of the summons. The bell continued ringing for at least another ten minutes before slowly fading out.

By then Lira estimated that most, if not all, students at the school had emerged from the tower and were gathered in front of the steps. She could just see over the heads in front of her.

An elbow nudged her arm and she spun to see Garan sidling up beside her. "What do you think all this is about?" he asked.

"You don't know?"

"Not a clue," he said cheerfully, blowing on his hands. "Wish we could do this inside, though."

A whistling sound, high pitched enough to cut over the hum of conversation, came from above. Everyone immediately craned their heads upwards, blinking against the bright morning sun.

Lira couldn't help the feeling of awe that niggled in her at the sight of Alyx Egalion dropping out of the sky to land gracefully on the snow-covered lawn before the gathered student body. Finn A'ndreas' wiry form detached from the crowd to join her, as did Master Nordan's.

The moment Egalion held up her hand for silence, any remaining conversation died. "I'm sorry to drag you all out here so early, but I'm departing for Carhall this morning, and there are some things I wanted you all to be aware of before I leave." Egalion's voice was crisp and clear, even as far back as Lira was standing. She was clearly using magic to enhance it—a useful trick. "We've received information indicating that Temari Hall may be under direct threat from the Shadowcouncil. Your safety is our utmost priority, and as such, you will see some changes around the grounds."

As if on cue, the front gates of the school swung open, and into the brief silence came the steady thump of booted feet. Lira's eyes widened at the sight of several columns of Shiven soldiers marching into the academy, eventually coming to a stop in perfect rows behind Egalion.

The entrance of the soldiers changed the air of eager curiosity that had hung over the student body. Now Lira sensed unease and fear coalescing around them.

"That's a full division of Shiven infantry," Garan muttered under his breath. "The threat must be serious."

"More serious than Underground's ability to snatch us all out of here without anyone knowing a thing?" Lira said, gaze narrowed on Egalion.

He shrugged. "I don't think they'd have been able to do it with those guys here though. Even a razak would come up short against a full division."

"A detachment of warrior mages from Carhall will also be arriving shortly in Karonan to bolster the Shiven infantry presence here," Egalion continued into the silence. "Be assured that you will be well protected in my absence. Master A'ndreas will be in charge until I return."

"Not a few Shiven will be pretty unhappy about Leader Astohar using their soldiers to protect us," Garan said quietly. "Where are the Bluecoats, or militia, or even the Leopards?"

It was a good point. Mage students at Temari came from all countries, not just Shivasa. In fact, the majority of students were Tregayan, yet not a single green militia jacket was in sight.

"From here on out, curfew will be enforced for all year levels, not just initiates. You may still leave the academy grounds inside curfew, but you must do so in groups of no less than five." A pause as a few grumbles went through the crowd. Lira swore inwardly—this was going to make sneaking in and out even harder.

"Thank you for your time," Egalion finished up. "I look forward to seeing you all when I return."

But when Egalion leapt back into the sky, and A'ndreas and Nordan headed back into the tower, the students lingered rather than dispersing. They seemed shocked. For the first time in their lives the danger of the outside world had reached into theirs. The sight of fifty Shiven warriors moving off in neat rows—presumably spreading through the grounds—was a stark reminder of that.

"This must have been what it was like before," Garan mused. "When my parents were at DarkSkull. The Shiven loyal to the Darkmage used to launch attacks on the school regularly."

Instead of the usual anger at the reference to her grandfather, Lira felt an unexpected stirring of sympathy. Egalion had vanquished the enemy and spilled a lot of blood doing it.

This wasn't supposed to be happening again.

CHAPTER 4

The student assembly meant that Lira's routine of arriving and leaving the dining hall early—so she could avoid conversation with anyone—was impossible. Everyone went straight from the assembly to eat, and the hall was packed, although the normally lively atmosphere was dulled today. Students were talking about what had just happened, but the chatter was conducted in low, worried tones. The usual laughter was completely absent.

After a long wait in line for food, Lira made it to her table unaccosted, glad that Fari and Garan hadn't taken it into their heads to come and talk to her again. But she also found herself feeling a surprising hint of disappointment. Her gaze lingered more than it should've on the cluster of tables where the popular students sat, frequently sliding to Tarion, who was the only one of their group who hadn't tried to talk to her yet.

The unexpected way she'd come to like and respect the privileged mage purebloods she'd been kidnapped with made her uncomfortable and confused. Her life had taught her that people always betrayed you, but *they* hadn't, not even when their lives had literally been at risk. Yet they were pureblood mage royalty who had no idea what her life, what real life, was like.

Best to stay clear of them altogether. Lira dismissed them from her thoughts and re-focused on what *was* important.

She had to assume that given this latest threat to Temari, Dawn A'ndreas and the Magor-lier would order Lira to stay away from Underground. Lira's only option was to get to Greyson and win her way back in before those orders came. At least then she could offer the incentive of confirmed re-access to the group—and another way for the council to learn about the threat facing Temari Hall.

Would Dawn travel here personally to pass those orders to Lira? Or would she tell her brother about Lira's mission and have him pass it on? If it was the latter, then Lira had no time at all—Dawn could telepathically contact her twin at any time. Her foot tapped restlessly against the floor as she ate. She hoped for the former, but in case the latter eventuated she'd have to avoid Finn A'ndreas like he had an infectious rash until she could get to an Underground meeting.

Easier said than done.

She toyed with approaching Ahrin, getting her to take Lira directly to Greyson today, but Ahrin would immediately be suspicious if Lira made such a request without a good reason. No, she'd have to wait until she got a message from Greyson.

Frustration making her unable to sit still any longer, Lira rose, dumped her tray, and left the hall.

The morning was cold despite the sun, and Lira shivered. Most students took the direct route from the back tower entrance to the dining hall, but Lira always took the longer way through the gardens around to the tower's front entrance so she didn't have to run into anyone.

It was an old habit. Even if she didn't have to keep up appearances for any spies watching, the walk gave her a momentary break from the dark looks and muttering she'd face for the remainder of the day—a consequence of being the only living heir of the Darkmage—until she could escape to her room at night.

As she walked, her thoughts shifted to her first class of the day, Languages. Lira hadn't yet mastered basic Tregayan verbs, and she was finding the class particularly difficult now they'd moved to more advanced subject matter. Of course, it would help if she actually gave two coppers about learning Tregayan verbs.

Even after two and a half years of unrelenting hard work she'd only barely caught up to the basics of what her fellow third year apprentices had mastered. Sometimes the weight of that on her shoulders was so heavy that Lira just wanted to stop. Stop fighting and scraping. Give up trying to be better. Give up on making them forget about Shakar and just let it all go.

But she couldn't. It simply wasn't in her. She didn't know how to do otherwise.

The muddied snow from hundreds of students gathering had already been swept from the main steps by a hardworking initiate, and Lira took them two at a time, allowing the exertion to loosen her sore and stiff muscles.

The winter sun shone through the open doors to bathe the entrance foyer in golden light. It was such a stark contrast to her recent memories of it—darkness faintly lit by moonlight and a razak trying to get through the doors while she and Fari and Tarion pressed all their weight against it to keep the monster out—that it was *almost* possible to forget the entire thing had ever happened.

Banishing those memories before they could take hold, she crossed the threshold and stopped dead at the sight of Lorin standing just inside. His right leg was in a splint, bandages wrapped around parts of it, and he leaned heavily on his left leg and a wooden crutch. A bulging duffel bag sat at his feet. His bony shoulders sagged and he was staring at the ground. Misery shrouded him like a blanket.

For the first time since Lira had dragged him out of his bed that night in the tower, Lorin Hester looked like the fifteen-year-old boy he was. He hadn't seen her yet, too lost in obvious misery, and she almost started walking again, leaving him to himself. But the sight of the bag at his feet stopped her.

"Lorin." She kept her voice brisk, no warm greeting in it. "You're out of the healing wing. What are you doing down here?"

He looked up, startled from his thoughts, but the subsequent clatter of hooves on cobblestone behind her—horses drawing a public carriage—answered the question before he could. His glance shifted outside, going dark with grief, then lingering. He seemed unable to look back at her. "They saved the leg, but Master A'ndreas says I'll have a limp for the rest of my life." His jaw clenched and tears glistened in his eyes, even though he didn't let them fall. He hefted the crutch. "I might always need this."

"That explains what happened to your leg," Lira said. "Not why you're leaving."

He took a breath, finally turned his gaze back to her. "I can't be a warrior mage. Not with a limp and a walking stick."

She frowned. "Who told you that?"

"Nobody needed to," he mumbled. "I can figure that one out all on my own, even if it wasn't obvious in all their pitying looks."

"Well, you're an initiate, even though you stepped up passably well during our recent... whatever that was... so I'm going to forgive your stupidity and correct it." She spoke firmly, letting impatience edge her tone. "I've seen your concussive magic. It's powerful. A limp doesn't take that away. I don't know what logic got you to thinking you can't be a warrior mage, but whatever it is, it's wrong."

His jaw clenched harder, pale Shiven face going bloodless. "I can't fight with a limp."

"Says who?"

He said nothing. Lira couldn't help herself; she felt for him. She knew the grief he felt, the aching loss of a life you loved stripped away from you without warning or mercy, completely out of your control. But her situation and Lorin's were different. His could be fixed. All she had to do was make him see it.

"You didn't strike me as the type to give up so easily." Lira sighed, glancing around to ensure they were still alone. This conversation needed to end quickly before whatever spies Underground had in Temari Hall saw it and decided she was suddenly going soft. "Are you afraid of working harder than everyone else in sparring class? Spending long hours with the healers to strengthen your leg so you can lose the crutch? Of the pain you'll likely always feel when you push yourself?"

"No, of course not!" he said indignantly, jaw jutting out, bony shoulders straightening abruptly. "I'm not afraid of any of that."

"So why are you standing here instead of heading back to your classes?"

"I..." He glanced around, looked down at his bag, lifted his gaze to meet hers. Hope dawned in them, bright and powerful. "You mean it, Lira?"

"About the fact it's going to hurt and you're going to have to work extra hard? Damn right I do. We done here?" There was no give in her voice, even though... she squelched the sympathy that wanted to rise up. It wouldn't help him.

"We're done." He bent to pick up his bag, fumbling and almost dropping the crutch as he did.

Lira didn't offer to help. But she did linger an extra second before walking away to make sure he didn't fall. A few steps away, she paused, turned back. "Lorin?"

His bag was over his shoulder and he was already taking one careful, limping step towards the stairs. "Yes?"

"Anyone tells you anything different to what we just discussed, Master A'ndreas included, you send them to me."

"Thank you, Lira, but I can handle my own battles from here on out," he said, that imperious Shiven dignity returning in full.

A smile crept across her face, and this time she let it out. She wondered what it would have been like, back in Dirinan, to have someone like Lorin on their crew. "I'm glad to hear it."

He nodded, took another step, winced with pain. Then took another one. And another.

She left him to it.

"PLEASE DON'T TELL me you've gone soft in your old age?" Ahrin was leaning against the wall of the corridor Lira turned into, clearly waiting for her. She fell into step with Lira when she didn't stop, brown robe swishing around her long strides. Lira squelched the irritation that rose up at the fact Ahrin was taller than her.

"Initiates don't talk to apprentices. Leave me alone." Her plan to win Ahrin to her side would have to progress slowly. If Lira's attitude suddenly changed, Ahrin would figure out what she was doing in a heartbeat, so she kept her voice brisk. She'd have to make Ahrin think *she* was winning Lira over.

"Soft *and* elitist. Should I point out you were just talking to an initiate. Not to mention making an attempt to *help* him." Ahrin gave her a once-over. "What happened to the callous street rat that ran with me for seven years?"

Lira hid her wince at learning Ahrin had overheard her conversation with Lorin. Best to brush it off as if it were nothing. "She's long forgotten about. You're the one who told me I was better than that."

"Ouch. I never realised you took what I said so much to heart."

Lira stopped, gave Ahrin a hard look. "Why are you still talking to me?"

"You know why." Ahrin stepped closer, a smile playing at the corners of her mouth.

Lira stifled a sigh, warning herself not to soften too soon, helped in that goal by irritation at Ahrin's usual game playing. "I have class. So do you. Unless you're here to tell me about the next Underground meeting?" Hope kindled.

Amusement warmed Ahrin's midnight blue eyes. "You do remember that unlike everyone else here I'm not actually scared of you, right?"

That very fact had once been the most wonderful thing in Lira's world. Now it was her only vulnerability in a game where she couldn't afford any vulnerabilities. Ahrin's loyalties were only to herself. Lira had to use that.

"I remember," Lira said with a shrug. "But you're the one who needs to remember that we're done, that we're not friends anymore. Just because we're both working on the same *project* doesn't mean we have to talk."

"Does the fact I let you walk away really count for nothing?" Ahrin's eyes searched hers. "I would have let you go, Lira, if you hadn't made that ridiculously foolish choice to help those idiots and risk your life in doing so. A choice I still don't understand."

Lira's mouth curled in a smile. "I have orders from the Shadow-council too. Ones I don't intend to share with you."

"Why not?" Ahrin shifted even closer, playing havoc with Lira's equilibrium. "I'll tell you mine if you tell me yours."

"I thought we weren't allowed to talk because of all the powerful telepaths roaming the halls." Lira scoffed

"Egalion just left, remember, after that rather dramatic assembly. Pureblood mages do like to get all high and mighty, don't they?"

Lira had abruptly had enough of Ahrin's attempts to charm her into submission. They worked too well, and only made her dwell on how false it all was, so she allowed her anger to surface. "You showed me who you really are when you abandoned us in Dirinan, and if that hadn't convinced me, then you serving me up on a platter to Lucinda certainly did. I won't be blinded again. I can't *trust* you, Ahrin!" The heartfelt words spilled out before she could stop herself, so she cleared her throat, tried to recover, to use the moment of vulnerability. "If you want to earn my trust back, tell me something true. What is this new threat to the school that the council have discovered?"

Ahrin hesitated. "I can't tell you."

"Then tell me why you're here."

"I can't—"

Lira walked off before Ahrin could say anything to stop her, something clever to charm her and peel back another layer of her shields. Ahrin was a clever liar.

She shouldn't have to keep reminding herself of that.

CHAPTER 5

Lira tried paying attention at the beginning of Languages class, but it was a losing battle. Schoolwork had bored her before the kidnapping. Now, squeezing herself into the persona of the perfect mage apprentice chafed unbearably, and she couldn't find the unrelenting dedication and focus she'd needed to keep up with her studies.

She regularly found herself losing track of the master's words in class, her thoughts turning to how she was going to win Underground's trust back, or how she could convince someone to tell her *something* about how the council search for their captors was going. Or even worse, she found her mind drifting to memories of the remembered joy of running the Dirinan streets after a score, or smoking a cigar by the potbelly stove in their crew's loft.

Today her mind lingered on her encounter with Lorin earlier, then went to that pitch-black room where they'd been strapped to tables by iron bars that drained their magic and left them unable to move.

His words in the darkness kept replaying in her memories, despite how often she pushed it away. They'd all made confessions about their worst days as a distraction to hold the terror at bay. The mere sound of their voices had helped distract her *just* enough to keep her panic from taking over.

She kept darting glances to the front of the classroom, where Tarion Caverlock sat, his too-long raven hair hiding his face from her. She hadn't spoken to him since the celebration party after their return. Unlike Garan and Fari, he hadn't sought her out since—probably for similar reasons to why she hadn't sought him out.

It had utterly astonished her to learn that he was so withdrawn because he was *shy*, because he hated attention and felt like a failure because he wasn't a powerful mage like his mother and aunt. There wasn't a trace of pureblood arrogance in him, only a desperate desire to avoid attention.

She'd never forget the sight of him fighting, the confidence and sureness in the way he moved. It had looked more like a dance, graceful and rhythmic and beautiful. Another thing he kept hidden from the world.

When class ended, she pushed her way forward to the front of the room, ignoring the protests and black looks as she bumped shoulders and elbows with students going in the opposite direction.

Tarion was still scribbling down the last of their master's instructions, ink staining his fingers. When he finally looked up, his hazel eyes blinked in surprise to find her standing at his desk. "Lira, hi."

"I need a favour."

"It's good to see you too." He smiled, closed his book. "What do you need?"

"It's not for me, it's for Lorin," she said quickly. "I saw him earlier."

Tarion flinched as she relayed the diagnosis on his leg. "Being a warrior mage is everything to him. That's terrible news."

"He can still be a warrior mage. But he'll need help." She paused, huffing in irritation when Tarion only lifted a questioning eyebrow. "Extra sparring training, for example. With someone patient enough to spend time with a student who will be slower to develop."

"Why are you asking me? Why don't *you* help him?" Tarion stood, pushed his chair in neatly, gathered his books.

"Do I strike you as the patient type?"

His smile was sudden and bright. "No. That doesn't mean you're not able to help him though."

"I can't."

He lifted his eyebrow again. "Can't or won't?"

"And I'm officially out of this conversation." She turned away. "Help him or not, it's up to you. Bye, mage-prince."

"Lira, wait." He reached out to grab her wrist as she walked away. His fingers were warm and dry as they wrapped around her skin, and the physical contact was a shock—she'd so rarely been touched with anything but violence.

"What are you doing?" She yanked her hand away, and he let go without protest.

"I just wanted to ask if you were okay," he said. "After everything."

She *did* roll her eyes then. "This is not a sharing session, Caverlock."

"It's been over a week," he persisted. "Have you heard anything about how the council investigation is progressing?"

"I don't know why you're asking *me* that. You're far more likely to hear things than I am."

He looked away. "Not even Da will tell me anything. He just keeps saying that they're working hard on finding our captors. But Underground still have Athira. I can't bear the thought that she's in that nightmare while we all made it out. It eats at me."

Lira bit her lip, glad he couldn't see her face. She understood what he was feeling better than she was comfortable with. Athira was alone, probably hurt, definitely afraid. She wasn't equipped for survival like Lira, she was a girl who'd grown up in a protected bubble. It made her unlikeable, annoying, but it didn't mean she deserved what had happened to her. "She's not my problem. I wasn't the one who kidnapped us. I'm just glad I'm out safe." All true. But still...

"I know you care more than you let on." His gaze was back on hers, a little smile on his face. "You leapt into a sea of razak for Lorin."

She rolled her eyes. Hard. "I'll see you around."

"Bye, Lira," he called after her.

As Lira's quick strides took her to her next class, her determination to win Ahrin to her side increased. If Lira succeeded, she might be able to learn where Underground was holding Athira. If the council could rescue her without breaking Lira's cover, well, then...

Her brain might stop replaying that blasted memory of Athira holding that stupid door open for her, no matter the razak bearing down on them both, no matter that she could have saved herself by closing the door on Lira and running.

She didn't like the feeling of owing someone. It made her itch.

HALFWAY THROUGH HER NEXT CLASS, Mapping, an initiate knocked tentatively on the door and carried a note over to Master Eren. The elderly mage blinked a few times at the note, then he looked up and searched the room, gaze eventually falling on Garan before switching to Lira.

"Astor, Egalion, you're to report to Councillor Egalion's office right away."

"Why?" Lira asked as Garan obediently rose from his chair and headed towards the door.

Eren gave her a sour look. A Shiven mage, he remembered the war with the Darkmage well—several of his family members, including his wife and children, had been killed by Shakar for refusing to join his army—and as such he disliked Lira intensely.

He hadn't made any attempt that she could discern to acknowledge that she might be an entirely different person to her grandfather, but to be fair, she'd taken one look at his face the first time she'd had class with him and been aloof and rude ever since.

Lira didn't give people the chance to see that she might be different. By the time she'd arrived at Temari at fifteen years old, it had become such a deep-seated survival instinct that she couldn't change it. How to burn the child who had been rejected by the world and had to learn to survive by any means necessary out of herself?

Even now, she only asked the question because she knew it would annoy Eren. She was inwardly thrilled at the unexpected break from the tedium of class. "Because this note says so," he snapped.

She rose from the desk, gathered her parchment and book, and followed Garan out the door. He was characteristically unkempt, but in an artful way that—she assumed—he thought made him more hand-some. She struggled to comprehend such ridiculous behaviour, but found it no longer annoyed her. Underneath it all Garan had proved himself steady and brave. Again that uncomfortable feeling of wanting to *like* him reared its head. She scowled and pushed it away.

"What do you think we're in trouble for?" he asked, slowing his long strides so she could keep up with him. His smile was warm, as if they were two good friends taking an idle stroll in the sun.

"What makes you think we're in trouble?"

"I only ever get called to my aunt's office when I'm in trouble," he said cheerfully. "Never seen you there before, though."

"That's because I don't get into trouble."

"You mean you don't get caught." He gave her a knowing look.

She held back a smile. They remained silent for the rest of the walk up the tower stairs. Garan didn't seem to mind. She felt comfortable in his presence, the same way she did now with Tarion or Lorin or Fari, even when they annoyed her. The wariness that was her usual outer layer faded around them. She allowed herself to admit that it was a nice feeling.

The double doors of Alyx Egalion's office stood open. Lira's gaze went straight to the floor where the door handles she'd ripped off that night had fallen. The floor was clear, the handles already replaced, shiny and new.

Garan's grin widened when he saw who was inside, but Lira's pace slowed as they crossed the threshold, her natural wariness instantly returning.

Tarion and Lorin were there, as was Fari, and they sat along a row of chairs facing the main desk. Behind the desk were Master Finn A'ndreas, General Dashan Caverlock, and an unfamiliar man who looked a similar age to the other two. Behind them, visible through the floor-to-ceiling windows, was the snow-covered vista of the city of Karonan, perched in the middle of a frozen lake.

A'ndreas sat straight, his mage cloak sitting neatly on his shoulders, hair slightly too long but neatly brushed. Dashan leaned back perilously far in his chair, booted feet crossed on his wife's desk, fingers toying with a folded piece of torn parchment.

On Dashan's left, the third man sat as straight-backed as Finn, legs crossed, a supercilious look on his face. Perfectly coiffed blonde curls and bright blue eyes, along with his perfectly tailored council-blue cloak, made him handsome. *And* marked him as a pureblood mage with influence. His gaze flicked over Lira and dismissed her in the blink of an eye.

She perched on the edge of an empty chair on the far end of the row beside Lorin, body braced to rise and leave in a blink. The initiate gave her a little smile in greeting. She ignored it, all her senses focused on being prepared for whatever this was about.

"Thank you all for coming," A'ndreas began. "I'm sure you all know Councillor Duneskal?"

Finn was perfectly polite as he said the words, but Dashan's faint eyeroll at the introduction was all Lira needed to know about what he thought of the man. Interest flickered through her.

So this was Rawlin Duneskal, the Mage Council's representative to Karonan. *And* the author of the stolen letter she had secreted away in her room. Lira had memorised everything she could find on the man after the Shadowcouncil had asked her to steal his letter. He was the brother of Cario Duneskal, an unbelievably skilled telekinetic mage who'd been one of Alyx Egalion's closest allies. Cario had died during the war, and Rawlin had inherited the Duneskal seat on the council after their father's death—he'd been posted in Karonan since before Lira had been born.

A'ndreas continued once they'd all nodded. "While Alyx is away, she asked us to continue learning what we could from your experience to help with the council investigation into Underground. It has been just over a week now, and you seem to be settling well back into school, but if you're not ready to talk about things yet just let us know. We can postpone this conversation until you feel up to it."

Lira rolled her eyes. Across the table, Duneskal caught it and gave her a hard look. She held his gaze until he was the one to look away. A small smile curled at her mouth and she mentally ranked the councillor in the category of spineless fop.

"Our *experience?*" Fari's eyebrows shot up. "That's what we're calling

44

it? Not our 'kidnap and almost death' or our 'two of our students died and one is still missing'?"

Lira smirked. Normally attitude like that would have a mage apprentice doing dishes for a week, but Finn merely frowned, while Dashan lifted his hands in the air, as if to say, *'fair enough'*. Rawlin's lip curled, like a disapproving parent.

"She's got you there, Finn," Dashan said.

"You're right." A'ndreas leaned forward, expression earnest. It made Lira uncomfortable. Any attempt at sincerity always did. "I should have asked you first how you're all doing. Do you need more time off from your studies... someone to talk to? Anything."

Garan glanced left and right along their row, seemed to decide he would be their spokesperson, then flashed a reassuring smile at the two men. "We're fine, Uncle Finn, Uncle Dash."

"Really?" Dashan asked mildly. "Because after what happened to all of you, I wouldn't be."

His brown Shiven eyes landed on Lira then, and she immediately looked away. She *was* fine. Or at least, she would be. As soon as she took down Underground.

"Athira is the one you should be worried about," Fari pushed.

"I agree," Lorin said.

"Me too." Tarion was barely audible, and he shifted uncomfortably as he spoke.

Lira stared at him, unable to help herself. How could someone so articulate, so skilled, be so uncomfortable around others? It made no sense to her.

"We'd like to help with the search for her. I assume there is one?" Garan said pointedly.

Lira opened her mouth, closed it. The memory of Athira holding the door open for her, razak almost on both of them, closed off her instinctive protest about volunteering to help with anything before the words could be spoken.

"It's understandable that you're all upset," Rawlin answered Garan, cool and arrogant. "But the council hardly needs the help of a group of traumatised mage students in searching for your friend."

Caverlock looked pointedly at A'ndreas, who gave a helpless shrug.

Every single person sitting before the desk, Lira included, stiffened in affront.

Garan was opening his mouth to respond—from the look on his face it wasn't going to be a polite response—when Dashan shot him a quelling look. He immediately subsided, though his green eyes remained dark with anger. Lira contemplated getting up and walking out. Instead she focused on how she was going to get Duneskal kicked off the council the moment she achieved her ultimate goal and was named to the council herself.

While she was at it, she'd make sure there were no more Duneskals on the council ever again. Calmed by that thought she settled back into her chair.

Dashan lowered his feet and leaned forward, his handsome features turning sober and full of purpose. "I think the councillor is simply trying to say that what we really need from you is information. Our first priority is locating Athira, but we've yet to find a solid trail to follow. Is there anything more that's come to mind, or that you've remembered, since you first gave your reports? Anything that might provide an indication of where they would have taken her?"

An uncomfortable silence followed. Lira looked away, crossed her arms. She'd been doing her best *not* to remember anything of that time. It was already haunting her subconscious enough. Part of her desperately wanted to know what had been done to her in that room, but the rest of her wanted to forget it had ever happened. And she had enough to focus on with trying to work out what Ahrin and Underground were up to next, not to mention getting herself back into the group.

None of them knew Dawn had asked her to infiltrate Underground, except for maybe Dashan—she suspected he'd been told from the little knowing glances he was throwing her way. Her head had started throbbing, and she had to stop herself from lifting a hand to rub her temples.

"Can you be certain that she isn't still where they held us, Papa?" Tarion murmured. "Maybe you should start there."

Lira answered before Caverlock could. "Wherever it was they held us, they won't still be there," she said flatly. "The Shadowcouncil would be fools to risk that we saw enough to find it again and lead the council back there."

"Maybe." Dashan's gaze landed on her, expression inscrutable. She got the distinct sense he knew something he wasn't saying, but it could be anything. Irritation flared and the throbbing at her temples increased. The desire to get up and leave surged.

"I can't think of anything I haven't already told you," Garan said. "I'm sorry."

The others all nodded in agreement, looking sad and uncomfortable. All avoided Rawlin's gaze and looked directly to Caverlock and A'ndreas. To amuse herself, Lira shot Duneskal the occasional smirk. He mostly ignored her.

"Lira, one thing I did want to ask is whether you had any sense of travel time?" A'ndreas spoke. "The drug they gave you wore off faster than the others, right?"

"Yes, but not until we were almost at the location they held us." She shook her head. "They deliberately made it difficult for us to tell time passing, or even whether it was day or night, by drugging us," Lira said. "They were trying to mess with our heads."

"Successfully," Fari muttered.

"Do you think that was the sole purpose of drugging you?" A'ndreas asked. "To make sure you had no idea where you were or how long you'd been travelling?"

Lira thought back to Lucinda's face, those flat eyes, the way she'd gripped Lira's chin. "They enjoyed messing with us, but I think there was more to it than that. I assume Fari told you her theory—that they were using our sense of fear and dislocation as a factor in their experiments?"

A'ndreas nodded. "The idea has merit, but without a better sense of what those experiments were, it's really only speculation."

"You and your healers didn't detect anything different about us when we were returned?" Lira asked, trying to hide how badly she wanted to know the answer.

A'ndreas look troubled. "You all had injuries of varying seriousness, but we noticed nothing wrong that was inconsistent with those injuries. Still, some drugs fade quickly from human bodies, and the experiments conducted on you didn't necessarily leave physical markers."

"I have more questions." Fari spoke into the ensuing silence, cutting off Duneskal as he moved to stand up and presumably dismiss them all. Lira would have applauded her if she didn't worry it would distract the men from answering. "What happened here when we were taken? Nobody has been clear with us on that point. The other students who were in Temari when we were kidnapped won't say a thing. They say they've been ordered not to."

"Only because we don't want rumours flying around and panicking everyone," Dashan said. "The night you were taken, the Shiven soldiers on the gates were killed quickly and efficiently, execution style. Those students that weren't taken with you were drugged, the same as you, but left in their beds. They woke as normal in the morning to find the guards dead and you missing."

Lira knew this from what Dawn and Tarrick had told her during her debriefing, but it was comforting to have corroboration that they'd told her the truth.

"How was Master Alias killed?" Garan asked grimly.

"The same way as the Shiven soldiers and guard dogs." A'ndreas' unease was obvious in his voice. "There's no evidence he was given a chance to use his magic to fight back."

Ahrin. Lira shivered. It had been her. The way Dashan described the kills... it was how she operated. And now the Darkhand was loose inside Temari Hall. Lira fought back the niggle of guilt that wanted to worm through her. The mages could look after themselves.

"Do you have any idea how they were able to overwhelm so many guards without a fight? Or how they got us back in here in the middle of the day without anyone seeing?" Fari asked, mostly managing to hide the tremor in her voice. "I've heard you think it's illusion magic?"

"We're confident that drugged candles were used to knock you all out. Once they got you out of the school, the most likely answer is that they kept you drugged until you arrived wherever they took you," A'ndreas said, but he wore a little frown, like he didn't fully believe it. "A mage with strong illusion ability could have gotten you inside the grounds the day you were returned. We didn't have any Taliath on guard that morning, and it was early enough that most students were still in the dining hall. There was only a small risk of a Taliath student spotting them bringing you in. I can't be certain, but it's the most likely explanation for what happened."

"So either they got lucky or they already knew the guard roster for that day?" Tarion said quietly.

His father looked at him. Nodded.

A shiver rippled down Lira's spine. Ahrin again. That was how she planned her jobs, carefully and with all her bases covered. She'd known the guard roster and the students' movements before Underground had returned Lira and the others.

"I assume there aren't any council mages with a powerful enough illusion ability to do what you're describing?" Lira asked.

"There are not," Rawlin said coolly.

Caverlock and A'ndreas shared a glance. "We have to assume it was a member of the Shadowcouncil, or a mage recruited to Underground. Even though until recently we didn't believe Underground had any mages not on the Shadowcouncil," Dashan said.

"There weren't any Taliath on guard the night we were taken, either?" Garan asked.

"No." Dashan was grim. "Apart from Derna, the guards, and Master Alias, they didn't kill anyone else here—nobody that left their rooms, anyway. Which tells me it was a targeted operation not looking to draw extra attention by killing mage students unnecessarily."

"Yet they took your son and nephew," Fari pointed out. "Which kind of draws a lot of attention."

Lira glanced at her. "They always intended to return us."

"I believe so, yes," Caverlock said heavily. "Whatever they needed you for, they weren't planning on killing you and bringing down the wrath of the entire mage order on their heads."

"Surely kidnapping us does that anyway?" Tarion said quietly, gaze on the floor.

"Exactly. Why even risk it?" Garan sounded puzzled.

Impatience surged through Lira. She was learning nothing new here. If she could just get to another Underground meeting, she'd be able to find out more. Lira hated waiting.

"One more question." Again Fari cut in as it looked like the men were about to dismiss them. "This new threat Councillor Egalion talked about at the assembly yesterday... do you think they're going to try and take more students from Temari?"

Caverlock and A'ndreas shared a glance but before either could reply, Duneskal did. "That is sensitive information and not for students to know. You don't need to worry about any of that."

"We don't believe the threat relates to another kidnapping, no," A'ndreas said hastily as both Garan and Fari bristled at Duneskal's dismissive tone and Lira let out a contemptuous snort. "But the councillor is right. The information *is* sensitive and the circle of knowledge has been deliberately limited—mostly to ensure the safety of those here at the school. You'll be safe. We'll make sure of it."

Lira's gaze narrowed. It was on the tip of her tongue to ask about the dead guard dog she'd stumbled across, to try and probe whether the discovery of the corpse had prompted Egalion's address to the school. Did they think someone or *something* had successfully infiltrated the school and killed the animal? Her neck prickled. Whatever had happened, instinct warned her it wasn't good. But that didn't change the fact that asking would lead to a lot of uncomfortable questions about why Lira had been up in the library that night. So again she held back.

A'ndreas continued, "We'll meet together weekly, if that's all right. It will give us a chance to ask you any questions that come out of the council investigation, and you can let us know if you've remembered anything that might be relevant."

"And you'll give us updates on any developments in the investigation and the search for Athira, of course," Garan said, not making it a question, his gaze locked on Duneskal. Like with Fari earlier, Lira wanted to applaud him.

Dashan smiled. "We'll tell you what we can."

"There's one other thing before you go," A'ndreas said. "Given what you've been through, and particularly given the presence of mind and mage skill you displayed in surviving and helping each other, we'd like to make you one of our combat patrols. You're the only student mages who have—"

"Absolutely not."

"I can't be in a combat patrol, I can't even pass Languages."

"Uncle Finn, are you sure, because—"

"With my leg, I'm not sure I'd—"

All but Tarion spoke at once, drowning each other and A'ndreas out. Lira stared at the three men across the desk in horror. A combat patrol? With *her*? Working with others? It was absurd. The most insane thing she'd heard all year.

"As I was saying," A'ndreas continued patiently once they'd all gone quiet. "You're the only mage students here with combat experience. I feel that's a benefit for us. Garan, Tarion, you're already assigned to guard shifts on the grounds, and as a third year apprentice, Lira, you should be. Given what you went through, I think it's silly to make distinctions of the fact Fari is second year and Lorin is an initiate. All we'd need is to select a Taliath student to round out the patrol."

Lira had never been assigned to guard shifts because nobody had ever been willing to work with her. That suited her just fine. It didn't seem wise to point that out, though, judging from the look on A'ndreas' face.

Fari raised a hand. "What about the fact I'm failing half my classes?"

"That's not because you're stupid," Lira grumbled unthinkingly.

All eyes shot her way. Lira's scowl deepened. "I'm not joining a patrol. I don't care who's in it."

"I'd like you to think about it. We won't force it on you." A'ndreas sat back. And there marked the biggest change for mages under the stewardship of Alyx Egalion and Tarrick Tylender. Students were respected and given choices. Not every apprentice—unless they were training to be a warrior mage—was required to join guard shifts or combat patrols. "That's all for now. You'd best get back to your classes."

They filed silently out of the office, letting Lorin limp ahead of them with his crutch. Lira made straight for the stairs while the others hovered awkwardly in the foyer.

"Do you guys still hear the rattling too?" Garan asked suddenly, making her stop dead and turn around. His shoulders were stiff, eyes dark, but he had a determined expression on his face.

Tarion looked at the floor. Fari's eyes went wide, but then she nodded.

"Every night," Lorin said simply. "I'm afraid to go to sleep, because I know when I wake up I won't be sure whether I'm back there again. The weakness shames me but I won't lie about it."

"How long does it take you to get out of your room in the morning?" Garan asked next, then, when nobody said anything, he cleared his throat. "I've managed to get it down from about ten minutes to five."

Fari took a breath. "I can't get out of bed until it's fully light. It's why I'm almost always late for breakfast now. Some mornings I miss it entirely."

"I can't get out of bed until I hear the birds start to sing so I know it's dawn," Lorin said, again without hesitation. The boy wasn't afraid to admit his weakness, and Lira couldn't understand it.

"Tar?" Garan asked quietly. All his charm and bravado was gone. Now it was just simple warmth.

Tarion's head came up, he gave a little smile. "Same as you, Garan."

All their gazes swung to Lira then. She swallowed. "I don't know what you're talking about."

"You've got some nice dark shadows under your eyes there, Lira," Garan commented. "How are you sleeping?"

She scoffed. She wasn't admitting her weakness to them.

She didn't know how.

But maybe... if she couldn't admit her weakness, she *could* at least try and help them. It wasn't like fear and lack of sleep were unfamiliar to her. So she ventured tentatively, "You know, back in Dirinan when we couldn't sleep because it was too cold or we were too hungry, sometimes we would sneak into the inn upstairs and drink the dregs of the ale glasses left on the tables until we were drunk enough to pass out."

Four pairs of eyes stared at her in confusion. She flushed, whirled, and headed straight down the stairs.

So much for trying.

CHAPTER 6

A sharp knock sounded at Lira's door.

She paused halfway through leaning over to blow out the candle on her bedside table, about to crawl under the covers to begin her nightly battle with falling asleep.

Nobody had ever knocked on her door before. Maybe she'd imagined it?

A moment later, another knock came, followed by Fari's voice. "You decent?"

What on...?

Lira went to the door and yanked it open, making sure her scowl was truly intimidating. Instead of quailing, the apprentice healer flashed her a smile, then slipped past Lira and into the room. She glanced left and right before she tossed the large bag she carried onto the spare bed.

"What are you doing?" Lira snapped. She was tired, cranky, and in no mood for Fari's perkiness.

"Moving in." Fari began unbuckling the straps on her bag.

"No you're not."

"Yes I am."

"You can't." Lira recognised the inanity of her words, but couldn't seem to stop herself. "You're a second year. This is the third year dorm level."

"Master A'ndreas gave me special permission." Fari finished undoing her bag and began tossing clothes into the empty chest at the foot of the bed. Lira wasn't sure the girl had attempted folding them before putting them in her bag—they looked like they'd been scrunched up and thrown in. "You know, due to the trauma of what we went through and everything."

"He did *what*?" Lira shook her head. "You can't stay here. I don't *want* you to stay here."

"You know what the problem with that is, Lira?" Fari finally turned, hands on hips.

"What?"

"I'm not scared of you anymore."

Lira's mouth fell open as Fari turned back around and finished transferring belongings from her bag to the chest. Once done, she tossed the bag in after the clothes and closed the chest with a thud. Then, she rested her staff beside Lira's near the door and began changing into the sleeping shirt she'd left out. Her grey robe she hung beside Lira's on the wall.

"I don't want a room-mate," Lira tried again.

"Yeah, well *I* don't want a room-mate who looks at me like I'm crazy every morning because I'm too terrified to leave the room," Fari said. "Besides, you've never had one before. How do you know you won't like it?"

"I have, actually." Lira thought about the loft in Dirinan, the snores of several sleeping bodies drifting through the darkness. How familiar and comforting it had been. Until it was all torn away and she'd adjusted to being on her own. "Trust me, I really don't want a room-mate."

"Who did you live with before you came here?" Curiosity filled Fari's voice. "I mean, I know you're an orphan, but I never really thought about where you came from. That story you told us earlier made me curious. *And* afraid for your general health. You do know that drinking at such an early age is bad for you, yes?"

Lira folded her arms, mutinous. "You can keep on being curious because I have no interest in telling you anything."

Fari shrugged, crawled into bed, then drew the covers around herself. "Suit yourself. Night, Lira."

Frustration rose in a tide, hammering to get out. "Look, there are reasons I can't have a room-mate, Fari. Please, can you just—"

"Reasons like what? And I told you to call me Ari."

Lira bit her lip. Swore inwardly. She couldn't exactly come out and say that she needed to be able to sneak in and out at late hours to attend Underground meetings. "I can't say, but they're good reasons."

"I'm too sleepy to argue. Let's talk about this tomorrow." Fari turned over, her back to Lira, her breathing evening out.

Lira stared, at an utter loss. Maybe she could march to Finn A'ndreas right now and demand he kick Fari out—but that was just going to make her look like she couldn't solve her own problems. Plus, she had a sneaking suspicion he'd refuse. She could throw Fari out herself... her magic was stronger and she was a better fighter. But that would mean hurting her, which shouldn't be a problem. Except she didn't *want* to hurt Fari.

"I'm going soft," she muttered under her breath.

"Do you sleep standing up?" Fari asked drowsily.

Lira huffed a breath, turned around, and got into her bed. The room settled into darkness once she'd blown out the candle.

She'd figure out this problem in the morning when she wasn't so tired.

THE ARROW HIT the centre of the target with a satisfying thud. Lira considered the shot, then lowered the bow, giving her aching fingers a break. She'd gone for an even longer run this morning—still no note from Greyson—and since returning she had been firing at a steady, relentless pace, pushing herself harder and harder to try and work out the residual anxiety and panic from another nightmare-ridden sleep. Now her muscles were sore, her breathing fast, but the ragged edge of emotion had smoothed out.

It hadn't gone entirely though. It was still there, a pressure weighing on her chest, and for a moment she allowed herself to give in to it, shoulders sagging.

She wished she were anywhere but here. The tedium of lessons and routine at Temari provided nothing to distract her from the yawning hole inside her, the one her mother had left when she'd died, that had only gotten bigger after Dirinan. Ahrin's presence only made it worse, a constant, painful reminder of what she wanted and could never have.

Suddenly having a room-mate, losing her only private space, made it worse. She felt trapped inside the walls of the school. A large part of her just wanted to leave, walk out the door and find somewhere else to go. Learn her magic on her own. Maybe she should forget trying to win over the Mage Council and just join Underground properly. Their fight would distract her, fill her time, give her something to be interested in.

The thought was tempting. Surprisingly strong. By doing that, she could forget about all this pretence and just be her.

But she wouldn't escape Ahrin that way. And that's what she really wanted, deep down. To have the Darkhand gone so she could forget her and Dirinan and leave it all in the past.

Lira shook herself. Straightened her shoulders. No. She just needed to start *doing* something. That would ease the growing frustration. If Ahrin didn't come to her today, she'd sneak out to Karonan tonight and find Greyson on her own.

Chest still heaving, feeling better for having made a decision, she glanced at the sky. The sun hadn't quite crept fully across the horizon yet. There was time for more practice, though she should probably start on another weapon. She'd improved to the point where she rarely missed what she aimed for with the bow.

The problem was, the most useful weapon to learn would be something bladed; a knife, dagger, or ideally, a sword. And for that she'd need someone to teach her. Someone to spar with.

"Morning, Lira!"

She spun at the sound of Lorin's voice. He limped across the yard towards her, walking stick clacking on the stone. Tarion lifted a hand in greeting as he paced at Lorin's side. Irritation surged at the sight of them—after the previous night with Fari, Lira was in absolutely no mood for more incursions into her private time. She valued the silence, the peace, more than anything else... especially when the rest of her world was about hiding, pretending, lying.

"Go away," she said flatly, turning back to the target and lifting the bow.

"We're not here to bother you," Lorin said, unfazed by her rude greeting. "Tarion offered to help me with extra practice, that's all, and this is the only free time initiates have. After classes this week I'm on kitchen duty every night."

She gave him a sceptical look. "And Master A'ndreas is okay with you sparring on that leg already?"

"He says I need to work on rebuilding the strength in the muscles and joints."

"I'll make sure he doesn't do too much," Tarion said quietly, ignoring the scowl Lorin shot his way.

"Fine. But find somewhere else to train." She fired the arrow. It hit the centre of the target with another satisfying thump.

"Lira?"

Tarion's voice made her turn, lower the bow, and snap, "What?"

"When we were locked in that cell together, you told me you hated the fact that everyone assumes you're a dangerous person just because you're Shakar's granddaughter. That you hate that everyone either fears or distrusts you."

The comment was so unexpected that she didn't know what to say in response and Tarion continued before she could come up with anything. "You ever think that maybe people treat you that way because you don't give them a chance to do anything different?"

She took a steadying breath, unsure if the emotion choking her throat was pure fury or something else. She *had* thought of it, knew it was at least partly true, but he had no right to go delving around in her private business. "You have *no* idea what you're talking about. And that was a private discussion, not for airing in front of initiates."

"Fine." He stepped closer, forcing her to meet his gaze. "But Lorin and I are not everyone else. We don't fear you and we don't distrust you. We are your friends and you can trust *us*."

"You gave up your only chance at escape to come back and help me that night. You saved my life and my leg," Lorin said in that quiet, dignified way of his. "You can glare at me and tell me to go away. You can be cruel, even, and I won't waver. I am your friend, Lira, and that's that."

She took a helpless step back, not knowing how to even begin dealing with those words. She went with honesty. "In the world I live in, there is no such thing as true friendship. People eventually betray you or walk away when you're not useful anymore. I learned that lesson the hard way and I'm not foolish enough to let it happen to me." *Again.*

"We live in the same world here at Temari," Tarion said.

She huffed a bitter laugh. "No, we don't. Lorin knows that, it's only you purebloods that don't. Some because they like that it's different, they *want* to be superior, and others—like you, Tarion—because you don't realise it, you *can't* see it."

Tarion looked at Lorin, who gave a little shrug. "She is right."

"Even if that's true, isn't saying that *everyone* will betray you a sweeping generalisation akin to calling you an evil mage because of who your grandfather was?" Tarion pointed out.

She looked away. "When I first came here, I capitalised on the fear and unease I saw because I wanted to survive. Where I come from you survived by making yourself stronger or more fearsome than everyone else, or hiding from those stronger than you. But I didn't create those reactions to me. I've dealt with them my entire life."

"And now you think it's too late to change how people think of you here?" Tarion asked softly.

"No, Tarion. I don't *want* to change it," she said bluntly, annoyed by the disappointment that rippled over his face.

Lorin took a limping step closer. "I don't agree with you entirely, Lira. Tarion's rich and noble. My family survived but never with ease. You were poor and took to crime to survive. But despite those differences all three of us are mages, *warrior* mages. We belong together. We fought for each other because that's what mages do, even if we don't like each other. It's who Tarrick Tylender and Alyx Egalion want us to be."

His words shook her to her core, because they spoke to the depth of what Alyx Egalion had promised her at six years old. What she'd found temporarily with Ahrin's crew and had torn away, revealed as an illusion. What she'd then desperately hoped to find at Temari but hadn't.

It was, deep down, what Lira most wanted. Why she fought so hard to get respect, to force them to think of her instead of her grandfather. She craved somewhere to belong.

She just didn't believe that option existed for her anymore.

"Why can't you at least give us a shot?" Tarion pushed when Lira said nothing.

"I..." She *hated* how her voice shook on that word, and didn't speak again until she was confident her voice would be firm. "For the same reason you can't manage to speak at normal volume in a group of people, Tarion. Because I don't know how." She didn't have a clue how to trust someone else again. Didn't *want* to open herself up to that pain. "I don't know how."

"I didn't know how to stay here after they told me I'd need this for the rest of my life." Lorin lifted his crutch. "You showed me how. Maybe I can help do the same for you."

Tarion glanced at the initiate, surprise flashing over his face, before turning back to Lira. He smiled. "You'll learn. They don't call you the best student here for no reason, Lira."

She swallowed. Part of her wanted what they were offering, a part of her she'd rarely acknowledged. It was weakness... surely it was weakness? And stupidity. These people were no different than Timin or Ahrin or the others from Dirinan; they just had more money and wore nicer clothes. But they *had* stood with her. Against a sea of razak. They'd held the door. "I..."

"Wait!" Tarion said suddenly, sharply, eyes narrowing in concentration. "There's something—"

A whisper rippled through the air.

All three of them spun toward it. Lorin's crutch clattered to the ground, and he swore before reaching down awkwardly to pick it up.

Lira stilled, senses straining, instincts warning her that the quiet peace of early morning had turned to danger as quick as a blink. All she could see was darkness in the direction the sound had come from, the golden glow of early dawn a faint line on the eastern horizon. Tarion and Lorin were silent, a step behind her, just as still as she was.

59

The whisper came again, more like a hiss this time. Closer. From above. It had a pitch to it that irritated her ears, made her want to block them.

It felt like being back there. Like they were in that dark, half-falling-down estate again. Like something was *hunting* them.

A thrill leapt through her, hot and seductive. Suddenly the world grew sharper, the air clearer. Her fingers curled tighter around the bow while her gaze scanned the skies for danger. Danger she welcomed with a fierce hunger.

She heard Lorin's gasp in the second before she saw what caused it.

Three winged shapes—several times larger than an eagle, but looking nothing like a bird—dropped out of the sky. If not for the creatures' eyes, their approach would have been entirely hidden in the darkness. Flickering like flamelight, they gleamed bright copper. One of the creatures banked sharply, and the light from the rising sun glinted off what appeared to be ridged edges to leathery wings; talons or claws... or something worse.

Pearlescent blue light flashed as a concussive burst flew from Lorin's raised hand. It lit up the training yard, headed straight for the three flying creatures, and exploded in an electrical roar that ripped the morning silence to shreds. The pressure hit Lira's chest a moment later, squeezing like a vice before letting go.

But the explosion did nothing to the creatures apart from causing a momentary buffeting to their flight path. The closest one dived straight at the three of them, another hiss rippling through the electric echoes of the concussive magic.

Lira froze for the briefest of seconds, grip white-knuckled on the bow. These weren't razak, but...

"They're invulnerable!" Tarion shouted, and then he vanished from her side.

He reappeared a heartbeat later in front of her, staff already sweeping towards the plummeting tangle of dark wings and snapping teeth. The creature swerved to avoid his swing, but he flashed out of sight again, a quick blur, reappearing behind it and swinging hard.

The second blow connected with the creature's side and it let out a shriek as it careened off course and hit the ground sideways, feet scrabbling for purchase. Tarion followed after as it scrambled to right itself, his feet dancing gracefully to avoid lashing talons, clearly aiming to bury his staff in the thing's eyes.

Clever boy. That was how they'd killed the razak.

"Lira!"

Lorin's warning had Lira's gaze snapping towards another creature swooping toward Tarion's head, scaled forelegs extended from a solid, muscular body covered in dark, iridescent scales. Wickedly-long claws sharp enough to rip into Tarion's face were poised to strike.

Lira didn't hesitate. She lifted her bow, took aim, fired. The arrow whistled through the air and buried itself in the creature's left eye. It screamed, shrill and pained, its determined plummet arresting mid-air as it writhed in agony. She drew another arrow, nocked the bow, tracked the creature as its flight wobbled crazily, then fired again. This one hit the second eye. It dropped to the ground and lay still, dead.

Another shrill scream sounded as Tarion buried his staff in the first creature's eye. A few more seconds and he'd gotten the other eye too.

Two down. One to go.

Lira scanned the sky, taking a few seconds to place the third flying creature. It had circled around them and now went for Lorin, clearly having picked him as the weakest remaining target. The initiate held his ground, balancing mainly on his good leg as he lashed out with his staff to force the monster to divert away with a frustrated hiss. Tarion flashed into the space beside him a second later, hovering protectively.

"Lorin, concussive burst to its left!" Lira shouted.

Lorin let his magic loose without hesitation. Bright concussive magic exploded into the morning sky seconds later. The creature veered right with a scream, right into Lira's line of sight. She loosed another arrow, but it had learned from the fate of its companions. The thing folded its wings so that it dropped rapidly out of the sky. Her arrow whistled inches over the top of its head.

It landed on powerful hind legs, wings spreading wide, narrow snout opening in a hiss to reveal rows of razor-sharp teeth. Outspread, each taloned wing was double the length of the creature's body, and on its hind legs it was a little taller than Tarion.

Lira re-nocked and aimed her bow, but the creature gave a mighty flap of its wings and dove toward her at the same time as she loosed. The arrow plunged into its scaled body without any obvious effect and she was forced to drop to the icy ground and scramble out of the way of lashing wings and claws. She caught a putrid scent as the thing's hot breath washed over her, teeth snapping inches from her face.

Lira kept rolling, the creature pursuing. Lorin went after it without hesitation, bringing his staff up and slamming it down hard on a wing. The creature screamed in fury and spun, quicker than thought, toward the initiate. Face set, Lorin swung his stuff in a frantic attempt to hold it off. It delayed the creature long enough that Tarion had time to get close and drive his staff into an eye.

Lira rolled to her feet, drew her own staff, and brought it slamming down into the second eye.

The thing slumped, dead. The copper light in its eyes faded to darkness.

"Well." Tarion took a panting breath, eyes running over the three dead corpses. "That was probably a little more advanced than I'd planned for your first lesson, Lorin. Well done."

Lorin stared at him, then looked at Lira.

"Don't look at me." Her gaze kept returning to the carcass at her feet. "I've got absolutely no idea."

Except for one thing.

It seemed razak weren't the only monsters out there hunting them.

CHAPTER 7

"Hey, what is going on out here?" A raised voice came from the direction of the tower. One of the apprentices on guard had obviously heard Lorin's concussive blasts and come to make sure everything was all right. Seconds later a few of the guard dogs let out a sharp bark at his tone of voice. Lira swore. Probably anyone awake had heard the explosions—although hopefully the concussive roars had masked the snapping and hissing from the now-dead creatures. The dogs were trained to ignore the sound of mages practising, but would respond quickly if the humans on guard became concerned or scared.

"That was Perin, right? Go and cut him off before he sees this," she snapped at Tarion. "Tell him we're fine and we were just practising with Lorin. If the guards don't raise the alarm, then anyone else who is awake and heard it will just think it's an apprentice out here practising too."

"Until someone sees those bodies," Lorin said. "Or the dogs catch their scent."

"Just go!" Lira snapped at Tarion. "One thing at a time."

Tarion didn't hesitate, presumably understanding as well as she did the panic that would sweep through the student population if the alarm was raised. He flashed out of existence, reappearing at the far side of the yard and then walking a few steps into the shadows beyond it, one hand raised to stop whoever was approaching. Several more questioning barks filled the silence.

"The Shiven soldiers will be next," Lorin muttered, glancing at the bodies. "Even though they're guarding the exterior walls, they'll have heard all that."

He was right. Several tall figures materialised from the shadows in the direction of the western wall gate, drawn swords glinting in the growing light. Lira froze, desperately trying to come up with something to say when they got close enough to see the bodies. They wouldn't panic, but she didn't want anyone knowing what had happened until she could figure out the best way to manage the situation.

"Lira." Lorin shifted nervously. "What do we—"

Her shoulders sagged in relief when Tarion flashed into sight before the Shiven, making them all lift their swords in reaction before realising it was a mage apprentice standing before them.

They weren't close enough for Lira to hear what Tarion was saying, but she and Lorin did their best to look casual and relaxed, and *not* glance toward the bodies lying in the shadows behind them. Lira's unease rose until Tarion gave a nod, then turned and began making his way back towards them. The Shiven warriors went back the way they'd come.

"Told them we were just out early practising," Tarion said. "Perin was fine, just glad that nothing was wrong and he could go back to his warm guard post and calm the dogs. The Shiven captain was very displeased. He told me in no uncertain terms that next time I was to warn them if we were out training early." His gaze searched them both. "Are you okay? You didn't get hurt?"

The earnestness of his question prompted a smile she did her best to hold back. "We're fine. You stepped in front of me."

"You had my back too." He gestured to the air above his head. "Friends?"

She hesitated. Even if she wanted to accept what Tarion was

offering—and she had to admit that deep down she *did* want it—she still had Ahrin and Underground spies watching her.

But.... eventually she nodded. "Only here. Where nobody else is around."

"I'm your friend whether anyone can see or not." Lorin was scanning the sky, presumably keeping watch in case more flying creatures appeared. "But I accept your terms."

"Me too." Tarion smiled at her, unforced and simple.

She allowed her smile to break free then. It stretched her mouth in a strange way, felt odd, but somehow good.

"You!" She swung on Lorin, unable to hold Tarion's gaze any longer. "You reacted faster with your magic just then than two third year apprentices. Don't ever try and tell me again that you're not a warrior mage!"

Lorin's shoulders straightened, a proud smile spreading across his fierce Shiven features. But it quickly faded, followed by a worried look. "We've still got three bodies in the yard. Students will be out here sooner rather than later, or one of the masters."

"He's right." Tarion sighed "We haven't got long to figure something out."

Before either Lira or Lorin could reply, the thud of running feet had them all turning, weapons lifted, until they saw it was Garan and Fari. Lira lowered her bow in disappointment. The thrill of the fight was already fading and she wished it would come back.

"What are you doing out here?" she demanded, trying to keep her voice down.

"We heard... felt... something. It was like being back there," Garan said. He was quieter than usual, less of a presence, and she understood why. It was the same thing that had made her freeze when those creatures first appeared out of the darkness. Fear. Remembered horror. And yet...

"And you decided to run *towards* it?" she asked.

"What in magical hells are those?" Fari asked, pointing at the corpses lying scattered on the yard.

Lorin answered, "They came at us out of nowhere. Lira and Tarion killed them."

"They were impervious to magic like the razak," Tarion added quietly.

A grim look settled over Garan's features. "Were they after you?"

"Impossible to tell because we were the only ones out here. They may have attacked whoever they found," Lira said. Even as she said it, she didn't believe the words, and from the look Tarion shot her way, he didn't either.

"They didn't go for any of the Shiven warriors on guard outside the walls," he murmured.

"What were you all even doing out here so early?" Fari asked in confusion.

"Tarion offered to help me get some extra training in, because of my leg." Lorin answered when neither Tarion or Lira did. "And Lira has been out here every morning since we got back, learning how to use weapons other than her magic. Because the razak were impervious to it and our staffs are pretty useless against them too."

Lira spun towards him. "How did you know that?"

"The first thing I heard about you when I got here is that you know how to survive, to adapt, that despite everyone here hating you, you've stayed unharmed and alive. It's part of the reason they fear you so much," Lorin said. "So when I saw you out here last week practising with the bow, I figured you had to be doing it for a reason."

"It's a good idea, Lira," Garan said. "We should all start doing it. Tomorrow morning, together?"

Lira's horror deepened, killing the rush still warming her from the attack a few minutes earlier. More intrusions on her private time?

"I'm not sure if you can call anything that results in less sleep than we already get a good idea." Fari sighed, then looked at the bodies. "Are they like the razak, sent by Underground?"

"Again, it's impossible to tell, but it seems like quite the coincidence if not." Lira's gaze narrowed as she glanced at them. "The fact the two of you sensed the attack... that's strange."

"Very." Garan frowned, then shook himself, as if trying to dislodge the same odd feeling from under his skin. "First though, we'd better go and report this to Master A'ndreas before any students see those corpses."

Lira froze, her stomach sinking at the implications of doing that. If A'ndreas knew the five of them might still be targets... "If we do that, the masters won't ever let us outside the tower without an escort again. Do you want to have a babysitter everywhere we go for however long it takes for the council to find Athira and catch Underground? I don't know about you, but I don't get the impression they're anywhere near close to doing either of those things."

"If we don't report it, Tarion's mother will melt us into a puddle of mage goop," Fari pointed out. "And I'm all for babysitting if it means I don't get eaten by scary monsters."

"She's right," Garan said heavily. "If something happened to any of you, and I hadn't reported this..."

"Oh rotted hells, you're not responsible for all of us," Lira snapped. "I've never had a parent, and I certainly don't need one now. I can look after myself."

"What are you suggesting exactly?" he asked mildly. "That we drag away those bodies, bury them, pretend this never happened and hope the guard dogs don't sniff them out? And then what, wait for more of them to attack us again? Or attack someone else out here early one morning? What if another student here got hurt because they weren't warned?"

"This could be the part of the threat my mother was talking about." Tarion stared at the ground, voice barely audible. "The masters need to know about it so they can protect the school properly."

She tried to come up with a good counter to those arguments. Failed. While Lira might not care two coppers about the other students on most days, if Dawn or Tarrick learned she'd been hiding things that affected student safety, she'd be pulled from her assignment with Underground.

But if they learned that Underground had possibly tried to kill her again, the same thing would happen. Frustration surged. She *hated* how limited she was.

"I'm sorry, Lira, but I agree with them," Lorin said before Lira could come up with anything.

"Fine. Do whatever you want." She let out an annoyed breath. How was she supposed to get to the next Underground meeting if she was on some sort of protective lockdown inside Temari Hall? It had already been difficult enough sneaking past those rotted Shiven guards earlier. Determination surged. She'd figure out a way. Somehow.

Garan took charge then. "I'll stay here and make sure nobody stumbles across those bodies. Lorin, will you wait with me just in case I need help? Tarion, you go and let Uncle Finn know what's happened."

"I'm going to go and get some breakfast," Lira said before she could be issued any orders. "I'm hungry and you seem to have things well in hand."

"Me too." Fari sketched a wave and fell into step with Lira. "You okay?"

"Do I not look okay?"

"I heard you leave early this morning." A wistful note entered the girl's voice. "It was still so dark. I wish I could be as brave as you."

"It was still pretty dark when you came running out here with Garan," Lira said.

Fari was quiet a moment, their footsteps carrying them towards the front doors of the dining hall, then she said, "It was the hardest thing I've done since coming back. I just wanted to stay curled up under the blankets and pretend it wasn't happening."

Lira hesitated, then said, "Thank you."

Fari started in surprise. "You're welcome."

"I'm still not letting you sit with me at breakfast."

Fari laughed. "Fair enough. I'll see you later, Lira."

TRUE TO HER WORD, Fari split from Lira once they'd received their trays and went to sit at one of the crowded tables in the middle of the room. Lira settled at her usual table, her thoughts dwelling on what had just happened.

Lucinda and the Shadowcouncil were surely responsible for the attack—the chances that some other adversary out there possessed monsters impervious to magic were slim. Still, though... Lira's head ached trying to figure out the logic behind it. Underground had returned them all to Temari less than two weeks earlier. It didn't make sense that they'd changed their minds so quickly and now wanted them dead.

It was possible that Lucinda was merely carrying through on her decision to have Lira killed. After all, the Shadowcouncil's spies inside Temari would have reported Lira's regular early morning routine by now. They would have known she would be out on the practice courts at that time. But that didn't make sense either... if they'd wanted only Lira dead, Ahrin would have been a much more discreet and reliable way of getting that done.

Lira had to get to Greyson. With A'ndreas and Ahrin both refusing to tell her anything useful, he was her only remaining source of answers. She'd go into the city tonight, try and find him by herself.

A whisper of air at her side announced the Darkhand's arrival—as if Ahrin had been summoned by her thoughts. The tension in Lira's shoulders tightened by several degrees as she pulled out the chair next to Lira's and sat down.

Ahrin got a few odd stares as students wandered past, probably confused that a new initiate was sitting with not only a third year apprentice but the school's outcast. It was the worst thing a student could do in their first few weeks of attending Temari Hall if they ever wanted to be accepted. The breakout of whispering from the nearest table was particularly obvious.

"I'm starting to get it," Ahrin commented, waving a hand towards the popular tables, presumably referring to the looks and the murmurs. Her face was hard despite the casual tone of her voice.

"Get what?" Lira spooned up oatmeal, debating whether to confront Ahrin about what had just happened. It might be better to see if she mentioned it first. If it had been a hit on Lira, then Ahrin had to have known about it.

"Why you joined." Ahrin lowered her voice, despite her oblique wording. "When I learned of it, I couldn't figure it out."

All thoughts of the attack slid from Lira's mind and she was turning towards Ahrin before she could stop herself. Her heart thumped in sudden fear. She couldn't afford for Ahrin to be suspicious about why Lira was a member of Underground. "What do you mean?"

"They didn't welcome you here, did they? Not like I thought they would." Her expression was cold. "They behaved no differently than the villagers where you were born, or the people at the orphanage where they dumped you."

Ahrin sounded genuinely angry on Lira's behalf, and she had to remind herself how good the Darkhand was at manipulation. After a moment's hesitation as she figured out how best to play this conversation, Lira decided on trying for more information. "When *did* you learn I'd joined?"

"Recently." Ahrin's gaze turned to her breakfast. The edge was back. The dangerous coolness that warned off any further questioning or discussion. They were in the middle of a busy dining hall, after all. But Lira couldn't stop the urge to poke at the Darkhand's armour, try and break through it. She'd have to figure out how if she wanted to win Ahrin over.

So she shifted a little closer, lowered her voice to a cold, demanding whisper. "What in rotted hells was that little incident earlier?"

Ahrin chuckled, the coldness vanishing as if it had never been. "I love that you're always in a sour mood in the mornings. Timin used to literally cower from you until mid-morning at least. Is there something in particular causing this morning's temper?"

Lira stared at her, trying to read whether Ahrin was faking her ignorance. It *seemed* genuine but it was impossible to tell.

Ahrin's gaze narrowed, seeming to sense something amiss. "Lira. What's going on?" But before Lira could say a word, Ahrin's quick mind was figuring it out. "The concussion bursts earlier. The alarm wasn't raised so everyone thought it was just an apprentice out unusually early to practice. It wasn't, was it?"

Committed now, Lira decided there was no point holding back. "We were attacked by three flying creatures out on the practice courts this morning. They were immune to magic, like the razak, only they had wings. More pets of the Shadowcouncil's, I'm assuming. Was it a hit on me?" Lira's words were barely audible, her desire to know the answers not entirely trumping her good sense.

Ahrin went still, and while her expression was unreadable, that in itself was telling. Ahrin was rarely truly unsettled, so when it

70

happened, she carefully removed all expression from her features. Surprise rippled through Lira. "You didn't know?"

"No." Ahrin returned to her food. "It must have been someone else."

"You're kidding, right?" Lira wrapped her fingers around Ahrin's wrist, leaning in close so she could keep her voice low. "Someone *else* sent violent creatures to kill the same group of students that were recently kidnapped and hunted by violent creatures immune to magic?"

Ahrin frowned. "You were out there with Garan and Tarion and the others?"

"Are you playing at being *jealous*?" Lira's mouth thinned. Ahrin was trying to divert her attention, and she had no patience for it. "Don't waste my time. You really didn't know about this?"

"If there was a hit on you, I'd know about it."

Lira waited a moment, but that was all Ahrin said. "Then tell me what this morning was all about. They might not have told you anything, but we both know you've probably already figured it out."

Ahrin glanced around, then murmured, "They were moving something along the main road overnight. Whatever it was came off a ship in Dirinan four days ago. I don't have the details because it's a minor logistical activity and I'm rarely involved in those."

Lira blinked, astonished that Ahrin had given her an answer. But she rallied quickly. "Why would they be moving monsters to Karonan? Where were they even going to *keep* the things?"

"They weren't coming *to* Karonan, just passing by. The cargo was large, big enough to require a transport that can only travel the bigger roads, and they mostly go through the capital." Ahrin made a sharp cutting motion with her hand before Lira could say any more. "That's all I know, and more importantly, all I'm willing to discuss inside this school."

Lira held her gaze, seeing an opportunity to sow division between the Darkhand and her masters. "Why wouldn't your friends have told you if they planned to attack me this morning?"

"I told you, they would have." Ahrin's mouth tightened.

"Are you sure about that?" Lira taunted softly. Here was leverage

71

she could use. "You're not as important to them as you think you are, are you?"

"Nice try at poking my ego, but it's not working," Ahrin snapped.

Lira simply smiled. Even though her plan was to win Ahrin over, it was oddly enjoyable to get such a rise out of her. Besides, if she could drive a deeper wedge between Ahrin and Underground, that would only work in her favour. "Isn't it?"

Ahrin's eyes flashed in warning. Very deliberately, she reached out to tuck a strand of loose hair behind Lira's ear, shifting close enough that her breath was warm on Lira's skin. Heat rushed to Lira's face despite her attempts to stop it and her heartbeat quickened. "There's a meeting tonight. Usual place and time. Greyson is expecting you, which seems unlikely if they were planning to kill you this morning, no?" She lingered, a little smile of triumph flickering over her face as she read Lira's reaction to her closeness. Lira fought the urge to move even closer. "And I wasn't playing at being jealous, Lira, I *was* jealous."

Before Lira could manage to gather her thoughts and figure out something cool and aloof to respond with, Ahrin abruptly moved away, lifting her tray and stalking off. Irritation surged. Every time Lira thought she'd scored a point, Ahrin would go one better.

She tore her gaze away from Ahrin's departing figure and stared down at her breakfast, working hard to regain her composure and push away that familiar ache in her chest. She wasn't at all sure about her ability to do this, draw Ahrin in close and bring her to Lira's side while simultaneously staying emotionally detached so that she didn't end up in pieces once Ahrin inevitably walked away again. She took a deep breath.

She could do it. She *would* do it. There was no other option.

A moment later, relief surged as Ahrin's message finally processed through her thoughts. She wouldn't have to go hunting Greyson tonight—there was a meeting. She could write to Dawn as soon as it was done, forestall any attempt to withdraw Lira once the lord-mage received news of the morning's attack.

A voice sounded at her side. "At the risk of receiving a deathly scowl, I've been sent to fetch you."

Fari's voice made Lira look up, startled. "Where?"

"Master A'ndreas wants to see us. Right away."

Lira sighed, stood reluctantly. "I bet he does. Let's get it over and done with."

"What did the new girl want with you?" Fari asked as they walked. "Someone needs to tell her that initiates don't talk to third years, especially heirs to Darkmages, if they ever want to make friends here."

"She was curious about me," Lira hedged. "I guess someone told her who I am."

Fari tipped her head back and laughed. "Oh that's delightful. No wonder she had such a strange look on her face as she left your table. Absolutely priceless. Did you give her the intimidating glare or the ice-cold voice that indicates you couldn't be less interested in her if you tried?"

Lira glanced at her, mouth twitching. "Both."

Fari's laughter deepened. "Seriously though, think you could introduce me? She is *gorgeous*."

"I take it you're past your deep and abiding grief over Derna then?" Lira asked dryly.

"No." Fari's entire manner changed, the light fading from her face. "I still miss her every day."

"I didn't..." Lira cleared her throat, feeling bad and not liking the feeling. "How do you cope with that?"

"What? Missing her?"

Lira nodded.

"It's not something that I can control. I know I don't talk about her much, and maybe it looks like I wasn't too affected by her death... but..." Fari paused, biting her lip. "We were together since we were initiates, since our second month here. I was in love with her. Still am. Sometimes I'm so sad that I literally can't do anything but think about how much I miss her, and I struggle to even get out of bed or go to class. And sometimes it's more like an ache that I can ignore *just* enough to pretend I'm fine." Fari swallowed. "I'm hoping those occasions get more frequent as time passes."

Lira didn't say anything once Fari had stopped speaking, pretending to catch her breath as they climbed the seven flights to Egalion's office. She had no idea *what* to say. After a while the girl gave Lira a curious glance. "Why do you ask? It's not like you to be concerned about other people's feelings."

"I just wondered..." Lira tried to find the words, but didn't understand well enough herself what exactly she wanted to know. "If it was the same for everyone."

Fari paused on the landing. "You lost someone too?"

"I've never had anyone to lose." Not after her mother had died, anyway. Lira kept her voice businesslike. "I thought I did, but it was a lie. I'd stay away from Ahrin if I were you. She doesn't strike me as the warm and fuzzy type."

"Who cares about warm and fuzzy?" Fari's good mood was quickly restored, and she gave Lira a knowing look. "Don't tell me you haven't noticed how utterly stunning she is. I can be warm and fuzzy enough for the both of us."

Lira laughed, but then sobered, searching again for words but not finding anything that didn't feel trite. "I'm sorry about Derna."

Fari paused, surprise on her face. "Do you mean that?"

"Well, I don't care two coppers about Derna and whether she lived or died." Lira hesitated. "But I'm sorry that you feel so sad that it's hard to get out of bed some days."

Fari let out a strangled breath, like she didn't know whether to be angry or amused. Then she shook her head and started walking again. "You're lucky, Lira. I'm going to accept that you're trying to be nice."

Lira frowned. That was exactly what she had been trying to do, yet Fari seemed angry about what she'd said. She shook her head and started walking too.

She wished she hadn't even brought up the subject.

CHAPTER 8

Lira and Fari were the last to arrive in Egalion's office; Garan, Lorin, and Tarion were already arrayed in chairs before the desk. It was only Master A'ndreas seated behind it this time—though Lira had no doubt A'ndreas had already sent a message to both Caverlock and Duneskal to tell them what had happened.

"Thank you for coming," A'ndreas said as Fari and Lira sat down. He looked more serious than usual, taking the tone of acting head of Temari Hall rather than helpful library master. "After this morning's events, I'll be instituting some changes and wanted you to hear them directly from me."

"What might those be?" Fari asked.

"Let me guess. Six more divisions of Shiven infantry are about to march through the school gates?" Lira muttered, warmed when Fari chuckled and Garan smirked.

A'ndreas ignored her. "All five of you are to remain within the boundaries of Temari Hall for the foreseeable future. If you want to leave the grounds for any reason, you'll seek permission from me first," he said. "Further, outside daylight hours you will not leave the tower unless it is in the company of one of the masters. During daylight hours, you're not to be on the grounds in anything smaller than a group of four. Am I clear?"

Lira shot a mutinous look down the row. They all avoided her stare, except for Tarion, who gave her a little shrug as if to say, '*what did you expect?*'.

"Uncle Finn, I really don't think—" Garan started, but stumbled to a halt at the look the master levelled at him.

"I asked you to form a combat patrol, and you all refused," A'ndreas said flatly. "With the extra training that comes with being part of a patrol, I'd be more comfortable with you leaving the tower, but otherwise I'm afraid I can't take the risk."

"I'm a student here, not a prisoner," Lira said, hating that A'ndreas thought he was protecting them by doing this. Not to mention how difficult it was going to make sneaking out to Greyson's meeting that night. "You can't keep me trapped inside the tower if I don't want to be here."

"That's not what I'm doing. I'm merely ensuring you're appropriately protected when you leave the safety of these walls." He gave her an uncompromising look. "If you want to be trained as a mage here, you'll follow the rules we set. Otherwise you're free to leave and make your own way."

"I see. So if I left the council's control, your care for my safety suddenly vanishes?" She lifted an eyebrow. "Good to know."

"You're twisting my words," he said, refusing to be goaded.

"Am I?" she pushed. When he said nothing, she continued, "Confining us to the tower is unnecessary. We were all tucked up warm in our beds when they took us. How does stopping us from going outside prevent that happening again?"

"My decision is final." An edge of warning filled A'ndreas' voice. His patience was fading. "And I don't want to hear any further arguments on the matter."

"If we were to agree to become a combat patrol, would you let us outside on our own?" Garan asked.

"Once your training had sufficiently progressed that we could be comfortable that you're able to protect yourselves, then yes."

"And how long would that take, do you think?" Fari asked.

A'ndreas merely gave her a look.

"This is ludicrous. We fought off those creatures this morning all by ourselves, not to mention surviving worse while we were held captive," Lira snapped. "You're treating us like we're helpless children. By all means wrap your precious family members up in a protective bubble like you always have, but I don't need it and I don't want it. Nor do they, if you ever wanted to stop and notice that."

All gazes swivelled to her. Then back to A'ndreas, whose calm finally broke. "That is enough, Lira."

She met his furious look with one of her own. "I do not need to be confined in this tower, sir. If you don't believe that, then we have a problem."

Fari spoke defiantly into the tense silence. "Master A'ndreas, I agree with Lira. We've already demonstrated that we can take care of ourselves. Surely you'd be better off figuring out how to identify if these creatures approach the walls of the school again. They flew right over the Shiven soldiers outside the walls this morning without being spotted."

"I'd like to discuss this with my father," Tarion added, barely audible, but stubborn.

Lorin cleared his throat, sat up straighter...

"Don't," A'ndreas warned him. "I am in charge of Temari Hall while Councillor Egalion is gone. Your welfare is my primary concern, and *not* just because one of you is my nephew. I am the master, you the students, and I consider these measures necessary. You're all going to have to live with them. Am I clear?"

He wasn't going to back down no matter how hard Lira pushed. And if she called his bluff and walked out... she could go to Underground, join them fully. But that would mean giving up on her plans where the council was concerned. Not to mention proving every single suspicion anyone had ever had about her right. Even then, it was tempting. She was sick of the council and Temari Hall and was starting to wonder exactly why she cared so much about making the Mage Council respect her anyway.

"Sir, you promised to give us updates on your investigation into our kidnapping. Have you found any link between Underground and the protests and strikes?" Lorin asked into the ensuing stony silence.

"The *what*?" Lira's gaze swivelled to Lorin.

A'ndreas ignored her. "What do you know about those, Initiate Hester?"

"My parents write to me every week, sir." He took a breath. "I know there have been strikes on some of the larger farms in the south over the past month, and protests here in Karonan. Da says food shortages are likely to occur if the strikes spread."

"Is he right, Uncle Finn?" Garan turned to A'ndreas, brows furrowed.

"Unfortunately, yes." A'ndreas sat back in his chair and let out a long breath, looking suddenly tired.

"It's Underground, isn't it?" Tarion asked quietly.

The look on the master's face was enough to answer the question. A grim note settled over the room.

"And the attack this morning. Is that connected to the mysterious threat to Temari that Councillor Egalion told us about before leaving?" Lira asked.

"It happened barely an hour ago. We don't know yet," A'ndreas said. "But I hope this helps you understand why I feel the need to take extra precautions."

"Are the strikes happening anywhere else, sir?" Fari asked suddenly.

He hesitated. "Yes, in some of the more rural areas of Tregaya."

Lira sucked in a breath. Underground's activity was spilling beyond Shivasa. Strikes, protests, that was in the Karonan cell's longer term plans, but they'd been nowhere near doing any of it before her kidnapping, let alone spreading their activities beyond Shivasa's borders.

They'd kept so much from her.

She'd been an arrogant fool, assuming just because she'd seen nothing happening that meant nothing was. She wouldn't make that mistake again. Determination flared, and she wished the day would hurry up and pass so she could get to the meeting tonight and find out what in rotted hells was going on.

"What about Athira?" Tarion mumbled.

"Nothing, I'm afraid, not yet anyway. But I promise you we're doing everything we can."

"We'll do as you say, Uncle." Garan rose to his feet, clearly unhappy but willing to bow to his uncle's orders.

"Thank you. I'll keep you apprised of developments as best I can."

Lira trailed after the others out of the room. A glance at Tarion showed him deep in thought. Lorin's stick clacked as he moved for the stairwell... it must be painful to drag that still-healing leg up and down so many steps, but he hadn't made a word of complaint.

"Lorin." Fari went after him. "Let me at least give that leg a little jolt of magic, ease some of the ache."

"I'll be fine, thank you, Fari."

Fari tutted. "It's all well and good to be tough and pretend nothing is wrong, but you don't want to push that leg too soon and have it heal badly, do you?" she asked, hands on hips.

"Let her help, Lorin. It's not weakness to take care of yourself," Garan said as he passed them both to head down the stairs. "And Lira, I don't want to hear your complaints."

"I wasn't going to say anything," she retorted as Lorin reluctantly let Fari approach him. "But maybe next time you'll listen to me."

"Listen to you and place everyone else at Temari in danger?" Garan's face was hard as he stopped and turned on her. "You *are* aware that there are students here without warrior magic, who would have had nothing but a staff to defend themselves with if they'd been out on the courts this morning? And it's not like those with warrior magic are much better equipped since those things are impervious to magic."

Lira's ire rose unchecked—she had no restraint left after sitting through that meeting. "I don't make a habit of paying any attention to the students here, as you know, or caring two coppers about their welfare. And nobody was out on the courts this morning except us. If you think that attack was random, then you're not as smart as I thought you were—and that bar wasn't high to start with."

"Why don't we just do what Master A'ndreas wants and become a combat patrol?" Fari intervened before a full-blown argument could start. "Then we'd have our freedom. Maybe they'd even let us help search for Athira."

"I think it's a good idea," Lorin said.

"Sure, and how long do you think it would take before they decided we were trained enough to look after ourselves?" Lira snorted. "My bet is on months, if ever. You can do as you like, but I'm not interested." She turned and started down the stairs.

"Lira!" Garan called after her.

She waved him off. "I've already missed half of Mapping class, and unlike the rest of you, I'm barely passing."

She let the irritation run its course as she stomped down the stairs. Joining a combat patrol was out of the question until she was on better footing with Underground, but of course she couldn't tell them that.

The Underground meeting couldn't come fast enough.

CHAPTER 9

T hat evening, Lira sat at one of the tables at the far edge of
the library atrium. She was trying to concentrate, but it was a
miserable endeavour, and not just because she was impatient
for time to pass until the meeting later.

She'd never sat in the atrium before her kidnapping, at least not in
the hours straight after dinner when everyone was there. She'd always
waited until closer to curfew, found a private spot amongst the stacks,
or studied in her room. But the first time she'd tried settling alone in
the stacks since her kidnapping, she hadn't been able to get rid of the
damn rattling sound echoing through her head, or the sweeping sense
of dread that sent her heartrate skyrocketing.

On two subsequent attempts, the same thing had happened. On
the third attempt she'd forced herself to sit in one of the empty stacks,
homework in her lap, for a full half hour. By the end of it, her
breathing had been fast, her chest tight as a drum, and she'd been
unable to scrawl more than a couple of lines of her homework.

The shame of her failure to conquer her fear ate at her, almost as
much as her frustration at the sheer stupidity of it. She had no
problem wandering around anywhere else in the dark, including her
early morning runs. It was only sitting still in the dark of the library

stacks she was beset by the panic. Her inability to defeat the night-mares that plagued her each night was equally infuriating.

Around her, parchment rustled, quills scratched, and there was the occasional whispered conversation. She ignored the frequent looks sent her way and tried her best to concentrate on her Languages' homework. When she heard her name murmured before an outburst of soft chuckles, she clenched her jaw and hunched further over her parchment. A headache throbbed at her temples.

It didn't help that Ahrin had walked in a short time earlier, tearing what small focus Lira was able to muster to pieces. She sat on the opposite side of the space with a handful of other initiates. They all looked hard at work, but even though Ahrin appeared to be reading and scribbling on parchment too, she seemed somehow distant from them, as if in her own world.

A frustrated breath escaped Lira. She'd read the same sentence in her book at least six times over now, and still the words were a hazy blur. None of it was making sense.

She rubbed at her aching temples. Maybe she should just study up in her room. But Fari might be there... talking. Which meant she'd have to talk back. As impressed as she'd been with Fari earlier in backing up Lira with A'ndreas, she didn't want a conversation right now. She just wanted quiet and privacy to finish her homework.

Taking a breath, she forced herself to focus only on the books and parchment before her for the next little while, ignoring the repeated temptation to glance over the room to see what Ahrin was doing.

She got through a good quarter of the assigned homework—or at least the parts she understood—before her mind drifted to her plan for attending the Underground meeting. She'd have to sneak off the grounds... difficult with all the Shiven solders around, but something she'd done successfully the past couple of mornings. But with A'ndreas' new orders, she not only had to get over the wall, but also out of the tower, without being seen.

The meeting was scheduled for after curfew, so she'd have to slip out just before the doors were closed for the night, and hope Fari just assumed Lira was down in the library studying.

Getting back in would be even harder, but she'd worry about that when it came to it. She was so deep in thought it took her a moment to process when someone pulled out the chair beside her and sat down.

"Hi, Lira." Tarion placed a heavy tome on the table's surface, glanced at her work, then started flipping through the pages. "You're nearly done, lucky you. I don't mind Shiven verbs. Much easier than Zandian pronunciation."

Lira looked up, saw several glances shift in their direction followed by whispered muttering, then turned to Tarion. "What do you want?"

He smiled. "That sounded like a genuine question. I detected no underlying hint that I should remove myself as soon as possible to avoid the loss of a limb."

She rolled her eyes, fighting a return smile. "I wasn't in the market for company, mind, but at least you don't talk incessantly like the others."

The smile widened. "I heard Fari is your new room-mate."

"You better not be laughing at me, mage-prince."

"I would never," he said earnestly, looking worried she was serious. "I had a good reason to come over here. I think I've worked out where we were held captive."

It took her a moment to realise what he was saying. Then interest flared. "What? *Where?*" she demanded, dropping her voice and shifting closer.

He went back to flipping through his book. "Think about it... a thickly forested valley wall. Rubble littering the ground, all grown over, indicating the damage happened years ago. Half-destroyed buildings with charring on *stone*. Somewhere not so far away we couldn't have been taken there and returned within a few weeks."

"I've *been* thinking, Tarion." She scowled. "Without any luck. So whatever your idea is, spit it out."

"DarkSkull Hall." He landed on the page he was looking for and pointed triumphantly. It was an artist's image of what the mage school had once looked like before her grandfather had destroyed it. She leaned closer, running her eyes over the placement of the buildings, comparing it with the mental map she'd put together from her memories.

It worked. The alignment of the buildings. The obvious remnants of a battle. The dormitory-like buildings so similar to Temari Hall's dorms. That massive hall where they'd fought the razak. She frowned as something occurred to her. "Did DarkSkull ever have underground cells? That would seem an odd thing for them to have."

"No, but we already thought the cells where they held us had been newly constructed, right? I think Underground dug them out after they moved in."

True. "You might be onto something," she murmured, mind racing. What did it mean that Underground had taken them to DarkSkull Hall? Was it a permanent base, or had they only used it temporarily? No, it had to have been in use for some time, especially if they'd gone to the effort of building cells underground. Years, probably.

Her eyes narrowed in suspicion as another thought occurred to her. She doubted very much A'ndreas, Egalion, and the rest hadn't figured this out already. They'd known DarkSkull Hall intimately. Which meant—

"I think Underground had been there a while before they took us," Tarion said, bringing her back to the present. "The equipment they had set up, that takes planning and preparation. Not to mention how much of the place had been restored to make it liveable. Even bits of the main hall had been rebuilt. From my mother's accounts of the final battle there, part of the roof had come down."

"We don't know for sure they were the ones who restored it... but I agree they're the mostly likely candidates," Lira murmured. From what she'd heard, people had stayed clear of that valley ever since the final fight between Alyx Egalion and Shakar; it had very quickly gained the reputation of being haunted. Like with many of the underlying reasons for why the war had started in the first place—people hadn't just followed Shakar because he was a powerful, evil mage—the council and everyone else seemed to prefer forgetting it had ever existed.

Which made it the perfect location to set up a secret base. Isolated, but with enough infrastructure left to support what they needed to do. And symbolic, too, for those aligned with a cause all about restoring mage power and using Shakar as their figurehead.

"Why, though?" She spoke her thoughts aloud.

"Why restore so much of it?" Tarion cocked his head thoughtfully. "I don't know. We'd have to ask them, I suppose."

Without thinking, Lira glanced across the room at Ahrin, only to find the Darkhand already watching her. She looked wary, like she'd picked up that Tarion and Lira were discussing something important. Why had Ahrin refused to tell her where they'd been? Could it be that Underground were still there in some capacity? Maybe Lira could use this. Unable to help taunting, Lira winked. Ahrin's eyes flashed, then she looked away, back to her homework.

"Do you know her?" Tarion's voice jostled her out of her thoughts.

"What?" Lira turned back to him.

He nodded his head towards Ahrin. "I saw her talking to you at breakfast a couple times. Since you've never eaten breakfast with anyone, *ever*, I noted it as an oddity. And you seem familiar with each other."

"Are you watching me at breakfast, Tarion?" She deflected with a mock scowl.

"I can't help it," he said quietly. "It's the same with all of you after what happened. Whenever we're in the same space I have this urge to check on you all, make sure you're still there and safe."

"You're ridiculous," she muttered, pretending his genuine concern didn't affect her. That she didn't sometimes have the same instinct, even if she ignored it.

"I know." He smiled briefly. "So, you know her?"

She hesitated, then decided to tell some of the truth. She couldn't see any harm in it, and the fewer lies she had to juggle, the more likely she would be able to keep them all straight and not betray herself. "I knew her back in Dirinan."

Surprise flooded his face. "Really? How?"

"I was in her crew for a while. It kept a roof over my head and food in my stomach... at least, enough food to survive."

At that revelation, Tarion's mouth dropped open, exactly what she'd been aiming for. She smiled at his shock. "Still want to be friends?"

"Absolutely." He smiled back. "Good to know we now have two

criminals with us at Temari. What happened? She broke out later than you, obviously, but—"

"There's nothing to tell. I ran with her for a while, my magic broke out and I came here." She waved off any further questions. "Not a sharing session, Caverlock."

He nodded, accepting that, then sobered and pointed to the picture of DarkSkull Hall. "What do you think we should do about this?"

"I presume you want to go running straight to your father and Master A'ndreas with your discovery?" she asked carefully.

"It seems like the best course of action. They could put together a force of Taliath and mages and go straight there. Athira could still be there." Concern deepened on his face. "I couldn't forgive myself if we delayed and she was hurt or killed."

Lira was far from convinced his parents hadn't already figured it out, but saw no reason to upset Tarion with her suspicions. If they knew, he'd find out soon enough. "If Underground are still there," she said instead, "surely they had to have planned for the fact we'll eventually figure out where we were. And even if they haven't left, wouldn't it be smarter to watch them, see what they're up to? Make sure Athira *is* there and hasn't been taken elsewhere? Learn more about Underground and what it wants before going in swinging Taliath swords and magic?"

"I agree with all of that. But I think we can be confident that trained warrior mages and Taliath strategists will come to that conclusion too," he said with a little smile. "What's your real hesitation?"

"I don't trust them. You forget who I am," she said simply. "They still haven't found Athira, or those who kidnapped us."

"So you want *us* to be responsible for tracking Underground and rescuing Athira?" There was no bite in Tarion's voice, no condescension. It was a genuine question.

She opened her mouth to reply, but hesitated when no obvious answer presented itself. Not an honest one, anyway. Part of her wished she could just tell him she was spying on Underground, that she was going to meet with them later and might get some answers. But she couldn't let him in on that secret. It would be too dangerous for them both. "I don't know. I just don't like leaving everything in someone else's hands."

Tarion thought about that for a moment. "I understand why you feel the way you do. But I trust that my father will know the best way to handle this information."

She let out a breath. Even if she was successful at getting more information out of Underground tonight, what could she do about it? Her first priority was maintaining her cover with the group, which meant she couldn't afford to do anything to risk that, like joining the others in a search for Athira—even if they were allowed out of the tower. And Tarion was right, his father was no fool. "All right. Tell him, if you think that's what's best."

"I do." Determination crossed his face. "But I will also ensure everything that can be done for Athira *is* being done."

The sound of whispered giggling rippling through the atrium had Lira and Tarion looking up from the book. Garan had appeared and was leaning over a table of apprentices, the source of their laughter. He murmured something to them, then headed over to the table where Ahrin sat, wearing his most charming of grins.

"I give him two minutes before he's taking her off to one of the private study rooms," Tarion murmured.

Lira's eyes narrowed. "I was halfway to thinking he was all right, but does he really have to behave like that with *all* the pretty girls?"

"To be fair, she is stunning... in an icy, aloof, scary kind of way."

Lira levelled a look at him. "You too?"

Tarion smiled. "Would it make you feel better if I said I thought you'd beat Garan in a fight over her any day?"

"No," she grumbled.

"Am I to discern from this exchange that Spider, heir to the evil Shakar, the most aloof student at Temari Hall, sometimes pays romantic attention to others?"

"Garan?" Her eyebrows shot skywards and she made a face. "Ew, no!"

His mouth quirked. "I was talking about your old friend from Dirinan."

"Oh, I..." Before she could come up with a response to that, their

87

attention was drawn by Garan rising suddenly from his chair, hands in the air, a flush creeping up his neck. Ahrin's scathing once-over of his retreating figure explained the situation nicely.

Lira snorted. Tarion grinned. They bumped shoulders in shared amusement.

"You ever take someone into the private study rooms, mage-prince?" she asked, wanting to needle him like he'd been needling her.

"No," he said simply, annoyingly un-needled. "I have a girl back home."

"You do?" Astonishment had the words spilling out before she could stop them. She really didn't want to care about Tarion's personal life, but still...

"Yeah. Her name's Sesha." A light came into his eyes at the mention of her.

"Sesha?" Lira stared. "As in, Princess Sesha, the king of Rionn's only daughter and heir to his throne?"

"That's her. We pretty much grew up together." He smiled. "Mama says it's fate. She and King Cayr were sweethearts when they were our age."

"Fate? So you just have to wait until Sesha finds her version of Dashan Caverlock and breaks your heart." Lira snorted and turned to pack up her books. She'd have to leave for the meeting with Underground shortly—curfew was almost upon them.

"Don't be mean," he said mildly.

"I'm not. I'm being honest." She hefted the books and parchment. "I'll see you, Tarion. Let me know how it goes with your father. Will you tell the others what you've figured out, see what they think?"

"I'll let Garan recover a little first, but yes, absolutely. You might see Fari sooner than me though now she's your new room-mate."

She gave his teasing smile a glare, then walked away. When she glanced back, he was heading towards the stacks, a little frown of concentration on his face.

When she shifted her glance to where Ahrin had been sitting, the Darkhand was gone.

Lira strolled through the corridor outside the library, taking the main stairs down to the first level, then ducking into one of the corridors holding several classrooms. Making sure the hall was empty, she slipped into one of the empty rooms, left her books and parchment on one of the desks, and headed straight for the windows.

Within moments she'd unlatched a window and slipped outside, closing it after her almost all the way—enough so that it looked closed, but would allow her to open it again later.

Once sure nobody had spotted her climbing out, she straightened, breathing in the cold night air and welcoming the darkness of the cloudy night. She tapped the pocket inside her robe holding the letter to ensure it was still there, then she set off, slipping through the shadows.

Finally, a chance to do something.

CHAPTER 10

Lira arrived at the Underground meeting alone and slightly late.

The number of soldiers guarding the exterior walls of Temari had meant waiting for a break in their patrol pattern to slip over the western wall via the tree, then a longer walk to the causeway —forced to keep to the shadows and move through the thick forest along the lakeshore until she was out of sight of Temari. A frustrating endeavour given how unnecessary it was. Maybe if she succeeded tonight, she'd write to Dawn, ask her to tell her brother to give Lira an exemption to his stupid new rules.

She'd half expected Ahrin to appear somewhere along the way, but she hadn't. The Darkhand's absence made Lira uneasy.

Once across the northern causeway, she'd made her way to the abandoned house where she'd previously stashed a bag of clothing to wear to Underground meetings. It had still been sitting there, buried under the same bush, undisturbed. She'd shivered in the cold night air as she changed, leaving her apprentice robe and staff behind.

As soon as she was dressed in the ratty breeches, shirt, and jacket, she felt better. More comfortable. Less out of place. Her stride changed, her manner became more watchful, her old street instincts kicking back in. It felt like a weight had been lifted from her shoulders and she could breathe properly again.

Abruptly any unease she felt about the coming meeting vanished.

At the back entrance to the tailor's shop, she paused, considering. Ahrin's absence could be a strong signal that inviting Lira to this meeting was a trap. Lira was banking on the fact that Greyson liked her, that he would give her time to explain herself and win her way back in. But if he'd had a kill order direct from the Shadowcouncil...

A smile flickered over her face. Stepping into that dark stairwell could be one of the riskiest things she'd ever done. The hot rush of danger spread through her, and she started down the steps without hesitation.

By the time she reached the bottom, her palms were sweaty and her heart was beating quickly. Her body was oddly warm, as if she were burning from the inside out. Before stepping out from the shadows of the stairwell, she did her best to make her expression cool and aloof, shoulders relaxed, as if she didn't have a care in the world.

The usual assortment of attendees were milling in the dim cellar, and the familiarity of it calmed her. This was the rabble she was used to. None looked at her sideways, and they all had friendly greetings, seemingly happy to see her. Nobody asked where she'd been.

Even Greyson looked pleased at her arrival. He waved her over as soon as he saw her. "Lira, I'm glad to have you back with us."

"It *was* Underground that took us, then?" she asked immediately. As much as Lucinda had convinced her of who she was, the possibility that she'd been lying had lingered in the back of Lira's mind. She dropped her voice lower. "Lucinda is on the Shadowcouncil?"

"Yes, and I'm sorry for not warning you." Regret flashed over his face. "We had no choice but to do it the way we did—I know you're always careful, but we couldn't risk the telepaths at Temari Hall learning anything about our plans. The Darkhand led the operation, and she was insistent we tell you nothing ahead of time."

Lira tensed, fiercely biting down on the rush of betrayal and pain that wanted to rise so that she could stay focused. "Did they tell you what they did to me?"

"No, just that your presence on the project was necessary to the cause." He frowned, wariness replacing the regret, and his voice lowered until it was barely audible. "I received a note from the Shadowcouncil instructing me to watch you carefully for any signs of disloyalty, and report all your activities in detail. What happened?"

She should be relieved that Greyson hadn't been instructed to kill her, but him being told to watch her meant she was far from earning her place back. She couldn't trust Greyson any more than she could Lucinda or Ahrin, but the fact he'd told her about the instructions he'd received proved he felt some loyalty towards her. She could use that. "Their purpose in kidnapping me with the others was more than just maintaining my cover with the council," she said in a low voice. "She had me tortured and locked up. I didn't respond well to being treated that way."

A troubled frown marked his face, and he lowered his voice. "Lira, we must do as the Shadowcouncil asks, no matter what it is. Loyalty to the cause comes above everything. We can't win this if we don't hold to that."

"I understand that, I do," she said. "But I deserve more than lies and secrets. If you want something of me, just ask. I'm here willingly."

His hand settled on her shoulder, warm and paternal, and she fought not to flinch away. "That isn't always possible—we must be prepared to do as asked without question. If we can't be trusted, this whole thing could come apart before it even begins. We're up against powerful mages, and they have powerful allies."

Lira suddenly wondered if *that* was what she'd missed. The blind loyalty and devotion expected by the Shadowcouncil... the same thing Shakar had expected from his followers. The Mage Council didn't have that same devotion. Especially now, since the war, when it insisted on giving everyone *choices*. She'd underestimated what could be achieved with blind devotion.

It was a mistake she wouldn't make again.

"I agree," she said firmly. "And to prove it, I got what you wanted." She pulled the letter to Finn A'ndreas from inside her shirt and passed it to him. "I had no time to copy it, so that's the real thing. He'll notice it's missing sooner rather than later."

"Well done, Lira." Greyson looked thrilled, and quickly tucked the parchment into his jacket.

"The Shadowcouncil still wants it, then?"

"Very much so. We weren't able to get it while you were away." Fear flickered briefly in his eyes before vanishing as quickly as it had come.

Interesting. "Greyson, did you know—"

Ahrin's husky voice cut in. "A pleasure to see you again, Greyson." She'd approached without a sound, startling both of them. Her gaze dismissed Lira and focused on the cell leader, cool and considering.

Greyson's shoulders straightened and a flicker of wariness flashed over his face. "Darkhand. A pleasure to have you at our meeting. Is everything going smoothly at Temari Hall?"

She shrugged. "It is, though I can't say I enjoy being an initiate at my age, or pretending to only have one ability."

"I hope you went with the telekinesis," Lira said sharply. "If they know about your ability with vegetation, they might make a connection to what happened to all of us."

Ahrin gave her that easy smile. "I made sure there was nothing too remarkable about me. Boring old telekinesis, broke out late, the usual story."

Lira stiffened, no doubt Ahrin's intention. She bitterly regretted the fact she had only telekinesis magic, nothing like the sheer power her grandfather had wielded. It was why Ahrin had found it so easy to manipulate her into being experimented on by Lucinda. Lira had thought they'd make her more powerful, but now she had no idea what they'd really done, only that she'd played right into Lucinda's hands.

Greyson seemed to pick up on the taunt too, and surprisingly defended her. "My understanding is that Lira is considered to be the most skilled telekinetic mage student since Cario Duneskal."

Ahrin glanced between them, and Lira didn't like what she saw in that look. It certainly didn't bode well for her or Greyson. But then Ahrin shrugged, reaching out to touch Lira's arm. "You'll get what you want, Lira. It won't be long now."

"What does that mean?" she snapped.

"It can take time, that's all."

"*What* could take—"

Greyson spoke over her, presumably having not missed that look of

Ahrin's either. "We should start, they're getting impatient. If that suits you, Darkhand?" He smiled, ushering them to go over and join the waiting attendees.

Ahrin merely nodded and steered Lira away. Greyson moved to take his spot at the top of the room.

"I haven't had any new magical abilities appear, if that's what you were referring to," Lira hissed. "And I'm still not convinced you were telling the truth about that." The memory of Lucinda's expression of triumph still made her shudder when she thought of it. What had the woman wanted of her?

Ahrin said nothing.

Lira's mouth thinned, but she persevered. "Where did you come from, anyway? I didn't see you on my way here."

"I had things to do." Ahrin shrugged and leaned against the far wall behind the assortment of crates and boxes that made up chairs for the attendees. Tonight she'd ditched the initiate brown and wore a black velvet coat that fell to her ankles. A hood covered most of her face. She exuded an air of dangerous authority. Like Lira, she'd dressed for this meeting. Only while Lira sought to display her solidarity with those who made up the rank and file of the group, Ahrin emphasised the power she held over everyone there.

When Greyson introduced Ahrin, a hush fell over the room, several eyes darting toward them before shifting away just as quickly. The Darkhand was legend amongst Underground members; the blade of the Shadowcouncil, ruthless, efficient. Now that Lira knew it was Ahrin, she could understand why such a mystique had built up around her. It was the same thing that had drawn Lira in back in Dirinan. The thing that had held her there, with no intention of ever leaving. Until Ahrin had abandoned her without a word.

"The Shadowcouncil is impressed with our recent efforts, and has dispatched the Darkhand to assist us in building on that momentum," he informed the room, keeping hidden the fact that Ahrin was posing as a student at Temari Hall. "Now, our main priority is increasing the numbers of those protesting in the city. We want workplaces empty, businesses shuttered. We want Leader Astohar and his advisors to feel the pinch."

While Greyson talked, part of Lira filed away what he was saying while the rest studied him for any sign that her explanation earlier hadn't worked. He'd seemed pleased to see her, disturbed that she'd challenged Lucinda, but clearly comfortable in welcoming her back even though he'd no doubt be following the Shadowcouncil's instructions to the letter and keeping a close eye on her. Nor did he seem to have any idea what had actually gone on during her kidnapping.

It was an interesting but disappointing revelation. It made her wonder if Greyson knew *anything* about the experiments, about the Shadowcouncil's larger plans. How much was the Shadowcouncil keeping from their followers? And were they holding back the true nature of their plans purely out of a paranoid desire for secrecy... or was there some other reason? Lira shifted against the wall, frowning. Some instinct warned her she was still missing things, and it made her uneasy.

Greyson didn't have the information she needed, and Lucinda still didn't trust her. Lira needed better access to the Shadowcouncil.

She'd have to go through Ahrin.

AHRIN FELL into step beside her as she left the meeting. Lira had come out last, after staying to acknowledge the attendees personally on their way out, so the Darkhand had clearly been waiting outside for her.

"What is it you didn't want me to tell Greyson?" Lira asked. "You cut in right in the middle of our conversation, don't think I didn't notice."

"Cell leaders are important, but can also be a vulnerability. They are informed only of what they need to know."

"So he doesn't know about the experiments? The razak?"

"He knows everything he needs to."

That was a no. Lira cursed inwardly. She could wrap Greyson around her little finger and it wouldn't do any good. He was no more than a puppet of the Shadowcouncil... although that in itself was useful to know. She'd make sure to include it in her next report to Dawn.

She tried a different tack. "How many cell leaders are there?"

"Enough."

Lira snorted and increased her stride. Ahrin matched her without comment, breaking the silence a few seconds later. "Fancy a chat with Lucinda?"

Lira stopped dead, eyes narrowing, a leap of fear arrowing through her chest despite her best efforts to ignore it. "She's here in Karonan? Why wasn't she at the meeting?"

"Underground keeps its cells carefully separated from each other for security reasons. In turn, the Shadowcouncil members keep themselves separate from the cells. Only Greyson has ever met Lucinda, and they primarily communicate by coded message. He can meet her directly if the need arises, but only when he has critical news or information. I'm sure you understand why."

"Telepath mages," she murmured. More useful details she filed away to write to Dawn later. "But coded messages can't always be sufficient..." Lira's eyes narrowed. "You're the go-between. For the Shadowcouncil and its cell leaders."

"Correct. I run things on behalf of the Shadowcouncil so they don't have to expose themselves."

A little thrill went through Lira. Ahrin was in an even better position than she'd thought. "Have you met all the Shadowcouncil members?" It was rumoured there were eight of them, matching the number sitting on the Mage Council in Carhall. But that was pure speculation.

Ahrin looked away.

"If you *have* seen their faces, that's dangerous information to possess," Lira said quietly, trying to push harder without making Ahrin think she was too interested in the information.

Ahrin didn't bite. "Whatever I'm allowed to see or know is leverage I can use if I ever need to."

Lira almost smiled, but held it back. Ahrin's complete lack of ideological commitment to the group would be how Lira would win her away from them and onto her side. All she had to do was offer Ahrin *more* power, *more* wealth, than the Shadowcouncil would give her. The Mage Council could give Ahrin what she wanted. Lira would just have to convince them recruiting Ahrin was worth it.

She wondered what it was Lucinda *had* promised her Darkhand.

The woman was clever enough to know what motivated Ahrin, to understand she had no true belief in the cause. Yet there was something about Ahrin that prompted the Shadowcouncil to make her their blade anyway.

Ahrin broke the silence again. "Lucinda is showing you an impressive amount of trust by allowing you to see where she's staying."

"An odd amount of trust, given last time we met she tried to kill me. Not to mention she instructed Greyson to keep a close eye on me, which indicates the opposite of trust." Ahrin could be walking her straight into another trap. Lira hated that it was a possibility, hated that she had to treat Ahrin with wariness and distrust... that she had to expect betrayal from her. They'd once been such a good team. She missed that with a fierceness she rarely let herself acknowledge. Feelings like that were dangerous given the game they were both playing.

"He shouldn't have told you that." Ahrin's voice was flat.

Lira swore at herself, came up with a quick lie. "He didn't. I figured it out on my own. I half expected to be killed the moment I stepped into the cellar. When I wasn't, I figured Lucinda had withdrawn her kill order... but that doesn't mean she trusts me."

"She does understand your value, Lira, but she doesn't tolerate insubordination. You can get what you want with Underground, but you'll have to play the good little soldier for a while."

"Like you?"

A wicked smile. "Like me."

Lira sighed. "If we're going to see Lucinda, I'd best get changed out of these clothes. I'd rather fend off another murder attempt in my mage robe and staff."

Ahrin laughed.

Lira chuckled with her, but it was mostly for show—she quailed at the thought of facing Lucinda again, but told herself it was the opportunity she needed. If she played this right, she could take the first step in regaining the woman's trust. And maybe even learn a little more about what lay between her and Ahrin—something she could use in her bid to recruit the Darkhand.

Even more importantly, though, maybe by facing down Lucinda again, she could destroy this new fear that lived inside her.

CHAPTER 11

Ahrin took her to a non-descript townhouse that formed part of a row of identical-looking townhouses on a quiet Karonan street. It was in the ideal spot for someone wanting to keep their presence in the city discreet—not in the business or wealthy quarters of the city, but in the district populated by those who were neither rich nor poor, but comfortable.

The Darkhand pushed open the front door without knocking, and although Lira glanced warily around as she followed, she detected no signs of guards on the exterior of the house. Her instincts were dormant, indicating no particular threat lay ahead.

Lucinda was in a lounge inside the first door to the left off the dim entryway. A fire crackled in the hearth, and several plush chairs were grouped together around a table in the middle of the room. On the table sat a steaming teapot and three cups.

It would have been a cosy setting if not for its occupant.

The curtains were drawn over the windows, and the rest of the house—from what Lira could tell peering down the hall from the front door—was dark and silent. It appeared like Lucinda was the only one there, but Lira doubted that very much. No Shadowcouncil member would be alone and unguarded in a place so close to Alyx Egalion and Temari Hall.

Dread and unease tightened in the pit of Lira's stomach, unexpectedly strong, at the sight of her captor. She half expected Lucinda to freeze her to the spot with her paralysis ability, and only barely stopped her own magic flaring enough to bathe her hands in violet light.

The thrill roused again, and she wavered, almost accepting it, knowing it would make her braver, clearer, better for this coming interaction. But it would also make her reckless. And Lucinda was too clever and controlled a foe to be reckless with. So instead Lira made herself take a deep breath and forced her thoughts to focus. Then, summoning every bit of composure she possessed, she managed a cool tone. "This is quite a different reception than I'm accustomed to from you. Are you sure you wouldn't like to tie me to one of those chairs?"

At her side, Ahrin barely repressed a snort.

Lucinda smiled. "The last time we saw each other, Lira, you were trying to attack me. Ahrin assures me you're still loyal, but is that really the tone you're wanting to take with me to prove it?"

"The last time we saw each other, you sent a razak to kill me. You're lucky that I was willing to come back to Underground after that." Lira held Lucinda's look, and despite herself, the heady rush of danger surged again, this time shattering her internal barriers. A little smile curled at Lira's mouth and she let it take over.

"I think I've adequately demonstrated that your utility to us only stretches to a point." The room turned cold, even though the fire burned on. "You're clever enough to understand the reasons why I must demand absolutely loyalty."

"That's where we disagree," Lira said coolly. "The chances of you successfully drawing together the resources you need to succeed increase dramatically if you have the Darkmage's heir. And Shakar would never have bowed down to anyone." The little smile remained on her face. "I believe in your cause, but I won't be treated as a tool. I am your partner. I am your symbol. I am what makes your rebellion work. We must come to some agreement on this or I will walk."

"If you walk, I *will* kill you this time. You're too dangerous to us in the Mage Council's hands."

Lira's smile widened, challenging and confident. "You can try."

The silence held, tense and icy. This was the riskiest gamble Lira had ever taken. Lucinda could freeze her to the spot and kill her now and they both knew it.

She didn't dare look away from Lucinda to see what Ahrin's expression was. She wondered what Ahrin would do if Lucinda ordered her to kill Lira. Letting her escape while Lucinda wasn't watching was one thing, but openly defying the woman would risk her life, and Ahrin was as much of a survivor as Lira was. If Lucinda asked, Ahrin would obey. If Lira wasn't so focused on her battle of wills with Lucinda, that thought would have sucked the wind right out of her.

Lucinda eventually settled back in her chair, breaking their gaze. "I do admire your strength, and you are correct in that we can't use a weak-willed descendent of Shakar. Will you come and sit?"

Lira dropped her smile, assumed a more obliging expression, and kept the triumph of winning this first battle of wills from her face. Not looking at Ahrin, she crossed the room in confident strides to take the seat opposite Lucinda. Heat prickled under her skin, and her magic stirred, sensing the danger she was in and rising in readiness. "I stole the letter you claimed you wanted and gave it to Greyson earlier. I would have brought it directly here if I'd known we were meeting."

Lucinda's expression betrayed nothing of what she thought of that. "Thank you, Lira. I'll be very interested to read it." She glanced at Ahrin as she spoke, lifting an eyebrow.

Ahrin moved then, coming to sit in the chair between them, posture relaxed. She reached into her jacket, withdrew the letter, and passed it to Lucinda. Lira almost rolled her eyes but settled for a nod in Lucinda's direction. Then she cursed herself for missing Greyson passing Ahrin the letter.

Lucinda took it and placed it on the table without glancing at it. Ahrin settled back in her chair, her gaze hooded, the way it always had been when she was at her most watchful. Interesting. As much as she gave the appearance of it, Ahrin wasn't at ease either. Not that it would be smart to relax in Lucinda's presence.

Ahrin dug into another inside pocket in her jacket, withdrew a cigar, then reached over to light it in the fire. Taking a long drag, she looked at Lira. "Would you like one?"

"No."

Seconds later the sweet scent of vanilla smoke filled the room. Lucinda leaned forward to pour a cup of fragrant tea and pass it to Lira. Lira took the cup. "Is it poisoned?" she asked flatly.

This elicited a laugh from Ahrin and an almost genuine smile from Lucinda. "I assure you it's not."

After a quick discreet sniff to ensure it didn't smell odd, Lira took a sip—mostly to prove she wasn't afraid—and put the cup down. "Not to my taste, I'm afraid."

"I'll have something different next time." Lucinda crossed her legs, settled further into her chair. "How are you adjusting to being back at Temari, Lira?"

"Fine. Although I assume your spies have already told you everything you need to know." This was exactly where Lira needed to be, the access she needed, but it wouldn't do any good to seem too grateful. She had to keep that edge, keep pushing back, or Lucinda would become suspicious.

"They're there to keep an eye on you, yes, but not just to ensure you can be trusted. We want to make sure that you're safe."

Except when they were trying to kill her, of course. Lira almost scoffed.

"I'd like to address our relationship." Lira took a breath. "I think we've been operating under a fundamental misunderstanding. You consider me a symbol only, a face you can put to your cause, a puppet. That doesn't work for me. I joined Underground because I am Shakar's granddaughter. Because I want what he had. I don't want to be your symbol. I will be your leader, or nothing."

This was the approach she'd been crafting for days, since being returned to Temari and getting Dawn and Tarrick's permission to continue spying on Underground. While it was a high-risk strategy— gambling on Lucinda considering Lira critical to her plans—it played to Lira's strengths and fit nicely with her behaviour during the kidnap. If Lucinda bought it, she'd have much less hiding and pretending to do.

Lucinda said nothing for a long moment. The fire crackled into the silence. Ahrin took another lazy drag of her cigar, her expression not betraying anything either.

"I know that I'm still young and need to earn my way," Lira continued, after letting her words sit. "But there has to be a middle ground between our two positions."

"Understood." It was all Lucinda said. Her gaze remained on Lira, expressionless, hands neatly clasped in her lap. Everything about her was perfectly arranged. Not a single thing out of place. The level of control she exerted on her surroundings was masterful.

Unclear whether that was agreement or not, Lira forged ahead as if it were. "Good. Now, I'd like to know why your Darkhand has been entrusted with so much while I was left to languish here attending Greyson's useless meetings." Lira didn't shift her gaze away from Lucinda. "It's become very clear to me how widespread your reach and activities are, and how little I know of them."

An amused smile curled at Lucinda's mouth. "While those meetings are far from useless, I take your point. Ahrin is our blade. She's been with us much longer, and has demonstrated her loyalty and capability in ways that you have not."

That was part of an answer. Lira suspected Ahrin was useful to Underground in some critical way, important enough they couldn't afford to keep her out of everything. Ahrin thought she was in control when it came to Lucinda and Underground, thought she was using them to get wherever she wanted to go, but Lira was far less certain of that. Lucinda simply didn't operate without being certain she could control everything in her sphere.

"I could have become that for you. It's why I joined in the first place. Why choose her and not me?"

"We have our reasons," Lucinda said coolly. "You are both important to us in very different, but complementary, ways."

Lira's gaze flicked briefly to Ahrin. Lira could ruin her right now. Tell Lucinda that Ahrin had helped Lira escape DarkSkull. Take the bet that Shakar's granddaughter was more important to Underground than a street orphan from Dirinan, no matter how clever or capable.

Ahrin's eyes darkened, that dangerous look flashing in them, as if she knew exactly what Lira was thinking.

But Ahrin could be more useful working for Lira inside Underground to bring it down. She told herself to stick to the plan, and simply smiled at Lucinda. "Like I said, I understand that I have to earn my way, I'd just like you to explain to me how I can do that."

"Ahrin and our watchers report that the students you were taken with have made several attempts to befriend you since your return?"

It stung. As much as she didn't trust Ahrin, as much as she knew Ahrin would betray her without thought, it still hurt that she so clearly had.

"Attempts I've repeatedly rebuffed. I assume your Darkhand has told you that too?" She levelled at look at Ahrin, who said nothing, before returning her gaze to Lucinda. "I don't need friends," she said flatly, adding for good measure, "Especially not spoiled pureblood mages who have no idea what the real world is like. I look forward to the day we can remove them from their pretence of power."

"Oh, we have no doubts about you on that score." Lucinda waved a hand, sounding sincere. "But we think this could be an opportunity for us."

"How?" she asked warily. Once again Lucinda had her on the back foot. She tried not to let it show.

"You are of great use to us because of your bloodline, your ability to be a living symbol for our cause." Lucinda leaned forward. "We are not at such cross-purposes as you have assumed. The end goal is to have you join us completely. Be a fully integrated member of the Shadowcouncil."

"But?" Lira lifted an eyebrow.

"But you yourself have said that you can contribute in other ways too, especially while you are at Temari Hall. Imagine if you were close to the children of the leaders of Rionn, Shivasa, and the Mage Council. Imagine the information you would have access to."

Lira's chest tightened painfully. She ignored it, tried to sound disgusted. "You *want* me to make friends with them?"

"You don't agree it would be an excellent opportunity?"

She did. She let out a breath, making sure she looked interested. It took an effort to ignore the squeezing in her chest. Spying on Underground for the Mage Council. Spying on the Mage Council for Underground. Her world had just gotten a lot more complicated. But there was no good reason to say no to this. "I do."

"I know it won't be easy." Ahrin took another drag, blew out vanilla-scented smoke. "It would make my skin crawl having to pretend to like that lot. But the benefits for us could be immense."

Lira sat up straight, smiled. "You're right, they have been making overtures. Despite who I am, they feel a kinship with me because of what happened to us. I can use that to get close to them."

A smile spread over Lucinda's face, predatory and cold. "Excellent."

"I will do as you ask. Now, I'd like to know why Ahrin is at Temari Hall. She's been keeping your secrets." Lira tossed a look at the girl. "But if she's planning harm to anyone, then I need to know before it happens so I can ensure I'm not blamed for it. I won't be a very good spy if I lose my privileged access."

"Ahrin means no harm to Temari Hall, at least not for now. That's all I can tell you." Lucinda glanced at the door. "Good luck, Lira. If you need to reach out to me for any reason, please do so through Ahrin, not Greyson."

"I have more questions before you throw me out." Lira lifted a hand, shaking her head at Lucinda's dismissal. "What happened this morning?"

A troubled look crossed Lucinda's face. "Ahrin relayed to me what happened. That wasn't us, Lira, I assure you."

She huffed a disbelieving breath. "Who else would it be?"

"We're going to find out—I've already got people looking into it."

"I don't believe you," Lira said flatly.

Fury rippled across Lucinda's face, quickly hidden. Lira forced herself to hold that stare anyway, allowing the heat of danger to dispel her growing weariness, keep all senses alert. Displaying weakness in front of this woman would be a deadly mistake. She leaned forward. "The creatures that attacked us were too much like the razak not to be from the same source. Either you've found a mage with the ability to create nightmarish creatures, or you've got one who can control them, or both. Either way, it's a rare ability, and my bet is there isn't two of them." Lira paused. "I don't challenge you for the fun of it. If I'm to be part of this group, I need to understand the weapons at our disposal. Middle ground, Lucinda."

Tense silence held for a long time. Ahrin had turned dangerously still in her chair, as if ready to explode into movement at any second. Lira wondered how long she'd last if Ahrin was ordered to kill her.

"We'd been moving the creatures from Dirinan to another location. The mage who can control them was supposed to join the group here to ensure the creatures remained docile; they'd been drugged until that point," Lucinda said eventually. "He was late in meeting the group and the drug wore off."

"Why come for us specifically when they escaped?"

"Like the razak who patrolled the grounds where we held you, the creatures crave mage blood. When they escaped, they headed straight for Temari Hall, which presumably stinks of magic to them. It's what they do." Lucinda lifted her hands. "They weren't targeting you. If other mage students had been outside at the time, they would have been attacked."

"And you couldn't tell me that straight up?"

"I don't trust easily, Lira, or often. And I still don't trust you completely." Lucinda stood. "You're going to have to earn it. But I assure you it was an accident."

Lira smiled, stood too. "One that resulted in the death of your beasties. I hope that's not too big a loss?"

"We'll manage." Lucinda waved a dismissive hand, casual enough Lira guessed she wasn't overly upset about the loss.

She wanted to ask more questions, but Lucinda's impatience was growing more and more obvious. Even so, Lira was about to push harder, spurred on by reckless courage, but Ahrin's fingers suddenly closed, vice-like, around her arm. "Time to go."

Lira yanked her arm out of Ahrin's grip, snapping furiously, "Don't touch me."

"Don't be a fool and I won't. You've taken up enough of Lucinda's time." Ahrin's midnight blue gaze had gone dark, genuine warning in it.

She wanted to ignore that warning, but the sensible part of Lira understood she was letting the rush overwhelm good sense. She'd won herself back inside Underground without getting killed. Pushing too hard now could ruin it all.

So she turned away from Ahrin, smiled at Lucinda. "Fair enough. Hopefully we'll talk again soon."

"Good night, Lira."

Lira turned and strode out the door without looking back.

"THAT WENT WELL," Ahrin said once they were several blocks away from the townhouse and stepping onto the northern causeway. Her expression was tight, words clipped. "You only almost provoked her into killing you twice."

Lira didn't respond immediately. The rush was fading and weariness coursed through her body, leaving behind a contented warmth. It took her a few seconds to realise Ahrin had spoken, that she was *angry*. Lira shot her a look. "And what would you have cared if she had? Stood by and watched again, I imagine. Or done it yourself while she held me still with her magic."

"Lira!" Ahrin sounded exasperated. "Lucinda is not someone to take lightly. I thought you had your addiction to danger under control."

"Says the girl who thinks she's got one over on the Shadowcouncil."

"And that took a long time and a lot of careful work."

"Well, I'm not like you. Lucinda can either deal with me as I am or throw me aside. It's her choice, but I'm not bending myself to fit what she wants so that she keeps all the power and control," Lira said. "I have the bloodline they need, not the other way around."

Unexpectedly, a smile flickered over Ahrin's face. "That's what I like best about you. You don't compromise yourself. Even though it's dangerously foolish in this particular situation."

"You never used to compromise yourself either. Not for anyone or anything." Lira couldn't help the words. The Ahrin she knew had been unyielding in her sense of self. This game she was playing with Underground was unlike her, and it made Lira ache. She wanted to know that the Ahrin she'd known still existed, that not *all* of it had been a lie, an illusion. She'd admired that girl so fiercely.

"I still haven't." Ahrin shrugged. "Underground see a part of me.

Not all of me. It's a charade, just like we used in some of our jobs back in Dirinan."

"Why you?" she asked, unconvinced. "What is it they want from you? And don't tell me it's because you're good at killing people and carrying out their orders. They could have found anyone to do that."

Ahrin didn't reply, her hand unconsciously tugging at the sleeve that covered the tattoo on the inside of her right wrist. Lira frowned, but didn't push it, reminding herself she was trying to win Ahrin to her side, not push her further way by asking questions she'd already been warned not to ask. The answers would come with time if she succeeded.

They turned off the causeway, strolling along the shadowed road lined with trees that led to the grounds of Temari Hall. Lira started to turn her mind to sneaking back in without getting caught, then how she was going to make it into bed without Fari noticing her creeping in and asking questions she couldn't answer.

Ahrin stopped suddenly, taking one of Lira's hands to gently tug her to a stop too. "I told you, Lira, I want us to be in this together."

"You didn't—"

"Don't!" Ahrin cut her off. "Don't bring up Dirinan again. It's in the past. You're the one who said back there that you didn't want to be Underground's pawn."

"I don't." She wanted to raze them to the ground. "But that doesn't mean I want to ally myself with you either. Shall I list again *all* the ways you've betrayed me?" Exasperation filled Lira's voice, weariness making her words spill out with too much honesty despite her goal being to win the girl over. Why did Ahrin keep pushing this?

"You have no idea—" Ahrin cut herself off, stalking a few paces away before turning back. She visibly calmed, her voice turning warm. "You and I are more important than anyone else in that group. The Shadowcouncil won't acknowledge it, but they know it."

"I ask again, what is so important about you?" Lira raised her eyebrows.

Ahrin flashed her wicked smile, deferring with teasing. "You know me better than anyone. You really have to ask?"

This was it. The opening she needed... Ahrin on *her* side rather than Lucinda's. So instead of rolling her eyes, Lira smiled, conceded with a chuckle. "No, I don't."

"Underground serve a purpose, I know that's why you joined," Ahrin said quietly. "But *we* should be the ones directing their resources. The Shadowcouncil should be working for *us*."

"So we'll *make* them acknowledge us," Lira murmured, caught up in the fire in Ahrin's midnight blue eyes, the rise of anticipation in her chest, the remembered excitement of how they'd once worked together, a seamless team. With Ahrin's help, bringing down Underground would be so much easier... and Ahrin didn't have to know Lira's true goal, not until the last moment. She felt flushed again, this time with excitement, despite the cool night air.

A smile curled at Ahrin's mouth, dangerous and delighted all in one. "We will."

Lira forced her gaze away from that captivating smile, glanced down towards the walls of Temari Hall, and took a steadying breath. She had to clear her thoughts, her mind, before she forgot where the lines where, what her true purpose was. "Any ideas on how we sneak back in? I don't particularly want to—"

Ahrin moved closer. "Lira..."

"What?"

"Why won't you look at me?" she murmured.

Lira forced her gaze back to Ahrin's. "Because I don't trust you."

"Liar," Ahrin challenged softly. "You smiled when I shut down Garan in the library before. I saw you."

"So?"

"So you were pleased I did."

Lira *had* been pleased, though she'd refused to let herself acknowledge it. Refused to admit it to Ahrin now, too. So she shrugged. "I don't care what you do with Garan. I just figured you're too busy plotting nefarious activities at Temari to bother yourself with courting."

"Courting?" Ahrin's laughter pealed out, genuine and unforced.

Lira couldn't help but grin in response. It had always been hard to make Ahrin laugh, and every time she'd succeeded she'd felt a bright ember of joy in her chest. That same joy leapt up now, despite the years and betrayals between them.

"I'm an orphan street rat, Lira. Courting isn't for people like us," she said when her laughter faded.

"You mean *caring* about others isn't for people like us," Lira said, a trace of bitterness she couldn't hide in her voice.

Ahrin took her hand, entangling their fingers. "You know I care."

"Only so far." Lira wasn't sure what was coming out of her own mouth anymore: truth, manipulation, or some twisted mixture of both.

Ahrin swallowed and stepped closer, her hand lifting to cup Lira's jaw, her touch feather-light. Her thumb stroked slowly back and forth over her cheek, making Lira dizzy, too hot again. "Farther than you'd think."

She refused to let Ahrin win this little game. *Couldn't* let her win. So Lira closed the distance first, reaching up to slide her hand around Ahrin's neck and draw her down to kiss her.

The moment froze.

The years stripped away. Everything that had happened since that hallway outside the gambling hall where they'd fought, where Ahrin had told her to leave, where she'd lingered so close, *too* close, and then turned and walked away. The last time they'd spoken privately before Ahrin left her.

It was as if neither could believe it was finally happening. Or that Lira had been the one to make it happen.

And then the moment shattered and Ahrin moved, deepening the kiss, tugging her closer, one arm wrapping tightly around Lira's waist. A series of cascading revelations careened through Lira's head then, a rush of sensation and heat and touch; the awkward realisation that Ahrin was *much* better at this than Lira was, the delight of Ahrin's hand tangling in her hair, the warmth of skin under her palms, the taste of her; vanilla and smoke and something else that was sweetness and danger both. The desire, long buried, leaping to life in the pit of her stomach.

When air became a requirement, Ahrin pulled back slightly, eyes darker than Lira had ever seen them, and smiled her wicked smile. "I've wanted to do that for a really long time."

Me too.

Lira didn't say the words, held them back. Instead she shrugged. "It wasn't bad for a first kiss."

"Then let me make sure the second is even better," Ahrin murmured. She slid her hand through Lira's hair and pulled her in.

And Lira went willingly.

LIRA LAY AWAKE for a long time once she got back to her bed, only half-waking Fari in the process. Her eyes stared up at the stone ceiling, but they weren't seeing anything.

The plan was working. She was winning Ahrin over. Making her a tool to be used *against* Underground rather than against Lira. But Ahrin was an enemy too. She'd abandoned her. Helped Underground kidnap her. Helped them experiment on her. Lira had to remember that.

But earlier, out on the dark road, she hadn't remembered it. All she'd cared about, all she'd wanted, was Ahrin. To be close to her. With her. Together in some grand scheme.

Lira shivered, turned over in her bed.

Who was playing who?

CHAPTER 12

Lira woke early despite the late night. For once, though, the snatches of sleep she'd gotten had been free of memory dreams and fever sweats. Fari snored softly in the bed opposite while Lira dressed, shrugged on her robe, and crossed to the door. There she paused, glancing back.

Heaving an inward sigh, she summoned a hint of magic and yanked the covers off Fari's sleeping form. When that failed to rouse her, she used more magic to lift the girl's hair and brush it over her nose.

Fari swatted at her face, eyes sleepily blinking open. "What?"

"It's time for training. Remember our lord and master Garan Egalion proclaiming it so yesterday?"

"Since when do you follow anyone's orders, let alone Garan's?" she mumbled.

"I'm not. If you remember, I was the one already down there training. Now you're all just invading my personal time."

Fari's gaze went to the darkness outside the window, and she seemed to curl up even more in the bed. "I think—"

Lira held back an irritated sigh. "I'll walk you down. I promise I won't let any razak or flying monsters get you."

"Why are you being nice to me?"

"I'm not. I'm dragging you out of bed before dawn."

Fari blinked. Glanced at the window again, then rolled off the bed and stood up. "Give me a minute to dress."

Lira let the sigh out this time. "Any longer than that and you can fend off the dark hallways all by yourself."

"They already knew," Tarion said as he loosed an arrow. It thudded into the centre of the target, where all his arrows had landed so far.

The five of them were lined up practising their archery, their new mage bodyguards hovering at the edges of the sparring yard, eyes on the sky. At least they were far enough away that Lira and the others could talk softly without being overheard.

Lira, who'd secretly been taking great satisfaction from the fact that Garan was a far worse shot than her, blinked at the uncharacteristic irritation in Tarion's voice and turned to him. "Who knew what?"

"Apparently, as soon as my parents heard our descriptions of where we'd been held, they knew it was DarkSkull Hall," he said. His shoulders were tight, face like stone.

Lira huffed a breath, thoroughly unsurprised. She'd guessed as much. "I—"

"Why didn't they tell us?" Fari shrieked, cutting over Lira and causing all the bodyguards to stare over at them in alarm.

Tarion shifted uncomfortably. "They didn't want word to leak out that they knew where we'd been held. In case Underground are still there," he said, then looked at Lira. "You're not surprised."

"They spent years at DarkSkull Hall. I would have been more surprised if they *hadn't* figured it out from what we told them."

"Then why didn't you *say* anything?" Garan snapped, looking just as frustrated at Lira as he was angry at Tarion's revelation.

"I..." She floundered, not understanding why he was so annoyed at her. "I didn't want to upset you."

"Cut it out, Garan, she was trying to be thoughtful," Tarion said, uncharacteristically firm.

Garan let out a breath. "Maybe we wouldn't have liked hearing it, but we would have wanted to know," he said.

Fari huffed, hands on her hips. "Back to the main point—now we're not only helpless fools that need to be protected at all times, but we also can't be trusted with important information relating directly to us?"

Lira sympathised, feeling similar stirrings of anger, even though she'd already guessed. Dawn should have told her, *Tarrick* should have. If they were willing to risk her life using her as a spy, they should have trusted her enough to tell her this.

"What are they doing about it, Tar?" Garan had stopped pretending any interest in practising archery. His voice was clipped, angry.

"Da says they've got discreet watchers stationed in the valley surrounding DarkSkull. They want to see if Underground are still there, and if so, get an idea of what they're doing before going in."

"What if Athira is still there? How is watching going to help her?" Lorin said, speaking for the first time. His mouth was pinched, hand white-knuckled on his bow. Lira spared him a glance—she knew he still grieved for his friend.

"This is unacceptable," Garan said. "I'll write to my father this morning and insist that we be kept informed of everything going on."

Lira snorted. "You think your parents didn't know if Tarion's did? Wake up, Garan."

"She has a point," Fari chimed in.

"Then we'll talk to Uncle Finn this morning."

"And say what? Insist on being told all the things they clearly don't want us to know? He'll just pat us on the head again and tell us to keep obeying his stupid rules." Lira began pacing, her anger growing.

"My father said we'd be told what we needed to know. He said we should concentrate on staying safe at Temari and learning our magic so that we can protect ourselves better." Tarion was deeply unhappy, obviously conflicted.

"Does that include forming a combat patrol?" Lorin spoke for the first time.

"Maybe we should think about it," Garan said, sounding troubled. "It might get this lot off our backs." He jerked a thumb in the direction of their bodyguards. "And if they had more confidence in our abilities they might trust us with more information too."

"No," Lira said flatly. "If they don't trust us after what we survived, forming a combat patrol won't change that."

"What do we do, then?" he asked her.

She was taken aback—while she was slowly growing used to these apprentices treating her like one of them, like a respected equal, she wasn't quite there yet. She just wished she had an answer for them. "I don't know."

"They wanted to meet with us every week, right?" Fari spoke into the silence. "Let's take the opportunity to start asking more questions. Specific questions. Either they'll answer us, or they'll look uncomfortable because they're lying. That's better than nothing."

"And we'll start with where they're searching for Athira." Garan nodded. "Because if they're not, then we either push them to do more, or we do it ourselves."

"I agree," Lorin said.

"So do I," Tarion added quietly.

Lira smiled. "Me too." And maybe *she'd* start doing some bargaining too. If the council wanted to know what she was learning from Underground, maybe she'd insist they tell her what she wanted to know first.

"Good, glad that's sorted. Now I'm starving, could we please go inside and get some breakfast?" Fari asked plaintively.

"You haven't even hit the target yet," Lorin pointed out.

She rounded on him, hands on hips. "And?"

Lira smirked. So did Tarion.

Lorin cleared his throat. "Nothing."

"I think that's enough for today. But we're back here tomorrow morning," Garan said with a smile, and they filed off to put weapons and targets away. "We should aim to reach Lira and Tarion's level with the bow, then we'll move on to other weapons. Tar, you'll teach us to use a sword?"

"I can do that," Tarion said.

Lira glanced at him, surprised that he'd spoken instead of just nodding. He joined her as they walked towards the breakfast hall, a little smile on his face. "We may as well be in a combat patrol, the way Garan orders us about."

Her mouth quirked. "I don't think he can help himself."

He was silent a moment, then said, "I understand, you know, why they're so insistent on protecting us, on keeping us out of this."

"Don't tell me, it's because they love you." She rolled her eyes.

"It's not just Garan and me they're trying to protect," he said. "My parents lived through a war. They lost people they loved, and that kind of grief leaves scars. Their worst fear is the same thing happening again."

"Just because they lived through a war doesn't mean they're the only ones that can deal with what's happening now," she said. "We're not children. Garan and I could pass the trials any day, and so could you. Lorin and Fari won't be long after."

"They want us to enjoy our lives before we become full mages. They want to protect the innocence we still have."

"I've never had that innocence and I don't want to be protected from anything."

He looked away. "I know. But have you considered that maybe we do? It's not like you make the real world sound all that great."

She opened her mouth, closed it. If she could go back to the time when she was small and had a mother who loved her and shielded her from the world, would she? The answer was quick in coming, as reluctant as she was to admit it. So instead of answering, she merely sighed, then bumped his elbow with hers. "Let's get something to eat."

EARLY RISERS WERE FILING into the dining hall when the five of them entered. Once they'd collected trays of food, they separated with promises to speak later, and Lira went to sit at her usual spot alone by the wall. She was comfortable assuming Underground's spies would report the fact she'd come in with the others—sitting and eating with them seemed a little too much progress to be credible so fast, and besides, she preferred the time to herself.

She put off thinking about what would happen once Underground started asking her for information from Garan and Tarion. That was an obstacle for future Lira to face. Current Lira had enough to juggle.

The room filled up, soon becoming noisy and chaotic, reminding her why she'd started coming early for breakfast. Most of the loud chatter and laughing came from the handful of tables in the centre of the room. Garan was amongst them, his latest girl beside him. Fari was part of the group too, though she sat closer to the outside, and Tarion sat in his own little bubble, a book open before him as if he were studying.

She'd never paid any attention to Athira sitting at that table before, but all of a sudden her absence was obvious. Lira thought back to that night, unable to hold back the memory of Athira holding the door open even with a razak bearing down on them both. She wondered where the girl was. Hoped she was okay.

"What are you staring at?"

Ahrin's voice in her ear made Lira start. "None of your business."

Ahrin smirked, sat down beside her. "Fine. Now that you've had time to sleep on it, what did you think of last night?"

Lira eyed her, trying to detect whether there was any hidden meaning to Ahrin's words, but her voice had been casual and her attention was on her food. Lira wished she could be so casual when she thought about what had happened *after* the meeting. A door long held tightly shut inside her had swung open and now she literally couldn't think of anything else unless she concentrated. "I'm pleased I was given something useful to do." She chose her words carefully, mindful of where they were.

"But you're still unhappy."

Lira cursed how well Ahrin knew her. "I'm not unhappy, just frustrated that I still don't know anything."

"Lucinda doesn't trust easily. When you start bringing her information, she'll reciprocate. I promise, it will get easier." Ahrin gave her that quicksilver smile. "Just remember the end goal."

"You and me running the Shadowcouncil?" she asked dryly. "When that happens, can we fire Lucinda?"

Ahrin laughed, the notes of it catching the attention of a handful of apprentices sitting nearby. They looked over curiously, probably wondering about the initiate laughing with Spider. Lira loved that laugh, even though she didn't want to.

"I know you held us at DarkSkull Hall," she said in an undertone, eyes on Ahrin's face, hoping to surprise her into a revealing reaction. "I haven't said anything to anyone, of course, but I figured it out after doing some reading in the library."

Ahrin smiled a little. "I knew you'd work it out. Although I doubt it will take the Mage Council much longer to figure it out—many of them lived at DarkSkull for years. They probably have already and just not told you."

Lira had to hide a wince at Ahrin's accuracy, but annoyance soon replaced it. "Then why didn't you tell me?"

"It was more fun watching you try to figure it out yourself."

Lira snorted. She couldn't help herself. Ahrin chuckled and returned to her breakfast. Lira did the same, taking a moment to re-focus on the fact she was supposed to be winning Ahrin over, not allowing the reverse to happen. But her traitorous gaze landed on where Ahrin's hand rested on the table inches from hers, long graceful fingers that had been trailed down her cheek the night before, slid through her hair. It would take only a small movement to reach out and tangle their fingers. Ugh, she was being ridiculous.

Focus, Lira.

She tore her gaze away, stared at her porridge instead, and tried to decide how hard to push for more information. When she felt steadier, she let out a deliberate sigh. "You're right, you know, about the council not telling me anything. And these stupid rules restricting our move-ments are making me furious. It's like they think I'm a child."

Ahrin's expression turned chilly. "Fools. They'll regret it."

Lira smiled slightly, liking that idea very much. "They will. You know, if you're serious about you and I working together, then I need to be able to trust you, which means you need to tell me what you know."

"You know better than to think I'm falling for that one." Ahrin gave her a faint smile. "Especially not in here."

"Convenient answer."

Ahrin shrugged.

Lira sat back in her chair with a huff. "You're completely exasperating."

"And yet, I am unmoved."

With a sigh, and before she did something stupid like kissing Ahrin again, Lira lifted her tray and stood. "I'll see you later."

Ahrin winked. "I look forward to it."

"Is that why you never, *ever*, socialise or spend time in the common rooms outside of lessons?" Fari's voice broke Lira's concentration. "Because you're always up here or in the library doing schoolwork?"

Lira put down the quill and stretched her aching hand. "I'm sure there are far more interesting theories circulating this place, but yes, that's pretty much it. I mean, apart from the fact I just don't like most of you. When I came here, I had no education at all beyond the basics of reading and writing. I was so far behind I'm still catching up."

Fari blinked, looking surprised at Lira's straight answer.

"Why do *you* struggle at school so much?" Lira asked before the girl could follow up with any more questions. "Surely a Dirsk receives the finest of educations before toddling off to mage school."

Fari shrugged. "I did, but I've always struggled at lessons. It takes me at least double the amount of time to read a piece of parchment and figure out what it's saying, or write out homework, than it does everyone else."

Lira frowned. "But not because you're stupid."

"Sometimes I think it is." Fari looked away. "My cousins used to make bets on how long it would take each private tutor my parents hired to give up on me and quit."

"You're not stupid," Lira said shortly, turning back to her Languages homework. "Trust me, I can spot a stupid person from a good distance, and you're not it."

"That's a very nice thing to say, Spider."

"I'm not being nice." Lira frowned in bafflement. "I'm just telling you the truth."

"You just made me feel good about myself. That's being nice." Fari smiled, then waved a hand. "What's distracting you tonight?"

"What?" Lira rubbed at her eyes, struggling to keep up with this conversation.

Fari got up from her bed, wandered over. "You keep turning back to that page to re-read it. Four times now. This is the third night I've watched you do your homework and you've never done that before."

"It's going to be five if you don't stop chatting at me."

"Fine." Fari heaved a sigh and dropped face-first onto her bed. "I may as well go to sleep since you're being boring and Garan insists we get up at a ridiculously early hour. Night."

"Night," Lira said distractedly, already back to re-reading a passage about verbs.

Once Fari was asleep, Lira put away her Languages homework and got out a spare piece of parchment. With frequent glances to make sure her room-mate was still sleeping, she wrote a report to Dawn that summarised her meeting with Greyson and Lucinda and described the location of Lucinda's townhouse. With every line she emphasised how confident she was that she was in no immediate danger from the group.

She wanted Rionn's lord-mage to get the report as soon as possible, to forestall any orders to stay away from Underground. To that end, she sealed the note the moment she finished, then slipped out of the room and went downstairs to add it to the school's mail box—meaning it should go out with the next day's post.

Relief relaxed her shoulders when she returned to find Fari still sleeping. She piled her homework into a single stack, blew out the lamp, and climbed into bed.

SOMETIME LATER LIRA woke screaming from a nightmare. At first it was hard to work out that she *had* actually woken and wasn't still in the dream. Darkness surrounded her and her skin was on fire... it literally felt like she was burning from the inside out. Sweat soaked through her sheets and plastered her hair to her skin. She let out a hissing gasp at the intensity of the sensation, her vision spotting and turning blurry.

All she could do was lie there and struggle desperately to breathe through it.

But she couldn't. Her breaths came in quick, panting gasps that she couldn't slow. Her chest heaved like a bellows. Everything burned. Her blood was so heated it felt like it was boiling inside her.

She thought she heard Fari's voice calling her name, but try as she might, she couldn't anchor herself to the sound or summon the ability to respond. The burning intensified, and she writhed on the bed, gasping, unable to get enough air. A palm touched her forehead, bringing momentary relief, but then it was gone.

A door was yanked open. Running feet left the room. Time passed... minutes, hours, Lira had no idea. Then more running feet sounded, voices calling out to her and each other.

Then another palm on her forehead.

And unconsciousness.

CHAPTER 13

T arion's face swam into view when Lira came back to herself. It was still dark, but she was no longer in her dormitory room, and she got the distinct sense more time had passed than just an hour or two.

He straightened in his chair when he saw her eyes blink open, leaning forward and lifting a hand to push his dark hair off his face. "Hey there. How are you feeling?"

She swallowed, considering that for a moment. Her thoughts were groggy and every muscle in her body felt as if it had been stomped on. She still felt too warm, as well, though nothing like the searing furnace her body had been before she passed out. "Strange. What happened?"

"Uncle Finn isn't sure, but he's pretending like he is." Tarion's eyes were dark with concern. "He says you had a particularly nasty fever. The healers think you're on the mend now, though you'll have to stay here a couple of days so they can keep an eye on you."

"Where's here?"

"The healing rooms."

She made a face at that thought. More missed classes meant falling even further behind, meaning even more long hours to catch up. She blinked, re-focused on Tarion. "What are you doing here?"

He hesitated, frowning as if her glib question concerned him. "Lira, without mage healers you would have died."

"Master A'ndreas said that?" she asked, surprised.

"He didn't need to. I've never actually seen him look worried before, which was telling enough."

That checked her. Deep down, instinct told her that whatever had caused the fever, it was linked to what had been done to her at Dark-Skull Hall. Ahrin *had* said that subjects sometimes died, and it sounded like Lira had come pretty close.

She shuddered, her chest tightening with fear and anxiety. She couldn't get that triumphant look on Lucinda's face out of her head. She'd been unconscious under that woman's hand for who knew how long. Nausea rose in her and she forced it away with an effort, turning her attention to Tarion in the hopes of being distracted.

"Consider the seriousness of my illness acknowledged," she told him. "Back to my original question—what are you doing here?"

"Seeing as the masters aren't really keeping us informed about anything right now, we wanted to keep an eye on you ourselves. We've been taking turns." His lips quirked in a smile. "And Garan decided since it was *my* mother who runs this place, I was the best choice for risking getting caught out of bed so late after curfew."

Tears rose in her eyes. Horrified at herself, she fought them back. They'd wanted to keep an eye on her so much they were willing to risk breaking curfew to do it? She coughed, clearing her throat. "Is someone planning on telling Garan at any point that he's not the boss of us?"

Tarion grinned, and her spirits leapt. "That will take a braver man than I."

As nice as their concern was, her old instincts roused. She didn't want to rely on them for her safety. "I appreciate the thought, but I'm awake now. You don't have to be here. Go to bed, I'll be fine."

"We know you can take care of yourself. We just feel better if one of us is with you, that's all." Tarion settled back in his chair. "Lorin even missed dinner so he could wait for me to show up so you wouldn't be left alone."

Lira chuckled then coughed. "Now that's a sacrifice. The kid never stops eating."

"You laugh and smile a lot more when you're on Uncle Finn's medicinal herbs." Tarion echoed her chuckle.

"So do you when there's nobody else around."

His face turned serious, and he didn't shy away from meeting her eyes. "They did something to you, didn't they? At DarkSkull, I mean."

She stiffened. "You didn't tell Master A'ndreas that, did you?"

"No. I know you don't trust the masters completely, and I respect that. You can trust us, though. *Me*. What did they do to you?"

"I don't know," she admitted, unable to hold his gaze and glancing down to where her fingers toyed with a loose thread on her blanket. "They did something to all of us. Or at least... they might have. We were unconscious for long periods of time."

"True, but none of the rest of us have ended up in here with a life-threatening fever so bad that it frightened the Mage Council's most powerful healer half to death," he said calmly. "There's something you're not saying."

"I truly don't know for certain what they did to me," she said. "I swear it. I wish I did."

He let out a breath. "I think you should talk to Uncle Finn. If this isn't a bad fever like he thinks, it could happen again. What if it's worse next time? Fari said you were screaming when you woke up."

"No." She couldn't. Because she didn't trust A'ndreas. Didn't trust what he'd do with the knowledge that Underground might have tried to give her, Shakar's granddaughter, more mage abilities.

"All right." He sighed, sat back in his chair. "Be ready, though. Uncle Finn is the smartest and most curious man I know. Even though he told us it was a fever, I doubt he's certain of it, so you'll likely get some questions from him."

She managed a faint smile. "Thanks for the warning."

His gaze searched hers. "You know, or you've guessed, what they were experimenting for, haven't you?"

She wanted to tell him. Get it off her chest. Get his advice, because Tarion was both smart and thoughtful. And he accepted why she was so wary of the council. But she couldn't... something inside her couldn't manage to bring down those walls and trust enough, even though she badly wanted to. That survival instinct was too strong.

"Think about it. I'd never betray your trust." He smiled. "Now, are you sleepy? Or do you want to play cards or something to help pass the time? I can't imagine you do well at being bed-bound."

Lira's response was forestalled by the ward door clicking open and light footsteps approaching. Tarion instantly turned wary, one hand reaching for the mage staff leaning against his chair, body angling towards the direction of the footsteps. Lira tried to reach for her magic, but she didn't have the control or strength to do it, and it sputtered away from her grasp. It took a moment to smother the instinctive panic that roused.

Moments later, the curtain around her bed slid open and Ahrin stepped inside. Her midnight blue eyes were dark, and an odd urgency vibrated from her. Her gaze went straight to Lira. "I just heard what happened, are you—" She cut herself off when she saw Tarion sitting there.

He glanced between them, then stood. "Hello. I don't think we've officially met. I'm Tarion Caverlock."

"Ahrin Vensis." She took his hand, but her voice was cool, distant. "I'll leave you to it. Sorry for interrupting."

"No, please, I suspect Lira would far rather have your company." Tarion turned to Lira with a little smile. "I'll be just outside the ward door, hiding from the healer on night duty, if you need anything."

"Go to bed, Tarion. I'll be fine," she told him.

"And I'll be fine out in the corridor." He gave her a little wave and left.

Ahrin stood where she was, unmoving, until the door had clicked shut behind Tarion. Then she drew the curtain back across the space to give them privacy. Lira watched her curiously. Her heart had leapt into her chest at the sight of Ahrin, the drugs and exhaustion meaning her usual instinct to shove away her weaker emotions was gone completely.

"How are you feeling?" Ahrin asked briskly. Without waiting for an answer, she crossed to the bed and placed her fingers at the pulse in Lira's neck before pressing her palm to her forehead.

"About as good as the last time you had to patch me up." Lira brushed away her hands and tried to sit up, just managing it, though weariness coursed through her at the movement.

Ahrin's mouth tightened and she sat on the edge of the bed, studying Lira's face. "You're pale. You could almost pass for Shiven right now."

"This is because of what they did to me, isn't it?" she asked, lowering her voice.

"It can be a side effect." Ahrin nodded, her gaze out the window above Lira's head.

"What did she do to me?" A pleading note edged her voice despite her best efforts to hide it.

Ahrin didn't seem to hear the question. She let out a breath, reaching up to rub her forehead, her shoulders sagging. "When I heard what had happened, you have no idea..."

"Hey." Without thinking, Lira reached over to take her hand. She'd never been able to bear it the handful of times she'd seen Ahrin in distress. It so rarely happened it made her unbalanced every time, desperate to fix it. "What is it?"

Ahrin jerked away from Lira's touch and took a breath, her usual cool demeanour sliding into place. "They use razak blood."

"What?"

"In previous experiments, they've established that razak blood injected into humans can result in the recipient developing a mage ability. Not always, but sometimes. Only, in their initial experiments, the injections caused side effects that killed most of their subjects." Ahrin's voice was terse. "Next they tried injecting into humans with existing mage ability. The consequences were less severe, though still fatal about half the time. They've refined the process even further now."

"Let me guess," Lira murmured. "The side effects include dangerous fevers."

Ahrin merely nodded.

"Wait..." Lira shook her head as she processed the implications of that, cold closing over her chest, all her exhaustion gone in a blink.

"Ahrin, you let them do that to you? When there was such a strong likelihood you would die?"

"I didn't know those were the odds at the time." She shrugged, as if it were nothing. "It's part of the reason I'm so useful to them, because my body can handle the injections even though I was born without mage power. I've survived three treatments."

Lira stared at her, deeply upset but not fully understanding why. She pushed herself up higher on the pillows. "Why? Why would you put yourself in someone else's power like that? It isn't you. I don't understand."

"You did it too," Ahrin deflected. "You offered yourself up."

"You manipulated me into doing that. I let you because I..." Lira trailed off.

"I told you *nothing* that was untrue." Ahrin exploded off the bed, anger flashing on her face. "I offered you extra magical abilities and you didn't hesitate to accept."

Lira stared at her. "You didn't tell me I might die."

"The odds were far better with you. Are you telling me you still wouldn't have said yes, even if I'd said there was a chance it could kill you?" Ahrin caught and held her gaze. "I know you. I knew what you wanted more than anything. I figured at least if you'd gotten yourself caught up in... I could make sure..." She made a sharp, dismissive hand gesture, looked away again. "It doesn't matter."

Lira studied her face, sad and upset and angry all at once. "Did someone you trust convince you to do it? Were you tricked? Explain to me why Ahrin Vensis, fearless crew leader and merciless killer, handed herself over to strangers to possibly be killed, because I can't even begin to understand that."

"Leave it, Lira," Ahrin snarled, voice dangerous and full of menace. "I wanted power, just like you. And now I have it."

Not afraid, but recognising when Ahrin couldn't be pushed any further, Lira changed tack. "Tell me what you meant about refining the process... wait, let me guess. It works better when the subject's blood chemistry is altered by fear and stress?"

"Yes. They believe the deaths and side effects are caused from human blood rejecting the foreign razak blood, but when high levels of fear or stress are present in the body, results indicate the binding process has a higher success rate."

"And it's even more improved when the subjects are young?" Lira hazarded. "That's why you took us and not older mages without warrior powers."

"Yes."

"Why not take unimportant students like Lorin, though? Why risk the reprisals from the Mage Council that taking their precious relatives would cause?"

Ahrin merely shook her head. Either she didn't know or wouldn't tell.

Lira relaxed back into the pillows. Having some answers calmed her, though she still couldn't let go of the fact Ahrin had offered herself up to be experimented on. It just didn't make any sense. "Am I going to die?"

"The side effects can be lingering and serious, but as far as I know, deaths always occur within the first few weeks after injection." Ahrin's face remained tight, shoulders stiff. "You might have more fevers, but they won't be as bad as this. I suspect this one was your body fighting to either accept or reject the razak blood."

"So it worked? I have another mage ability."

"Probably. But it could take some time to break out, and the first time is usually the longest. For me it was about six weeks."

Ahrin was being so forthcoming that Lira leapt at the chance to learn as much as she could for the council, despite how ill and exhausted she felt. "Why are the Shadowcouncil doing these experiments? Are they trying to build a mage army we can use to challenge the council?"

"That's my guess. The non-mage humans they've recruited to join Underground serve a vital purpose, but the Shadowcouncil isn't taking down the Mage Council without powerful magical strength. They've recruited non-council mages to their side, but the majority of mage-born folk are aligned with the council."

Lira eyed her. Ahrin was holding something back, she could sense it. "What aren't you telling me?"

Ahrin let out a breath. "So much. But what I've told you tonight is already too dangerous. If Lucinda knew I'd done it, we'd both be dead."

Another piece of leverage Ahrin had handed to Lira to use against her if she chose. Another utterly uncharacteristic thing for her to do, unless, of course, she was lying for her own purposes. Lira's eyes narrowed as she grew wary. "Why would you tell me any of it, then?"

Ahrin merely shook her head, crossing back to the bed to sit on the edge. She pressed her palm against Lira's forehead again. "How are you feeling? Anything other than a fever?"

"Fever would be somewhat of an understatement, but other than that, some muscle soreness and weariness."

Ahrin nodded and continued her prodding. She tested Lira's temperature before sliding her fingers down to check her pulse again. Eventually her hands rested at Lira's jaw and she took a shuddering breath. "I think you're going to be okay."

"Good." Lira murmured, far more aware of Ahrin's touch now than anything else. "What's wrong?"

Ahrin had gone rigid, as if holding back some fierce urge or emotion. It was so unusual that it worried Lira. "Nothing." Ahrin shook herself and leaned back, the cool expression there as if it had never left. "I should let you get some rest."

Not wanting her to go, Lira unthinkingly reached out, took hold of her wrist. "What does this tattoo mean?"

Ahrin stilled, and a chill rushed into the space between them, making Lira shiver. "I told you never to ask me about that."

"It's got something to do with why they want you, doesn't it?" Lira searched her face, ignoring every signal that she should let this be, drop it. "Is this tattoo why you submitted yourself to them, let them test you with something that could have killed you? I know you better than that. Make me understand, Ahrin."

Ahrin's gaze flicked up to hers, and in that look was the deadly killer that had kept other crews at bay and made her so successful as the Darkhand. The wicked smile, the easy laugh, it was all gone in a blink—only ever a surface thing. "Don't make the mistake of thinking I have the same softness in me that you've worked your whole life to bury in yourself. I didn't ever know a mother's love. I don't know affection, Lira, I was never taught it. I never experienced it. You are a fool if you push this further."

Her words rang true. Ahrin was always wearing a mask of some kind, shaping her reactions to what she wanted her audience to see, cleverly studying those around her so she could perfectly fake the same expressions, mannerisms, emotions. Lira had watched her do it for years. But she'd also seen real emotion under all of it, even if there had only been glimpses, even if those glimpses had been rarer than diamonds. "My question stands," she said quietly.

Ahrin yanked her wrist away and stood, genuine fury rippling over her face. "As does my answer. Next time you ask we'll be done."

Part of Lira knew she was being foolish, risking the progress she'd made to win Ahrin over. But she was weary, drugged, and in this moment she needed to break through the barrier Ahrin held between them far more than she needed to destroy Underground. And that little thrill of danger was egging her on, tantalising her with the idea that if she could break through, winning Ahrin to her side might go even faster. So she held Ahrin's gaze. "I don't believe you and I'm not afraid of you. You know that."

Ahrin's mouth tightened. "You think you know me—"

"I *do* know you," Lira said evenly, holding her gaze. "Despite your best efforts otherwise. We both know that's true. You might have tossed me aside like I was nothing, like you did to Timin and Yanzi, but you weren't nothing to me."

"I am a monster, Lira. A tool shaped for killing and nothing else." Danger filled the room, an eerie menace exuding from the way Ahrin stood, the way her hand hovered near what was no doubt a knife concealed beneath her robe, the flat killing look in her eyes.

"I know that too." Lira pushed anyway. "It doesn't change anything."

Ahrin spun and left without another word. She yanked the curtain aside and strode away on almost silent footsteps.

Lira wanted to call after her, to ask her to come back. Wanted Ahrin to curl up beside her and stay with her until morning. She wanted to feel Ahrin's touch soothe away all her fear and pain. But she couldn't bring herself to ask.

Not because she would be a fool to let Ahrin through her guard more than she already was, or because Ahrin had abandoned her and manipulated her and would probably do both again without hesitation or remorse. And not because Ahrin wasn't the person who would be there to share Lira's burdens when they grew too heavy, even though—deep down in the dark place she hid all the things that scared her—there was nothing Lira wanted more.

Because Ahrin was right about one thing. Lira had spent her life since six years old pushing away any feeling, any weakness, refusing to acknowledge it. Doing that to survive.

And like with Tarion earlier... she didn't know how to bring that vulnerability back anymore.

CHAPTER 14

T he following night, Lira was woken in the early hours by the sound of footsteps and hushed voices outside the main door to the healing ward. She'd managed to assure Garan earlier in the day that she'd recovered well enough that she didn't need a night-time babysitter, so she was alone, the ward around her dark and silent.

Within a heartbeat of her eyes opening, she'd read the underlying urgency of the voices and movement, and her instincts roused in response. Something had happened, something bad, but they were trying to keep it quiet.

She turned under the sheets, habit sending her gaze searching her immediate surroundings for a weapon. The main doors swung open a moment later, and she stilled and feigned sleep, eyes just barely cracked open.

Two men—Shiven soldiers—passed by the end of her bed carrying an unconscious girl. Her head lolled back in their hold and her eyes were closed. Even in the dim light, Lira didn't miss the multiple dark patches of blood soaking through the girl's apprentice robe, but that was all she got before they moved out of her eyeline. A man wearing a master's cloak followed close behind—Nordan, she thought. All were making an effort to move quietly.

She stayed where she was a few moments, then slowly turned over to face the direction they'd gone. The apprentice had been carried to a bed at the far end of the room, but a privacy curtain was drawn around it.

Damn.

The main doors opened again and soon after light footsteps passed the end of Lira's bed. Finn A'ndreas moved into sight, and Nordan stepped out from behind the curtains to speak with him. They had a murmured conversation, then A'ndreas disappeared behind the curtain while Nordan headed back out of the ward.

Lira caught a glimpse of Nordan's face as he approached. The normally unflappable warrior mage wore a deep frown, his hands shifting constantly at his sides as if he didn't know whether to tuck them in his pockets or not.

A little thrill went through her. What had happened?

Judging by the amount of blood Lira had seen, either an apprentice had gotten hurt in an accident or had been attacked. Nordan's agitation and the late hour told her an attack was the most likely scenario. She thought back to the corpse of the dog she'd found the night of the party... how it had been removed and hidden from the students.

She'd mostly forgotten about it in the weeks since, too caught up with her desperation to get back inside Underground, though she hadn't forgotten how uneasy it had made her at the time. The masters had never mentioned it, and there had been no other reports of dead animals being found by anyone on the school grounds.

But what if there *had* been more and the masters had covered those up too? Lira sank back down on her pillows, suddenly preferring to stay awake rather than go back to sleep.

What if something was stalking the grounds of Temari Hall?

As Tarion had predicted, Finn A'ndreas came to see Lira the next morning. Apart from his apprentices checking her temperature every morning and night, it was the first time any of them had come to talk to her. That was good. A'ndreas' kindness in allowing her to recover before questioning her had given her time to prepare answers.

Not to mention his arrival presented an opportunity to try and figure out what had happened the previous night.

After briskly checking her over, the healing master pulled up a chair and sat beside the bed, legs crossed and curious expression in place.

"What happened there?" she asked before he could say anything, pointing to the still-curtained bed at the end of the room. Maybe she could not only get some answers, but also distract him from her entirely. "Everyone in here this morning is casting worried glances in that direction."

"That's not your concern," he said briskly. "I'm here to talk about you."

"Time for the interrogation, is it?" she grumbled, annoyed by his brush off.

"You had a particularly nasty fever. I haven't seen one that bad for years, and the child who had it died."

"Lucky me, then." Two could play that game. If he was going to hide things, she didn't have to be forthcoming either.

"It doesn't bother you, how close you came to dying?" He lifted an eyebrow. "You're not curious about what caused the fever?"

"I'm very curious." She met his look. "Maybe you, as the expert healer, could tell me what caused it?"

"We're feeling particularly irascible today, I see." When she didn't respond to that, he sighed. "I don't think your fever was natural. Let's not do this dance. What did they do to you, Lira?"

"I don't know." Her gaze narrowed. "How are you so sure that my fever is related to what happened to us during our kidnapping? None of the others have been in here with life-threatening fevers."

His head cocked. "Well, Tarion was running a mild fever when you all first arrived back, but yes, you're correct. That could mean one of a few things. Either something went wrong with whatever they did to you, and you responded differently than the others for some reason, or they did something different to you."

"Or, alternatively, I just happened to catch a nasty fever. It *is* winter."

He was quiet for a moment, then said, "I do wish you'd stop taking me for a fool. I understand why it's difficult for you to trust anyone, but you have to know by now that I have your best interests at heart."

"Maybe I'll stop holding things back when you do," she said pointedly. "I saw what happened last night. There's an apprentice in that bed who was carried in here covered in blood,... hurt enough that she needed your help. She was attacked. Did it happen on school grounds?"

A'ndreas' clever gaze contemplated her for a moment, clearly weighing the best course of action. After a long moment he gave a little shrug and sat back in his chair. "Yes, it did."

"Do you know who did it?"

"It looked like an animal attack, actually, so I doubt whatever was responsible was human. And before you ask, no, we haven't caught whatever did it, but half the Shiven division posted here is searching the grounds as we speak." He smiled faintly at the look of surprise on her face. "Fair is fair. I can also tell you it wasn't a razak. Will you tell *me* something now?"

"Was last night the first time something like that has happened?" she asked casually.

"I think you'd have heard if any other students had been attacked in the middle of the night and hurt so badly they were brought here," he said dryly, relaxed and at ease, no hesitation at all. "I imagine by the end of today last night's events will be all through the school."

And with that answer he'd adroitly told the truth without revealing that a guard dog—and possibly other animals—had been attacked too. He was a clever man with clever words. Lira told herself to remember that when dealing with A'ndreas. "Fine, here's an answer to your questions. I'm confident Underground experimented on me while they held me captive, even though I don't remember anything specific." She gave him a little bit of truth. "The others, I'm not sure, I never saw them being taken away or being experimented on. I think you're right that my fever had something to do with the experiments."

Curiosity filled his expression. "What makes *you* think that?"

"I woke up once, during whatever they were doing... it was only a few seconds, and everything was hazy. But I have faint memories of feeling fevered, too hot." A half-truth. Before he could ask her any more questions, she kept going, pointing towards the bed at the end of the room. "Do you think there will be more attacks?"

The curiosity on his face vanished, replaced by a blank mask. "You're safe here, Lira. We'll make sure of it."

"That's a yes." Lira shook her head. "Was *she* safe last night? You have no idea what attacked her, do you?"

"We will, very soon. It's only a matter of time." A'ndreas rose to his feet.

"You have a hundred elite soldiers guarding the exterior of these walls, and an extra complement of warrior mages and Taliath backing them up," Lira said, studying his face. "Whatever did this didn't come from outside, did it?"

"That is yet to be determined."

Lira pushed again. "The information Councillor Egalion talked about at the assembly—the threat to Temari. What was it?"

He hesitated. "A handful of Underground members were arrested by Dash and his soldiers immediately after you were all returned. My sister sat in on their interrogations. They told Dashan nothing of value, and there wasn't much more in their thoughts either. They knew nothing about your kidnapping. However, Dawn read in one of their minds that the Darkhand is in Karonan."

Lira huffed a breath. "That's it?" Ahrin would be thrilled to know that an entire division of Shiven soldiers had been dispatched to Temari because of her. Lira resolved never to tell her.

"The timing concerned us deeply. And like I've said many times, the safety of students is our utmost priority."

She shook her head. "Nobody is safe in here right now, Master A'ndreas. If last night is anything to go by, your measures aren't working."

"You might try having some faith in those whose only concern is your protection," he said mildly. "Besides, since when do you give two coppers about the other students here?"

He had her there. She conceded gracefully. "When are you going to let me out of here? I feel fine."

"I want to make sure there are no lingering aftereffects of the fever before I release you."

She held back a sigh with some effort. "How long will that take?"

"Another day or two at least." He paused at the end of her bed before walking off. "Think of it as a good opportunity to learn some patience."

She scowled after him.

GARAN WAS the first to visit that morning, and from the expression on his face when he sat in the chair by her bed, the news about the attack had gotten out. Lira smiled inwardly—even sooner than A'ndreas had predicted.

"It's Neria," he said quietly when Lira asked. "A fourth-year apprentice with ice magic. She's almost guaranteed to pass her trials at the end of the year."

"So whatever attacked her took down an almost fully trained warrior mage?" She whistled. No wonder Nordan had looked so worried.

"Exactly. Security inside the tower has increased at night." Garan's voice lowered even further. "And there's a rumour going around that there have been other attacks in the past few weeks. One of the guard dogs was killed, apparently, and a couple of the wild cats that roam the grounds. There was a ruckus in the stables three nights ago, too, some of the horses going wild in their stalls in the early hours—the groom on duty sleeps there, so he may have scared off whatever it was when he went to settle them."

Shock rippled through Lira. The dog she'd found hadn't been the only creature killed by whatever this was. Her thoughts went straight to the flying creatures that had attacked them a few mornings earlier, but no... Lucinda had said they hunted those with magic, not animals. Besides they would have made enough noise killing the animals, or attacking Neria, to have woken people, surely? "How credible are these rumours?"

He shrugged. "You know what student talk is like."

Lira hesitated only briefly. A'ndreas refused to tell her what was going on, and her curiosity was strong enough that she was willing to engage the help of those she was beginning to trust to figure it out. "It's true that one of the guard dogs was killed. I saw the body."

His eyes widened. "How did—"

"I was studying late in the library and saw it on my way out. Whatever did it had left the corpse sprawled in a pool of blood on the floor outside the main doors. I didn't say anything because I didn't want to be linked to it or caught out of my room so late," she said in an undertone. "It was gone the next morning and since I heard nobody talking about it, I figured the masters had come across it and covered it up before any students could see it."

"When was this?" He frowned.

"The night of the party after we were returned."

He fixed her with a look. "You were studying in the library after the party?"

"My actions are not the point of this story, Garan."

He smiled a little, but then sat back in his chair, clearly thinking it through. "I'll talk to Tarion, see if his parents have told him anything about it."

"Nobody else," she warned him. "Panicking the school won't help us find out what's going on."

"Agreed. I imagine that's why the masters have been keeping it quiet. Do you think the attacks are linked to our kidnapping?"

"I think it's a mighty coincidence if not," she said. Especially the timing of it. Her thoughts drifted to Ahrin. The attacks had started just after her arrival. But none of it felt like the Darkhand. Lira couldn't even begin to think of a reason why Ahrin would be killing dogs and cats. And if she'd wanted to kill Neria, the apprentice would be dead.

Garan frowned. "What could be the purpose of it all? Why animals and then an apprentice... and why leave Neria alive? If some vicious creature capable of inflicting those kinds of wounds was wandering the grounds, someone would have seen it by now. We're packed wall to wall in here with students, masters, Shiven solders, Taliath and mage warriors."

"Agreed." Lira lifted her hands helplessly. She didn't understand it either.

"I wondered whether it might be those flying monsters who attacked you the other morning, but from your description, they're far too big and noticeable to have been creeping around killing dogs and cats," Garan said.

"Also agreed, although we probably shouldn't rule it out. Maybe their immunity to magic helps somehow." Lira resolved to ask Ahrin next time she saw her, *if* the Darkhand was still talking to her. Maybe she'd be willing to confirm whether Underground was behind these attacks.

Garan let out a breath. "I just wish it was all over, that Underground were gone and we could go back to our normal lives."

"You want to go back to your bubble," she said without rancour. "That's not normal life, Garan."

He accepted that with a terse nod, then stood from his chair, gaze moving down the room.

"What are you doing?" she asked.

He gave her his charming grin. "I'm going to go and check in on Neria, see how she is. Maybe even drop in a question or two about what she remembers."

Lira brightened. "What an excellent plan. If any of the healers come in, I'll distract them for you. I can fake a good relapse if needed."

"Sounds good, partner." He winked and was gone, striding towards the still-curtained bed.

GARAN HAD JUST LEFT Neria's bedside and was almost back at Lira's when Finn A'ndreas entered the ward. The sight of his nephew made him dart a suspicious look between him and the curtained off bed at the end of the room. "Garan. Aren't you supposed to be in class?"

"I was just on my way, Uncle Finn." He smiled widely. "I came to visit Lira, see how she is. We've been worried about her."

"If you could get rid of him, Master A'ndreas, that would be very welcome," she said sourly. "He won't stop talking at me and I'd really rather be left in peace."

"She complains, but she loves my visits." Garan's grin widened at her scowl. "You're right though, I should get to class."

Lira winced at how thick he was laying it on, but A'ndreas merely gave a resigned sigh. "Get out of here, Garan."

"Yes, sir!"

Garan gave Lira a little shake of his head as he passed by the end of her bed, and her heart sank. It seemed like Neria hadn't been able to tell him much. His follow up wink, then his cheerful whistling as he left the ward, came close to making her smile though.

"Careful, Lira," A'ndreas said mildly as he headed for Neria's bed. "You seem to be getting dangerously close to making a friend."

She scowled at his back, then settled more comfortably in her bed, already bored. A moment later she realised she was looking forward to her next visit; probably Tarion, if she'd memorised their ridiculous roster of babysitting correctly.

Rotted hells. She was most definitely going soft.

Pushing that thought aside, she glanced at her hands, a habit that had formed since Ahrin's revelation. A useless thing, as there were no answers written there to tell her about what mage ability she might have obtained from being injected with razak blood.

A little shiver went through her at the thought, anticipation and unease both. She couldn't help hoping the mage ability was a powerful one. One that would make her stronger, better, more capable of destroying Lucinda and her group.

Though how she'd ever explain it to the Mage Council... at the time Ahrin had offered it to her, Lira had dismissed her nagging worry about how the council would react, too eager to take what was being offered. Too desperate for more magic, more power, something she could use to dispel Shakar's lingering echo.

But now, thinking more rationally about it, the realisation of what it meant had much more of an impact. The council would have no choice but to accept it, accept her, especially once she handed them Underground and the Shadowcouncil on a platter.

But they weren't going to like it.

She told herself it wouldn't matter if they were upset at first, ignoring the little voice in her head—the one that had experienced the looks and mutterings her entire life—that warned her it might not be so easy. She'd win them over. She'd figure out how.

A little thrill burned in her chest at the idea of her new ability, whatever it might be, and council objections be damned. She wouldn't give it back even if she could.

CHAPTER 15

L ira remained in the healing ward for another two days. The
fever didn't return, and though she had unsettled dreams, the
nightmares didn't come back either. Fari, Garan, Tarion, and
Lorin came to check on her regularly. Garan had filled them in on his
discussion with Lira, and so each brought snippets of information
for her.

Garan's conversation with Neria had resulted in a description of
her wounds that was consistent with what Lira had seen on the dog's
corpse. More unsettling, however, was Neria's recollection of burning
copper eyes chaotic with madness, a vaguely human-shaped form, and
unusual strength.

"Garan said she really doesn't remember anything but that. She was
surprised, the attack coming from behind. She was knocked hard in
the head, so she was dazed, her vision blurry, by the time she hit the
floor. After that, she remembers the eyes, and pain, then waking up in
bed here," Fari relayed. Fari also confirmed there hadn't been any
unusual blood loss apart from that to be expected from the wounds
Neria had sustained. "So not a razak," she said, almost cheerfully.

"It sounds like the attacker could be human, and maybe terror and concussion distorted her memories," Lira mused. The description firmly ruled out Ahrin, too. The Darkhand was a cold, efficient killer. Not a maddened murderer.

Tarion informed her that he had been told nothing by his parents, a little flash of ire crossing his face as he said it. Caverlock was busy leading the search for Underground and the Darkhand in Karonan, and Egalion was still in Carhall. The job of figuring out what had happened to Neria and the dead animals had been left in the hands of A'ndreas and the Temari Hall masters.

Lorin told Lira that it was a fellow initiate, his new room-mate, who'd found one of the dead cats on the grounds, torn apart like the guard dog, out near the training courts. He'd been sworn to silence by the masters. It all formed a very disturbing picture.

"Do you think it's significant the animals were killed while Neria was left alive?" Lorin asked her.

"Maybe, maybe not," Lira said. "It could just be that dogs and cats are easier to overpower than an apprentice mage with warrior magic, or that the attacker was disturbed in its attack on Neria before it could finish the job."

And that was all they knew. It was frustrating, being kept on bedrest when all her instincts wanted to be able to move, protect herself if necessary. And unlike the others, Ahrin hadn't visited again. Either she was busy on Underground business or she hadn't felt it necessary to visit once she'd assured herself Lira was fine. It was more likely the latter. Ahrin didn't bother about things once she considered them taken care of—especially after Lira had angered her so profoundly.

She wondered what Ahrin had told Lucinda about Lira's illness, and whether she'd also passed on the fact she'd found Tarion at Lira's bedside. No doubt Ahrin had noticed the others keeping a close eye on her as well. Lira hoped she had; it would only reinforce that she was doing exactly what Lucinda had asked of her.

An apprentice healer finally released Lira early on the third morning after she flatly refused to lie there another minute unless she was able to speak directly to Master A'ndreas. She derived from that exchange that A'ndreas was either absent from Temari Hall or extremely busy.

Other than a faint headache that still lingered at her temples, she felt mostly back to normal as she came down the stairs, planning on a late breakfast before returning to classes. She reached the ground floor to find several initiates and apprentices gathered by the open doors in the entry foyer, staring outside with great interest.

Tarion and Lorin stood at the back of the group, still in their sparring clothes, skin flushed from exercise despite the cold air. It looked like they hadn't even been to breakfast yet.

Her spirits unaccountably lifted at the sight of them, even as she was simultaneously annoyed with herself for her reaction. Hesitating only briefly, Lira walked over to join the two boys. Both flashed smiles of greeting, Lorin's reserved, Tarion's warm. She followed their gazes to where several horses were being saddled in the yard, blue-cloaked mages and graceful Taliath wearing their magnificent swords moving around with bulging saddlebags. There was an odd efficiency to it all, even though on the surface it looked chaotic.

"What's going on?" she asked.

"They're riding out today for DarkSkull Hall. Da had one of the telepaths here contact Mama, and she and Uncle Tarrick are going to travel from Carhall to meet them there." Worry flashed over Tarion's face.

Interest sparked. "They've finally had enough of watching the place, I take it?" she asked.

Tarion nodded. "Da says the scouts report no sign of any activity in the valley, but they can't be certain given how cautious they've been— apparently they were holed up a good distance away from the valley floor. They're going in expecting to find at least a few guards left behind, and potentially razak too. Hence the small army of mages and Taliath in the courtyard." He paused. "If Athira isn't there, then Da hopes to find enough traces of her or Underground to give us an idea of where she was taken."

Lira's gaze narrowed thoughtfully as she watched the courtyard bustle. While she'd meant it when she told Tarion she didn't trust anyone to manage the approach to DarkSkull, she did agree that Dashan Caverlock was smart enough not to do anything foolish.

Her thoughts turned quickly to whether she should tell Underground that the mage force was coming. Given Ahrin—not to mention Lucinda's spies at Temari—would eventually find out and pass the information on themselves, it was going to be hard for Lira to pretend she knew nothing of their plans. At the very least Ahrin would immediately report the sudden departure of a group of Taliath and mage warriors from the school. Maybe Lira could wait a few days before telling Underground, try and give Dashan's force time to get most of the way there before—

"Hey, Lira, are you paying attention?" Lorin's voice nudged her out of her thoughts.

"Sorry, what?"

"I was saying you'd better go pack."

She blinked. "Why?"

Tarion gestured outside, voice lowering so nobody around could overhear. "We're going with them." His smile widened at the look on her face. "We spent days running around all over the ruins of Dark-Skull—who do you think has the best chance of finding any information still there on Underground and Athira? I managed to convince Da of that, and so we're all going."

Delight flashed over Lorin's face, though he too kept his voice quiet. "All of us? I figured it would just be you and Spider."

"I don't think—" Lira began.

"Yes, all of us. We'll need Garan with us if anything goes wrong," Tarion said firmly. "And it wouldn't be fair to leave Fari alone here. What if those flying creatures came back? Not to mention whatever is creeping through the halls at night ripping bodies to shreds."

Lira opened her mouth, then closed it, the ache in her head sharpening at her competing reactions to Tarion's revelation. On the one hand, the idea of getting out of these walls, going to Dark-Skull, and being able to dig around herself for information on Underground and Athira was an unexpected win. Action instead of endless boring lessons. The thrill inside her threatened to burst free.

But how was she going to explain to Lucinda and Greyson her sudden disappearance from Temari without a word? Not to mention she'd be leaving behind the Darkhand to roam free at the school without Lira being able to keep an eye on her.

"Lira?" Tarion was frowning. "I thought you'd be more excited."

"We're going to miss a lot of classes." As soon as the words were out, she cursed herself for how unconvincing they sounded, but she hadn't been able to come up with anything better on the spot.

"I thought you wanted to find Athira too." He sounded disappointed, like he'd expected better from her. "You and Garan were the ones raging the other day about being left out of everything."

"I do want to find her," she said. It was true. It was just that she wanted Underground gone even more, and this might risk that.

"Then what's going on?"

"Nothing." She forced a smile. "I'll go and pack. I'm glad we're getting the opportunity to help with the search."

"Da's going to keep us wrapped up in about ten layers of protection, so don't get your hopes up too much." Tarion made a face. "But at least we'll be doing *something*."

And with that she couldn't help but completely agree.

They were about to disperse when Caverlock himself appeared, taking the front steps two at a time and crossing to them in quick, graceful strides. He was an impressive man. One, despite his good-humoured façade, it would be foolish to cross.

"You've told them the news, I take it." Caverlock looked at his son with a quick smile.

"Yes, Da."

"Good." His glance shifted to Lira and Lorin. "Not a word to anyone else, understood? Nobody here knows where we're going, and the word I'm putting about is that we've decided the five of you aren't safe here given the recent attack on Neria. As far as everyone is concerned, the warriors outside are escorting you to a safer, undisclosed location until we deal with the Underground threat."

Lira was impressed despite herself. She'd suspected Caverlock had

145

been told by Dawn about her spying on Underground, and now that suspicion was confirmed. He'd clearly designed a cover for Lira with Underground, and a clever one too. True excitement began to burn inside her then. It was strong enough to dispel any irritation she might have felt over Dawn extending the circle of knowledge. "Who else knows what's really going on?"

"My wife, the Magor-lier, and the men and women out there, all handpicked and trusted by me," he said. "You'll all be safe, as long as you don't talk to anyone."

"We won't, Da," Tarion said sombrely.

"I'll go and get Fari and tell her the news—we have the same Mapping class this morning," Lorin said. "I'll make sure she doesn't tell anyone. See you back here soon."

Tarion's gaze lingered on Lira as Lorin and Caverlock left them. "Is something wrong?"

"No, of course not."

"You can talk to me. About anything."

She scowled and backed away. "I don't do sharing, you know that, mage-prince. See you soon."

ANTICIPATION SHIVERED through Lira as she packed, enhanced by the excitement of getting out of these walls, making her hands clumsier than usual.

Her brain tripped over itself, busy trying to figure out how to pass Caverlock's excellent cover story to Underground before she disappeared and they got suspicious of her lack of contact. Finding out which initiate class Ahrin was in, interrupting it, and making the whole thing damned obvious, was out of the question.

After a long hesitation, she'd also taken the unsent letter about Ahrin's presence at Temari out of her drawer and asked a passing initiate to ensure it was mailed to Dawn A'ndreas while she was gone. She couldn't risk leaving Ahrin behind to carry out Underground's bidding without knowing what her purpose at the school was, not when Lira didn't know how long she'd be away. If anything happened… it would be Lira's fault, plus she couldn't accept the risk of how the council would view it if Lira's link to Ahrin was ever discovered. She would just have to hope that Dawn would be discreet enough in dealing with Ahrin that it wouldn't blow Lira's cover with Underground. And that Ahrin wouldn't be hurt in the process.

Still, handing the letter over had hurt more than she was willing to admit, and not because of her fear that it would ruin her ability to spy on Underground. By doing it, she was betraying Ahrin to the Mage Council. It shouldn't have been hard. After all, Ahrin was freely telling Lucinda and Underground things about her. Why shouldn't Lira do the same?

But even that logic didn't help. There'd been a time when the thought of either one betraying the other had been utterly unimaginable. It tore some deep part of Lira to know a day had come when it was possible.

Ahrin's appearance at her doorway moments later brought jolts of relief and guilt in equal measure. Lira told herself to focus on her purpose—Ahrin showing up meant she'd be able to pass on a message for Lucinda and Greyson about her absence from Temari. Her mission was what mattered. Anything else was vulnerability she couldn't afford.

"I heard you were released from the... going somewhere?" Ahrin lifted her eyebrows, coming to a halt at the sight of Lira's packed bag. Her demeanour was relaxed, easy, no trace of the cold fury from their last interaction.

"Yes." Lira filled her voice with frustration, keeping her gaze on her bag so Ahrin couldn't read her face to detect the lie. "General Caverlock and Master A'ndreas have apparently decided the five of us aren't safe enough here. We're being taken somewhere where we'll be better protected."

"Where?"

Lira focused on buckling the duffle up. "No idea. They wouldn't tell me. Apparently nobody knows apart from those escorting us wherever it is."

"Curse them all," Ahrin snapped. "Don't they know you're not a baby lamb that needs to be wrapped up in pillows and blankets?"

Lira couldn't help it; she chuckled, finally turning to look at Ahrin. "Apparently not."

"The sooner we get you out of this, the happier I'll be, Lira." Ahrin was all seriousness as she came closer. "You deserve better."

Lira ignored the little shiver of agreement that went through her, and shrugged. "At least it will be a perfect opportunity to work on the project Lucinda gave me the other night. By the time we return, I should be in a good position to start reporting on them." At which point she'd have to figure out exactly *what* to report, of course, but she had time to plan for that.

Ahrin smiled and took a deliberate step closer. At her nearness, Lira's mind flicked back to the Darkhand's odd intensity that night in the healing ward, the way she'd switched from that to a cold fury in a blink. Now there was only a teasing smile on her face as she murmured, "Speaking of the night we saw Lucinda..."

"Yes?" Unbidden, a matching smile crossed Lira's face.

"You're going away for who knows how long. Shut up and kiss me already."

It was all so tangled between them. Desire and loyalty and betrayal. Ahrin wasn't someone Lira could trust, but she was someone Lira needed in order to bring down Underground. Balancing the two was beyond hard, and the lines were becoming more and more blurry. But Lira wasn't going to pretend that kissing Ahrin wasn't exactly what she wanted to do in that moment, and so she did.

The Darkhand tasted like the cinnamon oatmeal she'd had for breakfast, and her skin smelled like the citrus soapweed they all used in the bathing rooms. That was pretty much all Lira noticed about the world for the next few minutes. Ahrin gradually moved them backwards, hands tugging on Lira's hips, until her back was pressed against the wall and she could draw Lira more closely against her.

"You really do learn fast," Ahrin murmured when they broke briefly for air, voice gone husky in a way that had Lira's stomach doing flips.

"I'm not telling you you're a good teacher," Lira breathed, kissing her again.

"Oh, I *know* I am, Lira Astor." Ahrin's hands slid under her tunic and brushed over bare skin. Lira bit her lip, eyes closing at the sensation. Her own hands grew bolder, sliding from Ahrin's back and over her hips and stomach before absently beginning to work on the

148

buttons of her shirt. Her lips moved to Ahrin's jaw, her neck. Ahrin pulled her even closer, so that there wasn't an inch of space between their bodies.

"How long until you have to leave?" Ahrin breathed.

"Now."

"Damn." Regret filled Ahrin's voice.

Damn indeed. Ahrin kissed her again anyway and Lira didn't protest. Another few minutes surely wouldn't...

"Spider, what is this about us going off on some hare-brained... Oh!"

Lira pulled away from Ahrin as Fari walked in, and an awkward silence fell over the room. Ahrin pushed off the wall, straightened her shirt, then winked at Fari and sauntered out. "See you when you're back, Lira."

"Bye." Lira's gaze tracked her leaving, but Ahrin didn't look back.

She was a fool. She was playing with fire, and chances were it was all going to blow up in her face. Going away, keeping some distance from Ahrin, was probably a good idea. By the time she returned, maybe she'd have managed to summon better resolve where her nemesis was concerned. But it ached, more than she was comfortable with, the thought of being away from Ahrin.

"So you..." Fari's eyes went wide as she looked out the door after Ahrin and then back at Lira. "Care to explain how the school's outcast manages to land the most gorgeous student here?"

"It's not..." Lira waved a hand, then went back to finish buckling her bag.

"It's not what? It looked very much a thing to me."

"Not talking about it." Lira hefted her bag, turned. "Want me to help you pack? They'll be waiting for us."

Fari eyed her, hands on hips. "You like girls. I knew it! Should I be worried that you've secretly had a crush on me this entire time?"

Lira burst out laughing. "No. Rest assured, your virtue is safe with me. You are far too talkative and *cheerful*."

"I have no virtue remaining." Fari snorted, then grinned. "But I'm glad to hear it nonetheless. It'd be very awkward, and I don't do awkward."

"You don't say," Lira said dryly. "We're late already, you know?"

"How much will you pay me not to tell the boys we're late because you were making out with your girl?"

"She's not my girl." But she was. Always had been and always would be. Lira pushed that little voice down deep. It was impossible. Ahrin was the enemy now.

"Oh boy, I'm going to have so much fun with this." Fari finally moved to drag her duffel out and began loading clothes into it.

Lira's grin faded. If Fari knew who Ahrin was, she wouldn't have fun with it. She'd feel betrayed. Hurt. Ahrin had led the group who had kidnapped and tortured them all, who'd left Lorin with a permanent limp, who'd killed Haler and Master Alias. And Ahrin felt no guilt about it either. No remorse. She was ruthless, focused only on achieving what she wanted and nothing else.

Lira was no different. A little wriggle of guilt rippled through her. She felt no real loyalty to the Mage Council, or anyone else. She had no reason to. Her actions were driven purely by her desire to find a place for herself in the world of mages—if not of welcome and acceptance, at least of respect.

"You feeling okay?" Fari glanced over, concern on her face.

"Yes, fine. Can you not talk about Ahrin to the others, please? It's not... I shouldn't have let myself... I mean." Lira took a breath. "It's complicated."

Fari's teasing expression faded. "Sure. I'm your friend, remember? If you don't want the boys to know, then it stays between us. Simple as that."

"Thank you."

"And for the record, you're too rude to be attractive to me."

Lira snorted, and a comfortable silence fell as Fari finished packing. In a few minutes the healer appeared at her shoulder, bag hanging from her hand. "Let's go."

As Lira followed her out, Fari's words still settling through her, she thought about how she'd risked herself for Lorin's leg. Wanted to find Athira. How they'd all sat at her bedside to ensure she was safe while she was unconscious and sick.

Maybe there *was* acceptance to be found. Not with everyone. Not even with most. But with some... some that she liked and respected in turn. It was an odd feeling, something she wasn't sure how to settle within herself.

But it was nice. Warm.

It was a feeling she'd fight for.

CHAPTER 16

They arrived in the village of Weeping Stead—a bustling town only a half hour or so ride from the valley enclosing Dark-Skull Hall—just over a week after setting out. On arrival, Dashan Caverlock directed everyone to a large inn. After issuing orders to his warriors to take their horses to the adjacent stables, he ushered Lira and the others inside and upstairs to shared rooms on the top floor.

Lira sat in the nearest chair, almost letting out a groan at being able to rest her aching muscles. While learning to ride was mandatory for mage students, she never had the time to ride for leisure, and her legs were woefully underprepared for long days in the saddle.

Fari and Lorin followed suit—Lorin's face tight with pain—but Tarion and Garan remained standing, arms crossed.

"It's only just past midday, plenty of time to get out to DarkSkull," Tarion said in confusion. "What are we doing here?"

A knock sounded, and Caverlock took a piece of parchment from one of his Taliath with a quick nod before closing the door again. His gaze shifted from the parchment to his son and nephew as he responded. "We're riding out for DarkSkull. You'll stay here until we return."

"You're seriously going to leave us here? What was the point of bringing us then, Uncle Dash?" Garan demanded. He'd been in a jovial mood the entire journey, thrilled at being included, but this clearly wasn't what he'd envisioned would happen once they arrived. His amiable demeanour transformed quickly into full imperious mode, shoulders back, tone polite but firm.

Dashan lifted the parchment in his hand. "The scouts I had watching the place confirm they haven't seen any movement in or out of the valley since they arrived weeks ago. I'll go in first, make sure there is no danger waiting on the grounds—clear out any nasty surprises they left behind. Then we'll bring you in tomorrow to help search for anything that will help us either find Athira, or figure out more about what Underground were doing there."

Silence followed those words. Clearly reading the brewing mutiny on all their faces, Caverlock gave a firm shake of his head, directing his next comment at Tarion. "Your mother is already going to kill me for bringing you along. Don't ask me to risk certain death by putting you in danger."

On one hand, Lira considered it a sensible plan. Caverlock wasn't going to put their safety in jeopardy any more than necessary, but he was at least willing to admit that their presence might be useful once the area was secured. On the other hand, she utterly detested the fact that he thought *she* required this level of protection, and had to quell a tide of frustration at the idea of sitting on her hands at the inn and waiting.

She gathered the others felt similarly, because Dashan left them with a parting, "You leave this room and you will not like the consequences, I promise you. We'll be gone until tomorrow. We'll hold in the cover of the valley wall until dusk and use the darkness to hide our approach. I promise I'll let you know as soon as we're back."

"Be careful, Da," Tarion called after him. Worry shadowed his hazel eyes.

Dashan turned back with a grin. "It's been a while since I've walked the grounds of DarkSkull Hall, but trust me when I say I've been in far more dangerous situations there than this."

The knowledge of what he meant settled around them once the

door closed, their glances flicking to Lira. Dashan had fought Shakar at DarkSkull Hall—it had been Dashan's blade *Heartfire* that had dealt the death blow to the Darkmage.

"Lira, he didn't mean to—" Garan started.

She waved him off. "I know what my grandfather was and who killed him. There's no need to tiptoe around it for my sake."

"Good." Garan dismissed the topic. "Now, this waiting here business is rubbish. What do you say to waiting until Uncle Dash leaves, then sneaking after them?"

Lorin frowned. "But we—"

"I say no," Fari cut over him. "They'll expel us from Temari Hall if we're caught. I'm already enough of a failure to my family. If I get expelled, they'll throw me out with nothing but my apprentice cloak. Zandia is warm, but I still don't fancy a life on the streets."

Lira stiffened at that comment, even though the girl was only half-serious. Fari had no clue what it was really like to live like that, and she never would. It grated on Lira, made her think of Ahrin, wish Ahrin was there with them. Which was both stupid and impossible.

"They've been keeping things from us this whole time," Garan argued. "I want to be there when they go in so we can see it for ourselves. I want to know exactly what they find. Uncle Dash said it himself, the place is most likely empty. There's no danger to us. And even if there was, there's a whole force of mage warriors and Taliath marching on it. We'd be well protected."

"What do you think, Lira?" Lorin asked.

"I agree with Garan," she said without hesitation, the little thrill in her stomach speaking up before she could stop it.

Part of her knew it would be smarter to wait. There was no way to be certain the valley was empty, given how cautious it sounded like Caverlock's scouts had been. If any Underground members remaining on the grounds spotted Lira and the others and got away to report the information... Dashan's cover story for their departure from Temari would be blown.

But she didn't care. Whatever was still there, Lira wanted to see it before Caverlock's force had the chance to remove or cover up anything they thought she needed to be protected from.

Most of all, she was sick and tired of being cosseted and doing what she was told. Her ability to deal with the frustration of the past weeks at Temari had worn thin. If there were Underground members still at DarkSkull, she'd just have to make sure they didn't see her.

And if they did... well, she'd make sure they never made it out of the valley to report to Lucinda.

"Then I'm in too," Lorin said immediately.

"Tar?" Garan sought his opinion.

"I trust my father," he said quietly. "But I don't want to sit back and do nothing while Athira is still missing and Underground haven't been stopped. They took *us*. That makes us part of this, even if the council wants to keep us out of it." He hesitated. "And you're right about them hiding things from us. I know their intentions are good, but I'd rather know the truth, whatever it is."

A surprised silence filled the room, and Lira sent Tarion an approving nod.

"That's what this is about for you, Lira?" Fari gave her a shrewd look. "Revenge?"

"Damn right it is. I want them taken down for what they did to me." Lira's voice rang with conviction—it was a relief to actually say something that was completely and utterly true.

"To *you*?" Garan asked quietly.

She met his look and didn't flinch. His insistence—*their* insistence —on making her out to be something she wasn't grated. Not to mention the uncomfortable guilt it roused. She liked them, yes, wanted to be their friend, even... but not by fitting herself into the box they wanted to put her in. "I'm not the team player or hero you keep trying to make me out to be. I'm not like you all. I look out for myself first, I've *always* had to do that. So yes, I want to take Underground down for *me*. To protect myself."

"You don't trust us," Fari said in disappointment.

"I don't trust anyone." Lira's temper sparked at the disapproving looks on their faces. "None of you have any idea. You grew up never having to worry about food being on the table or staying warm enough to survive in winter. Guards always around to protect you from harm. A fancy education. Smooth entrance into Temari Hall."

"Lira, we—"

"I almost starved multiple times when I was a child. Nearly died from the cold even more often. Do you know how I survived that world?" The words spilled out of her, unstoppable now. "I stole food or I died. I stole clothes and blankets, or I died. I found others who could protect me from those who would prey on an orphaned girl, and in return for that protection, I stole *for* them. And the moment I turned my back on them I knew I could expect a knife in the ribs, so I never did." Except Ahrin. Her heart ached so fiercely her words trailed to a halt. Ahrin had always protected her. Until she'd left. Why had she left?

She swallowed, taking a shuddering breath and trying to restore calm to her voice. "The world outside your precious Mage Council and royal courts is harsh, and it's unforgiving. There's no luxury of right or wrong, there's only survival. I survived because I learned that lesson quickly, and you all stand there and disapprove as if I made some bad choices. As if I *had* any other choices. As if I can simply unmake those choices or forget those instincts now because I have food and clothes on my back."

The silence after her words halted was thick. It was hard to tell what any of them were thinking, though their discomfort, and their annoyance, was palpable. Part of Lira was horrified that all of that had spilled out of her, but the rest of her was glad. Relieved almost. Because she wanted them to understand. Understand *her*.

"I acknowledge what you're saying, but you're not entirely right," Tarion said softly, eyes on the floor, uncomfortable as always with disagreeing. "My parents and their friends only defeated the Darkmage because they trusted each other. Because they cared about each other. You've read the accounts. You know that."

"They defeated him, sure. After he killed how many?" Lira said. "I *have* read the accounts. They beat him because your mother eventually outwitted him. She figured out that brute mage power couldn't win, and used her Taliath warriors against him. He wasn't prepared for that. He made a foolish mistake."

"And you're suggesting you'd do better?" Fari asked sharply.

"Fari, don't!" Garan snapped. "She's baiting us, and you're letting her. Lira is no Shakar, despite how she'd like us all to think she is."

"I'm not what you're trying to make of me either," she snapped back.

He met her gaze. "We'll see."

They would.

"So are we going after General Caverlock or not?" Lorin's voice broke the silence, eyebrow raised in haughty disapproval of their bickering. A little chuckle rippled through the room, breaking the tension.

Garan looked at Lira. She nodded.

"I think we are," he said.

Fari peered out the window. "How are we going to sneak past those guards?"

"That's easy," Tarion said. "I'll transport us all from here to the stables, one by one. The guards are watching our room, not the stables next door—the distance is just within my range. We'll ride out on the horses we came in on."

Fari's frown only deepened. "Your father, famed Taliath strategist, didn't think of that?"

"I'm sure he would have. But I don't think it crossed his mind that Tarion would disobey him," Lira said quietly, for once gentling her voice to lessen her words' impact.

Garan reached out to squeeze Tarion's shoulder in silent support. Tarion's gaze remained firmly on the floor as he spoke. "Lira is right. Da won't have set a guard on the stables."

"Come on then, let's get moving," Lira said crisply. "Garan, you're the heaviest, you first."

Fari sighed. "This is a terrible idea."

It might be. Lira didn't care. Anticipation surged through her. Finally, she was going to go back to DarkSkull Hall.

CHAPTER 17

"Think it's been long enough?" Garan asked.

"What *I* think is that we should turn around and go back," Fari muttered.

The five of them sat on their horses in the middle of an empty road. Ahead, it led onto a bridge stretching across a deep gorge. Wooden support struts crisscrossed down from the bridge and disappeared into dimness. Wide enough for at least six carriages travelling abreast, the structure had a deserted air about it.

At its opposite end stood a pair of broken iron gates.

Lira stared across the space into the murky light of late afternoon. The area was utterly deserted. The gorge stretched away to the left and right, encircling a row of hills. A cold wind whipped around them, the fading day taking on a grey, overcast tone. Leaves scuttled across the surface of the bridge every time it gusted. She tried not to let the lack of birdsong disturb her.

"Do any of you remember being over the bridge before? Does *anything* look familiar?" Garan asked.

"No." To Lira it was as if this were the first time she'd ever laid eyes upon the bridge leading over to the valley that held DarkSkull Hall. A little shiver crept down her spine. The cart she'd woken up in must have already been in the valley when she'd escaped from it.

"Maybe they didn't bring us this way," Fari said. She sounded less upbeat than normal, and her brown eyes were shadowed with the same unease in Lira's bones.

"They must have," Tarion said, soft voice being picked up and carried away by the breeze so that Lira could barely hear him. "Carrying seven unconscious students, plus transporting themselves? There's no other way into the valley for a cart like the one Lira described waking up in."

"Unless they used magic?" Garan suggested. "Something like Tarion's ability?"

"No, I woke up in a cart being drawn by horses," Lira said. "If they had access to teleporting magic, why not use it to transport me all the way? Less risk of me escaping that way."

"General Caverlock is well ahead." Lorin spoke into the silence, a hint of impatience in his tone. "Can we go?"

Garan nodded, but still all five of them hesitated. Eventually Lira rolled her eyes and kicked her horse forward, suppressing a wince as her sore leg muscles complained bitterly.

The day grew darker as the horses clip-clopped over the bridge at a walk, a bank of dark clouds moving in from the east obscuring what remained of the day's light. But the increasing dimness only made Lira feel more comfortable. Despite what had happened to her in this place, the duel she fought with danger was always a familiar place, bringing with it a seductive excitement that wanted to break free. She tried to hold it back, despite the strength of its lure. The struggle sent lines of tension locking through the muscles of her shoulders.

"I still feel like this is a terrible idea." Fari broke the silence as they reached the gates at the end of the bridge.

"Would you like to say that another seven times, just to make sure we understand what you really think?" Lira muttered.

"Rude." Fari scowled at her. "I'm just trying to point out that Underground kidnapped us—as in, they wanted *us* in particular, even if we don't know why. And now we're just waltzing right back into the place they held us prisoner."

"Behind a powerful unit of mage warriors and Taliath led by the greatest Taliath in the world." Lorin frowned at her. In his voice was the resounding belief that nothing could stand against such a force.

Lira was less certain. She'd already badly underestimated the Shadowcouncil, and even if they didn't appear on the surface to have the same resources and strength as the Mage Council, Lucinda was dangerous. More so than anyone Lira had met before. At the thought of her greatest adversary, the thrill surged again, and it took more of an effort to hold it back this time.

Maybe there would be something here they could use to bring the woman down sooner. But as much as the thought spurred Lira, she couldn't completely ignore the little voice in the back of her mind that was beginning to wonder what she'd do once Underground was gone. Her life would return to lessons at Temari, the trials in a year, then becoming a warrior mage. And she would have to keep fitting herself into that box of what the council wanted. There was no other way to carve out a place for herself—a place she wouldn't have to fear could be snatched away at any second.

Lira shook those thoughts from her mind. None of that was important right now. The future was still a long way off, and Lira didn't live in the future. She lived only in the present.

One of the iron gates was torn from its hinges and hung halfway to the ground. The other was charred in places, but stood open. Lichen crawled over the iron surface, and some of the bars were a deep red with rust. Two enormous trees stood on either side of the gates, their branches hanging almost to the ground, whispering to each other in the breeze.

Garan glanced at Lira. "We should move off the road. Uncle Dash would have set up guards at his rear."

"Before you suggest it, no, we're not going to approach the guards," Lira cut off Fari as she opened her mouth. "We do that, and we'll find ourselves escorted right back to Weeping Stead before getting anywhere near DarkSkull."

Fari scowled at her. "I was merely going to suggest we leave the horses here. Lorin is hiding his pain well, but walking would be better for his leg. Not to mention, if we're avoiding the road, the forest along the valley wall is thick and will be slow going for the horses."

Lorin looked mutinous. "I'll be—"

"We'll do as Fari says," Garan spoke over him. "Lorin, I suspect what is best for your leg right now would be resting it back at the inn after days of riding. Be glad I'm letting you come along at all."

Lorin opened his mouth, an angry flush climbing his cheeks, but eventually he closed it and dismounted. Lira wasn't sure whether to be impressed or annoyed with Garan. He'd made the right decision, but she hated his assumption of command over them all.

They led the horses off the road and into a small clearing where they could graze, but were out of sight of anyone coming along the road in either direction. Each of them checked their mage staffs; Lira slung a bow and quiver of arrows over her shoulder too. The other four carried knives strapped to their waists.

By the time they set off through the trees, night had fallen and the forest had turned dark around them. Lira found herself in the rear with Fari, while Garan and Tarion took the lead, keeping Lorin in the middle—a silent but tacit arrangement so they could make sure they kept up with his limping pace and he didn't fall behind.

Lira couldn't help but remember her last trek through these trees, when they'd moved to stop her heading in any direction but down. That had been Ahrin all along. She'd had no idea. Lira shook her head, seeking distraction by turning to Fari. "What you said earlier about your family kicking you out if you were expelled," she said. "Did you mean it?"

Fari sighed, shot a glance her way. "I realise that I was being dramatic, and that I've had it pretty lucky compared to you."

Lira hesitated. She somehow felt better after her outburst earlier, clearer-headed. Like maybe they would understand her more and she'd stop having to explain herself all the time. "That doesn't mean you haven't had hard stuff to deal with too." As the words came out, initially just an attempt at a peace offering, Lira realised they were true, reluctant as she was to admit it. Tragedy, sadness, hard times; they weren't reserved only for her.

A brief silence fell, then Fari said, "The answer is, I'm not sure what they would do if I got expelled, and that terrifies me. They *might* throw me out."

Lira frowned. "Just because you couldn't be a warrior mage?"

"Not entirely." It was Fari's turn to hesitate. "In royal, noble, and pureblood mage families, what everyone cares about most is continuing their lineage; that's how you hold onto power and influence. It's how you gain more of it."

"Don't I know it," Lira muttered. The rich held the poor down to keep themselves where they were. Or that's how it had seemed in Dirinan anyway. And she'd seen nothing different in Karonan or Temari to make her think differently. It was what gave Underground such a foothold amongst so many.

"The only way to continue the lineage is to ensure you have heirs. Girls loving girls or boys loving boys is fine in the rest of the world. Nobody cares—why would they? But in my world, it means you can't produce an heir. And therefore, it is very much *not* okay."

Lira blinked in surprise. She hadn't thought about it from that perspective. "So if you can't add to your family's power and influence by being a powerful warrior mage, you'd be expected to give them heirs. And if you can't do either, then you're pretty much useless to them?"

"Ouch." Fari winced. "But yes. It doesn't help that I'm my parents' only child. They were never able to conceive another. So it's critical I carry on the line, or at the very least distinguish myself in some grand way. Can't let that Tylender family outshine us."

"That's..." Lira shook her head, her thoughts and perceptions resettling into a new framework at Fari's story. "That sounds just as harsh as the world I come from."

"We're not all that different, huh?"

Lira didn't reply, but her thoughts were busy as they kept hiking through the dark forest. She'd vowed from the moment she'd realised why the world feared her that she would never, ever, have a child. The fear and distrust would end with her. Shakar would end with her. His name, his memory, all of it.

That vow meant that the slow realisation as she grew older that she preferred girls had brought nothing more than a mild relief that it would make her vow easier to keep. Fari was right. In most of the world nobody cared who you loved or shared a bed with. There were far more important things to occupy your mind—like making sure you had a roof over your head, and food to eat.

But Fari's words made her consider... as privileged as the girl's life was, she was trapped too. While poverty and lack of opportunity had trapped Lira and Ahrin and those in their crew to a life of resorting to crime to survive, Fari was trapped within a golden cage of tradition and expectation. It was a lighter and prettier cage. And probably an easier one to break out of. But it was a cage nonetheless.

"What are we going to do if the forest starts attacking us?" Fari's voice sounded, breaking Lira from her thoughts. She was glad of it. She was juggling too many balls already—the last thing she needed was more distraction.

"It won't." She spoke without thinking. Ahrin was miles away. Lira ignored the ache in her chest at that thought. She refused to allow herself to miss Ahrin Vensis.

"How do you know?" Lorin asked.

"I don't, but if Underground is still here, which I doubt, I think we can assume they'll be too distracted by the arrival of an armed mage force to notice us creeping about," Lira said. She shouldn't rule out the possibility other mages had Ahrin's ability. After all, the group were apparently able to *give* people magic.

"You sound very confident." Fari shot Lira a dubious look.

"They'd be fools to still be here," Tarion said in his quiet way. "We saw enough of this place while we were here to eventually figure out where we'd been taken. They had to know that. And they wouldn't have returned us unless they were prepared for that eventuality. Whatever it was they were doing here, they're long gone."

"Not to mention if your father's mage force had encountered any trouble we'd be hearing those warrior mages at work," Lira pointed out. There'd been at least one concussive mage with them, and a wind mage. No way they'd miss those bright flashes of light or the boom of a concussive blast, even at this distance.

"You're both right," Garan said. "Even so, we approach slowly, and

163

we stay well back from the grounds of DarkSkull until we can work out what Uncle Dash and the mages are doing. Clear?"

Lira bristled at his commanding tone, but settled for shooting him a scowl as she continued following them through the night.

"Yes, boss," Fari muttered, making Lira grin.

Lira glanced at her hands as the group kept moving, slower now. She had razak blood flowing through her veins, and at some point, a new mage ability would break out. She'd done her best not to think about it—it wasn't her unease over what they'd done to her that worried her, that was an emotion she was well practised at burying. It was the anticipation, the excitement... it made the thrill inside her stronger, less controllable. And what she feared most was more disappointment. So she didn't want to let herself hope too much.

But now, as they approached the place where she'd allowed them to experiment on her, she couldn't help thinking of it. What would the new ability be? She hoped fiercely for concussive power, another warrior ability, and despite herself she couldn't ignore that hope. She wanted to be more powerful. Not just because she wanted to make them forget Shakar and see her, but because she loved the leap of magic through her veins. Loved how it made her feel. Loved the ability it gave her.

She wanted more.

Much more.

CHAPTER 18

The clouds cleared away as they headed down the valley wall, and watery moonlight bathed the shadows of the forest. Dashan would have entered cautiously, prepared for an ambush, but even so, instinct shivered beneath Lira's skin, warning her that something wasn't *quite* right. Not enough to put her finger on, to tell the others to turn back, but enough to make her wary. Alert. Ready to fight or flee in an instant if necessary.

Apart from the same type of tree and brush, nothing looked familiar to her from that night when she'd first awoken in the cart and fled into the forest, but they were approaching DarkSkull from the south this time, and she was fairly certain her last hike through the forest had been down the western valley wall.

As the incline levelled out, the trees began to thin, and all five of them slowed to a halt before breaking the cover of the forest. There they gathered, staring out over the dark valley. There was no mist tonight, and the buildings and grounds were far more visible. A frozen lake glittered silver in the moonlight.

Lira shook her head. If she'd seen it like this, laid out in its entirety before her, she'd have guessed their location much sooner. The mage with mist or weather ability that Lucinda had used to keep everything hidden had been a nice touch.

What had Underground been doing here? The group had fixed up portions of the school and dug out a cellar. Something else had been going on well before Underground had kidnapped them. But what?

Lorin was the first to speak, breaking into Lira's musings. "It must have been an impressive place when it was all still standing."

"It still is," Fari murmured.

Closest to them was a lake, and to the northwest of it sat the hulking, shadowy buildings of DarkSkull Hall. The main road from the bridge snaked down out of the trees to the east and ran along the edge of the lake before going all the way up to the main hall. The damage wrought on the school by Shakar was obvious even from this distance, but Fari was right, it was still an imposing edifice.

Another chill went through Lira at imagining what had happened here. The final fight with Shakar. The Mage Council almost entirely wiped out apart from Alyx Egalion and what remained of her followers.

A single mage had almost brought down the entire mage order, twice.

She was his heir.

And decades later a group fighting to restore his legacy had brought her here. Ahrin had *helped* them hold her here. Lira took a shuddering breath, trying to push back the bitter pain that roused.

Did Underground truly think they could replicate what Shakar had done? If Lucinda was representative of the rest of the Shadowcouncil, then they were certainly powerful and clever. But none in the world had magic like Alyx Egalion—the only mage who'd come close to matching the Darkmage in sheer power and ability, and even she hadn't been able to defeat him alone.

Lira glanced idly at her hands, turning them over. Presumably that was what Underground expected of her. Could she meet those expectations? Her gaze shifted back to DarkSkull Hall, considering. Could *she* face down someone as powerful as Alyx Egalion and emerge the victor?

The thrill spread hot and seductive through her blood until she ruthlessly cut it off. She couldn't allow herself to be distracted by thoughts like that. Not yet, anyway.

"This is where we were. I'm sure of it." Tarion spoke suddenly, breaking the thoughtful and uneasy silence that had settled over all of them.

Lira glanced to where he stood beside her. His jaw was clenched, fists curled at his side. She gave him a little nudge with her elbow. His shoulders loosened slightly.

Garan visibly shook off the same weight of memory. "I hope we can help Uncle Dash and the others find something useful in there."

"I can't see any of them," Fari said doubtfully.

"They'll be creeping around just like we are, in case Underground are still here or left any traps behind," Tarion said. "The telepath with them will be searching for the thoughts of anyone hiding or planning a trap, that sort of thing. Da knows how to be careful."

They knew this already, but saying it aloud clearly helped keep them calm. Lira bit back a sharp retort and let them have their comforts.

"Make sure your mental shields are up," Garan said unnecessarily.

"Remember last time some of the windows in the restored sections were lit up?" Lorin pointed out. "Everything looks dark now."

"He's right." Garan gave the initiate an approving look. "But we don't move until Uncle Dash and the others do. I say we bunker down here, get some rest. We'll take turns keeping watch in case something happens. Once they're out in the open, provided there's no ambush or attack, we'll approach them, endure the yelling and remonstrating with appropriately apologetic looks, then help them search the place."

Tarion shook his head. "I don't think we can afford to wait too long. My mother is on her way, remember? As soon as she arrives with Uncle Tarrick, her telepathic magic will take about three seconds to notice I'm here in the valley. I can't shield from her."

Lira didn't dispute Tarion's assessment of the reach and strength of his mother's ability. And while Lira's shielding was flawless, she doubted the others' was as good. "Not much we can do about that except hope your father moves before your mother gets here," she said.

"Sounds good to me." Fari turned and glanced around, eventually walking a few steps to a nearby tree and settling against its trunk. "Lira, you can take first watch, don't worry."

Lira opened her mouth, frowned. "I—"

"We know you're not comfortable trusting anyone else to have your back, so the first watch is all yours," Garan said cheerfully. "You *are* going to need some rest though, so if Uncle Dash doesn't move soon, you might have to trust us enough to let us take watch for a little while."

"I'll go after you," Lorin assured her. "You can trust me not to miss anything."

"And Tarion after that. Fari and I will go last." Garan settled against his own tree. "Night all."

In a few moments they were all curled up, eyes closed, leaving Lira standing there in the dark, staring at them.

They were starting to *know* her. More... they knew her and were fine with it. Not only fine with it, but happy to sleep, be vulnerable, with her on watch. They trusted her.

Fools. That was the immediate thought that went through her mind. But wasn't that what she'd wanted all along... people that saw her and trusted her? Because of who *she* was. And they were giving that to her. Warmth kindled in her chest. Steadier, less powerful, than the thrill she yearned for. But *good.*

She glanced from the shadowed remains of DarkSkull back to their resting figures. Maybe being in a combat patrol with them wouldn't be the worst thing in the world. Once they passed their trials, it would increase the chances that they'd be posted on assignments together. Maybe not all of them, but some.

After all this with Underground was done—and she fully intended it would be over well before her graduation as a mage—maybe she wouldn't always have to be alone as a warrior mage working for the council.

Not to mention ongoing association with these pureblood apprentices would make her path up the ranks smoother and faster. If they accepted her, others would too.

Maybe she *could* learn to trust again.

· · ·

LIRA WAS JUST ABOUT to wake Lorin to take his turn at watch when blue mage light flashed from the direction of the DarkSkull buildings. She woke them instantly, and they clustered around her, groggy from sleep. Together they watched pinpoints of orange flamelight flicker to life and start moving around to the eastern side of the main hall.

"Looks to me like they're spreading out to search. Underground is definitely gone then," Garan said.

"Which means it's safe for us to go and join them?" Lorin asked, impatience in his voice. The boy didn't like standing around waiting for anything.

Garan braced his shoulders. "And endure a good long telling off."

Fari heaved a mournful sigh. "We have all been spending way too much time around Spider, you know that, don't you?"

Garan chuckled. A small smile flickered over Tarion's face and he leaned into Lira briefly.

Lira didn't know what to say, but mercifully Tarion spoke into the silence. "I think we should circle around the valley before approaching, look for signs of anyone leaving. Da's priority will be searching the buildings first. If Underground took Athira away on foot, horseback, or cart, there might be signs of it—a direction Da's people can follow. The sooner we go after her, the better, and I don't want to waste any more time than necessary. We'll veer around to the west. Let's go."

Garan cast a look of amused surprise at them all as Tarion headed off into the trees. "Our boy is finding his voice."

"Don't be mean," Lira snapped as she strode past him after Tarion.

THEY FOLLOWED TARION, remaining inside the tree line, moving quietly, gazes focused on the ground for any sign of tracks or disturbed shrubbery. Lira thought it unlikely they'd find anything but was happy to follow Tarion's suggestion in the interest of being thorough. After all, given how confident she was that Underground had been doing far more at this place, and for longer, than holding captive a group of mage students to experiment on, it would be foolish to assume their activities had been confined to the buildings.

They were halfway along the western side of the valley, almost directly across from where the shadowy dormitory buildings stood in the distance, when Tarion stopped moving and pointed at the ground.

It took a moment to make out in the gloom, but then she saw the narrow ruts gouged deep into the soil, heading west up through the trees of the valley wall and east back towards the grounds of Dark-Skull. Cart tracks. There were several trails, indicating the cart had made a number of journeys back and forth.

"They had to get supplies in and out of the valley, not least all those sacks of food they had in the kitchen storeroom," Garan murmured. "But why not use the road?"

"What if this is how they got us out? Or Athira?" Tarion said.

"Again, though, why not use the road?" Fari asked. "And I don't see any hoofprints interspersed with the tracks... they were dragging a cart up here themselves."

Lira cast a dubious glance up through the dark trees. It was possible the forest was thinner in this section of valley wall, explaining the utility of bringing a cart this way. But she'd studied maps, with Tarion's help, on the journey here. The closest village was Weeping Stead to the south. To the west, after crossing the valley wall, there was only more rugged country between them and a distant village. Which meant days of travel pulling a cart by hand.

"The distance to the nearest village is too far heading west, not to mention it's a tiny village where strangers would stand out." Garan echoed her thoughts. "Nobody was hauling a cart that far. And for what?"

"So if they weren't taking the cart out of the valley, what were they doing?" Fari glanced between them.

"It doesn't make sense," Lira murmured distractedly, still staring up into the trees where the tracks disappeared into darkness. Instinct shivered across her skin.

Tarion was standing still, shoulders tense. He kept glancing between the buildings of DarkSkull and the direction the tracks were leading. "The mages are covering the buildings. I say we follow the tracks and see where they *were* taking the cart," he said quietly. "It could be important."

"It delays the time until the yelling starts, too," Lorin pointed out.

Fari nodded approvingly at him. "I like the way you think."

Garan merely nodded. Lira didn't dispute the plan. It *was* worth checking out. There was too much they didn't know about what Underground had been doing in this place.

She turned after the others, following the tracks, leg muscles burning on the incline. The trees *were* thinner here, but that was because several had been cut down to make room for the cart to pass through, leaving raw stumps dotting the ground. Surely Underground hadn't chopped a path all the way up to the summit and beyond... no, Lira was growing certain these tracks weren't made by anyone leaving the valley. Her wariness deepened and her steps quietened without thought, senses turning to high alert.

"The depth of these tracks," Tarion said softly, almost to himself. He was frowning, unhappy.

"What?" Lira asked.

"Whatever the cart was carrying, it was heavy." Lorin answered before Tarion could. He glanced at Lira, and something in his gaze told her he had an idea of what that might be, like he'd seen something similar before. Before she could ask him any further questions, Fari froze.

"Stop!" She lifted a hand, her face taut with concentration.

They all came to a halt, Lira included, one hand unconsciously reaching for her staff. But no enemy came looming out of the darkness, and she relaxed slightly. They were about a third of the way up the forested valley wall. It was so dark and quiet, the air a heavy weight. She breathed it in. Sank into the moment.

Garan murmured, "What is it?"

Fari's eyes opened. "I can sense blood."

Lira's attention snapped to the girl. She hadn't forgotten Fari's healing affinity was with blood. Her instincts shivered again, not enough to presage imminent danger, but a warning that something lurked ahead.

Garan straightened. "Someone is hurt nearby?"

"No, it's old blood. I can barely..." She frowned, clearly digging deeper into her magic to try and figure it out.

"Athira's blood?" Dread filled Garan's voice.

"Impossible to tell." Fari turned in a circle, then determinedly set off through the trees, away from the tracks.

"Maybe someone was in the cart and tried to escape—they might have been bleeding," Garan said as they walked, hope peaking in his voice. He clearly thought it might be Athira.

"Maybe Athira fought with one of the guards and *they* were bleeding," Lorin suggested, face brightening.

"Or, much more likely, whoever was hauling the cart up here had an injury. Maybe a nosebleed, or a cut from a sharp tree branch," Lira pointed out. "Especially if they were stumbling around in the dark."

"Then why were they heading *away* from the tracks?" Tarion asked.

Fari ignored them, her strides low, shoulders hunched as she focused her attention on the ground around her. "Whoever it was wasn't bleeding much, just a few drops with each step."

"They must have been in a hurry. No time to stop and bind the wound," Tarion said with a glance in Lira's direction.

"Or it wasn't bad enough to need binding," she couldn't help saying.

Garan was looking ahead. "There's nothing but more forest in this direction."

"There's nothing where those cart tracks were leading either." Lira glanced back over her shoulder, an odd kind of dread shivering through her. If the source of the blood *was* Athira, where had they been taking her in the cart?

They walked on in silence for a few minutes, Garan's anticipation almost palpable. Fari insisted she could still sense blood spatter.

"I can't see any sign that anyone was following," Garan said at one point. "No broken branches or obvious footprints."

"I'm not sure that means anything. Whoever was bleeding didn't leave much trace either," Lorin said.

"It's been at least three weeks. Wind or rain could have washed away any traces," Lira said. If this was Athira—or someone else Underground had been holding here—fleeing, then why hadn't Ahrin tried to stop her? The Darkhand could have, easily. Maybe she'd had a reason to let Athira go. Ahrin was always playing her own game, after all. Or maybe she'd been gone already, arriving at Temari Hall and pretending to be an initiate whose magic had just broken out.

Ahead of them, Fari abruptly stopped. The trees cleared just short of the banks of a swiftly flowing stream that cascaded over a short drop into a series of rock pools. Lira's gaze scanned the muddy ground along the water's edge, but there were no traces of someone passing through she could make out in the dim light.

"I can't sense any more blood." Fari gave a frustrated sigh. "I'm sorry."

"Don't be," Tarion said quietly. "You got us this far."

"Athira is clever. If it *was* her running away, she would have crossed the water to try and evade any pursuit." Garan hunkered down, dipping his fingers idly into the water.

"I still don't think we should assume it was Athira, but I agree it could have been *someone* trying to escape." Lira stared into the darkness, thinking over the possibilities before letting out a reluctant sigh. "We should go back and tell Caverlock. He and his warriors can search the other side of the valley wall, see if whoever it was sought shelter somewhere."

They all turned to stare at her, astonished.

"Don't look at me like that," she snapped in irritation. "I'm not an idiot. If we keep going we'll only be wandering around in the dark getting increasingly tired and lost. Councillor Egalion can fly—she can search the area much faster than we can."

"And depending how recently this person moved through here, a powerful telepath mage might be able to pick up a trace of their thoughts," Fari added.

Garan stood up. "Then that's what we'll do."

"Actually, I think we should see where those cart tracks lead first." Tarion spoke up. "Make sure there isn't anything there that could help us."

Nobody argued, proving they were as uneasy as Lira was about where that cart had been going.

Silence fell between them as they walked. Hope had been lit in the others by the signs that someone had fled, and they clearly now felt there was a real chance whoever it was would be found. Lira was far less certain. If Athira had made it across the river, she would have been stumbling around in thick forest—hurt, days away from help, and without any supplies. And that was only if Underground's mages hadn't caught up to her. They probably knew the area far better than she did.

"Do you think they'll kick us out of Temari Hall for disobeying General Caverlock?" Fari asked, breaking the silence.

Lira snorted. "The sons of Alyx and Ladan Egalion kicked out of school? A Dirsk? You'll get a nice talking to and then be safely delivered back to your silver spoons and comfortable beds."

"Careful, Spider, you're betraying your prejudice," Garan said mildly.

"She's kinda right, though," Fari said.

"Mama isn't the old council," Tarion said quietly. "She cares as much for Lira or any other student at Temari as she does for me or Caria."

Nobody disagreed with that. Not even Lira.

The cart tracks didn't continue much further past where Fari had sensed the blood spatter, but Lira began to realise what lay ahead when she caught the edge of a familiar nauseating scent on the night breeze. "Rotted..." Her voice trailed off and she pushed past the others, breaking into a run.

"Lira!" Garan called after her, but she ignored him.

The tracks continued up the incline for a short distance before stopping at a natural plateau in the valley wall. The flat section of ground had been cleared, but was surrounded on all sides by thick trees.

A few paces behind Lira, Fari suddenly took a deep, gasping breath, her dark skin going bloodless in the moonlight. Lorin reached out to steady her. "What is it?"

Lira looked at Tarion. "It might be best to keep her back."

He nodded without protest and went to join Lorin in steadying Fari. Garan hurried to Lira's side, jaw set. A long, horrified breath escaped him a moment later.

A pit had been dug in the centre of the clearing, roughly rectangular in shape, and deep. It was filled with bodies.

"Gar, what is it?" Tarion called out.

Garan reached up to run a hand through his hair, shaking his head slightly, unable to form the words.

"It's a grave," Lira replied. "I count maybe seven to ten bodies. One's almost skeletonised, but a couple look recent."

"Athira? Haler?" Lorin began moving up the slope, limping furiously with his stick. Fari pushed off Tarion and followed suit.

Lira glanced at Garan, then took a shallow breath and moved closer to the pit so that she could get a better look at the bodies. None of the fresher corpses had blonde hair. It was impossible to tell with the older ones, but by the state of decay they'd been there months if not years. One of them, still fleshy but ravaged enough to have been there a few weeks, wore a grey apprentice robe. "Athira's not here," she said heavily.

Her words dropped into the horrified silence, clear in their meaning. Lorin limped over, gaze desperately searching the bodies until falling on the one in the grey cloak. "Haler." He bit his lip hard, tears glistening in his eyes even though he wouldn't let them fall.

Without thinking, Lira reached out and squeezed his arm, then turned away to give him a moment.

"They were experimenting on them, those people, weren't they? It wasn't just us." Fari held a trembling hand to her mouth. "And they died."

"Probably." Lira saw no reason not to be blunt. "Either that or they tried to escape and were caught and killed."

"How can you do that?" Garan's eyes were sheened with tears. "Just stand there and be so... calm."

"I've seen death before, Garan. Many more times than I can count." She didn't tell him that the thought of being experimented on and then thrown away into a pit horrified her.

"Wait, why is there no predation?" Lorin asked suddenly.

Tarion tensed, gaze scanning the area around the pit. "This grave is open. There should be wolves in these hills, bears too. Not to mention carrion birds."

A chill wrapped itself around Lira's chest. "They must have had someone guarding the pit."

"Or *something*," Fari whispered.

Tarion spun to face Lira, eyes widening. "Those bodies aren't touched at all, but that smell would have drawn every carrion bird within scenting distance."

She nodded. "Whatever was guarding the pit was here. As recently as a few hours ago. Maybe even less."

"It was a razak, wasn't it?" Fari spoke bluntly, a hand rubbing at her temples as she walked a few paces away, like a nasty headache was brewing.

"Impossible to tell."

They all stared off into the darkness as if a razak were about to jump out at them with a tell-tale rattle. Lira pushed away that instinctive fear. The air wasn't cold enough for one of those things to be nearby. If it had been a razak guarding the pit, it had moved on. And if it had been a person... well, Lira would have sensed the presence of danger in the night if they were still nearby.

"Breathe," she told them softly. "We're not in immediate danger. If someone or something was here, it's gone."

Garan shook himself, that look of command snapping into place. "We should go. Uncle Dash needs to know about this right away."

They followed without hesitation. Lira came last, casting constant glances behind them. The wariness she'd felt earlier had deepened into a sharp sense of danger at their discovery.

Something was very, very wrong.

And it wasn't just a pit full of dead bodies.

CHAPTER 19

Lira was the first to see it.

She led the way back along the cart tracks, tread sure and confident despite the darkness. The thought that there might be danger after all, that a razak or some other adversary could be lurking in the darkness, spurred her, made her heart beat faster and senses come alive. The boredom and frustration of the last few weeks at Temari began to slough away.

Lira didn't hesitate on reaching the treeline, stepping out into the overgrown grass of the valley floor, gaze scanning all directions as she turned toward the bobbing torchlights visible in the distance.

Her searching gaze caught the body an instant before she would have tripped over it. She stepped quickly to the side, one hand reaching out to grab Tarion's arm before he, too, tripped over it.

The body was lying facedown. It wore a blue mage cloak.

A staff lay on the ground barely a metre away, like it had been dropped and rolled a short distance. Lira knelt beside the body, reaching out to press her fingers against the clammy skin of his neck. "Fari, I can't feel a pulse."

"He's dead." The healer didn't move from her spot a few paces away. Her face was stone, fear flickering in her dark eyes. "I can't sense much blood, though, indicating no large open wounds that bled extensively."

Lira stood, wiped her hand on her breeches. Her gaze scanned the area, magic readying for a fight to throw herself into, to win. The thrill stirred.

"It's Wurin." Garan crouched on the other side of the body, sadness and regret making his voice shake. "He was one of my guards growing up. He's a telekinetic mage like us, Lira."

Lorin glanced at Fari. "Can you tell what killed him?"

"Not specifically. The lack of blood makes it difficult." She shrugged. "I'm not great with understanding the rest of the body, not yet anyway."

At Lira's side, Tarion flinched as if a thought had occurred to him. "What is it?" she asked.

He shook his head, went to kneel by Garan. "Let's turn him over."

Garan hesitated only a moment before nodding. The two boys gently turned the body over, both of them deathly pale in the moonlight. Wurin's chest was wet with drying blood, making it hard to tell exactly where the wounds were, but there were no signs that the blood had run down the body to pool on the ground. Garan reached out to close the mage's eyelids.

Jaw clenched tight, Fari went to kneel beside Tarion. Her voice shook when she spoke a moment later. "Two penetrating wounds in his chest, near his heart. But no corresponding pool of blood."

Lira stilled, gaze up and searching the night, even though there was no tell-tale cold descending on them. A razak had been here. But they were in an open area... where had it hidden, that it had taken out a warrior mage before he'd been able to sound the alarm?

Tarion stood, then moved a few steps away, fists clenched. "Razak wounds."

"How long ago did he die?" Lorin asked Fari.

"Maybe a half hour. No more," she said grimly.

"It can't be a razak," Garan said immediately. "We'd have heard the rattling."

"Not if we were too far away. *Something* was guarding that grave. Something that was gone when we got there," Tarion said.

A close call... or was it? Lira frowned. The others were silent, presumably wrestling with their fear. She reached up to unsling the bow from around her shoulders and nock an arrow. If a razak tried coming near her again, she was going to put a shaft into each of its three stupid silver eyes.

"We can't rule out an ambush, especially if the razak left its spot guarding the grave and headed in this direction," she said briskly. She doubted very severely that Underground had left behind only a single razak guarding a pile of dead bodies they didn't need anymore. "We should leave, now, before it can be sprung on us."

"If it's an ambush, it will be on Da and the mages, not us. Nobody knows we're here," Tarion said, beginning to pace in agitation. "We can't abandon them."

But Fari's words from much earlier were ringing through Lira's brain: *it was us they were after, and now we're just waltzing right back into the place they held us.*

"We have a lead on where Athira might have gone," she said firmly, ignoring the surge of excitement that was urging her to agree, to wade *into* the danger if it was coming. "Your father and his warriors can take care of themselves. We need to get out and make sure someone knows where to search for her."

Garan was already striding away. "I'm not abandoning them. They need to be warned."

With only a slight hesitation, the others followed. Lira glanced from their retreating backs to the forested valley wall, the way out before any trap could be sprung. With a shrug, she followed them.

Mage light flooded the darkness before they'd crossed half the distance, followed quickly by a screaming wind funnelled like a tornado rising above what was probably the area of cleared ground on the other side of the main hall. Even at this distance the night air whipped around them, crackling with magic.

Lira removed the arrow from her bow. There'd be no use trying to shoot in this gale. After a brief hesitation, Garan kept going, heading towards the source of the light and wind.

Lira's magic surged as it picked up the magic in use by the nearby mages, wanting to explode out of her, tugging relentlessly at her control. Her skin prickled with an unfamiliar heat. She held it back with an effort, though she couldn't stop the violet light flickering around her palms. Her pace increased, and she moved to the head of the group, breath coming fast.

She wanted to fight.

After a few more steps, she began to notice a sharp drop in temperature, and her heartrate kicked up a notch. The air grew colder the closer they got. Nobody said anything, even when the breath started frosting from their mouths. Lira's magic surged again—there was more than one razak nearby.

They moved along the northern side of the main hall, grass whispering around their boots, before rounding the corner and sliding to a halt. The mages and Taliath with Caverlock—twelve fighters in total— were gathered in the open space between the hall and the stables. At least, Lira assumed it was them; they were surrounded by razak, the creatures so numerous that their inky blackness shrouded the group in a cloak of shadow so thick that it was impossible to make out the mages' features.

"Oh no." Garan's shoulders were rigid.

The monsters' rattling filled the air, chains scraping over stone, setting Lira's teeth on edge and allowing the old panic a foothold at the base of her stomach. Memory drowned her—of hiding under that bed as the creature's shadowy limbs crept over the floor towards her, totally rigid with panic, unable to move.

She fought the memory away with an effort. Sweat slicked her skin, and her bow hand trembled despite her fierce attempts to steady it. Damn Underground to the fiery pits of the Zandian desert for doing this to her. They'd made her weaker. More vulnerable.

She was going to ruin them for it.

All the mages had their staffs out, though they must know it would be useless to wield magic against the creatures. The mage wind had already died. No more concussion bursts lit up the night.

"How did they hide so many razak here?" Lorin asked.

"They were planning for the council to show up eventually," Lira said, her thoughts coming out unbidden. "So they set an ambush."

"Underground haven't struck directly at council mages before, the group isn't strong enough to provoke a direct confrontation like that," Garan said wildly, running a free hand through his hair in agitation. "It would be insane for them to do it now."

"It doesn't matter how crazy it is, it's happening," Lira said. What was Lucinda thinking? If the Shadowcouncil killed Egalion's husband, she would rain down fiery hell on Underground. There would be nowhere for them to hide. Nowhere for them to run to.

Were the Shadowcouncil even stronger than Lira had imagined? Could they be ready to make their move against the council so soon? Had Lira made the mistake of continuing to underestimate them?

Her stomach sank. She had. She was certain of it. Damn it.

If this ambush succeeded, Underground would have removed the council's strongest Taliath and greatest tactician, not to mention the fighting strength of ten other elite mages and Taliath, in one fell swoop.

The tenor of the rattling turned focused, dark, the circle of razak slowly closing in around the mage force. Lira's gaze narrowed. They looked awfully in sync...

Dashan Caverlock's voice sounded, shouting an order, and immediately the Taliath moved to circle the mages protectively. Like doused torches, the gleam of their magnificent swords was almost entirely swallowed by the darkness of the monsters surrounding them.

"We have to help." Tarion's gaze was spinning around in all directions, searching for a plan, an idea. She could sense the rising panic vibrating off him. It set the wick to hers, making it flare. She swallowed. Tried to take even breaths. Garan burst forward, but Lorin reached out to grab his arm and stop him.

"Going in blind won't help them," the initiate said, loudly enough to get his attention. "Not outnumbered as they are."

"Maybe Lira's right." Fari spoke too fast. "Maybe we should get out while we can, take news of Athira with us. We're not going to make any difference to that fight."

Lira *was* right. Caverlock's forces were doomed. The razak outnumbered them and none could use magic to defend themselves.

Lira said it aloud: "We can't save them." She had no reason to risk herself for those council warriors, not when it would only result in her death. It wasn't her responsibility to try. Underground had caused this, and destroying them from within was the only way to fix it. She couldn't do that if she was dead.

Walking away from the battles you couldn't win was how you stayed alive.

Garan spun, fury etched on his face. In that moment he looked so much like his father that Lira almost took a step back. "We are mages. It is our duty to help them, not run away like cowards."

"We are apprentices, not warrior mages," Lira snapped. "We can't help them. We *might* be able to help Athira if we leave now. We survived what happened to us, and now you want to throw that away and get us all killed? We can't change the outcome of this, Garan."

Her words hovered in the air between them, cold and stark. Not far away, the razak continued to close on the mage force. The anger on Garan's face only deepened, but before he could argue further, a whistling sounded on the air, barely audible.

Lira's eyes turned to the sky along with everyone else's. At first she couldn't see anything against the darkness, and she squinted harder, sure she wasn't imagining the sound. It grew steadily louder, and then she saw the dark shapes in the sky, two of them, dropping in over the valley wall.

They came down in a hurry, landing in the centre of the mages and Taliath, a thunderous boom echoing through the valley as they did. Lira winced as the force of it rolled over her.

Alyx Egalion had arrived.

Green magic lit up the night sky as she sent a concussive burst into the air above the razak, and then Tarrick Tylender followed with several pearlescent explosions. They boomed across the valley, momentarily dispelling the inky blackness.

Not an attack. An announcement. A warning.

Dashan Caverlock let out a roar, lifting *Heartfire* and rushing the nearest razak. Egalion was only a step behind, her magic lighting up his blade in green fire, her staff raised high. The Magor-lier bellowed orders, his voice deep and compelling, organising the mage warriors to fight with the Taliath. They formed a wedge behind Dashan and Alyx, clearly looking to break through the circle of razak so they would no longer be surrounded.

Garan said flatly, "You can all make your own choices, but I'm going to help."

He was striding away before any of them could try to stop him. Lira let him go, trying to fight down the urge to follow. She didn't want to see him dead, but they weren't winning this fight.

Lorin hesitated. "He's right. It is our duty. And I can't see any other way."

He was gone then too, limping as quickly as he could after Garan. Fari stared between Lira and Tarion. "I'm not a warrior."

"You're a healer. They'll need you after the fight," Tarion said. "Go find a spot in one of the nearby buildings. Stay hidden and safe, all right? Go, Fari."

Fari glanced between them, then turned and started running after Garan and Lorin.

"Are you going to run after them too?" Lira demanded, made angry by her own inability to keep her emotions out of this. She didn't want to abandon them even if it was stupid. "Or can we leave now, get out of here and find Athira?"

Tarion took a step closer to her. "I know you don't understand it, Lira, but there is nothing in this world that could make me walk away from my family right now."

"Fine. Go. Good luck." She turned to leave, but his hand reached out, caught her wrist. She snarled at him, "I'm not risking my life for them, Tarion. And they wouldn't want you risking yours either."

He ignored her. "I have an idea. I know that you noticed how coordinated the razak look, how carefully they were approaching the mage force."

She hesitated. Nodded. "Dasta is here somewhere, or another mage that can control them. They wouldn't have left the razak here without someone who could keep a hold over them." She hadn't killed him that night after all. Either that or they had more than one mage able to manage the monsters.

"I'm going to find him and kill him. It will distract the razak, make

183

them uncoordinated. Da's force will have a fighting chance then." His hand on her wrist tightened. "I need your help. Please?"

"Tarion..." She wavered.

"It's not just the mages anymore. It's Garan and Lorin too. Are you really going to walk away from them?" Tarion's mouth tightened. "From me? I know that's not who you are, Lira."

Lira yanked her arm out of Tarion's grip. "Yes it is! Have you listened to nothing I've been saying to you? I don't want to die for no reason."

"Fine." Frustration filled Tarion's voice. "Good luck, Lira. Be safe."

"Rotting bloody fish carcasses." She swore under her breath as he ran away from her, heading towards the main hall.

She was right. She *knew* she was right. She had to go. Get out of the valley. Survive. Pass on what they'd learned about Athira at the same time. Live to fight Underground another day.

And then she thought about Tarion facing down Dasta, a fully trained warrior mage, on his own. She doubted very much that Dasta would be unprotected either—not if he was controlling the razak.

Ahrin would tell her to run. That they weren't worth her death. And they weren't.

Her grandfather would say the same thing.

Muttering every curse word that immediately came to mind, Lira ran after Tarion.

CHAPTER 20

She caught up to Tarion as he pushed through the first door he found on the northern side of the main hall. "Where are you going?" she hissed, hoping he had a strategy for finding Dasta and didn't plan on wasting time running around searching aimlessly while everyone outside was killed.

He glanced back at her. "If he's controlling the razak, he needs to be able to see what's happening, right? Where the mages are, how they're fighting, where the weak points are to send the creatures to attack."

Of course. "You think he's on the roof somewhere," she said, her gaze searching for the nearest stairs. "What if it's not this building?"

"This one has the clearest view of where they're fighting. The dormitory buildings are too far away, and on the opposite side of the hall."

And the barn-like structure she'd seen, the only other building adjacent to the battle, was half-falling down and didn't look like it had an accessible roof. "We should be careful. Last time we were here this is where they lived and worked. Let's not assume the ambush is only outside." Lira spoke softly as they headed to the end of the hall where a back staircase led upwards. It was dark, full of shadows.

"No time for caution."

Lira sighed but conceded the point. If they were throwing themselves into danger, why bother creeping about and wasting time? The main hall of DarkSkull was five stories high, and the climb seemed endless. This part of the structure seemed mostly intact, though it had the same air of abandonment the rest of the place did.

Their boots skidded through dust and debris as they crossed a landing and started up the next flight of stairs. Lira's legs burned, the breath coming fast in her chest. Her magic glimmered under her skin, eager to be let out, and she fought to keep it under control. Constantly tapping at the back of her mind was the fact that if they found Dasta, she would have to make certain he died. If he made it out and reported back to Underground that she'd not only been here, but had actively helped protect the Mage Council force...

Tarion's long strides carried him ahead of her so that he was the first one to reach the top landing and look frantically around. Corridors led off to their left and right, empty and dark. Directly ahead of them, though, was a door set into stone.

With a single shared glance they went to open it, revealing narrow stone steps leading directly upwards. Tarion ran up, far faster than Lira, and pushed through the half-rotted wooden door at the top leading out to the roof.

Lira came sprinting up after him, taking the top step in a giant stride before sliding to a halt beyond the door and lifting her nocked bow in one smooth movement.

Both she and Tarion froze at the sight before them.

Rotted carcasses.

On the upside, they weren't going to have to keep searching. They'd found Dasta. The Underground mage stood on the opposite side of the roof, balanced on the edge, one hand lifted as he watched the battle unfolding below. The noise of it swept over the rooftop, mage light flashing brightly amidst the rattle of angry razak and shouts of the mages and Taliath fighting. It simmered through her blood, setting her alight.

On the downside, reaching Dasta was going to be impossible. Filling the roof space between Lira and Tarion and Dasta were six razak. The cold of their presence ate deep into her bones. Lira frowned, thoughts momentarily caught in puzzlement... why so many creatures dedicated to protecting a single mage? Surely one or two would be enough to—

The monsters turned as one, letting out a warning rattle and breaking Lira from her confusion. Alerted by their tone, Dasta glanced over his shoulder, face tightening when he saw them. His eyes narrowed even further when he saw Lira.

Damn. He was going to have to die this time.

After a single moment, Dasta dismissed them and turned back to his view of the battle below. But he must have done something with his magic, because a new edge sounded in the rattles echoing across the roof. The creatures were hungry, anticipatory.

"We should go back." Tarion was already taking a step towards the door. "We can't get through to him, but my mother... Lira?"

She took a breath, closed her eyes, and let go of all her barriers, the ones she used to keep focused, to think sensibly, to control herself. The thrill leaped like a flame, instantaneous, seductive, flaring through her in a giddy rush.

Six monsters and only Tarion and her bow and arrow between her and death. It heated her blood, gave her the reckless confidence she needed. For a moment she shuddered, feeling more herself than she had in weeks, warmed and euphoric from the prospect of risking imminent death. Then she opened her eyes and grinned. "We can take them, Tarion."

She moved before he could protest, loosing her arrow and firing two more in the space of seconds. Two shafts buried themselves in the eyes of the nearest razak and it screamed loudly enough to make both she and Tarion wince. The others screamed in quick succession, even some of those below echoing the screams.

Good, maybe the brief distraction would help Caverlock and the others.

"Lira, we can't—"

She cut off Tarion's shout, snapping, "Attack now, before they can organise themselves."

He hesitated only a moment, but then her confidence seemed to sweep him up too. "I have a better idea."

The air beside her blurred and Tarion vanished. Inside a heartbeat, while Lira was still lifting her bow to aim another arrow, he reappeared right beside Dasta on the edge of the roof. His staff was already moving, aiming for the man's head.

"Clever boy," Lira murmured, firing her next arrow. It hit another eye, but didn't bring the monster down. Its shrill cry rang through her ears.

Dasta reacted quickly, and the closest razak let out a furious rattle —anger at the attack on its master or in pain from a sudden, urgent command?—and lashed out with a razor-sharp scaled limb at Tarion's head. He was forced to pull back on his swing in order to duck the razak's attack.

Lira took aim at Dasta, but there was no clear shot through the razak between them, so she shot an arrow into the eye of the creature threatening Tarion instead. The distraction was enough to give Tarion the time to drive his staff into a second eye and kill the thing.

Two down.

Heart racing, blood singing, she ducked as the nearest razak swung out at her, its multiple limbs seemingly everywhere, the chill of the air freezing the sweat on her skin. Dasta moved, shuffling along the edge away from Tarion and allowing a razak to fill the space between them. His attention was still on the fighting below, but the rigidness of his shoulders told Lira that his focus was coming under strain. Good.

Tarion vanished from sight again, but Lira had to yank her attention away from him as three of the four remaining monsters abruptly turned in her direction, rippling with terrifying speed over the roof towards her. Her immediate environs darkened to inky blackness, but she was just able to see the fourth razak move to intercept Tarion as soon as he flashed into view in another attempt to get to Dasta.

Lira's mouth went dry, awareness kicking into extreme focus. In the mere seconds it took those creatures to reach her came the realisation of just how much danger she was in. Her energy surged, determination and anticipation both.

She got two arrows off before they were on her, but the second went wide. After that, she barely had enough time to drop the bow and scramble frantically out of the way as a scaled leg swept at her neck. Her heart pounded with unnerving force. That limb would have taken her head clean off if she hadn't moved in time.

She grinned, heart beating out a fierce rhythm. Gasping, scrambling, she fought back. If the razak wanted her, it was going to cost them.

Her magic surged then, stronger than she'd felt it before, flaring under her skin and turning it hot and slick with sweat. Violet light shone from her hands as she reached for her staff, drawing it just in time to slap away another lunging leg. The razak rattled, annoyed, and came at her again.

She tried to dodge left, but another creature seethed in to fill the space, and her awareness of danger increased to sharp clarity with the realisation they were herding her into a corner.

Ducking again and laying about with her staff, she tried to catch a glimpse of Tarion through the darkness of shadowy razak. He was flashing in and out of sight, battling the monster protecting Dasta. As she watched, he drove his staff into one eye in a move so fast she barely saw what happened. The creature screamed, scrabbling wildly about. Tarion flashed in and out again, then appeared to drive his staff into the second eye.

All the razak on the roof screamed in agony as it died, giving Lira a half-second to win herself some space. But it wasn't enough. She was trapped in the corner of the roof, a creature cutting off every possible exit. And once they'd recovered from the shock of the death, they closed on her, their rattling angry and vengeful.

She bared her teeth at them, daring them to try and kill her. Tarion had a clear shot at Dasta now. All he had to do was kill the man, and the mages below would have a fighting chance—and so would she and Tarion.

But Dasta was already turning to face Tarion... and Lira wasn't going to survive the next few moments, let alone for however long it would take for Tarion to defeat his opponent, if she didn't move faster, harder.

Lira swore, dragging herself out of her thoughts and taking a hurried step back as a long leg lashed towards her. She dodged right and swung with her staff. She was backed almost all the way to the edge of the roof now. Her magic burned like fire, desperate to be of use, desperate to explode out of her in some way. But her telekinesis was useless against these creatures.

"Lira!" Tarion shouted. He turned as if to move towards her.

"Forget me and get the rotted mage!" she screamed at him. "I'll keep them distracted."

All this would be for nothing otherwise.

She spun left as movement flickered in her peripheral vision, but she wasn't quick enough. She was already extended too far to the right, her staff sweeping out to block a lunge from the second creature, and there was no time, no space, to stop the closest razak's leg slashing down at her open and vulnerable left side.

Lira braced for the pain, felt bitter frustration rise up inside her, furious anger that this was going to be the end of her, that this time she was going to lose her battle with danger.

But before she could blink, before the blow could land, Tarion appeared in the space between her and the creature. He tried to bring his staff up to block, but there wasn't enough time. Its leg slashed down across his chest, tearing into him, blood spraying into the air, a triumphant rattling echoing over the roof.

Tarion crumpled.

Lira watched him fall as if in slow motion, certain that she hadn't just seen that happen. Certain Tarion hadn't just put himself between her and a death blow. But he kept falling, slumping to the ground, eyes wide, blood soaking the front of his tunic and flowing freely down to the stone beneath him.

Lira screamed.

She didn't know where the scream came from. Didn't know what the rising tide of burning fire in her chest was. But her magic exploded. One moment it was contained inside her and in the next it was erupting out into the world, uncontrolled and explosive.

Fire roared into life. White hot flames edged in violet. It filled the space around her, wrapped around the razak and everything else on the roof.

The razak screamed.

Dasta screamed as he turned into a pyre of burning flesh.

The roof was bathed in violet. Hot and fierce and cleansing. There was nothing in the world but the crackling of fire and the scent of burned skin.

And then the magic was gone. As quickly as it had come, it winked out of existence.

Lira swayed. Her vision blurred. Her body felt like it was empty, sucked dry of everything but skin and bone. She took a single, rasping breath. Then...

She dropped to her knees, partly because her legs wouldn't hold her and partly because her horrified gaze had landed on Tarion's body—untouched by the flames—lying at her feet. It was real. He was hurt. Really hurt. It drove everything else out of her mind.

He was taking shallow, gasping breaths, eyes fixed on her, his Shiven skin deathly white.

"Tarion..." She couldn't manage more than that, placing a hand over the bleeding wounds on his chest. They were so deep she could see bone and muscle. Her vision blanked out and she couldn't put a single thought together.

"I..." He gasped, eyes flickering closed.

"Tarion!" She tried to get him to stay awake.

He had to have known... When he put himself in front of her, he had to have known he wouldn't have time to defend himself. Why would he do that?

His eyes flickered open, but he was fading, she could see the life in them slipping away. She held his gaze, somehow thinking that might keep him there, with her. He let out a groan of pain, agony, and a strangely familiar light flashed in his eyes.

No. Her breathing stopped for a moment. She blinked, sure she'd imagined what she'd seen.

But then his eyes were sliding closed, and he was unconscious.

"Lira! Tarion!" Garan's voice. From the roof door. It startled her from the daze she'd been lost in.

"Where's Fari?" She tried to say the words, but they weren't audible. They sat somewhere in her throat, stuck, unable to come out. Her eyes were fixed on the blood pooling under Tarion's form, soaking the hands she had pressed to his chest. She couldn't look away.

"Tar." Garan slid to his knees across from her, tears sheened in his eyes. "Fari!" He bellowed the words, desperation filling his voice.

"I'm here, I'm here." The healer dropped down at Tarion's head, all traces of her flighty demeanour gone. She closed her eyes, reaching to place her hands over the horrible wounds.

"His mother." Lira swallowed and sat back to give Fari room, blinking, trying to put her thoughts in order. Tarion needed help, he needed... her frantic gaze swept over the roof, landing on Lorin. He was the only one still standing, looking shocked and helpless, like he wanted to help but didn't know what to do.

How had they gotten up here, or even known where they... focus. She had to focus. For Tarion.

"Lorin." She made her voice strong. She couldn't stand, let alone run anywhere. She was barely able to hold herself upright while a terrifying weakness coursed through her bones. Garan was a mess. Fari needed to stay and keep Tarion alive long enough to.... "Get his mother. His parents. Her magic... Fari needs it. Quickly, Lorin. Please."

Lorin didn't hesitate. He dropped his walking stick. Bad leg and all he *ran* for that doorway.

It felt like an eternity passed.

Lira sat there and stared at the wounds, watching as blood continued to run from Tarion's chest, dripping to the stone under him. She was unable to look away, barely able to stop herself collapsing to the ground. An odd scent filled the air... charring, maybe... but her brain couldn't quite function enough to work it out.

Garan gripped Tarion's hand, his whole body rigid, eyes fixed on the increasingly shallow rise and fall of his cousin's chest, as if by refusing to look away he could keep it moving.

Fari grew steadily paler as she used the brute strength of her magic to feed Tarion's strength and fight to hold him to life. If Lira hadn't been completely drained, there was no way she could have stayed still. As it was it felt like her insides were trying to crawl out of her body in fear and anxiety. At the same time her heart was racing too fast and she couldn't keep her thoughts straight. They kept flowing away from her.

"Tarion!"

Two figures landed on the roof before sprinting towards them. Lira's shoulders sagged in relief.

Alyx got there first, sliding to the ground by her son, biting her lip so hard she'd drawn blood. For a moment she swayed, the sight of Tarion's wound almost too much. But then Dashan crouched behind her, his hands coming to rest on her shoulders, steadying her.

Lira watched as Alyx took a deep breath, then looked at Fari. "I'm going to share my raw magic with you. I haven't absorbed much healing ability, but Finn's taught me a bit over the years, so we'll muddle through this together, okay?"

Fari's eyes flicked open, jaw set. "I'm just a second year, Councillor, I don't—"

"You'll be fine," Alyx said, voice cracking.

Fari shook her head, tears bright in her eyes. "I don't think I can, I'm sorry, I—"

"Fari!" Lira snapped, drawing the girl's attention to her, finding enough clarity and resolve for these hard words. "This isn't book learning. This is you and your magic. You can do this. If you don't, he dies. Got it?"

"She's right, Fari." Garan shifted around behind her, placing a hand on her shoulder and squeezing. "Blood is your speciality, remember? He's lost a lot, but you can help rebuild what he needs. Let my aunt work on the mechanics of the wound itself."

Fari swallowed. Nodded. Looked back at Alyx and met her gaze. "All right."

Both women's eyes closed then, and green light flared around Fari and Alyx's joined hands where they rested on the wounds.

"Are the rest of you all right?" Dashan's voice was taut with strain, gaze tearing away from his son to glance between Lira, Garan, and Lorin, who had reappeared without her realising.

"I think Lira has overused her magic." Lorin's face was tight with what had to be awful pain in his leg, and worry filled his eyes. "Otherwise we're all fine."

"Keep an eye on her," Dashan instructed. "If she looks like she's going to pass out, or she starts to have trouble breathing, you let us know."

"I will." Lorin's shoulders straightened and he limped over to stand beside Lira.

"I'm fine!" Lira tried to snap, but it came out as a rasp. Either way, Lorin ignored her, his Shiven gaze watching protectively. "At least get off that leg."

"I can stand a bit longer," he said quietly.

Thick, heavy silence filled the rooftop. Even their breathing was too quiet to be heard, everyone holding themselves so tightly it was like they'd become statues.

Eventually the wound on Tarion's chest started to close over, though not all the way, and the blood began clotting rather than flowing out of him. Alyx let out a gasp and her eyes opened. Fari swayed and almost toppled over sideways, but Garan reached out to pull her into his arms before she could hit the ground.

"Is he all right?" Dashan asked his wife, hands white-knuckled on her shoulders.

"For now, but he needs more if he's going to live. I want to take him to the healers in Alistriem. You'll carry him, I'll fly the three of us." Alyx sounded bitterly exhausted.

"Finn's at Temari Hall," Dashan murmured.

"They got to him at Temari Hall before, Dash. Jenna and Ladan are in Alistriem, and other skilled healers. We'll be safer there."

"Have you got enough magic for—"

"I'll be fine." Alyx pushed herself to her feet, fury, pain, and weariness warring for supremacy in her expression. "The rest of you will go and join the mages below and you will travel with them to Alistriem. You do *anything* other than follow obediently and you will learn exactly what the wrath of a mage of the higher order looks like. Am I clear?"

Garan nodded when the rest of them simply stared in awed wonder. Lira dazedly wondered if her grandfather had ever been that terrifying in full fury.

Dashan leaned down and gently lifted his son into his arms. The pain that flashed over his face was so raw Lira had to look away. Once he was standing, Alyx wrapped an arm around his waist and they leapt into the sky. In seconds they were gone from sight.

"Can you stand, Lira?" Garan asked. "Fari?"

"I'm okay." Fari sounded exhausted, but she untangled herself from Garan and managed to get to her feet. Blood crusted her hands and clothes. Tarion's blood. Lira couldn't tear her eyes away.

"Lira?" Lorin's hand wrapped around her arm and he helped her stagger upwards. She didn't have it in her to shove away his assistance. Once on her feet the world tilted and she almost went over again, but Lorin wrapped a steadying arm around her waist.

"What happened?" Garan's eyes fell on the charred remains of the razak. "Just as we were about to join the fight, we saw a flash of violet light on the roof up here and we... it doesn't matter. When I got up here Tar was on the ground and the creatures were piles of ash."

A blink of memory. Bright white flame lighting up the roof. Just as quickly it was gone, blurry exhaustion in its place.

"Tarion wanted to go after the mage controlling the razak. He thought if we killed him it would give you all a fighting chance," Lira said dully. "But the mage was protected by six of them."

"You and Tarion took out six razak?" Lorin asked, then frowned. "How did you burn them?"

"I..." She sucked in a breath. All the heat she remembered from earlier was gone, her magic a dry well. She couldn't stop seeing Tarion's body falling in slow motion, his blood splattering her hands and robe. "He jumped in front of me. He took a blow that was meant for me."

"Lira, are you doing okay?" Fari stepped closer. "You sound a little dazed."

"I'm fine." She swayed, giving the lie to her words. "Can we go please?"

"We can," Garan said gently. "Lorin's going to help you, and I've got Fari. We do this together, okay?"

She wanted to leave. Go away and never come back. A shudder wracked her wiry frame, a shudder that wanted to break into wrenching sobs that she fought to hold back. But where could she go? There was no home for Lira Astor.

So she simply nodded.

She would go where they went.

CHAPTER 21

I t was a two-week journey to Alistriem. The mage in charge—
Warrior Restan—pushed them hard, clearly worried they were
vulnerable to any follow up attack force.

The healer with them treated Fari and Lira in the breaks they took
to water the horses and get some sleep. Exhaustion constantly tugged
at Lira, the short rests they got not nearly long enough for someone so
badly affected by magic overuse—which was the healer's diagnosis for
both apprentices. Lorin's leg clearly pained him, but he said nothing
about it, instead hovering protectively around all of them whenever
they stopped while Garan marched off to ensure the healer came over
to check on Fari and Lira before she did anything else.

They didn't speak much. The shock of what had happened weighed
heavily, even on Lira. Her normal resilience seemed to have vanished,
gone to the same place her magic had disappeared to. All she could see
when she closed her eyes was Tarion planting himself before her.
Tarion falling. The look on his parents' faces when they saw how badly
hurt he was.

What she'd seen when he'd lost consciousness, that light... she
pushed that memory away every time, sure she must have imagined it.

But what weighed most heavily was the knowledge that it had been all her fault. Her need for the thrill of danger had meant Tarion was on that roof when she should have listened to him and retreated. Guilt twisted her stomach whenever she thought of it.

They rode close together during the days, and at night they set out their blankets in a group inside the cordon of guards. Once the healer had checked Fari and Lira, Garan made a point of ensuring they had enough water and food, that they were warm enough to sleep, and that Lorin got off his leg and gave it some rest. Only then would he curl up beside them in his own blanket.

Normally, this would have irritated Lira to no end. But not now. Now she was grateful for the presence of someone to look out for them, to take charge, when she didn't have the strength for it. She was glad of Garan. More, she found she trusted him to keep them safe.

Nobody asked her what had happened on the roof. Garan clearly hadn't said anything to Restan or the other mages and Taliath, and he didn't raise it with Lira either. He seemed only to care about making sure he got them all to Alistriem safely. Fari was too exhausted to muster conversation at all, let alone questioning, and Lorin rarely spoke anyway.

She should have taken the time to come up with a story to explain what had happened, practice it so she was ready for the interrogation when they reached Alistriem. But even if she hadn't been too groggy to string clear thoughts together, she wasn't sure she'd be able to come up with anything even remotely plausible.

Whatever she did, she couldn't afford the council finding out that Lira had broken out with another mage ability on that roof. Mages didn't have additional magical abilities—not unless they were one of the extraordinarily rare mages of the higher order like Alyx Egalion. And it had been far too many years since Lira had first broken out with a single ability to be classified as that. No, they would know something else had been done to her. Or suspect she'd been hiding more abilities this whole time.

While her memories of exactly what had happened were hazy, she recalled the fire with clarity. The heat and roar of it. How it had felt exploding out of her body.

It had killed the razak and left Dasta a pile of steaming ash on the roof.

Underground's experiment on her had worked.

THEY RODE into Alistriem late at night, Restan forcing a longer day to make sure they didn't have to spend another night outside. Lira was dazed from bone-deep exhaustion, barely able to do much more than concentrate on staying astride.

People crowded around them as they rode into the torchlit entry courtyard of the Alistriem palace. Blue-coated guards were everywhere and someone was calling out crisp instructions. Garan's voice was audible amongst it, and Lira and the others followed when he led them away with several of the guards.

"Garan!" A deep voice snapped out his name, and the young man turned, face crumpling in relief.

Ladan Egalion appeared a moment later, striding through the crowd, *Mageson* at his hip. He pulled his son into a brief hug before letting go. "You're all right?"

"I'm fine. Da, how is Tarion?"

Lira took a step closer, desperate to hear the answer.

"It wasn't good, but he's still fighting." Ladan's voice was edged with relief. "They think he'll be okay."

Relief swamped Lira, almost causing her to sway on her feet. Garan shuddered, his eyes closing briefly "Da, I'd like to stay at the palace tonight with Fari and Lira and Lorin, rather than coming home. I—"

Ladan reached out to grip his son's arm, his hard green gaze running over the rest of them. "It's fine, lad. Everything has been sorted."

"Good." Some of Garan's imperious tone returned. "And I want them to get some proper rest, and another look from a healer, before anyone starts asking them questions. If you desperately need to talk to one of us immediately, I'll do it."

Once again, Lira was grateful for Garan handling everything so capably. The last thing she felt up to was trying to give an account of what had happened on that roof. She still hadn't come up with anything to explain it.

Ladan smiled then, and it sat oddly on his grim-featured face. "I understand. Come with me, all of you. Garan, your mother will want to see you, but then you can rest with the others."

"Where are we going?" Fari asked, sounding as weary as Lira felt.

"Somewhere you can sleep. Rooms have been set aside for us in the guest wing," Garan said gently.

Lord-Taliath Ladan Egalion, second most important man in Rionn after the king, personally escorted them through the palace halls. He showed them to their rooms, pointed out where to go if they needed anything, then left them to it. Lira stumbled over to the bed and fell face forward onto it.

She was asleep in seconds.

WHEN LIRA WOKE, it was morning, and she was alone in the room Garan's father had brought her to. Warm sunshine shone through glass panes that looked out into a pretty garden. The faint sound of trickling water teased the edges of her hearing.

She sat up and tested her limbs, checking for injuries. The odd, heavy exhaustion that had been with her since the roof was gone, and she closed her eyes in relief. Her magic was back too, that intoxicating well inside her that had run terrifyingly dry. She sucked in a deep breath, eyes closing as she sank into it, revelled in its warmth and potence. Thank everything.

How long had she been out?

Tarion!

She scrambled off the bed, then made a face when she caught a whiff of her bloodied and travel-stained clothing. A basin of water and neat pile of folded clothes sat on a table near the window, so she stripped off and washed as best she could. It took several minutes to scrub away the dried blood on her hands and nails while she stood shivering.

As she stared into the red-tinged water, flexing her fingers, the events of the roof flooded her mind. Swallowing, she reached for a touch of magic and visualised those flames. It took effort and concentration, but a flare of violet-edged flame flashed into being around her fingers.

Joy lit up her chest.

Thoughts now alert and clear, the full import of what had happened sunk in. Not only did she have a new power, but she had killed razak with it. It shouldn't have been possible. The monsters were immune to every bit of magic that had been thrown at them so far. How had her new fire magic been able to kill them?

A more immediate question crowded to the front of her mind—what had happened to the razak that had ambushed Caverlock and his party? Too out of it to wonder on the journey to Alistriem, she hadn't asked how that fight had fared.

Her head began to ache, and she killed the flame, dressing in the fresh clothing before crossing to open the door.

Time to get some answers.

The corridor outside was completely empty. No guards. No servants. Shrugging, Lira turned right, glancing into the open doors of the rooms she passed. They were all empty, though the beds had rumpled covers and in one room she spotted a torn grey apprentice cloak tossed over a chair.

The last room on the right wasn't empty. Through the ajar door, Tarion was visible lying on the bed inside, gaze turned towards the windows to his right... more gardens. The king of Rionn clearly liked them.

Lira pushed open the door tentatively, her gaze taking in the sunlit room and the lack of other people inside. Tarion visibly brightened at the sight of her. "Lira! I was hoping you would visit."

For a moment she froze on the threshold, the memory of that night coming back as vividly as if it were happening all over again. What she'd seen in his eyes when he'd passed out, the way... no! She forced the memory away. She'd been exhausted and ill with magic overuse. Whatever she'd seen had been a fancy, or a trick of the light. It wasn't important.

"Lira?"

"Sorry!" She stepped inside and closed the door, managing a smile, the torrent of questions that had been building up inside her slipping out. "Where are your guards? How long was I asleep? Are you okay?"

He laughed. It was stupid, but she was so relieved to see him awake and apparently well that she'd let enthusiasm overwhelm her for a moment. She cleared her throat. "Sorry. I'm still a little..." She waved a hand.

"It's okay. I'm glad to see you well. To answer your questions, my parents know I hate being hovered over, so the Bluecoat guards are out there, just at a distance. We've been here three days, so if you just woke up, you slept a lot." He frowned. "They said you overextended your magic."

She dismissed his concern with a wave. "How are you feeling?" she asked, eyes running over him. The blankets covered most of his body, but his colour was good and he didn't seem to be in pain. "When we got here, Garan's father said the worst was over."

"I'm all stitched up and the healers are working on me every day. I'm going to be fine. You, however, look paler than usual."

"I'm still a little tired, but I'm fine." Lies. All lies. But what was the truth? That she felt fragile, shaky, vulnerable? She wasn't sure whether she didn't *know* what was wrong, or just wouldn't let herself face it. Ahrin's face floated into her mind and for a moment she almost crumpled with the force of how badly she wished Ahrin was here. But at the same time she hated wanting it, because it wasn't going to happen. Couldn't happen. She wasn't the comfort, the solid presence, that Lira needed, and never would be.

Tarion spoke into the silence. "Will you come and sit over here please? It feels extremely uncomfortable to yell across the room at you."

She huffed a laugh. "Sorry, I forget that you hate talking at normal speaking volume. Are the others all right?"

He nodded. "They were here a little earlier, then went off to find lunch. Are you really okay?" he asked as she perched on the side of the bed, trying not to jostle him.

"I wouldn't be, if you hadn't jumped in front of that razak." She toyed with a loose thread on one of the blankets. "Why did you do that? It was the stupidest thing I've ever seen someone do."

"I saw you were exposed and weren't going to be able to recover in time." He shrugged, as if it were no big deal. "I knew I might be able to get there to cover you, so I tried."

"Killing Dasta was your priority."

"You're my friend. I wasn't going to stand there and watch a razak kill you." Impatience edged his voice. "*That* was my priority."

She frowned. "And now you're annoyed at me?"

"You are very exasperating at times. Lira, you came up to that roof with me to help, because I asked you to. Because even though you refuse to admit it, we are friends. I will always try and protect you."

"I don't need protection." But her voice lacked the fire it usually held.

"You did on the roof." His hand moved to touch her arm. "It's not a weakness, you know? Everyone needs help sometimes."

"It *is* a weakness in my world. One I can't afford."

He nodded, shifting on the pillows. "I understand."

"You don't, not really. You have no idea."

"Maybe not. But I do understand how it's shaped you."

His hand dropped from her arm to the covers. She stared at it for a moment, contemplated reaching out to take it. Told herself she was being a fool.

"You're not him, Lira. You are worth saving."

Hand forgotten, her gaze shot to his hazel eyes. "You don't know that either."

"Sure I do. So do Garan and Fari and Lorin." His eyes searched hers.

She opened her mouth to say something, but no words came. They didn't know her, not really. They didn't know that she was secretly working for Underground, that half the time she didn't know which side she was truly on.

She'd started working with Underground not because she was loyal to the Mage Council, but because she wanted to win glory. To make them forget about who her ancestor was. Lira Astor didn't have a side. She looked out for herself. If they knew that, they'd hate her. But she didn't want to face that yet. So she met his gaze. "Thanks for saving me, Tarion."

His smile flashed, simple and true, and she couldn't help returning it. "You're welcome, Lira."

"Next time, don't," she said sharply. "I'm not worth your life."

Before he could respond, the door opened, and a cheerful voice spoke. "Tar, you're awake."

His smile turned several degrees brighter when he saw who it was. "Sesha!"

Lira stared as a blonde girl came into the room, a warm smile on her face, light blue eyes shining. She was incredibly beautiful. An artist given Sesha and Ahrin to paint side by side would feel like they'd won a pot of gold—night and day in all their stunning beauty.

Sesha sat on the opposite side of the bed from Lira and offered a welcoming smile, ignoring what had to be a gape-mouthed stare from Lira. "Hello. Let me guess, you're Lira Astor?"

"That's me." Lira's voice came out cooler than she intended, and she stood up, bowing her head slightly. She wasn't exactly sure of the protocol for addressing royalty, but figured a head bow was a good start. Much better than staring in fascination, anyway. "You must be Princess Sesha."

"Please don't use my title, not if you're a friend of Tarion's. It's nice to meet you."

She didn't mean it. She couldn't. This princess must have heard all the same stories everyone else had about Spider. But maybe... Tarion loved this girl. It was clear in the way he looked at her, the way he'd brightened the moment she'd walked in. Maybe Sesha did mean it. "It's nice to meet you too."

"Are you hungry, Lira? I could ask a servant to bring some food and hot tea, if you like?" Sesha offered. "We could eat together, the three of us. Tarion has been worried about you."

"No, thank you." Lira felt awkward now, like she was intruding. "I should leave you to it."

"There's no need to leave," Tarion protested, wincing as he shifted in the bed.

She managed a smile, throwing his words back at him from the night in the healing ward with Ahrin. "I suspect you'd rather be alone with Sesha right now."

He smiled back, warm and true. "I'll see you later then?"

"You will," she promised, then bowed her head again in Sesha's direction. "Your Highness."

She left the room without another word.

WEARINESS STILL NAGGED AT LIRA, so when she arrived back at her room to find a plate of food and jug of water had been delivered, she ate and drank her fill before falling back into bed.

Her initial plan had been to nap for a while then go and seek out Garan and the others to check on them, but when she woke again, it was dark. It took her a moment to realise she'd been disturbed from sleep by the faint murmur of voices. For a moment she lay there in the darkness, wondering if she'd been dreaming, if the voices were a result of another nightmare. But she hadn't awoken feverish or sweating. Instead she felt better again, her energy levels almost back to normal.

When she heard the whisper of voices again, she pushed back the covers and padded to the door. After making sure her staff was within easy reach, she quietly cracked it open and looked out.

Further down the dim hallway—directly across from Tarion's room —two figures sat with their backs against the wall. Surprise flickered through Lira as she recognised his parents. Their conversation was clearer with her door ajar, and so after she carefully reinforced her mental shields to ensure Alyx Egalion wouldn't pick up Lira's presence from her thoughts, Lira sat down by her door.

She wasn't entirely sure why she wanted to listen. Underground wanted her to get closer access to the council, of course, and what was better than overhearing the private conversation of a mage councillor and the Shiven leader's second in command? But that wasn't it—she wasn't planning on telling Underground anything useful about the council, nothing they could use to harm them.

No, as always, Lira was listening in so that she could protect herself. The better armed she was with information, the greater her chances of survival. She buried the twinge she felt at how disappointed Tarion and the others would be if they knew that.

"It feels like it's happening all over again." This from Alyx, her voice so soft Lira had to strain to catch it.

"It's not." Caverlock's voice, firm.

"Maybe. But there's something... don't tell me you don't feel it too?"

A sigh. "Yeah. But you know, whatever it is, we'll get through it. We always do, mage-girl."

"I thought it was over. I don't want to fight again, Dash. I don't want people getting hurt. I don't want to worry about people I love again. Tarion almost died. If I hadn't been there..."

She sounded so sad, her voice catching in grief. Lira remembered the look on Egalion's face when she'd seen Tarion lying badly hurt on that roof. As unfamiliar as it was to Lira, that emotion had been real and true and deep. Wistfulness rippled through her, a yearning for someone in the world who would feel about Lira like Alyx did about her son. The chasm in her chest threatened to gape open, and she hurriedly pushed those thoughts from her mind, concentrating on parsing useful information from the conversation.

Caverlock spoke gently. "Tarion and Caria are strong. They're your kids, Alyx, of course they are. No matter what comes at us, we'll all be fine." He sounded genuinely confident of that. But Alyx, when she responded, was less certain.

"It feels like him again."

A long pause. Lira stilled, holding her breath as Caverlock spoke. "When I spoke to Finn before I left, he said he thought he was getting closer to finding her father. He thinks if we find him, it's the link we need to get to Underground. We're going to end this, Alyx, I promise you."

"He's been searching for years, Dash. Her father could be anyone. He probably doesn't even know the identity of the woman he fathered Lira with."

Lira froze. She'd had no idea the council were trying to track down her father. What made them think he had anything to do with Underground? She racked her memories, but everything before that night—the one where her mother had never come home—was indistinct. Still, her mother had never given an indication her father was anything more than a man who'd not wanted a child and left her when he found out she was pregnant.

What would she do if A'ndreas *did* find her father? Lira's mind blanked at the idea. He'd never been a figure in her life, and he'd never wanted her. She certainly didn't want or need him. Busy with those thoughts, it took her a moment to realise another silence had fallen between Caverlock and Egalion. It felt heavy, with doubt and fear. Caverlock clearly sensed it too, because he made another attempt to reassure his wife.

"Just because he has an heir, doesn't mean—"

"But to see her there... his face, his eyes, that cool look he always wore, hovering over my dying son. I couldn't help but..." Egalion's voice caught, as if she couldn't continue.

"She's not him."

"I know, but..."

The voices fell silent then, and when Lira risked a peek through the open gap in her door, she saw Alyx curled up against her husband's side, his arm tight around her, his head resting on hers. Both had their eyes closed. All stress had smoothed from their faces and they looked content.

They would never see anything but him in her.

Lira stared into the darkness of her room for a long while, shivering despite the warm air, wanting Ahrin so badly she could taste it. Not Ahrin now, but Ahrin as she had been, the one that had never really existed except in Lira's head. Running a crew, making a home for themselves, facing the world together. It was the only true home she'd ever known, and it had come close to breaking her to lose it, and ever since then she'd been cast adrift.

She felt sick. Tired again. Beaten down.

Lira forced herself to take a deep, calming breath. Miring herself in self-pity was stupid.

She would keep fighting. To survive. To make them see her.

It was all she could do.

CHAPTER 22

Early the following morning, a knock came at the door just as Lira finished eating the breakfast that had been delivered to her room. She hadn't slept much after returning to bed the night before, and the gluggy porridge wasn't sitting overly well in a stomach tangled up with knots. When the knock came, a quick burst of hope flared that it might be Garan or Fari or Lorin.

But the hope died quickly when she opened the door to find Dawn A'ndreas standing on the other side. After a brief moment spent cursing herself for not preparing better for this meeting—magic overuse or not—Lira put all her focus into ensuring her mental defences were up. She was going to need them. "Lord-Mage." She kept her expression neutral. "I was wondering how long it would take for you to come and find me."

Dawn smiled. "I wanted to give you some time to recover. The Bluecoats on this wing say you've been keeping to yourself, and I worried that maybe you had been more affected than the healer mages thought. May I come in?"

Lira's eyes narrowed. Even though Dawn's question had been delivered with her usual warmth and concern, there was something cooler about the telepath mage than the last time they'd spoken, directly after Lira had been returned to Temari Hall with the others.

Her first guess was that Dawn had received her message about Ahrin being at Temari Hall, and wasn't pleased with how long it had taken Lira to tell her. She gave an easy shrug and stood aside to wave the mage in. "I'm actually feeling a lot better, but I think I slept for about three days straight."

"That happens after overuse. I know the feeling." Dawn smiled again, then paused, the smile fading. "Your mental shields are up."

"They're always up," Lira said, taking one of the chairs by the unlit fire, sparing a longing glance for the beautiful day outside. Winter was finally losing its grip to spring, making the world brighter. "You're the one who taught me how to make them infallible."

Instead of taking the chair opposite, Dawn wandered to the window, looking out into the garden and the bubbling fountain in its centre. "What were you thinking, disobeying Dashan's orders and taking the others to DarkSkull?"

Ah, so this wasn't about Ahrin. It was about Lira endangering her precious son and nephew. "It was Garan's idea, not mine, and though I agreed with him, it wasn't like I dragged them kicking and screaming with me."

"Even so." Coolness edged Dawn's voice.

"Even so, what?" Lira said snappishly, already irritated with this conversation. "When we arrived at Weeping Stead and were promptly locked in a room and told to stay put, Garan made the point that since you've all been hiding things from us since we got back, it might be a good idea to go and take a look for ourselves rather than waiting to be given snippets of information you all deem safe. I agreed. You're the one that put me inside Underground to spy for you. You can't pick and choose what I know, not if you want me to be successful."

Dawn murmured, almost to herself, "I'm beginning to wonder whether that was a good idea."

"What does *that* mean?" Lira asked. "Why are you really here, Lord-Mage? I'm confident Garan has already told you that disobeying orders was all his idea."

Dawn turned away from the glass to meet her gaze. "They all did. They made quite the effort to protect you, in fact."

Lira stilled, a heavy weight of despair settling in her chest, despite how much she hated that Dawn's obvious distrust affected her like it did. "You too, huh? What, now you're starting to worry that I'm trying to recruit my own little mage army to take over the world?"

There was a brief silence, and when Dawn spoke again, it was with an edged tone that Lira had never heard from the woman before. "I hope you haven't been thinking all this time that I'm a fool. That I didn't have my doubts about asking you to infiltrate Underground, knowing who you are, what you've been through."

Lira couldn't help it—she laughed aloud, bitterness turning it into an ugly sound. "You mean, you hope I didn't think you were different from any other person I've ever met? Don't worry on that score." She turned away. "This is a boring story I've heard too many times. Unless you've got something else to say, I'd rather be left alone."

Something rippled across Dawn's face, something she couldn't read. Surreptitiously, Lira reinforced her mental shield.

"I've told you many times that I don't think you are your grandfather, Lira. But that doesn't mean I don't worry about the effect this is having on you, or how dangerous it is to place a seventeen-year-old apprentice inside a group like Underground."

Lira merely stared at her. "And I've told you many times that I don't need protecting."

"I was sixteen when I started at DarkSkull." Dawn's gaze turned distant. "After some of the things that happened to me that year, I don't mind admitting that some protecting would have been nice."

"You and I are very different. My life didn't get dangerous when I started at Temari Hall, Lord-Mage. My entire life beforehand was far more dangerous than your cosseted school. I learned how to survive."

A thick silence held, then Dawn let out a breath and came to sit in the chair opposite her. When she spoke again, she sounded genuinely interested, her warm voice returning. "What can you tell me about what happened at DarkSkull? Yes, I've heard it from the others, but I want your account. You're the most informed of all of us."

"Like I said, I went with them because I thought I might be able to pick up anything the searchers missed." Lira paused, still on edge despite the change of subject. "Including any clues to what happened to Athira. Did they tell you she might have escaped, or at least that someone did?"

"Yes. Mages and Taliath are searching the countryside and villages surrounding the valley as we speak. If Athira made it to any of them, we'll know about it soon. Haler's body will be recovered and properly buried." Dawn's eyes held hers. "You weren't aware of the ambush."

"No, I wasn't. As far as Underground knows, I'm being hidden away somewhere with your precious relatives for my own protection." Lira frowned. "Was that cover story your idea or Caverlock's?"

"That was all Dash." Dawn smiled wryly.

"It was a clever move. But I take it that means Councillor Egalion also now knows about my position with Underground? I doubt very much those two keep secrets from each other." Lira pushed. She wasn't comfortable with the circle of knowledge expanding, but there wasn't much she could do about it.

"She does." Dawn offered nothing further, prompting, "Back to that night?"

"Fine. When the ambush happened, I tried to get the others to flee with me rather than joining the fight. I'm sure they told you that, too."

"They did. They said they didn't listen to you."

"Then what is it exactly that you're upset with me about?" Lira's eyes narrowed as realisation struck her. She cursed herself for a fool for not realising it sooner. "You've just been asking me all these questions to keep me distracted so that you could try and read any stray thoughts that fell out from behind my shield."

"That surprises you?"

"No. It's what I would do if I were you." Lira shrugged. "But I know you didn't get anything."

"That sounds dangerously close to arrogance, Lira. And you think I shouldn't be worried when you withhold important information about Underground?" Dawn's blue eyes flashed in irritation.

Lira's shoulders stiffened. Here it was. "You got my letter about the Darkhand."

"I did. I can't for the life of me figure out why you didn't tell me instantly. It concerns me deeply that you didn't."

"I explained why in the letter. I thought I had a good chance of recruiting her to our side. She's much higher placed in the organisation than me and she holds their trust. It will take time—years maybe—for me to reach that level of access. That's time we don't have."

"Putting aside the fact that wasn't your decision to make without approval, which you well know, *did* you recruit her?" Dawn lifted an eyebrow, clearly humouring her. It was a different tactic from the refusal to engage Lira got from the masters at Temari, so it had her on the back foot.

"It was going well," Lira said reluctantly. "Until Caverlock swept us all off to DarkSkull. And that's why I wrote to you... because I couldn't keep an eye on her while I was away and I didn't want to take that risk."

"Fine. But why didn't you tell us about her when you debriefed Tarrick and I after you were returned from your kidnapping?"

"Because..." She didn't have a good answer for this, had hoped Dawn wouldn't have the opportunity to ask it. "I was still shaken, not everything was clear. I didn't remember her."

"That's a lie." Dawn's mouth tightened. "I might not be able to read your individual thoughts, but I can tell when you're lying."

Lira said nothing. She wavered on the edge of telling the truth—would Dawn understand if Lira explained everything? She might... but Lira doubted the Magor-lier or anyone else would. "Lord-Mage, if we had the Darkhand on our side, we could bring Underground down so much faster, before anyone else gets hurt. And much more thoroughly too."

Rather than be mollified by Lira's argument, Dawn merely looked incredulous. "What exactly possessed you to think the Darkhand would allow herself to be recruited by you, as opposed to reporting your treason straight to the Shadowcouncil?"

Lira hesitated, knew as soon as she did it that it was a mistake, because any lie she spoke now would be picked up. She'd have to give some truth. "We knew each other. Back in Dirinan. I knew I could use that as leverage."

Fear... or shock... rippled over Dawn's face and she stood abruptly. Lira's heart sank—the telepath must have picked up something despite her shielding, but what? Whatever it had been, Lira needed to distract her from it. It was obvious Dawn was having serious doubts about continuing to use Lira as their spy. Lira needed to quell those doubts. "More than anything else, I want to bring Underground down, that is the truth." She lowered her mental shields briefly enough for Dawn to read her sincerity. "I swear it. You can trust that."

"Maybe, but I don't like that you're hiding things from us," Dawn said softly. "You shouldn't be doing what you're doing, you're still just an apprentice. Maybe it's best if we pull you out."

"I don't need this mothering that you keep trying to do," Lira snapped. "I'm an apprentice, yes, but I'm a mage like you. If I'm a tool you can use against Underground, you should use me. It's that simple."

Dawn nodded and rose, her face expressionless. "You'll all be going back to Karonan in a week or so, once Tarion has fully recovered—we can't afford anyone to know he was hurt, since none of you were supposed to be anywhere near DarkSkull Hall. I want more regular reports from you. If I get the sense you're leaving anything out, or lying to me, I'll pull you no matter your protests. Is that clear?"

"Very."

"And you keep Garan and the others out of it. This is not their fight. At least not until they're fully trained and have passed their trials."

"Agreed." Lira didn't want them involved either. At least they could agree on that. "Will you tell me what you did about Ahrin? Will I need to have an explanation for her being discovered when I get back?"

Dawn hesitated. "I sent orders to Finn, discreetly, to have watchers placed around her. Like you, I didn't want to tip off Underground that we knew about her and potentially place you in jeopardy."

Lira's heart sank at her tone. "But?"

"She was gone before my message arrived. She left a note with Finn to say there'd been a death in the family and she'd gone home to see them. Whatever Ahrin Vensis was planning at Temari, either she completed her task, or she was pulled away to do something more important."

213

Lira swore inwardly. "Maybe." Or maybe her purpose there had more to do with Lira and Garan and those that were kidnapped, and after they'd left, there was no point in staying. Still, apart from being annoyed on her behalf, Ahrin hadn't seemed particularly bothered by Lira's departure—not like she would have been if their leaving had meant obstructing plans she had in motion.

"Yes, well, we both know there's no death in the family, so she won't be back," Dawn added.

"No," Lira agreed. "And while we're on the subject, I need you to do something about your brother's overly restrictive rules. Being confined to the school grounds makes it extremely difficult to get to Underground meetings or do any spying."

"Those rules are there for your safety." Dawn shook her head. "Besides, you've already managed to sneak out at least once judging from your report."

"I'm not sure you understand how difficult that was. Lord-Mage, Underground are a much bigger problem than we expected. They just ambushed the most powerful mage alive and her husband, not to mention they kidnapped your son and nephew. I know you want them gone as much as I do."

"I'm reluctant to bring anyone else in Karonan into your work with Underground. Dashan is immune to telepathic magic, but neither Finn nor Councillor Duneskal are. Until we know for certain, we have to operate under the assumption that the Shadowcouncil has a telepath mage. I'm sorry, you'll just have to keep working around his rules." Dawn looked suddenly weary. "When you return, it's possible Underground will know you've been in Alistriem—your presence here hasn't been kept a secret—but that fits well with Dashan's cover story. I can assure you no word has leaked of any of you being at DarkSkull. No Underground member there that night was left alive."

"They killed all the razak, then?" Lira asked in surprise.

"You didn't know?" Dawn looked equally surprised. "The theory that they are hive creatures turned out to be correct. The queen must have been on the roof with you and Tarion and their mage. When it died, all the creatures attacking Dashan's force died too."

Lira frowned. None of the razak on the roof had looked any

different from the others. Maybe... "Either that or killing the mage killed all the creatures under his control?"

"Also a possibility," Dawn agreed. "What can you tell me about how the razak on the roof died?"

"I'm not sure." Lira allowed a flicker of combined puzzlement and irritation to cross her face as she lied without hesitation. "Tarion killed two, I think, and I took down at least one... when he fell I just remember being so upset, I lost control over my magic and it exploded out of me, draining my entire reserve in one hit. The telekinesis can't have harmed them... but the magic overuse made everything blurry. I don't remember exactly what happened after."

"As upsetting as it no doubt was, you'll need better control over your magic if you're to pass the trials," Dawn said gently. "Alyx and Dash thought the monsters looked like they'd been burned?"

Lira shrugged. "I remember the scent of something burning, that's really clear, but I don't know how it happened. Could Dasta have lost control of *his* magic somehow when Tarion attacked him?"

"Maybe," Dawn said thoughtfully.

It was time to change the subject before Dawn thought too much about what Lira had said, or came up with more tricky questions to answer. "When I get back to Temari Hall, I'll tell Greyson that we were taken to Alistriem for our safety." She thought it through. "And I'll say you sent us back because you believe the threat against us has passed, but you wouldn't tell us why. When they hear about what happened at DarkSkull, they'll assume that was the reason."

"Agreed, it's a good cover." Dawn rose to leave, but paused at the door. "Don't make it obvious, but if you can try and figure out why the Darkhand was withdrawn from the school, that would be helpful."

"I can do that."

"Good luck, Lira. Stay safe."

And she was gone.

Lira sank back in her chair, shoulders slumping, heart beating too fast. A faint headache throbbed at her temples, the result of the split focus she'd needed holding her shield and evading difficult questions at the same time against a telepath of Dawn's calibre.

Everything was becoming so complicated—trying to manage what

Underground wanted with what the council asked of her while fighting to maintain focus on *her* ultimate goal.

She rubbed at her forehead, trying to ease the ache in her temples. She wanted to wipe Underground from the face of the earth for what they'd done to her.

But she had to admit...she also wanted the magic they could give her.

CHAPTER 23

Time alone staring into the sunlit garden after her talk with
Dawn didn't help the tangle of Lira's thoughts at all. After a
while she stood abruptly, gaze searching for her boots and
robe. She would go and find Garan and the others, make sure they
were okay. If nothing else, seeing them, talking to them, would be a
welcome distraction.

Just as Lira was lacing up her second boot, another knock at the
door caused her to glance up sharply, a smile crossing unbidden over
her face when Fari peeked her head around the corner and announced,
"She's alive!"

"So are you." Lira finished the laces and stood, waving Fari in. Lorin
came limping after her, Garan not far behind. "Magic overuse isn't fun,
though, I don't recommend it."

"I take it my mother has been to see you?" Garan asked. "We got
our interrogations two days ago. The adults are thoroughly unimpressed with us."

"She just left. Don't worry, I blamed you for the whole thing." Lira
smirked at him. "Is Tarion still recovering well?"

"Much improved, but currently canoodling with the gorgeous

Princess Sesha." Fari sighed longingly. "So we thought we'd come look for you. Interested in a late breakfast, or early lunch?"

"I just ate, but I'll come sit with you," Lira said, falling into step with Fari as they followed the boys down the hall and ignoring the girl's start of surprise at Lira's friendliness. "She *is* stunning, isn't she?"

"Heartbreakingly so." Fari shrugged. "Tarion is one lucky man."

"Maybe." Lira frowned.

"Not maybe. She's clearly as besotted with him as he is with her."

"She's going to be queen one day," Lira pointed out. "You think Tarion wants to be a king?"

"Well..." Fari hesitated. "I'm sure he'll get used to it."

Lira wasn't so sure.

Garan winked. "You know, if you're interested in a title, Lira, as one of the more handsome heirs of the Alistriem court, I'd be happy to—"

He was cut off by Fari's burst of amused laughter. Lorin looked confused.

"I hate to break your heart, but Lira's with Ahrin, Mister Handsome Lordling," Fari managed between chuckles.

Garan momentarily looked confused, then indignation rippled across his face. "Is *that* why Vensis turned me down?"

"Lira isn't *with* anyone!" Lira said firmly before the teasing could continue. "Including you, Mister Handsome Lordling."

"Sure." Fari was still giggling. "That's why I walked in on you both wrapped all around each other before we left Temari."

Lorin shot a thoughtful glance Lira's way. She ignored it and scowled at Fari instead. "I thought we agreed we weren't talking about that?"

"All these secrets you keep, Lira," Garan said good-naturedly. "You continue to unfold like a flower."

"I'll shove a flower into uncomfortable places if you don't stop."

Everyone laughed.

They were almost at the end of the hall when a handsome soldier about Caverlock's age, wearing the same blue uniform and jaunty blue hat Lira had been seeing everywhere, strode around the corner. A warm smile creased his face. "Just who I was looking for."

"Lord-General." Garan straightened, looking pleased to see this man.

"I've told you, lad, call me Casta." His smile moved from Garan to include the others. "His Grace would like to see you all. I've come to escort you."

Fari, Lorin, and Lira promptly nodded, not sure what else to say to a request from the king of Rionn. Garan grinned in amusement, murmuring as they started walking, "Casta leads the Bluecoats— Rionn's elite cavalry unit responsible for the king's protection. Uncle Dash used to be a Bluecoat; he and Casta were in the same unit when they were our age."

They were led through several beautifully appointed hallways and into a wing guarded by more Bluecoats. Casta eventually came to a stop outside a non-descript door. The two Bluecoats guarding it saluted him sharply then opened the door.

"I'll leave you to it." Casta smiled at them again, then strode away.

Lira trailed in last, wariness taking over, preparing herself for how this meeting might go.

Cayr Llancarvan, king of Rionn, was leaning by the window, sipping at a cup of something, gaze distant. He turned instantly at their entry though, handsome face spreading into a smile almost as warm as Casta's. "I hope I didn't interrupt your breakfast. This time of day is usually the only spare moment I have."

"Not at all, Your Grace." Fari managed this for all of them, her Zandian confidence asserting itself.

Garan bowed his head. "It's good to see you, Your Grace."

"Garan." Cayr's smile widened. "Please, take a seat, all of you."

They were just perching gingerly on the edge of a comfortable sofa when a side door opened and a woman entered the room. She was tall, graceful, with long golden hair. Although she wore a stunning dress, the magnificent Taliath sword at her hip instantly marked her as Jenna Casovar, queen of Rionn. All apart from Garan immediately leapt back to their feet. Lira stared.

"Cayr, you can't—" The woman stopped at the sight of the rest of them, eyes narrowing slightly. "Apologies. I didn't realise you had visitors."

"What can't I do now?" Cayr lifted an eyebrow at his wife.

"Concede to Lord Mariom's insistence on cutting the tariffs at Port Rantarin by five percent. You know if you give in on that, he'll only ask for more."

"Then let him," Cayr said mildly. "He won't get it."

"The other northern lords will be thoroughly unhappy with you."

"When are they not?"

Jenna huffed a breath, gaze switching to the apprentices, then stilling on Lira. "Lira Astor, I take it."

"That's me," Lira said.

"You look just like him."

Her mouth thinned. "So I'm told."

A sharp elbow to her ribs from Garan followed, and Lira supposed she should be adding honourifics to her words when addressing the queen. "Your Highness," she added, with an edge.

Jenna smiled coolly. "Interesting. You sound just like him too." Two graceful steps brought the woman closer. She was taller than Lira, looming over her. For a long moment silence filled the room as the queen of Rionn studied Lira's face and Lira refused to look away. Eventually Jenna murmured, "Something tells me you'd give your grandfather a stern challenge."

"Stop intimidating Apprentice Astor, dearest," Cayr eventually said with a little sigh, as if this was something he had to say often.

Jenna smiled slightly. "Oh, she's not intimidated."

Lira matched her smile. She wasn't.

After a moment Jenna spun away, her gaze landing on her husband. "I hope Egalion knows what she's doing with this one." And then she was gone, striding from the room.

The king shot her an apologetic look. "You are very welcome here, Lira. My wife tends to be overly protective."

"It's fine." Lira shrugged. "Can we sit now, Your Grace?"

Garan made a choking sound at her side, but Cayr merely smiled. "No, I've taken up enough of your morning. I really just wanted to meet you all, and thank you for your efforts during the battle at Dark-Skull. Many people I love dearly were there that night."

This was far better than Dawn's chastising, so Lira's smile was genuine this time. "It was an honour to meet you, Your Grace. I appreciate your hospitality in allowing us to stay here."

"As do Lorin and I," Fari said gracefully. "You have a beautiful home."

"I hope to meet you again one day." Cayr straightened from where he stood and glanced at one of the guards by the door, a clear dismissal.

Lira trailed out after the others, finding herself thinking well of the king of Rionn. He might be the only person she'd met in Alistriem so far she'd like to spend more time with.

His wife was another matter. She would be a dangerous adversary. A little thrill shivered inside her at the thought.

Lira's sleep was restless that night. Her thoughts were too busy for her to relax enough to sleep. Part of her was caught up in juggling the many competing interests she had to manage. The rest of her felt unsettlingly adrift in a way she never had been before, and she didn't know what to do with that.

She needed to get back to Karonan, so she'd have something to do. Something to distract herself with. All this sitting around in Alistriem was only causing more and more frustration.

Eventually giving up on sleep, she tossed off the covers and crossed to the door leading out into the garden all their rooms shared. A night breeze stirred the trees, and the air was filled with the scent of flowers. Even at night she felt a hint of the warmth of spring approaching. As soon as she stepped outside, some of the stiffness in her shoulders relaxed and she took a deep breath.

"Can't sleep either?"

Startled, she turned towards the sound of the disembodied voice. "Tarion?"

He sat on a bench outside the door to his room, a blanket over his legs. He waved an invitation to join him, so she went over and settled cross-legged onto the bench. "Do you know that your parents were sitting in the hallway outside your room last night?"

"I'm not surprised." He looked at his hands. "They're really worried."

"And not just about you."

He nodded. Hesitated. "They think... everyone does... that after I was hurt you managed to kill the mage on that roof, and his loss of control was what reduced all the razak in the area to ashes. Either that or our hive theory is correct and one of the creatures on the roof with us was the queen, and you managed to kill her."

She froze. Dawn hadn't given anything away when asking Lira about what had happened on the roof, and it had been nagging at Lira ever since—whether she'd managed to successfully fool the woman or not. She hadn't asked Garan and the others either, not wanting to risk them asking questions she couldn't answer. "Is that what you told them?" she asked carefully.

He nodded. "It's the only thing that makes sense, right?"

Lira swallowed. "Are you asking me if I have another explanation?"

"No." He turned to her, smiling a little. "I know that wasn't what happened. I'd really like to know what *did* happen, but if you don't want to tell me, that's okay too."

She opened her mouth to respond, but nothing came out. To tell him the truth... that her magic had destroyed everything on that roof even though the razak were supposed to be immune to magic... She liked Tarion. Felt comfortable around him. Trusted him even. But trusting him with *this*? She wanted to, but some deep intractable part of her froze at the idea, unable to contemplate it. Too long had she been unable to trust. She couldn't get past that block now. She didn't know how.

"Maybe one day," she said. And by admitting that he was right, that she *did* know what happened, instead of making up a lie, she *was* trusting him. Even if she couldn't tell him the full truth.

"Okay." He accepted that without complaint.

"You lied to your parents, Tarion."

He looked away, guilt rippling across his face. "I hate that I did it. But... I know what they'd all think, if I told them you took out all those razak and the mage by yourself and you didn't use telekinesis to do it."

"So what?" she said coldly, annoyed by his attempt to protect her, despite the fact she'd worried about the exact same thing. "Don't feel like you have to keep protecting me. I don't need it and I don't want it. I can look after myself."

"I know, but it's not just that." He took a breath. "Whatever is going on, it's bad. My mother is worried and so is the council. If you're sidelined because they don't trust you, then that's one less weapon in our arsenal. I have a feeling we're going to need all the weapons we can get against Underground."

"I'm slightly mollified by that recovery." She couldn't help but smile, shoulders relaxing as she settled into the seat.

"Phew." He grinned.

She sobered. "You're still being foolish. You shouldn't trust me, Tarion, and not because I'm Shakar's granddaughter, but because I'm not like you. I won't stand on a precipice for your beloved mages or Taliath. You're smart enough to have figured that out by now." Despite herself, she wanted to be honest with him.

"Yet you came after me onto the roof."

"That wasn't because I felt undying loyalty for the mages and Taliath being attacked," she said softly. *I did it for you.* The words went unsaid, but he heard them anyway.

"I know," he said simply, then leaned closer, bumping their shoulders.

She huffed a breath and dismissed the topic. He'd learn eventually. Her thoughts returned to overhearing his parents the night before, and her words spilled out before she realised what she was doing. "They're looking for my father."

"What?" Surprise filled his voice.

"Last night, I heard your parents talking. Apparently Master A'ndreas thinks he might be linked to Underground, that they could use him to get to the group."

Tarion was silent a moment, then, "What do you know about him?"

"Just what my mother told me, that he hadn't wanted a child. She fell pregnant when she was living in Karonan, so when he abandoned her, she went home to have me."

"Do you think he abandoned you both because he knew who your mother was and was afraid of the consequences?"

"It's possible." Lira shrugged. "I was too young when she died to remember clearly, but I've always had the impression he never knew. One thing that has always stuck with me was how secretive she was about our identities. I think that's why she went home to have me, even though the villagers didn't want her. They knew. And so it was a kind of protection."

"That must have been awful for her." Tarion touched her hand in sympathy.

Lira shook her head, growing too uncomfortable with the topic to keep talking. She cleared her throat and changed the subject, shifting away from him slightly. "Garan said earlier we'd be leaving in a couple of days. Any idea how long the trip back takes?"

As nice as Alistriem was, she was growing desperate to return. To Greyson and Underground... especially after what had happened at DarkSkull Hall. She wondered if they'd heard about it yet. Probably not if Dawn was right that all the razak and mages there were now dead. It would take them a while to realise something was wrong, and then send someone to DarkSkull to investigate.

And Tarion was right. Underground had just attacked the Mage Council. They were growing stronger and bolder, and it made Lira deeply uneasy that she still didn't have a greater understanding of their plans.

"A week or so, I think. It's nice being here though." His head fell back to rest against the stone wall behind them, eyes closing. "Less pressure."

"What are you going to do after your trials?" she asked. "Come back here and marry your princess? Doesn't being queen-consort bring with it all the attention and pressure that you hate?"

A silence fell, and she realised she'd hit a nerve. She didn't retract the question though—if he truly loved Sesha, he would have considered this already. She wasn't sure why she was curious about it, but she was.

When he eventually spoke, it was an attempt to deflect. "Why, what are you planning to do after the trials?"

"I asked first." A smile flickered at her mouth.

There was another long silence, long enough she wasn't sure he was going to answer. But then he said in a quiet voice, edged with pain, "I don't know."

"Being queen-consort won't allow you to hide from the spotlight." She spoke gently, not aiming to wound. Tarion was so different from her, in some incomprehensible ways, and she found herself wanting to understand why.

He looked away. "I know that. But the thought of her marrying someone else, of living my life without her? That's worse than anything I could imagine. We keep saying to each other that there'll be a solution, that we'll figure something out, but..." He trailed off, breath hitching. "Neither of us has yet."

"You know, I don't mind attention at all. I'd be happy to take her off your hands and marry her myself," Lira teased, trying to lighten his mood. "It wouldn't be a sacrifice at all."

He chuckled. "I think Ahrin might have something to say about that."

"Ahrin has no claim over me." Lira waved that off. "Okay, put Sesha aside for the moment. You want to be a Taliath, right?"

Startled, he sat up straighter, hazel eyes flicking to her. "What?"

"I've seen you fight. You love the dance of swordplay, battle, strategy, that's what brings you alive. It's what you're best at." She shrugged. "You don't want to be a warrior mage."

"It wouldn't matter even if that were true. It's impossible." He shook his head. "Anyway, there's not much difference between the two."

"Yes there is. At least, there is in the ways that matter to you. Why is it impossible?"

"Did you forget that massive book we had to study for initiate exams already? I'm not a Taliath, I'm a mage with a single ability." Annoyance edged his voice. He didn't like having to say this aloud.

She scoffed at that. "I've seen you fight. You'd best any of the Taliath students I've watched at Temari Hall."

"You really mean that?" Surprised hope filled his voice.

She frowned. "Surely someone has already told you that? Your father at least. Isn't he the one that taught you?"

"No." He settled back against the bench seat. "They haven't. Your turn. What do you want to do?"

"I'll be a warrior mage, of course," she said promptly. It was the expected and standard answer. The only answer that would get her where she wanted, *needed*, to go.

"I don't believe you," he said mildly.

"Oh really? So what do you think I want to be?"

"I think you want to throw everyone's fear and prejudice back in their faces. I think you want to make them forget the name Shakar and remember yours instead."

The silence that fell was too long. It told him how accurate he was, how deeply unsettled she was that he'd guessed so accurately. Even so, she managed a laugh, tried to brush off his comments. "That's deep, Tarion."

He turned towards her, expression earnest. "Good, bad, or somewhere in between, you are your own person, Lira. And I happen to like that person. You're going to be great, just like you want, and you're going to do it by being the opposite of Shakar."

The pressure that always weighed in her chest tightened to an almost unbearable constriction. Tarion's assumptions, his belief that she was good, they were wrong. And even if she wanted them to be right, living up to those expectations was an unbearably heavy weight to carry. She simply wasn't that person. She had to *pretend* to be that person, and she was beginning to hate the pretending. She looked away, managed a dry, "Even when I'm being horrible to all of you?"

He smiled. "Even then."

"You wouldn't like me," she murmured. "Not if you really knew me."

He held her gaze. "I doubt that. Let me ask you something. Making them forget your grandfather, seeing you instead, what does that look like to you?"

"A seat on the council. Mages looking at me and thinking my name first, not his. My victories spoken about, not his darkness." Again, the words came quickly, the mantra well-rehearsed.

"And are those things what you really want? Wrangling mages, signing a lot of papers, living in Carhall with the pureblood mages you hate?"

"I—"

"Pretend you weren't Shakar's granddaughter. What do you, Lira, want for your life? What do you want to be?" he asked.

She had no answer for him. She didn't even know where to begin with answering that question. Her entire life had been driven and shaped by her name, by the circumstances of her life after her mother's death. There'd been no room for *wanting* anything. Only for making it to the next day. And then, making it so she could throw off the yoke of her name.

But after she'd done that... only blankness yawned. She didn't know what came next.

"I like signing things," she said glibly, then stood up. "You should get some rest, you're still healing. I'll see you tomorrow."

"Night, Lira." His soft farewell followed her all the way back to her room.

CHAPTER 24

T wo days later, an update came by way of a telepathic message to Dawn A'ndreas. The lord-mage came in person to tell them the news, finding them all together as they ate breakfast.

"There's no trace of Athira, I'm afraid." Dawn looked tired. "A thorough search of the hills and villages around DarkSkull Hall hasn't turned up any sign of whoever left the trail of blood you identified, Fari. It seems Athira—if it was her—was likely recaptured."

There was a brief silence as they processed this. None of them spoke aloud the other possibility, that—like Haler—Athira had been killed at some point during their captivity. It was on the tip of Lira's tongue to point it out, but at the look on all their faces, she refrained.

"Was there anything else, Mama? Anything found that could help you find and destroy Underground?" Garan asked.

"I'm afraid not. We'll keep searching, though." She rose from the table, squeezing her son's shoulder. "I'm sorry, I have a meeting with Cayr, but I'll see you all later."

Lira remained silent once Dawn was gone, letting the others' chatter wash over her. Her conversation with Tarion two nights earlier, not to mention having too much time alone with her thoughts while she waited to return to Temari, left her unsettled and restless.

If they all thought the way Tarion did, that Lira was fundamentally good, then that was perfect, because it meant she'd achieved Underground's mission. Their spies would report their new closeness and that would win Lira greater trust with Lucinda. It meant Lira was succeeding in what she'd set out to do.

But at the same time... it was growing increasingly uncomfortable to see it in their faces, in the way they treated her like one of them. How would they react if they knew she was lying to them? That not only was she a spy, but she'd *allowed* Underground to experiment on her, that she had more offensive magic that she was hiding from them?

Annoyance surged. She was getting too close to them, and it was interfering with her focus. Her goals. But at the same time... she wanted that closeness. She liked them. It was damnably frustrating!

"Lira?" Fari's sharp nudge brought her abruptly out of her thoughts.

"Sorry, what?"

Garan chuckled. "What were you thinking about just now? You looked completely absorbed."

"Nothing." She shook her head. "What did you want?"

Fari sighed. "Lorin was just complaining for the sixteenth time about how they're not letting us send any messages back home. I thought you might provide a change of subject."

"My family will be worried about me," Lorin muttered.

Tarion tried to reassure him. "I'm sure they'd choose your safety over getting a letter from you."

"How about some more practice?" Garan suggested when that seemed to have no effect on Lorin's dark mood. "I think I can beat Lira today."

"Ha!" A genuine smile crossed her face. "You're dreaming."

He crossed his arms over his chest. "Let's see, shall we?"

"You're on, Egalion!"

A FEW HOURS LATER, they were still all gathered in the garden outside their rooms. It was a gorgeous spring day—the sun warm without the oppressive edge of summer—and the sky a cloudless cobalt blue above. Snatches of crisp orders and the marching feet of Bluecoats at drill somewhere nearby drifted on the faint breeze. Occasionally, the sound of horses' hooves clopping on cobblestone sounded from the other side of the garden wall, where the palace stables sat. They'd all laughed when a loud, indignant whinny had rung through the morning right at the same moment Garan had lost his first practice battle with Lira.

As midday approached, they were on their fourth such duel, seated facing each other, gazes firmly locked. Garan leaned slightly forward, shoulders tense, face tight with concentration. Lira lounged comfortably in her chair, an unconscious smile tugging at her mouth as magic warmed her blood.

In the air around and above them, twenty soft balls darted in all directions, an equal mix of green and yellow. Lira's left hand rested on her leg, her index finger tapping slightly as she used telekinesis to send her green balls zooming about, her aim to catch one of the yellow balls being manipulated by Garan.

Lorin and Fari stood off to the side, one grinning and cheering, the other a study of fascinated concentration, while Tarion reclined on an armchair that had been carried out for him. He wore a little smile too.

Garan stiffened slightly as one of his yellow balls darted to the ground just in time to avoid being touched by one of Lira's. But she'd only been feinting, and quickly sent three green balls diving after another yellow one. Garan's magic flared as he fought desperately to respond in time.

A few tension-filled moments later and he was settled again, this time gathering the green balls closer together before sending them exploding outwards in a spinning circle. Showy, but not overly complex.

Lira shrugged. She'd been taking it easy so far, but it was time to end this.

Fari whooped with excitement as Lira sent her green balls after Garan's yellow ones with far more precision. Her timing and control, the subtlety with which she'd trained herself to wield her telekinesis, was exquisite.

In seconds one of her green balls collided with Garan's yellow. And then every yellow ball was hit, one by one by one, until all of them were on the ground. Lira's green balls flew in the air above, weaving and ducking as she made them dance in victory. Letting out a breath, Garan sat back in his chair and conceded with a smile.

She grinned back. Then waved her left hand and brought all the green balls settling gracefully to the grass.

Fari, Lorin, and Tarion burst into applause. Garan's smile widened. "I think I lasted a whole minute longer that time. That's improvement, right?"

"At least a minute, if not longer." Fari chuckled. "I reckon another year or two of practice and you could even go ten minutes against Spider."

"Mama!" Tarion's surprised greeting had them all turning toward the door from his room. Alyx Egalion stood there, her face set in an expression of puzzled recognition and surprise as she looked at Lira. Had she been watching the duel?

When everyone turned to stare at her, the strange expression dropped from Egalion's face, and she gave Lira an approving look. "That was an entertaining duel. Your control over your telekinesis is beyond impressive, Lira. I've rarely seen such skill."

Despite herself, Lira was warmed by Egalion's praise. "Thank you, Councillor."

"Garan, you're a little sloppy." A smile tugged at Alyx's mouth. "You need to work on your focus. It's not just about sheer power."

"I know, Aunt Alyx." He sighed. "But I am getting better."

"He is," Lira said. "We've been practising every day."

Garan gave her a surprised smile.

"Good." Alyx's gaze lingered on the balls that had fallen to the ground, her gaze distant, sad almost. To Lira, it looked like she was lost in an old memory.

"Is there something wrong, Mama?" Tarion asked.

"No, not at all." The expression on her face cleared. "I was on my way to join Cayr and Jenna for lunch, and I thought I'd invite you since I'm sure Sesha will be there as well."

His face brightened, and he rose gingerly. Alyx came to help him and the two made their slow way out of the garden.

Fari sighed. "I guess we're on our own for lunch then."

"Why don't you all come home with me?" Garan asked, looking uncharacteristically shy. "I'd love to show you the Egalion estate, and I know my parents would enjoy seeing you all. That's if Da's not busy at the palace, of course."

"I appreciate the invitation, but I think I'll leave you to it," Lira said, feeling no inclination to face Garan's mother and her powerful telepathic talent again anytime soon. "I'd like to get some more practice in."

"Will you at least join us for dinner here this evening, Lira?" Fari asked as they headed off.

"I will," she promised.

Once they were gone, Lira settled in her chair, tipped her head back and let the sun warm her face and the music of birdsong soothe all her worries momentarily. Time alone in this quiet garden to practice until all the confusing thoughts disappeared from her mind—

What a wonderful prospect.

LATER THAT NIGHT, Lira woke suddenly.

Her instincts warning her that something was amiss before she heard enough to rouse her, she rolled silently from the bed, dropped to a crouch and called her staff to her hand.

Then she stilled.

Nothing loomed out of the dark and it took only a few seconds to register that whatever had woken her, it wasn't inside her room. Rising to her feet, she dressed quickly and laced up her boots, making sure to do it quietly. Her senses strained the entire time, but there was no sound or movement in the night air to tell her what had triggered her unease.

The wood of her staff warming to her touch, she padded over to the door and cracked it open just enough to be able to see through. A glance in both directions along the dim hallway outside showed nothing obviously wrong. She watched for several long moments, but nothing moved in the shadows, and the calm quality of the silence indicated that whatever had tripped her instincts, it wasn't coming from that direction.

Lira closed her door, then crossed to slip out the garden door, closing it softly behind her before going still so she could breathe in the night. A glance to her left revealed Tarion's room dark, the door closed. The next one along—Fari's room—was equally dark. The bench outside Tarion's room was empty.

A slight breeze stirred the trees lining the walls of the garden. There was nothing obviously out of place, no...

A short, cut-off cry broke like a crash against her attuned senses.

It had come from beyond the garden wall.

Lira began moving the instant she heard it, even though complete silence followed and there were no further sounds. A burst of tele-kinetic magic bolstered her jump enough that her fingers could grip the top of the wall. Quietly as she could, she hauled herself up to lie flat and still on top of it.

The palace stables lay spread out on the other side of a pebbled path that followed the base of the wall. Her gaze roved over three long barns in a row with a circular exercise yard between each one. A fenced grazing field sat across from the barn furthest to Lira's right. She could only make out half of the field from where she lay—tall trees bounding the eastern side of the yard cast most of it into shadow.

The area appeared deserted, quiet, undisturbed. No guards were visible patrolling. Whatever Lira had heard, it didn't appear as if anyone else had. That didn't surprise her. Few possessed the instincts she'd learned as a child. Few needed to.

Lira's gaze returned to the field. She was no expert on horses, but the handful that had been left out overnight had moved to the far end of the field, and they seemed restless, heads tossing, moving rather than grazing or sleeping.

Something had disturbed them.

Lira slipped down the other side of the wall, landing in a crouch and drawing her staff again. She kept to the cover of the wall as she circled the field, heading for the area draped in darkness by the trees. Once she reached the fence, she paused until her eyes adjusted to the lack of light.

Still no evidence of anything untoward. But the horses continued to move restlessly, gathered in a tight bunch. Lira took a focused breath, sank into the familiarity of the night, let it settle over her shoulders like a well-worn cloak.

Then she slipped under the fence railing and headed deeper into the shadows. She'd barely taken four steps when her roving gaze spotted the dark shape on the ground in the far corner of the field.

She stilled instantly, gaze up and scanning for any adversary that might be lying in wait, magic rising through her veins, ready to deploy.

Nothing moved, so she warily approached the dark mass. It was a horse, lying on the grass near where trees clustered right up to the fence. Even in the dim light it was obvious the animal had been eviscerated, its warm blood still steaming as it ran in rivulets into a growing pool underneath the corpse. The rich scent of blood, mixed with the nauseating smell of torn intestines, filled her nostrils. She quickly switched to breathing through her mouth.

Not making the mistake of lingering too long on the body, Lira's gaze cleared the area again before she moved even closer, crouching to study the corpse more closely, hoping some other cause of death would reveal itself. But seeing it up close only confirmed her worst fears. The body been torn up, just like the guard dog she'd seen at Temari. Long, tearing gashes to the body and obvious violence in the kill.

Lira bit her lip, trying to come up with an explanation that wasn't what she was afraid of. They were a long way from Temari, and it was possible a wolf from the rugged hills just north of Alistriem had somehow gotten inside the palace walls.

But deep down, she knew that wasn't it.

Whatever or whoever had been killing animals at Temari Hall had followed them here. Her key question was why the perpetrator hadn't graduated to killing humans yet. It was clearly capable, if the attack on Neria was any indication. Part of her realised she might know the answer to that too. It didn't make her feel any better.

A faint rustle in the trees had her head snapping up, gaze staring into the darkness in the direction of the sound. If the attacker was still nearby, she should go and rouse the guards, bring help so they could

catch and kill it. But if what she was beginning to suspect was right...
that would be the worst thing she could do.

No, she'd have to handle this herself.

Lira stood and headed towards the fence railing, vaulting over it
and moving stealthily into the shadows between the trees.

She hadn't gotten far before a soft but blood-curdling snarl rippled
through the night. Lira honed in on it, taking several steps before
emerging into a small, moonlit clearing.

"Rotted carcasses," she gasped out, eyes growing wide at what she
saw ahead of her. She hefted her staff without thinking, magic surging
strongly enough that the violet light around her hands glowed bright
before she could stifle it.

The thing that had killed the horses was human-shaped, but that
was where the similarities to a person stopped. Burnt-copper eyes
flashed with a wildness that was chaotic, untamed, lacking any rational
thought. Overlapping dark scales covered the skin of its face and
hands, where long, curved claws stretched instead of fingers.

That was about all Lira was able to take in before the thing lunged.
It came at her so swiftly she was barely able to duck aside in time, her
staff sweeping out and missing it completely. She staggered away,
summoning and loosing her telekinesis magic in an effort to hold it at
bay while she regained her balance. But the magic passed uselessly
around the thing, just like when she tried to use it on the razak.

She thought about using her flame magic. But if she did that, and
she was right about what this creature was.... Damn it. Her hesitation
cost her. The creature let out a low growl, the sound edged with anger
and hate. It came at her, too-fast, a swipe of claws almost taking out
her face and ripping the sleeve of her shirt to shreds instead. Hot lines
of pain opened up on her right bicep and she swore.

Trying to gain the advantage, Lira leapt straight at it, unable to
think of anything else—it was too fast to engage in a conventional
fight—and raked her fingers at its face, aiming for its eyes. Her nails
scratched painfully over hard scales before hitting the eye she'd been
aiming for.

The creature snarled in pain and reared away from her, then turned
and ran.

Lira sprinted after it as fast as she could, ignoring the blood soaking the sleeve of her shirt and the pain in her arm, following the sounds of rustling through the trees, knowing there wasn't much distance before the thing would run into open spaces and the buildings of the palace where Bluecoats on guard would see it. She had to stop it before then.

In the end she didn't have to.

She burst out of the trees, recklessly fast given how violent this thing was, into another clearing and slid to a halt. The creature was slumped against the trunk of a tree, shivering, arms wrapped around its middle.

And it wasn't a thing anymore. Her heart dropped in her chest. She'd so desperately hoped to be wrong.

"Tarion?" she asked softly, holstering her staff as she moved closer to him.

He looked up, blinking, clearly confused. He wore only breeches. His right eye looked bruised and reddened in the moonlight, but the copper glow had vanished from his irises. His healing wound was a scabbed red line across his stomach and chest. "Lira?"

"It's me." She crouched before him. His skin had returned to its Shiven paleness, no scales to be seen. "Do you know what just happened?"

"I..." He looked wildly around, close to panic. "How did I get here?" He lifted a trembling hand to his face. "Why does my eye hurt so much?"

He was too unsettled to be pretending. Lira reached out to touch his shoulder, trying to keep her voice gentle, though that wasn't a skill of hers. "How about we get you back to your room, and we can talk there?"

He shook his head, almost conceding, but then his gaze fell on the blood-soaked sleeve of her shirt. "No. What happened? Why are you bleeding? Tell me, Lira."

"Well..." She held his gaze. "You killed a horse, then tried to kill me. A rather eventful night, all in all."

Her attempt at levity fell flat. He looked at her in horror. "What are you talking about?"

She sighed, then settled more comfortably on the ground. The throbbing in her arm was getting worse, but she tried to ignore it; she was fairly certain the wounds weren't too deep. "I'm not sure, actually. But I think you're the one who's been killing the guard dogs, and the cats, and tonight, a horse."

"That's impossible. Why would I...." He stared at his hands. They were clean. That was an interesting detail. "I don't remember doing it."

"Have you had any blackouts recently? Periods of time you can't remember?"

"No."

"Maybe it only happens when you're sleeping?"

Tarion's shivering worsened, and his eyes had gone glassy. "I don't understand what you're talking about."

Lira reached for him again. "Let's get you inside and warm. Come on. We can talk more there."

He swallowed, distress all over his face. "Lira, what's happening to me?"

"I think they did experiments on you at DarkSkull," she said gently. "And I think it changed you into something. But we will work it out, I promise you."

"You're saying they turned me into a monster?"

"No, I'm saying they changed you. We'll figure this out. You and me." She rose to her feet, offered him her hand. "Come on."

He took her hand and stood, swaying but eventually righting himself. "We have to tell my parents, the council. What if I hurt other—"

"I don't think you should tell anyone until we figure out what's going on," she disagreed firmly. "You haven't killed any people yet, and there has to be a reason for that. Let's just get you back to your room, warm you up, and we'll make a plan. Besides, I need you to clean up my arm before I bleed to death."

That seemed to galvanise him, and he took a shaky step. She managed to get them both over the wall in an effort to avoid the guards—Tarion didn't seem hurt in any way, just shaky with shock. Once they were in his room, she took charge, giving him crisp, steady instructions to clean her arm with the basin of water. Once the blood was wiped away, three shallow gashes were revealed; with stiches they probably wouldn't even leave a scar, but Lira had no intention of reporting this to anyone, so scars it would be.

His hands were steadier by the time he bound the cleaned wounds with strips from the un-ruined sleeve of her other arm. Once that was sorted, she told him to change, then settled him into the bed. He curled up under the covers, still shivering from shock.

"Get some rest," she told him, recognising he wasn't in any condition to have a rational conversation. "And we'll talk first thing in the morning. Don't do anything until then. Okay?"

He nodded.

She waited until his breathing evened out in sleep, then settled in a chair beside his bed to keep an eye out. If he turned into that thing again and tried to leave, she'd be there to stop him.

Her mind was too tangled to sleep, anyway. She'd told him she would help, and she'd meant it, but that was going to be a challenge. Tarion's parents would seek to protect him, but what he'd been turned into by Lucinda's experiments... people were going to fear it, and him. There would be limits to what his parents could do.

No, better it remained a secret until they figured out exactly what was going on.

As soon as Tarion woke in the morning, she'd convince him of that. Then they could figure out how to control the change, or stop it. Once they'd figured that out... once he knew what was happening to him and had mastered it... *then* they would tell everyone.

A shiver rippled unbidden through her as she watched his sleeping form.

Had the same thing been done to her?

CHAPTER 25

At some point close to dawn, Lira fell into a doze by Tarion's bed. When she woke, the sun was above the horizon, and Tarion was gone.

"Dammit!"

She leapt to her feet, swore as her stiffened arm protested with a stab of pain, then ran to the door. She yanked it open, only to almost run headlong into Garan.

"Whoah!" He scrambled out of her way. "What's the rush? Why were you in Tarion's—"

"Have you seen him this morning?" she snapped.

"No, I was coming to see if he wanted to... what's going on, Lira?" His voice lifted an octave. "Why is your arm bandaged and your shirt all torn and bloody?"

She ignored him, pushed past into the hall, and ran for the exit. Three steps away, she realised she had no idea where she was going, and turned back. "Do you know the way to his parents' quarters?"

He opened his mouth to question her, read the look on her face, then nodded. "Follow me."

Lira fell into step as he headed off with quick strides. Disappointment and worry filled her. It was too late, she knew that already, but even so, she wanted to try.

"Is Tarion okay?" Garan asked.

"I don't know. I think he might have done something very foolish."

Garan didn't ask any more questions, simply leading her through the palace on the most direct route to the rooms Egalion and Caverlock were staying in—not far down the hall from the king's suite. Garan's presence got them past every Bluecoat guard without protest.

Lira's heart sank the moment they rounded the corner into the hall. The space bristled with Bluecoats, and the mage healer in residence at the palace was just emerging from the door the guards were clustered around. Lira pushed through the Bluecoats, caught the door as it was swinging shut, and went inside before any of them realised what was happening. Garan followed close behind.

Alyx Egalion sat with Tarion on a plush lounge before an unlit fire. Caverlock was nowhere to be seen. Both mother and son looked drawn and weary. Tarion was the first to look up and see her. "I'm sorry, Lira, I had to tell them."

"Tell them what?" Garan asked, bewildered.

"You're a fool." She ignored Garan and responded to Tarion. "We could have taken the time to figure it out first."

"No." He shook his head firmly. "I trust my parents."

"And the rest of the council?" Lira's gaze shifted from Tarion to his mother, an unflinching stare. She was angry, furious at both mother and son, even though she wasn't entirely sure why. This was Tarion's problem, not hers. "This is a mistake. I could have helped you."

Egalion stood. "I appreciate that you wanted to try—"

Lira cut Egalion off. "You forget I know what it's like when the world thinks you're a monster. Now that everyone knows, how are you going to protect him?"

"Tarion doesn't need protecting from the Mage Council, Lira. Why would you even think that?"

Lira stared. "Don't tell me you really believe that's true?"

"Lira..." Garan tried awkwardly to intervene, but trailed off at the look on both their faces.

"This was my choice to make." Tarion rose to his feet now too, holding Lira's gaze. "Thank you for looking after me last night. For trying to protect me. I'll be safe, Lira."

Lira turned a challenging look on Egalion. "If that's true, tell me what you're going to do about this?"

The councillor's expression turned hard. "You're forgetting who *I* am, Lira. You have no business being here. Garan, you too, this is a private family matter. Leave us, please."

A moment's silence fell.

With a little shake of her head, Lira turned and left without another word. There was nothing she could do to help Tarion now.

Garan followed her out, matching her stride for stride. "Lira, if you don't tell me what's going on right now, I swear I—"

"Not here." She cut him off. "The others deserve to know too, and I don't want to say it more than once."

BACK IN GARAN'S ROOM, with the doors shut and windows closed, Lira relayed the events of the previous night and her assessment of what they meant. By the time she'd finished, Garan had turned Shiven-pale, Lorin grim, and Fari horrified.

"Are you sure it was...?" Fari mumbled.

"Certain. It was him." Lira nodded.

Fari looked between all of them, glance darting about as if searching for something reassuring to latch onto. "Is the same thing going to happen to us?" she asked.

"It's possible." Lira had thought of nothing else before eventually falling into a restless sleep by Tarion's bedside. "Neria and the dead animals at Temari might not have all been Tarion's work. It could have been one of us too. But I don't think so."

Garan ran an agitated hand through his hair. "Why not?"

Instinct. But they wouldn't believe that. "If more than one of us had been running around Temari ripping animals apart, there would have been too many corpses for the masters to successfully hide. Not to mention the odds that not one of us was seen? No, I'm fairly certain it's just him."

"'Fairly certain' isn't reassuring me. And even if you're right, it doesn't mean it won't happen to us," Fari pointed out.

"No." Lira let out a breath, more disturbed than she'd like to admit by that prospect. Lira welcomed more offensive magic, abilities that could make her more powerful, more likely to survive and win. But to be unconsciously and forcibly changed into a violent creature that didn't appear to be capable of rational thought... Terror shivered through her bones. The fear sparked more anger. Fury at Lucinda and Underground for their willingness to experiment on innocents without knowing what the effects would be. Risking lives and futures. And... if Lira was honest with herself, the anger had only become more personal.

She counted Tarion as a friend.

Fari let out a long sigh, then stood up. "You really should do something about that arm, Spider."

"It's fine, I—"

"Oh, let her look at it!" Garan snapped.

Lira stared, surprised more than anything else by his outburst. Her initial instinct was to snap back, but then she realised he was upset about Tarion, not angry at her. So she submitted with ill grace to Fari unwinding the makeshift bandages on her arm, then using Garan's basin of water to give the three gashes another good clean.

"You should really get those stitched up." Lorin peered at Fari's work, seemingly fascinated.

"No thanks."

Unexpectedly, Fari flashed her a smile. "I appreciate a good scar too."

A sharp knock came at the door before anything more could be said. It was Garan's father, his expression grim and forbidding. He was carrying a small leather bag which he passed to Fari before pointing at Lira's injured arm.

Garan shot to his feet. "Da. Is something wrong?"

"I see from your faces that Lira has informed you all," he said, gaze sweeping the room. "That's good. For what it's worth, I'm sorry this happened. Tarion will be looked after, you have my word."

"But?" Garan asked.

"The rest of you will be heading back to Karonan tomorrow. Alyx and I want Finn to look over you all and monitor you closely for signs of what happened to Tarion."

Fari pulled a small jar of ointment and fresh bandaging from the satchel. Lira's breath hissed as the ointment was applied—it stung like fireants—before settling into a cool sensation.

Garan shook his head. "I want to stay here, near Tarion. At least until we know if he's going to be all right."

Ladan reached out to settle a hand on his son's shoulder. "I'm afraid this is non-negotiable. You'll be able to write to Tarion, I promise, and you can come back to visit him when the school year ends in a couple of months."

Garan shrugged off his father's touch. "I—"

"Finn is the most accomplished healer in the mage order." Ladan's voice turned to iron. "I want him looking after all of you. Besides, with everything going on, it's imperative you continue to learn your magic. Temari is the best place for you right now."

"Then why isn't Tarion coming with us?" Lira asked as Fari finished bandaging her arm and stepped away. "If Master A'ndreas is the best healer you have, why isn't he looking at Tarion too?"

"It was considered, but Alyx needs to return to Carhall and she wants Tarion close. Besides, the scholars and healers at the council headquarters there will be able to figure out how to help him."

"And what does Tarion want?" Lira couldn't help but push.

Ladan's grim features softened as he looked at her, as if approving of her question. "He wants to be close to his family so they can help him deal with this."

Even Garan relaxed at that sincere response, though it made Lira uncomfortable because she didn't understand it. Still, she was satisfied that this was Tarion's choice, which meant there was nothing further she could do.

And *that* meant returning to Temari Hall and re-joining Underground was the best possible outcome. Not only might she be able to get some answers about what had happened to Tarion—and whether the same might happen to the rest of them—it was time to re-focus on her ultimate goal.

The Shadowcouncil's destruction.

And a seat on the Mage Council.

CHAPTER 26

They wound down the road into Port Rantarin as clouds scudded across the horizon and a stiff breeze whipped up, turning the grey ocean choppy. The city was a thriving harbour now that the war with Shivasa was over, and new buildings spread in all directions outward from the curving bay, where merchant and naval ships sat rocking at anchor.

The port belonged to Rionn now, what had once been called the disputed territory divided after the war in favour of its victor. It was one of many things the Shadowcouncil used to recruit more members to Underground.

Lira's horse tossed its head, and she tightened her grip on the reins in case it decided to play up, but her gaze remained on the distant city, thoughts dwelling in the past.

By the final years of the second war against Shakar, Shivasa had become a deeply divided society. The Darkmage had used the country as a base to build his mage army and in return he'd helped the Shiven in their war against Rionn. Once ready, he'd combined the two forces behind him in his invasion of Tregaya and the destruction of the old Mage Council.

He'd sought to rule everything.

The south of Shivasa had erupted into open rebellion as farmers and labourers protested the Shiven leader's alliance with Shakar and the effect war was having on their country. Tarion Astohar, the current Shiven leader, had led that rebellion, and those rebels now formed the core of his support base.

Yet two decades after Egalion had defeated Shakar, ending the war, Shivasa remained deeply divided. Too many remained who harboured the territorial ambitions of the previous leader... who still believed that had Shakar not made the critical mistake of pushing too far too fast and overstretching his forces, he would have eventually won the war. Lira was no strategist, but she'd studied every account she'd been able to find on her grandfather, and she thought those people had a point. These were the people who formed the Shadowcouncil.

But Lira was starting to wonder what they were truly after. The Mage Council—and Lira—had thought the group entirely Shiven. Born from lost hopes and those that believed her grandfather could lead the country to strength and power. She was beginning to think that was too simplistic a view.

The group's motives were more tangled than that—Underground was an uncomfortable mix of the Shadowcouncil's desire for mage supremacy and their recruits' resentment born from poverty and the lasting effects of a brutal war. It was like the Shadowcouncil were doing the same thing Astohar had during the war, stoking resentment against the Shiven leader for their poor living conditions in an attempt to start an open rebellion. But Lira was confident Lucinda didn't care two coppers for the poor of Shivasa.

On the surface, the theory that the Shadowcouncil's experiments were an attempt to build a mage army that could combat the Mage Council in power made perfect sense... but something about that pat answer niggled at Lira.

Where had they gotten the expertise to give people magic? It certainly didn't exist within the Mage Council. Even more importantly, where had the razak come from in the first place? There was no such recorded creature in council archives. Not to mention the flying creatures, related in some way to razak, that had attacked them that morning on the training courts. The monsters could both sense magic and were impervious to it. It was impossible that they could have existed on the continent for any length of time without the council knowing about it.

Underground's recent actions only added to Lira's puzzlement. They'd set up an elaborate ambush at DarkSkull, launching their first direct attack on council mages and Taliath. Why provoke the council before they were ready? Were they readier than Lira guessed? Or were the Shadowcouncil's goals something completely different to what they all assumed they were? Could they just be distracting the council's attention while—

"Can I ask you something?" Garan interrupted her musing. He'd brought his horse up beside hers. The usual cheerfulness in his demeanour was muted, and had been ever since he'd learned what happened to Tarion. Her chest tightened slightly at the thought of him, but she dismissed it. Feeling bad for Tarion wasn't going to help anyone.

She blinked to clear her thoughts. "Sure."

"How do you feel about Underground?"

She stared at him, wondering if he'd somehow guessed what she'd been thinking. "You mean, because they idolise my grandfather?"

"Well, yes, but not..." He considered his words. "You told us back in Weeping Stead that you're not one of us, not truly, that you feel no particular loyalty to the council. I guess it just makes me wonder what you *do* believe in."

She hesitated, but wanted to be honest with him. She was lying about so much else. "I don't believe in anything but myself. I've never really had the choice or opportunity to do otherwise."

He was silent a moment, then said, "Once you graduate, and you're given the choice of swearing loyalty to the council or the Shiven leader, what will you do?"

"Well I'm not Shiven, so I won't be swearing to Leader Astohar," she said lightly. "I've no idea who my father was, and my mother only ended up in northern Shivasa because of her ties to my grandfather's people, but neither of them were Shiven."

"Oh, of course." He blinked in surprise. "I suppose you'll have to swear to the council, then?"

"Yes, that's the plan." It would be the fastest way to achieve a seat on the council. "What about you?"

"That was never a choice," he said easily, as if that didn't bother him at all. "I'll be Lord Egalion after my father dies, so I'll be swearing to King Cayr, not the council."

"What do you think Tarion will do?"

Garan's face darkened. "You mean, once they figure out how to cure him?"

The assumption that Tarion needed fixing irritated Lira, even though she wasn't sure why, but she let it go, not wanting an argument. "He's got the best council minds looking after him, so yes."

"He's got a few tough choices ahead of him." Garan's frown deepened. "Sesha will be expected to marry well, and while Tarion is a Rionnan noble, the king will be looking for her marriage to strengthen Rionn's alliance with Zandia, Tregaya, or Shivasa. Not to mention being a queen-consort isn't exactly Tarion's goal in life."

She thought on that a moment, then said, "Why aren't you two close?"

He chuckled at the abrupt segue. "Since when is Spider curious about other people's relationships?"

"I'm not," she said defensively. "I just…" But she was, despite herself. She wanted to understand these apprentices she now called friends. "All right, fine. I *am* curious."

He beamed at her admission. "Tar and Caria lived mostly in Karonan growing up. Sesha travelled to Karonan quite a bit—King Cayr spent a lot of time with Uncle Dash and Leader Astohar helping them to rebuild after the war. And while the king was away from Alistriem, my parents administered Rionn in his place, so that meant I rarely left," Garan said. "Tar and I didn't see each other all that much until Temari Hall, and while I tried to get to know him better after he arrived, he didn't seem interested. Caria is the opposite—we're great friends. Temari became a lot less fun after she left."

Lira nodded. That made sense, especially now that she knew how shy Tarion was. "Garan?"

"Yes?"

"Thank you."

248

His eyes twinkled. "For which of my multiple gallant, chivalrous, or generous acts are you thanking me?"

She didn't smile. "For listening to me. In Weeping Stead. And thinking about it rather than dismissing it because you don't understand it."

His levity faded, and he opened his mouth to respond, but Fari's voice called out from behind them where she rode beside Lorin. "What are you both muttering about? You know I don't like missing out on gossip."

Garan threw his hands dramatically in the air. "Spider was demonstrating curiosity about her fellow students for the first time ever. Now you've gone and interrupted."

"Ooh, what was she asking?" Fari kicked her horse forward. "Do you want to know anything about me?"

Lira rolled her eyes, but played along. "You don't happen to get seasick, do you? That wind from the north is getting stronger. Could be a bumpy crossing tonight."

"We might be in more trouble than mere seasickness if our ship capsizes because of the sheer number of bodyguards we have," Lorin said gloomily, speaking for the first time that afternoon.

Lira made a face in shared annoyance. A full unit of Bluecoats along with twelve mage warriors and ten Taliath seemed overkill, even for the nephew of Alyx Egalion. Not to mention that rather than being allowed to leave via ship from Alistriem—a much quicker route home —they'd been snuck out of the city and sent via Port Rantarin so that nobody would know they were on their way back. Apparently the Egalion siblings hadn't wanted to open them up to the possibility of being attacked en-route.

Lira wasn't sure Underground spies were quite *that* good, but complaining wouldn't have gotten her anywhere so she hadn't bothered.

"Underground took us out of Temari Hall without anyone knowing and successfully ambushed a trained mage force," Garan said quietly. "We should be glad of the protection."

Lira's irritation deepened, but part of her acknowledged he was probably right.

· · ·

DUSK WAS FALLING as they boarded their ship, its female captain a brisk but cheerful sort who displayed no discomfort in the presence of so many mages and Taliath. The Bluecoats spread throughout the ship in protective formation while Lira and the others were shown to small cabins below deck.

"The winds are against us, but even so it should only be a day and a half journey across to Alanan, two at the most," the captain promised, referencing a busy port on Shivasa's east coast, northeast of Karonan. "You need anything, you let us know. Otherwise please stay out of our way. The crew need to pay attention in this gusty weather."

Lira dropped her bag on the narrow bunk, exchanged a glance with Fari who was sharing the cramped room with her, then immediately left to escape back up to the deck.

The wind grew stronger once they moved out of the shelter of the harbour and onto open ocean, but Lira relished its cool touch on her face as she stood at the port railing well away from where the crew needed to work.

Within a few days she'd be back at Temari Hall. She'd have to take the first opportunity she could to sneak out and go to the townhouse where Lucinda had been. If the woman wasn't there any longer, Lira would have to hope Greyson had left a message in the usual place to tell her where and when the next meeting would be.

Once again, she'd have to weave truth with lies, convince Lucinda she'd been safe in Alistriem all this time. A little spurt of excitement shivered through Lira at the idea of matching wits with that woman again. She wondered if Lucinda already knew about what had happened at DarkSkull—or whether she'd tell Lira even if she did. It would be a good test of how much Lucinda trusted her at this point.

Chances were high she didn't know yet, though. Lira and Caverlock's force had killed all the razak and Dasta, which meant until someone noticed the lack of contact from him, or went to DarkSkull to check, the news wouldn't get back to the Shadowcouncil for a while yet.

Lira would prepare to act shocked when the news did come

through. She would offer to try and learn more about what happened, further cementing her usefulness with the group. She and Caverlock could come up with something to tell them that would seem like good information without compromising the council. The excitement in her belly flared more strongly.

Lira wondered if Ahrin was still in Karonan. She hoped so. Though she told herself it was because recruiting Ahrin was still their best hope of bringing down Underground quickly, deep down Lira just wanted to see her again.

She hated that she did, hated that Ahrin was such a weakness in her armour. She needed to let go of the past. If she didn't, she'd end up compromising her mission. Dawn was already distrustful, and now Dashan would be watching her closely too as soon as he was back in the city. She couldn't afford to make any more mistakes.

She just wished she knew *how* to let go.

A FEW HOURS after departing port, the four of them ate together in the galley, which was above deck and lit by several gently swinging lanterns. Outside it was all darkness—the wind bringing thick clouds scudding across the sky as the sun had set earlier.

"How long do you think it's going to take to catch up on Master Tweller's class?" Garan asked gloomily. "I was already behind."

Fari snorted. "That's because you prioritise entertaining your girl-friend in the stacks over doing homework."

"That's... fair." Garan sighed.

"I don't expect any concessions from the masters. I'll just work harder," Lorin said in his usual dignified way.

"I can help, if you like? Passing your first-year exam is important, or you won't be able to stay on," Garan said. "Maybe we could all study together to catch up? I'm really good at Strategy class, but Lira is better than all of us in Shiven language."

She spiked him with a look. "If you're suggesting I'd waste my own catching up time helping all of you, you're sadly mistaken. I might be passable at Shiven, but I'm well behind on everything else and I need to work extra hard just to keep up."

"Ah, there's the Lira we all know and love." Fari beamed.

Chuckles around the table. Again, it made Lira feel off-balance, confused. She wasn't accustomed to good-natured teasing, wasn't completely certain it wasn't cruel teasing.

"What if we promise not to talk about anything *but* homework if you help us?" Garan asked, that charming smile on his face. "No gossip, no chatter, nothing but studies. And we'll help you too."

"I'll think about it," she allowed. Maybe catching up might be easier with their help. And if she didn't need to spend as much time on studying, it would give her more time to continue her work with Underground.

"Honestly, I don't know how you've done it, Spider," Fari said with a little shake of her head. "If I hadn't come to Temari with years of torturous lessons behind me I'd have failed in my first month. I can't imagine how many extra hours you must have put in just to stay afloat."

"It's a lot of hard work," Lorin said quietly.

Lira glanced at him, and they shared a little nod. Growing up on a farm, he probably hadn't had much education beyond learning to read and write Shiven either.

"No wonder you had no time for any of us," Garan agreed.

"I—"

Her words were cut off as the ship suddenly lurched violently to the side, coinciding with a gust of wind slamming open the galley door to send it crashing against the wall. Everyone reached out to stop plates and cups sliding to the floor. Lira's magic beat them all, holding everything frozen. Garan gave her an exasperated look—he'd been a second too slow—and she smirked.

"We must be sailing into that storm the captain warned us about." Fari looked gloomily out the window.

Garan stood up. "We should probably get below, out of everyone's way."

"Come knock on my door if you get seasick," Fari offered as they clambered below deck to the corridor holding their cabins. "I can help."

"Just don't do it loudly enough to wake me too," Lira grumbled. "We're sharing a cabin, remember."

Fari stopped suddenly in front of their door, almost causing Lira to run into her. "Can I ask the obvious question everyone has been ignoring since we first spoke about what happened to Tarion?"

"Absolutely," Garan said instantly, turning back from his door to give her his full attention.

"I know all the adults made comforting noises, and Master A'ndreas is a super smart and powerful healer, but how can we be sure the same thing won't happen to us?"

Unease churned in Lira's stomach—she'd been doing her best not to think about it. The thought of it happening to her... losing control, awareness, like that. It was horrific.

Lorin added quietly, "Why do you think they've sent so many guards with us? It's not just to keep us safe."

"You're right. But I think we can all agree, no matter how frustrating, that it's necessary," Garan said. "We have to hope that Uncle Finn will be able to come up with some answers for us. He's the smartest man I know, and I have faith that he will."

"Do you think Tarion is going to be okay?" Fari asked quietly, breaking the worried silence.

"He's got the best mage minds looking after him. It will just take time," Garan said confidently.

"And if it happens to us too?" Fari's eyes were bleak, no doubt imagining what her family would think.

"No matter what else happens, we won't abandon you, Fari," Garan said, clearly understanding her fear. "I promise. Leaving Tarion behind in Alistriem, with his mother and Sesha, isn't abandoning him. It was what he wanted."

"Even if it does happen to us too, then we can hope that by then the council would have figured out a solution to help Tarion," Lorin said. "It's not something we should worry about. Like Garan said, we keep an eye on each other, but that's the best we can do."

Fari waited until they were in their room before asking Lira, "It's been just on two months since they returned us. Do you think there could be more potential side effects that just haven't shown themselves yet?"

"You're the healer, you tell me." Lira dropped onto the narrow bunk. Ahrin had told her it could take several weeks, but both her new magic and Tarion's had broken out within five or so weeks. It seemed doubtful that more would be coming, but there was no way to know for certain.

"I have no idea. We don't even know what they did to us." Distress edged Fari's words.

"Lorin was right," Lira said, trying to be reassuring but not really knowing how. "It's outside of our control, and needless worrying won't help."

Fari snorted. "Sure. I'll just tell my thoughts to stop worrying. Problem solved."

"Garan was right too," Lira said quietly. "He won't abandon any of us."

A moment's silence fell, then Fari said, "You tried to stop Tarion telling anyone. You tried to protect him."

"Yes."

"Would you do the same for me?"

Lira didn't even pretend to hesitate. "Yes."

"Same here."

Warmth blossomed in her chest at the sincerity in Fari's voice.

Lira believed her.

CHAPTER 27

The docks at Alanan were crowded as their captain carefully tacked her way into the harbour. From where they stood on deck, Lira and the others listened to the crew speculating that the storm of the night before may have meant some crews had waited the bad weather out in the harbour rather than departing on schedule and risking their ships.

It was a grey morning, thick cloud hanging low over the city—promising more rain if not another storm—and flat farmland beyond it. It felt so similar to Dirinan with its ramshackle docks, the smell of salt and seaweed on the breeze, and the musical creak of ships rocking at anchor.

The longing in Lira's chest was sudden and fierce for how much she missed that life. Her hands curled on the railing, white knuckled. It didn't matter how many times she told herself it hadn't been real. That it had been false contentment. That she couldn't count on it or hope for it ever to return. She yearned for it anyway.

And now they were growing closer to Temari. Lira's excitement over re-joining Underground was quickly being overshadowed by the fact that returning to the school meant tedious lessons and a routine that bored her silly. It was getting harder and harder to force herself back into that box of what the council wanted.

The warrior in charge of their protection detail, Restan once again, organised them all onto the ship's boats as soon as the anchor dropped. After a short row across choppy ocean, they were clambering onto one of the numerous jetties.

There weren't as many workers on the docks as Lira expected given the number of ships at anchor, and though she'd never been to Alanan before, the chaotic hive of activity that she'd seen every day on the Dirinan harbour was oddly absent here. No street vendors shouted their wares. No overladen merchant carts trundled along the cobblestones at the top of the jetties.

Lira's shoulders began to stiffen as they left the harbour and headed into streets just as quiet as the docks had been. Her instincts roused. Something was off.

Restan noticed it too, exchanging a wary look with the lieutenant in charge of the Bluecoats. He stopped at the first inn they came to, a single block away from the harbour, shepherding them all inside and telling them to stay put while he disappeared with the Bluecoat lieutenant. Lira thought about protesting, looked at Garan, who stayed quiet, then rolled her eyes and said nothing.

Garan led them over to a table, rather imperiously told the remaining Bluecoats and mage warriors to give them space, then ordered cider and food from the waiter that came over. The man looked delighted at the influx of customers.

"Raise your hands if you think Warrior Restan is being just a tad overprotective." Fari sighed, scowling at the closest Bluecoat keeping an eye on them.

"Ridiculously so." Garan rolled his eyes

"Not at all," Lira said.

They both spoke at the same time, then scowled at each other.

Fari glanced between them. "No offence, but I'll take Lira's view on this one. What do you think is going on, Spider?"

"Couldn't say. But the harbour was far too quiet for the number of ships at anchor. Not to mention the streets outside. People don't stay indoors in the middle of the day for no reason."

Garan opened his mouth as if to argue, but then clearly considered her words. "You might have a point."

"How worried should we be?" Lorin asked, looking anything but worried.

"Not overly so, not with the sheer weight of protection we have," Lira said. Not yet, anyway.

"Then we can enjoy some food and drink until Restan gets back." Garan rubbed his hands together and dug in.

RESTAN RETURNED before an hour had passed, and Lira's eyebrows shot upwards at the sight of Councillor Rawlin Duneskal trailing after him. Duneskal looked severely unhappy, the annoyance in his expression only deepening when Restan brought him over to their table.

"I really wish somebody had told me you were coming," he said, snappish. The look on Restan's face suggested this wasn't the first time Duneskal said that. "This is the last place they should be right now."

"We didn't want anyone to know they were returning to Temari Hall, Councillor," Restan said, with the forced patience of a man who was repeating himself for the second or third time.

"Why *are* they returning? I thought the council had judged that they weren't safe there."

"While I'd be very happy to explain further, Councillor, perhaps that's something best not discussed in a busy inn?" Restan said politely. Lira was impressed by his composure. By now she'd have slapped the supercilious pureblood mage.

Duneskal's mouth tightened, but he nodded. "All of you come with me please. Hurry now."

Garan stayed right where he was. "What's going on?"

Rawlin made a gesture toward the door. "We'll explain when we get there."

"Get where?" Lira demanded, also refusing to move.

"The army barracks in the city. It's the safest place for you."

"Why do we need to be in a safe place?" This time Garan's voice was edged with command.

Duneskal was thoroughly unmoved by Garan's posturing. "If you don't move, I'll have you dragged like the spoiled children you are. There are enough mage warriors here to do it. Now come with us, be quiet, and keep your heads down."

His appalling arrogance had Garan turning red and Fari leaning back in her chair, arms crossed. Lira was tempted to refuse merely to needle the man. But when Garan, shoulders rigid, stood, she gave a little sigh and followed suit. At that cue, both Fari and Lorin stood too.

Still, Lira couldn't help but deliberately spend a few moments slowly pushing her chair in and then draining the last of her cider. "Should we expect danger?" she asked. "Or is all this hurry just because you've got a busy day and no time to deal with us?"

Restan coughed. Duneskal's mouth thinned. "You'll be fine if you do as I say and keep that mouth of yours shut." He turned and strode off, clearly expecting them to follow. Restan stepped aside for them to trail sullenly after him.

"Thanks for following my lead," Garan murmured as he fell into step with her. "I know he's being awful, but there's no point starting a fight with him in here."

She nodded. Garan had earned her respect with his behaviour since the ambush at DarkSkull, and the thought of following his instructions on occasion no longer made her annoyed. Not to mention, in the little battle of wills they'd just had, the son of Ladan Egalion had been the bigger man than a mage councillor. "When you're right, Garan, I'll listen."

He didn't say anything to that, but a little smile spread across his face as they kept walking.

WHEN THEY STEPPED out of the inn, the street was just as oddly empty as when they'd arrived. Duneskal glanced around briefly before turning left and heading away from the direction of the harbour. Restan's protection detail closed in around the apprentices.

The route they took was equally quiet. Lira spotted a handful of citizens out and about, but they all walked with a wary air, heads down as if wanting to avoid notice. In the distance though, somewhere to the south, a muddle of loud voices occasionally drifted in snatches on the breeze. Shouting, she thought, but the sound was too distant to be able to tell whether the tone was angry, afraid, or something else.

Whatever it was, it had to be what was making everyone stay indoors. Her gaze narrowed—was the storm *not* what had kept all the ships in the harbour? As much as Lira detested Duneskal, he was clearly worried about them being in the city, which meant *something* was going on. Curiosity itched at her.

"Was his brother like that?" Lira asked Garan as they walked.

"Cario died before I was born," Garan said. "But his name is always spoken in this strange way in our house, or whenever Aunt Alyx is around... I don't know how to describe it. Some mix of love and respect? Mama told me he was Aunt Alyx's closest friend, the one she trusted above everyone, and her smartest advisor. Did you know that he was killed leaping in front of an arrow meant for her? It was loosed by a Hunter assassin sent by your grandfather. Aunt Alyx has worn Cario's mage staff ever since."

Lira's eyebrows rose. She hadn't known that. What a foolish way to die.

"I assume Caria was named after him too?"

"Yep." Garan scowled as his glance fell on Rawlin ahead. "The rest of the Duneskals are just like Rawlin, though. I don't know how Cario ended up so different."

"Athira is Rawlin's niece, you knew that, right?" Fari asked.

"I did not." Lira shrugged. She didn't much care who Athira was related to, but it did explain her awful snootiness.

"Her mother is the councillor's younger sister. She married the Walden heir." Garan said, a flicker of sadness crossing over his face, presumably at the thought of Athira still being missing.

"Well, I for one am glad the Hunters are gone," Fari caught the sadness and changed the subject. "Your grandfather had some deviously clever schemes, Lira. I still can't believe he was secretly murdering mages for decades before the council discovered his Hunters even existed."

"They didn't discover them," Garan said darkly. "Shakar just started using them openly to go after Aunt Alyx and her allies."

Lira didn't know much about her grandfather's Hunters. In all the accounts of Shakar that she'd read, his elite assassins had only ever received passing mentions. She suspected that was deliberate—that nobody wanted future generations getting ideas about the best way to take down powerful mages.

"You sound afraid, but Hunters are long gone and aren't coming back, Fari," Lorin said dismissively. "Without the medallions that allowed them to repel all magic in their vicinity, they were just well-trained fighters. Today they'd be useless against warrior mages or Taliath."

Lira frowned, a thought snagging at the way he'd phrased those words. But it was too wispy to catch.

"Oh really?" Fari bristled at his tone. "And how do you know there isn't a secret cache of medallions hidden out there somewhere? You can't be certain the council recovered *all* of them after the war."

Garan looked amused. "If that's true, then why haven't they been used already?"

"Because the Shadowcouncil have found an even better way to kill mages," Lorin pointed out. "Razak."

"Quiet please!" Duneskal turned to snap at them. "You can talk all you like once we reach the barracks."

Garan made a face as soon as Duneskal turned away. Fari giggled. Even Lorin's haughty expression softened into a smile. Lira, unwilling to trust Duneskal's word, turned her attention back to their surroundings.

If danger came, she'd make sure they were safe.

WHEN THEY REACHED the walled compound of the city's army barracks, Restan's shoulders visibly relaxed, and several intimidatingly large and well-armed Shiven warriors came out to escort them inside.

Once through the gates, Restan's warriors and Bluecoats were immediately shown in a different direction to Lira and the others, only Restan remaining with them. Duneskal led the apprentices inside the main building and down a long hallway to a large office on the ground floor. A fire crackled in the grate, and a set of windows looked out into a drill yard.

Lira dropped immediately into the leather sofa by the fire, the others joining her, while Restan stood by the door and Duneskal crossed to scan the piles of parchment on the desk at the far end of the room.

After a few moments, he looked up and over at Restan. "Now that we're in private, please explain why Councillor Egalion thought it safe to send them back to Temari."

"Recent developments gave the council a level of comfort that they would be safe going back, as Underground had taken a significant blow." Restan laid out the cover story without hesitation.

Rawlin lifted a supercilious eyebrow. "Well, that information was obviously wrong."

Garan cleared his throat. "Are you going to tell us—"

"Several sections of Alanan's industry have gone on strike, including the dock workers and metalworkers." Duneskal left the desk and came to stand before them. "There has been rioting and looting in some areas, as well as violence directed against the city guards when they've tried to intervene and restore order."

Restan frowned. "Are you saying parts of the city aren't under Leader Astohar's control anymore?"

"Only a couple of small pockets now, but yes. I arrived a few days ago and we've managed to restore order in most areas without having to resort to violence, though the city jails are filling up quickly."

"Were the strikes and riots organised, or did they happen spontaneously?" Garan asked.

"It has all the appearance of being random and unorganised, arising organically from sector to sector," Duneskal said. "But no, we think it was carefully planned."

"Based on what?" Restan asked.

Duneskal smiled without warmth. "Their success. Almost half the city was out of control when I arrived."

Restan followed up. "Do the protesters have mages working with them?"

"No mage would join that rabble." Duneskal dismissed the question.

Lira spoke up then. "So this is the same thing that has been happening in Karonan and on the farms in the south of Shivasa? It's spreading north?"

Annoyance flashed over Duneskal's face, presumably over being questioned by an apprentice, but he seemed to decide it would be easier just to answer. "We haven't seen the same violence in those instances, but yes, we must assume they're connected."

"Underground." Lorin spoke quietly but they all heard him.

"Are the strikes and protests still happening in rural Tregaya too?" she pushed. "Anywhere else?"

"That's not information for mage apprentices to be privy to." Duneskal had clearly had enough of being questioned. "Now, your timing is unfortunate, but for now nobody but the soldiers on this base know you're here, and even they don't know who you are. It will take a few hours to prepare safe passage out, but we'll move you in the early hours tomorrow, while these rioting louts are sleeping. You have nothing to worry about."

Lira rolled her eyes. Hard. "Because I was *so* worried before you said that."

He gave her a filthy look. "Until then, I ask that you stay here in this room. Food and drink will be provided. If you need anything, ask one of the guards posted outside."

Duneskal left without another word, summoning Restan after him with an imperious flick of his hand.

"Prisoners, again," Fari said with a mournful sigh after the door had closed.

Lira managed a smile. "Imagine if they knew in Alistriem that they'd sent us into this?"

"It isn't funny." Garan rose to his feet. "Lorin, when you talked about the strikes weeks ago, it didn't sound as bad as this."

"It wasn't, not from the description my family gave me, but it's possible they didn't want to worry me," Lorin said. His face darkened. "If someone had let me write to them recently, I might know more."

"What is happening here fits Underground's escalation pattern," Garan said thoughtfully. "A matter of weeks ago they were comfortable enough to strike directly at the council by ambushing Uncle Dash at

DarkSkull, and now they've managed to take over parts of an important city."

Lira looked at him, wondering if he was beginning to ask the same questions she was. Were Underground really strong enough to start this fight now and win? And if so, what were they missing? Lira rose to go and stare out the window. On the ground floor, there was nothing to be seen but the exterior wall of the barracks compound.

How were the events in Alanan going to affect her? If the Underground cell in the city caught wind that Lira and the others were here... it still fit with their cover story of a return to Temari. It was a shame Greyson had never given her the details of other cell members. She might have been able to sneak out and meet with them, gather information for the council. As it was, it looked like she was going to have to sit in this room until Duneskal arranged for their departure.

"It's interesting that Councillor Duneskal is here, don't you think?" Fari spoke into the silence that had fallen, piquing Lira's interest. "Why wouldn't Leader Astohar send one of his advisors, or rely on the Alanan city governor? With the Shiven soldiers here backing them, they could have quelled the city without a mage councillor overseeing."

Lira turned back to them as Garan spoke. "My guess would be that the protesting and strikes aren't just about Leader Astohar's policies. Their discontent is connected to the council too, and they need a high enough ranking figure here for negotiations. Especially if Astohar doesn't want too much blood on the streets. If he kills any of the protesters, he's only going to inflame the unrest."

Fari snorted. "Who thought it would be a good idea to send Duneskal to negotiate anything? If he's in charge, I'm telling you now, he's not going to resolve things in three days. In fact, I wouldn't be surprised if they got worse again."

Garan nodded, jaw tight. "That's the fundamental problem, isn't it? There is still too much of the old traditional beliefs on the council. People like him shouldn't be representing us. That's why Underground has a voice and a foothold."

"Exactly." Lira gave him a surprised look, returning to the couch and dropping into it with a flourish.

"Lasting change takes time," Fari said. "If your mother and aunt tried to push harder, Garan, they might lose the support of the council and a good portion of the mages entirely, and then we'd be in an even worse situation."

"There needs to be fresh blood on the council. The Magor-lier and Councillor Egalion are the only new additions in decades," Lorin said. "Walden, Duneskal, Dirsk, the old pureblood families who refuse to change, they should all be removed."

"Are you suggesting instituting voting for council members?" Garan asked with a shake of his head. "Never going to happen."

"It should," Lira muttered.

"That's not what *you* want, Lira," Fari challenged her. "You want to be Magor-lier yourself one day, and you won't get there if mages are *voting*. Your only chance of winning a seat is by forcing them to give you one. And once you get there, you want to stay there, not rule with the chance of being voted out some day."

"I..." Lira stared at her. She blinked. Her words had come out without thinking, but Fari was right. "That's true."

Lorin and Garan both shot her disappointed glances. She scowled at them. "Underground would lose a lot of its appeal if more progressive mages sat on the council," she said. "But voting introduces too much uncertainty. You'd have councillors spending all their time figuring out how to win the mages' votes rather than actually running the mage order. You'd become weak and ineffectual."

"That's... probably true," Fari conceded. "Not to mention the voting process would favour those who could speak well and look good, as opposed to those who were actually competent and had the right ideas."

Garan lifted an eyebrow. "And who decides what the right ideas are?"

"I still think it would be better than what we have now," Lorin argued. "Mages would have a say. They'd be more engaged with the council and less likely to listen to the voices of someone like Shakar or those on the Shadowcouncil."

Lira stared across the room as they continued talking, quickly bored by such theoretical discussion. Her thoughts dwelled on what Underground was seeking to achieve with these strikes and protests.

They weren't anywhere near enough to topple Astohar or any of the other monarchs, let alone the Mage Council. Maybe they were just the first step in a larger plan... but in that case, what *was* the next step? Impatience set in. She wished they could just get back to Karonan, so she could talk to Greyson, or Lucinda.

"I hope Duneskal can get us organised to leave sooner rather than later. I'm not sure waiting is a good idea." Lorin's words brought Lira back to the conversation. He'd taken her spot by the window, gaze distant as he stared through the glass.

"Why?" Fari asked.

"A whole lot of Shiven soldiers saw us walk through those gates, and those that did will tell their comrades. By nightfall, most of the soldiers on this base will know we're here."

Lira stilled, realising quickly where he was going. Garan and Fari clearly did not. She cursed herself for not thinking of it already—she'd been too focused on her impatience to get out.

"Why is that a problem?" Garan enquired.

"Shiven foot soldiers are drawn from the rural populations, mostly, second and third and fourth sons with no future on their family's farm or business," Lira replied. "Only the officers come from the richer parts of society."

"That's pretty much how every army works, Lira," Garan said with a smile.

"Right. And who do Underground draw most of their support from?" Lira arched an eyebrow at him.

Lorin spoke in the silence that followed Lira's words. "I bet all the gold coins I don't have that there are at least one or two Underground sympathisers on this base."

"Underground are going to find out we're here sooner rather than later." A little shiver of excitement went through Lira. "Now it's just a matter of whether Duneskal gets us out before that happens."

Realisation crossed Fari's face. "Do you think Duneskal knows that?"

"As arrogant as he is, he's no idiot, and I suspect that's why he looked so worried when he learned we were here," Garan said reassuringly. "We'll be fine."

Lira felt that thrill growing stronger anyway. Lucinda wanted them alive—at least, if she hadn't been lying when she'd asked Lira to become friends with them to gain access to the council—but she very much doubted Lucinda was in Alanan. And if the local Underground cell leader learned two pureblood mage apprentices were in the city...

Well, maybe their return to Temari wouldn't be boring after all.

"Do you think you could try and exhibit some concern about the rest of us, Lira, despite your evident excitement at the idea of getting to fight things?" Fari sighed.

Lira blinked, the thrill fading as quickly as it had come. While she relished the thought of the danger inherent in trying to escape the city with Underground on their tail, it wasn't her they would be targeting. It would be Garan and Fari. In place of the thrill came a well of frustrated irritation. This was what happened when you let yourself care about people. She'd lost her autonomy, her edge. It forced her into a box. "I'll keep you safe," she mumbled in the end, meaning it, but hating the fact.

"I—" Fari opened her mouth, but then shot an astonished look in Garan's direction. He gave her a little smile but said nothing. Fari's mouth closed and she sat back in the chair. "Think it's time to order some food? I'm starved."

Garan and Lorin immediately echoed agreement and Garan went to the door. Lira stayed silent and stared at the opposite wall, annoyed with all of them. They left her alone, falling into school gossip that made no sense to her anyway—even from a distance, though, she could feel the unease underlying their chatter. Lorin kept glancing toward the window. Eventually, pushed by her own hunger, she joined them when platters of steaming food arrived.

"Want to practice some while we wait, Lira?" Garan asked once they were done. "You always feel better when you beat me."

Fari clapped her hands. "And I feel better when I watch you beat him!"

Lira conceded her bad mood with a smile. "Yes, all right, let's practice."

Instinct told her they might need it later.

CHAPTER 28

T hey set off two hours before dawn.

Restan gave them a set of clipped instructions as they gathered by a small side gate in the barrack walls. Duneskal was nowhere to be seen. "You stay quiet. You do everything we say. You keep up. You don't use magic unless we're attacked. Is all that clear?"

"Yes, sir," Garan answered for them.

"The route we've planned avoids all the pockets of unrest in the city. You may hear sounds of fighting—although there shouldn't be much at this hour—but be assured we're not going near any of it. Horses have been arranged and will be waiting a short distance outside the city, on the western road. We'll ride through the day to make sure we're well clear before stopping." His voice gentled a little. "We should be back at Temari within three days."

As he finished speaking, a small whistle came from the other side of the gate—the signal that the street beyond was clear of watchers.

"Let's go," Restan said.

They slipped out the gate, their protectors keeping close to the apprentices as they set off. Lira wasn't certain, but thought they were heading north. A soldier from the Shiven garrison, acting as a guide, led the group of Bluecoats and mages through the dark and empty Alanan streets.

The night was rich with the scents of seawater, refuse, and humanity; it was so familiar to Lira that it was hard not to feel like she was back in Dirinan, heading out to undertake a job.

Every part of her wished that was exactly what she *was* doing.

Although, if she were, she'd be slipping silently through the back alleys and shadowy roofs, not walking along main streets surrounded by guards. Lira's neck prickled, a sense of vulnerability making her uneasy. She didn't like being so obvious. Duneskal was a damn fool and Restan should know better.

A thudding boom was the first indication that something was wrong. The entire party froze halfway along the street they were on, blinking at the sudden flash of golden concussive light in the sky. The ground shuddered under their feet.

Lira shared a glance with Garan. Restan had mentioned they might hear some fighting, but so close? Unless...

"Rotted Duneskal lied to us," Garan swore.

Lira gave him an approving look for his use of the curse word. "It sounds like Underground have at least one mage here working with the protesters."

"Who are they attacking in the middle of the night?" Fari hissed.

The golden light flashed once more in the instant before another boom roared out. It seemed to be close, barely a block away. Lira could feel the ripple of magic on her skin.

Restan snapped an order to find cover at the same time as the Bluecoat lieutenant moved, turning with his men to close around the apprentices. Lira found herself being hustled to the edge of the street and pressed up against the wall of the nearest building while Restan sent two Bluecoats ahead to see what was going on.

Lira shifted closer to Garan and the others. "It could be a council mage, not Underground. Maybe they're just trying to clear out one of the remaining pockets of protesters—taking them unaware while they sleep. Anyone know a mage with gold concussive magic?"

Garan shook his head grimly. "Pretty sure none of the council mages are that colour. There aren't that many concussive mages alive. Lorin was the first at Temari in years."

"Duneskal wouldn't have sent us this way if they were conducting an operation in this part of the city," Lorin pointed out.

Lira and Garan looked at each other. The boy was right.

"Neither would they have deliberately sent us through a part of the city controlled by the protesters," Garan said, gaze still on Lira.

Lira let out a breath of realisation. "Our Shiven guide is Underground. He's led us into a trap." She felt that shiver in her blood that warned of danger. On its heels came the thrill, the clarity of her senses focusing into sharp relief, the quickening beat of her heart.

Fari shook her head, staring down the street where the two Bluecoats had almost reached the end of the block. "Underground have had the opportunity to kill us before and didn't take it. Why now?"

"The Underground cell here won't know who we are, just that a group of mage apprentices are trying to sneak out of the city. They probably hope Duneskal is with us." Lira reached up to draw her staff. "We're quite a prize for them, especially as hostages."

"Restan?" Garan waved for the man's attention. "Where's our guide?"

Restan frowned, but to his credit looked around, then went and spoke to the Bluecoat lieutenant. The man shook his head. While they spoke, the Bluecoats scouting the top of the street returned at a swift jog. The four of them had a murmured conversation, then Restan returned to Lira and the others.

"The guide has vanished," Restan reported back. "There's a left turn at the top of this street, and the road beyond is barricaded and manned by several armed individuals, presumably protesters. The Bluecoats couldn't tell where the concussive magic came from."

"Pretty sure the guide was leading us right into that barricade," Garan said. "Once we turned into the street, they would have cut off our retreat and we'd have been trapped."

Lira frowned. In that case, why the concussive magic that had warned them before they reached the ambush point? A mistake? That didn't feel quite right.

"Could be." Restan whistled, then made a series of hand gestures.

The Bluecoat and mage force closed in around them. "We head back the way we came and we move fast, before they realise we've been warned. Our goal is to get back to the safety of the barracks. From there we can plan another route out of the city."

Lira had no argument with that plan, and fell in with the others as they moved into a jog back down the street. They were approaching the first corner when the ground shuddered again, another golden concussive burst ripping through the night. This one was so close the force of it sent Lira stumbling into the wall of a stone building. She swore, straightened, and scrambled towards the corner. The others were close behind, coming to a halt behind her.

The golden light faded away and for a moment she couldn't see anything but darkness in the street beyond, felt nothing but the gusting wind whipping her hair around her face and the cold seeping into her bones.

"Go!" Restan shouted. "Quickly, now."

Bluecoats started into the street, moving in close formation with swords out, mages not far behind. Another golden burst flared, bright enough to make Lira see spots, before the tell-tale concussive boom sounded in the air. The crack of wood splintering followed as the wall of a house across the street was hit. The echoing ripples of the concussion squeezed at her chest.

When her vision cleared, several Bluecoats and two mages lay fallen, unmoving, in the street. Lira's heart thudded in realisation and anticipation both.

This was the real ambush.

A powerful wind whipped up, screaming through the street, as one of Restan's mages counter-attacked. Lira lost sight of everything as Restan and the others caught up and surrounded them.

Garan said to Restan, "They've blocked us in."

"I worked that out already, thanks." The warrior mage was looking ahead and behind, clearly trying to work out what to do. Then he began calling orders. "We push forward, try and break through. Keep the apprentices covered in the middle."

Around them the Bluecoats and mages moved efficiently in response. They ran forward, the wind screaming around them, only to slide to a halt as fire leapt into the night—several flaming balls of it, launched from behind a hastily constructed barricade at the top of the street.

Lira pushed through the protective cordon and kept moving. At least one fire mage lay ahead, but they had to break through somewhere if they wanted to get to safety. She certainly wasn't going to loiter in the street until the trap closed even more tightly around them.

Fortunately, Restan seemed to concur. Wind whistled as the wind mage joined with Restan's telekinesis to surround the barricade ahead, trying to tear it down. Lira snarled at a Bluecoat who tried to yank her behind them and out of the line of fire.

"Lorin, help them!" Garan ordered crisply.

The initiate didn't hesitate. With a grunt of effort he lifted both hands and sent two blue concussion balls toward the barricade. Both winked out of existence a few yards before hitting the barricade. The wind died too, swirling around the construction but not able to touch it.

For a long moment they just stared, unbelieving.

"Again, Lorin!" Lira snapped. "More focused this time."

He did as she bade. She felt the prickle of his magic on her skin, saw the tight focus on his face, how Fari hovered near in case he lost his balance on his bad leg. The blue bursts arced towards the direction of the ambush, bright and graceful, and then again winked out of existence.

Garan looked at her. "Razak in the streets?"

"Maybe." She couldn't think of anything else, but... "It's not cold enough. And no rattling, or that miasma of fear they carry with them."

Garan glanced between them, then closed his eyes, fists clenching at his sides. Lira felt him hurl his telekinetic magic outwards, trying to wrap it around the hastily constructed barricade protecting the ambushers.

Nothing happened.

His jaw tightened, shoulders going rigid with the effort, then he let out a bellow of frustration and opened his eyes. "I can't touch it. Lira, can you try?"

She frowned. Their ambushers weren't attacking. Even though their group was trapped, their aggressors seemed content to hold them in place. Why weren't they attacking?

Even as the questions went round and round in her head, violet light flared bright around her hands and she summoned as much telekinetic magic as she could hold then sent it flashing out towards the barricade like a whip. But before it could get there, her magic dissolved against some sort of numbing block. The magic slid out of her grasp.

Frustrated, she tried again. Same thing. No matter how hard she focused, she couldn't keep the magic together when it hit the barricade. And each attempt drained her energy.

"I can't." She opened her eyes, then went stumbling backwards as another concussive burst flew towards them. It hit the ground only a few metres in front of them, forcing them back but not killing anyone.

Still, Lira's magic responded instinctively, flaring bright and hot, seeking to help, to attack, to destroy anything trying to hurt her. And she had not yet had the opportunity to practice enough to build up the same control with her fire magic as she had with her telekinesis.

It flared to life in her hands, bright white flame edged in violet, curling around her fingers and up her forearms. Horrified, she slammed down on her magic in a desperate push, and the flames winked out of existence.

But it was too late. They'd all seen.

A heavy silence fell. Shock crawled over Garan's face. "It was you that burned the razak and the mage controlling them?"

"Yes," she said, because there was no point lying now.

Fari lifted a trembling hand to her face. Even Lorin seemed shaken at the evidence of her additional magic.

"Can you use it against the barricade?" Garan asked, mouth a hard line of tension.

She shook her head. "It's too far and I don't have the same control over it as my telekinesis."

"What else can you do?"

Lira ignored Garan's question, an idea coming to her. "Time for questions later." She glanced around to the mage guards hovering nearby and waved Restan over. "We need to get up to the roofs, escape that way."

The tall warrior nodded agreement. "I'll send half the force with you and keep the rest here to cover your retreat. We'll do our best to get you clear."

"There's an alley just down there." Lorin pointed. "It's a dead end, but there should be a roof access ladder somewhere along it."

They retreated down the street, weaving their way between fighting Bluecoats and mages, a growing number of their protectors falling in with them after orders snapped by Restan.

Right as they reached the alley, another golden concussion burst slammed into the street behind them, clearly trying to stop their retreat. The concussive force squeezed Lira's chest so hard she couldn't draw breath, and she staggered to her knees. The pressure was gone as quickly as it had come, but even as she was fighting to get back to her feet Garan was already leading them down the alley.

Why were their ambushers just trying to hold them in place?

"Restan!" she called out. "They're not trying to pick us off. I think they might be trying to grab us, not kill us."

Restan nodded. "My thoughts too. Either way, we need to get you clear. Go."

Ahead, Lorin had found a ladder, and they joined him, gathering around it. Restan sent Bluecoats and mages swarming up to clear the roof.

Garan addressed them briskly while Restan ran back to order the remaining guards in the street to retreat into the alley. "Once we're up there, you stay low, and you run. Each of you stick with two guards— you don't leave them for anything. If you get lost, keep heading in the same direction until you find your way out. Once clear, you circle straight back for the army barracks. Any questions?"

Even the guards were listening to Garan, and nobody disagreed with his course of action, Lira included. Her thoughts raced, focused despite the urgency of the situation. "You!" Lira pointed at the telepath mage amongst their guard force. "Can you reach back to Port Rantarin or Alistriem and tell them what's happening?"

"My range is strong enough, but I can't get through. My magic is being blocked." Panic turned the mage's skin white. He'd clearly never experienced being cut off from his magic before.

Another blast, along with a particularly violent gust of wind, sent them stumbling in all directions. Lira staggered backwards several steps, eventually losing her balance and falling hard, her body rolling along cobblestones. By the time she was able to stop herself and clamber back to her feet she was a long way from the ladder.

Restan came running from the alley entrance, the handful of remaining Bluecoats close behind. Lira waved them on past her as she scrambled back to her feet. "Is everyone clear?" she asked.

"Everyone alive." Restan paused at the base of the ladder, waiting as the Bluecoats clambered up. "They'll figure out where we've gone quickly though. Come on!"

"Go, I'm right behind you."

Lira waited, one eye on the end of the alley, one eye watching those climbing. She refused Restan's attempt to wave her ahead of him. She could roof-run faster and better than any of them... best they have the longest lead she could give them.

"Lira?" Garan was crouched on the roof's edge, clearly waiting for her. The others had vanished from sight, hopefully already clear. The Bluecoats ahead of Restan scrambled over the top. Restan was almost there. Lira gripped the bottom rung of the ladder, her glance flicking to the end of the alley, making sure they were clear.

And she froze.

A tall figure walked into the alley, strides loose and relaxed. Lira summoned a quick burst of magic. Then she stilled. It was Ahrin, long coat swirling around her ankles, blade in her left hand. Some unnameable tangling of emotion thrilled through Lira.

Joy. Despair. Fear. Confusion.

"Lira!" Garan again. Restan hovered beside him.

"Go!" she shouted at him, then stared down the alley at Ahrin, lowering her voice, unsure if Garan and Restan could see her from their position above. "What are you doing here?"

Ahrin's eyes were bright, despite the dark night. "I could ask you the same thing. I couldn't believe it when my spies reported you and the others sailed into port yesterday."

"*Your* spies." Lira stilled in realisation. "This is all you."

"That surprises you?" Ahrin came closer. "This is a real bit of luck. I've come for you, Lira."

She stared at Ahrin, mind racing. "The ambush is for me?"

Ahrin nodded. "To extract you, yes. The Shadowcouncil have decided it's time for you to join us completely. Once I was done in Alanan, I was supposed to go and get you."

"They want me out of Temari? What about Lucinda's mission, her—"

"Questions and answers later," Ahrin interrupted. "We have to go now, before your council mages come back for you."

"Lira!" Garan bellowed her name. He must be able to see Ahrin now, though she doubted he could hear their conversation. "Hurry, or I'm coming down there to get you."

Ahrin ignored him, hand outstretched, impatience edging her voice. "Come on."

Unexpectedly strong reluctance filled Lira. If she disappeared with Ahrin now, she had no way of knowing whether the others would be safe. Whether they'd gotten away. More importantly, Garan would see her leaving with Ahrin. He would tell his mother, surely, and knowing Lira's mission, Dawn would understand why Lira had done it. But Garan wouldn't know, and neither would the others. And if they learned Ahrin was the Darkhand... they would think she'd betrayed them.

But it sounded like Underground were finally allowing her into the inner sanctum, allowing her to join them full time. The exact position to be in if she wanted to bring them down.

And in the end, that was all she cared about. Lira wanted Underground gone, because of what they'd done to her, but also because of how it would increase her status with the council.

That mattered more than anything else.

Lira reached out and took Ahrin's outstretched hand.

She glanced up at Garan, part of her wanting to make sure that he was okay. It was foolish. They would be fine. They were smart and resourceful and they had mage guards and Bluecoats protecting them. They didn't need her.

Garan was staring down at her, confusion all over his face as he shouted, "What are you doing? Get up here."

She met his gaze, ignored the lurch of guilt in her chest.

And she walked away.

Another blast went off nearby and Ahrin quickened her stride. When Lira glanced back again, unable to help herself, both Garan and Restan had vanished from the edge of the roof.

Slipping past the barricade, Ahrin led Lira along a tangle of dark and empty alleys, the scent of brine growing stronger until they arrived at the docks.

A small boat bobbed at the jetty Lira was led to, the sails furled, crewed by two young Shiven men. They sat almost unnaturally still in the shadows of the boat, startling Lira when they stood at Ahrin's appearance. In a series of quick movements they readied the boat for departure.

Ahrin swung over the railing and landed in the boat. Lira didn't hesitate before following, her searching gaze noting the weapons worn by the crew. Though they looked practised at managing a boat, their demeanour told her they were trained warriors. Not Underground's usual type.

"Where did you find these two?" she murmured to Ahrin as they began rowing away from the dock.

"Answers later," came the short reply.

Ahrin in this mood wasn't worth pushing, so Lira shrugged and settled down in a spot out of everyone's way. Once they were clear of other boats, one of the men scrambled around to unfurl the sails. They quickly caught the night's breeze and the boat sped up, steering into a south-easterly direction.

Lira stared back at the city, wondering whether she'd just made a terrible mistake. Her friends' lives had been placed in grave danger again because of her, because Underground had wanted her. She didn't want to worry about them, or feel guilt about abandoning them, but she did. And she hated it.

"Are you okay?" Ahrin dropped down beside her. "You weren't hurt?"

"I'm fine." Lira forced herself to turn her gaze away from the city and settle on the ocean ahead.

"Why wasn't Tarion Caverlock with you?"

Lira looked at her, making a split-second decision. Would it be to her benefit for Underground to know what their experiments had done to Tarion? She wasn't sure... and she didn't want to give away anything that might help Lucinda in any way. Not until she understood more about the experiments, anyway. "He stayed in Alistriem. You know he's courting the princess?" All truth.

Ahrin made a grimace.

"Are you going to let them escape?" Lira asked.

"What do you care?" Ahrin laughed, settling back on the bench, long legs stretched out before her.

"Ahrin!" she snapped.

"Lira!" Ahrin mimicked.

"Tell me," she said coldly, making it clear she wasn't messing around.

Ahrin's face tightened. "The ambush was a diversion to grab you. I gave no specific orders to kill anyone, but nor do I care who got caught up in the crossfire. I don't know why *you* do."

"I don't." She turned away, refusing to show any relief in front of Ahrin. "I'd just like to be kept informed about exactly what is going on. You're the one who keeps insisting you want to be a team."

Lira took a long, steadying breath. She hadn't made a mistake. Underground had pulled her out. This was the opportunity she'd been waiting for—full access to the group and all its workings so she could bring them down from within. This would be her trials, surely. No more Temari, no more tedious lessons.

A warrior mage in her own right once this was done.

She pushed away the memory of Tarion asking her whether that was what she truly wanted. Pushed away all thoughts of Garan and Lorin and Fari. Locked them away in a small corner of her heart to bring out later, once this was all over.

Dawn and the Magor-lier would consider what Lira had done reckless and dangerous. She couldn't go back to them now, not until she had enough for them to take down Underground completely. That was the only way to guarantee they wouldn't expel her... or worse.

And to succeed she would need to be Lira of Dirinan again. Clever, ruthless, wary. The skin settled down over her like a perfectly fitted cloak, bringing enough relief that it eased the sting of regret over leaving the others. She no longer had to worry about anyone else—just herself. The thrill pushed at her internal walls and she let it in, let it heat her blood and make her excited, anticipatory.

Ahrin caught the smile curling at Lira's mouth and returned it, her eyes going dark. Confidence filled Lira. She'd win Ahrin too. Win her to Lira's side.

There was now no other option.

CHAPTER 29

D awn was breaking across the horizon as their boat scraped ashore on a sandy beach. They'd sailed through the day and the following night, and though the cloud cover had been too dense to be certain of the direction they were heading in, Lira thought they'd stayed on a roughly south-easterly heading.

The Shiven warriors crewing the boat—who hadn't spoken a word the whole trip—jumped into the shallows to drag it further up onto the sand. Lira climbed out behind them, taking a moment to adjust to being back on land, and then stretched as she stared around her.

Empty beach spread to the east and west, endless ocean to the south, and ahead, a line of forested hills too high to see over. Ahrin spoke to the men a short distance away. Their conversation was soft enough to be inaudible, but it was clear Ahrin was issuing orders. Tendrils of dark hair, loosened from the braid she wore, whipped around the Darkhand's face, her coat swirling around her ankles.

After a brief conversation one of the warriors left, heading east in a swift, graceful jog. The second disappeared into the brush. Perimeter guards, perhaps? Or did they have some other purpose? Lira made a note to figure out later.

Ahrin returned to Lira, some of her edge softening. "Lastor has gone ahead to warn Lucinda of our arrival. She'll be surprised that I've delivered you so quickly."

"Lucinda is here?" Lira said, startled. "Where *are* we?"

Ahrin flashed her that wicked smile. "Where do you think?"

Lira considered. "I'm confident we headed southeast most of the way, which rules out the Shiven coast. So either somewhere in south Rionn, though I'm not convinced we travelled far enough east to reach it, or... Shadowfall Island."

At Ahrin's pleased nod, a little shiver went down Lira's back. For generations before the construction of Temari Hall, all Taliath had trained on Shadowfall Island. Lira's grandfather had come here to learn after he'd absorbed Taliath abilities from his lover. This was where Shakar had gone rogue, his grief over her death—after she was assassinated by the council—crystallising into hatred and a burning desire for revenge.

Here he'd started planning a war that had cost thousands of lives and scared the Mage Council so deeply that they'd spent decades afterward hunting and killing Taliath potentials to prevent another Shakar ever existing.

Only for the Darkmage to begin a second war, one even more carefully planned than the first. Still, he'd lost that one in the end too.

Now only one mage of the higher order with Taliath invulnerability lived—Alyx Egalion. And she worked every single day to dispel the council fear of Taliath. Training Taliath potentials alongside mage apprentices at Temari was a big part of that... but it didn't mean the fear was gone. They'd been so terrified of Lira's grandfather, that fear had passed to her as well—strong enough to eclipse rational thought.

And while Egalion had proved she was no Darkmage and never would be... if another mage of the higher order was born—and that was inevitable—Lira knew without hesitation that people would live in fear of that person absorbing Taliath invulnerability too. She wondered what would happen to the fragile acceptance of Taliath then.

Ahrin touched her arm, breaking her from her thoughts. "Something wrong?"

"No. Just thinking about my grandfather... about what will happen when the next mage of the higher order is born."

"It will fracture the council," Ahrin said decidedly. "Too much fear still exists. I bet you a hundred bags of gold there will be those who will argue to have that person isolated from all Taliath, or worse, have the Taliath removed. Egalion has tried to quell the fear, but she's only papered over the cracks."

"What do you think it will take to lessen that fear?"

"My, we're philosophical today." Ahrin cocked her head. "I don't think it's possible. Lucky for us, we can use that fear for our own purposes. Now, shall we?"

Lira nodded, falling into step with her.

"We often come ashore on the beach here because it's the southward side of the island and there's less chance of being spotted, though we have access to the eastern beach as well," Ahrin explained as they walked. "Even though the Taliath training academy is no longer functioning, there are several fishing villages along the north and western sides of the island. We'd rather they not see us coming and going. They have no idea Underground have a base here."

Lira shot her an amused look. "You're a font of information all of a sudden."

"I told you there'd be answers when we got here. You're one of us now."

Lira doubted that. Questions crowded to the front of her mind, clamouring to be asked while she had Ahrin alone. She particularly wanted to ask about Tarion, whether what had happened to him would happen to her too. But she held herself back. Ahrin wasn't any more trustworthy than Lucinda. Safer not to betray her interest or knowledge until she had a better understanding of why she was here. Why Underground had chosen now to extract her.

After a short walk, the shifting sand under their boots turned solid as they entered a forested area and turned northeast, following a narrow track worn by passing feet. Birds trilled happily overhead, tree branches rustled in the breeze, and the scent of salt tickled her nose.

"It's really quite pleasant here," Lira remarked. "Maybe I'll quit Underground, build a little cabin near the sea, and live a quiet life."

Ahrin snorted, eyes dancing with amusement. "You'd get bored by day two."

Lira's smile widened to a grin, warmth filling her. "Yeah. Probably by nightfall on day one, actually."

"We're going to do great things, you and I." Ahrin bumped their arms. "There will be no time for you to get bored."

Lira's momentary happiness vanished, replaced by aching sadness. They weren't going to do great things together, no matter what Ahrin said. Because Ahrin wasn't hers.

They continued to veer toward the east, the terrain growing steeper as they ascended one of the hills. After about an hour of walking, they finally emerged from the forest onto a grassy clifftop above the ocean. Wind whipped past her face and tangled in her short hair. Not far to her right, a set of steps carved precariously into the rock wound down to the beach below where a jetty stuck out into the water.

"No fishing villages on the eastern shore—the cliffs are too precipitous." Ahrin pointed, then spread her arms wide. "And this used to be where the Taliath trained."

Lira blinked a few times against the brightness of the day, then her gaze roved the grassy field spread out before them. It was long and wide, perfect for drill training, she imagined, but was hemmed in to the north and south by forested hillside, and to the east by rugged cliffs. Also perfect for privacy.

To the west, rough, rocky ground rose upwards on a slight incline. Perched on it, constructed amongst the trees of the hill rearing above, was a series of wooden structures all interconnected by stairways. Ivy crawled along surfaces cracked and worn from weather and time.

Lira smirked. "Don't tell me, you brought me here to murder me where nobody will ever find the body." The place looked utterly deserted, like nobody had been here in decades.

"If we'd wanted to murder you, we could have done that a hundred times already," Ahrin responded, far too casually for Lira's liking. It reminded her of just how fragile her position was with Underground. "We haven't touched the exterior. The original builders of this place dug into the hillside, and the cliffs below us, presumably for more space. We only use those parts—to avoid a passing fishing boat, or ship out of the usual shipping lanes, spotting us."

"Clever," Lira murmured.

"Follow me." Ahrin walked across the field toward the nearest staircase. A door at the top stood half open, nothing about it indicating it had been used recently. A wide corridor beyond the door was similarly unkempt, the floor covered in leaves and other debris that had blown in. Rooms branched off to either side but they were all empty, covered in dust, the walls and floor weathered by time.

At the end of the corridor was a room enclosed by a wall of rock, rather than wood. A wide tunnel had been dug into it. A fresh breeze drifted through from somewhere at its other end.

"Neat." Lira approved.

Ahrin reached for a torch—several sat leaning against the tunnel wall, the only sign so far that people might be living here—and lit it with a flint from her pocket. "Shall we?" she asked, and they headed deeper into the tunnel.

Lira looked around, a little smile curling at her mouth. "A masterstroke by the Shadowcouncil to use DarkSkull Hall and Shadowfall Island as places to hide out and plan against the council. The symbolism is delightful."

Ahrin flashed her that wicked smile. "You must be thrilled we've finally gotten you out of that cursed council's clutches."

The right play was to grin back, to agree, but instead hot anger sparked through Lira as the image of Garan on that roof flashed through her thoughts. "Sure, but did you really have to attack a whole group of people to do it? Surely a little more finesse would have been smarter." The words spilled out before she could stop them, but she tried to make them sound casual, just a little curious, like it meant nothing to her.

When Ahrin's eyes narrowed, Lira knew she'd failed. "What I did was follow orders. An ambush was the easiest way to extract you."

Instead of allaying Lira's anger, Ahrin's words only made it worse. "Right, of course, you're the Shadowcouncil's pet killer and personal assistant," she said bitterly.

"Since when do you care about those bratty apprentices?" The edge was in Ahrin's voice now, the warning one. "You're acting like you're upset that I attacked them to get you out, when it was clearly the best move to make. It worries me you can't see that."

"I care since they risked their lives to save mine," Lira snapped, then immediately regretted it. She knew where she was, knew she couldn't afford to betray herself here of all places. Especially not with Ahrin. She'd been here all of an hour and was already putting her cover in jeopardy. But something inside her ached at the thought of what had happened, and she couldn't hide it. Rotted carcasses, she was losing her edge. She had to push those feelings away or they'd get her killed.

"Tell me what that means," Ahrin demanded, eyes flashing dangerously.

Lira wrestled with herself, then said, "Will you find out for me if they survived your little ambush?" Maybe if she knew they were safe, she could focus properly on surviving her mission.

Ahrin went still, eyes locked on Lira's for a long moment. Lira held that look, knowing to shift her glance now would reveal weakness she couldn't afford. Eventually Ahrin spoke. "If that's what you want. I wouldn't go raising it with Lucinda, though." Ahrin lowered her voice, moved closer again. "What happened?"

Lira closed up every inch of her expression and ensured her mental shield was airtight. "Maybe after I get some answers, I'll give *you* some answers. Now, are we going somewhere, or do you want to stand here and chat all day?"

Ahrin stared at her for a moment longer, that dangerous stillness hovering over her, but she eventually stepped away and started walking. "We're going to see Lucinda."

A short time later they reached a wooden door set into a rocky wall and Ahrin knocked sharply. Throughout their entire walk, Lira hadn't seen a single other person, and instinct told her that was deliberate. Either whoever else was here had been told to stay away and keep out of Lira's sight, or Ahrin had taken her through unused walkways. The knowledge fuelled her anger and irritation. She'd had enough of Underground's lies and secrets.

She hadn't walked away from Garan and the others, left them in danger, for this.

It was time for answers.

CHAPTER 30

As the door opened, Lira cleared everything but her mission from her mind. She'd already made a mistake with Ahrin on the journey in. She couldn't afford any more of them, not if she was going to pull this off.

She took a breath, letting go of every part of herself she'd acquired over the past three years to fit in at Temari Hall.

"Lira!" Lucinda smiled coolly. "Welcome. It's good to have you finally with us."

The welcoming words didn't fool Lira for an instant. Lucinda's decision to bring Lira in now would only have been made because it served the Shadowcouncil's purpose in some way. That was fine—she could work with that.

Best to start off strong.

"I'm done on all the secrecy and mystery," she said, using the cool arrogance her grandfather had been known for. "Your Darkhand says the Shadowcouncil has decided to fully bring me into the group, but if that's the case I insist on full disclosure. If not, I walk, or you kill me, but pick one, because like I told you in Karonan, I'm not your malleable puppet."

Lucinda's smile widened and she stepped aside from the door, waving her in. "Come in, Lira. Ahrin, you'll wait outside."

The Darkhand didn't like that. Lira could tell from the tapping of her left hand against her leg—not noticeable to anyone who didn't know Ahrin's tells. But to Lucinda, Ahrin merely bowed her head gracefully and stepped away as she closed the door.

The room inside was cosy and firelit, containing several bookcases, a desk, and a cluster of comfortable chairs surrounding a low table. At one of the chairs sat a familiar figure.

"Greyson!" Shock echoed in Lira's voice. Genuinely taken aback, she came to a halt.

"Hello, Lira." He gave her his warm, paternal smile. "It's good to see you. Please come and sit down."

"Greyson has been helping us finalise our plans for Karonan," Lucinda explained. "He was scheduled to leave this morning, but Lastor brought Ahrin's message to say you were here, and of course he wanted to see you before he left."

"I was pleased to hear that the Shadowcouncil feels it's time for you to properly join us," he said, glance shifting between Lira and Lucinda. "Welcome, Lira, we are honoured to have you."

Lira sat, crossed her legs, looked at Lucinda. "I thought you wanted me to gain access to the council's inner circle by befriending Garan and Tarion and the others? I was doing nicely at that until your Darkhand decided to attack them just to snatch me up."

Lucinda's jaw tightened imperceptibly, but she didn't sound angry when she replied. "That *was* the plan, and I apologise for not being able to warn you of our intentions. Our situation has shifted rather more quickly than we expected. Access to the Egalion brats is no longer a critical requirement for us."

Lira didn't allow her expression to change, but foreboding shivered through her. What did that mean exactly? Unless Lucinda was lying—always impossible to tell—Underground seemed to keep upping the ante with a precision and confidence Lira didn't understand. There was still so much she was missing. "What about my access to the council? Wasn't that the reason you recruited me? I can't go back to them now."

"Lira, you know that you're important to us, far more so than just being a spy," Greyson said, leaning forward in his chair. Lira's gaze narrowed as she spotted the sweat beading on his brow. Why was he nervous? "Here, with us, helping to lead Underground, is where you truly belong. This is the place where you'll be welcome, respected, wanted. With us, you can be who you were born to be. The true heir to the Darkmage."

Lucinda gave Greyson an approving nod before turning her attention back to Lira. "It's what you demanded of me, no?" She lifted an eyebrow, her words containing a hint of a challenge.

Lira took a shuddering breath, trying to ignore how Greyson's words resonated with her. Because this wasn't Temari Hall or rural Shivasa, or anywhere else. This was a group who valued her *because* she was Shakar's granddaughter. And as much as she hated what they'd done to her, as much as she burned to bring them down, she couldn't pretend she didn't feel the lure of that welcome. That acceptance.

That power.

She didn't let the feeling linger. Greyson might mean what he said, but Lira wasn't foolish enough to believe Lucinda did. Or the rest of this mysterious Shadowcouncil. "Why is the Darkhand here instead of at Temari Hall where I left her?" she asked, changing the subject. She wanted to understand why Ahrin had been sent to infiltrate Temari in the first place, and why she'd so abruptly left. "And why can't she hear any of this? I thought she was your right hand."

"The Mage Council became aware of Ahrin's true identity." Lucinda's voice turned icy with disapproval.

Lira fought to stifle the jolt of instinctive fear that tone caused. Ahrin hadn't been withdrawn from Temari because she'd completed her task or something else more important had come up.

Underground had found out the council knew she was a spy.

And there was only one way the council could have learned that for certain, because only one person apart from Lucinda and Greyson had known about it... Lira. Had Dawn lied to Lira about telling nobody but her brother? Lira blinked, realising Lucinda was still talking. "... she at least owned up to her mistake, but the damage was done and we had to pull her out."

What?

287

"Your precious Darkhand made a mistake?" Lira managed, fighting to hold onto her casual tone with every bit of resolve she had.

"That's what I just said." Irritation filled Lucinda's voice. "She's useful to us, Lira, almost as valuable as you, but she must be clear on the consequences for those who endanger our mission. Mistakes won't be tolerated."

Lira shifted, trying to betray neither the relief nor confusion flooding through her. She knew even better than Lucinda that Ahrin didn't make mistakes. Ahrin was far too clever, too prepared, too capable. "What was she doing there in the first place?"

"It doesn't matter." Lucinda still sounded cold. "She failed. We'll move on."

Lira was about to ask what exactly that meant, but Greyson spoke before she could. "After being pulled from Temari, the Darkhand was sent to oversee the operation in Alanan," he said. "A chance to make up for her error. Fortunately for her she's done exceedingly well there."

"Time for you to give *us* some answers now, Lira," Lucinda said smoothly. "It seems a strange coincidence that you were in Alanan at the same time as the Darkhand. I didn't expect Ahrin to deliver you for some days or weeks yet, not until she'd seen things through in Alanan."

Lira took a breath, letting the thrill make her sharp, confident. She gave a little shrug, added a dash of impatience to her voice. "It was an odd coincidence, I agree, but that's all it was. Ahrin presumably told you we were taken from Temari to a safer location because the council didn't think we were safe at Temari?" Lira waited for their nods, then continued, "We were taken to Alistriem, kept locked up in the palace under guard for weeks. It was mind-numbingly boring, though a good opportunity to work on my friendship with Garan and Tarion. They sent us back via—"

"Why send you back now?" Lucinda cut in.

Lira shrugged, not having to feign the irritation she felt. "They decided the situation was safe for us again back in Karonan. At least, that's what they told us, but I honestly don't know the real answer—the council isn't big on keeping apprentices and initiates informed of what's going on. It's damned infuriating."

"Curious." Lucinda sounded more suspicious than curious, and she looked at Greyson. "Let's get our contacts to find out why their position changed."

"As soon as I get back," he promised.

Lira glanced between them. "When you find out, I expect you to tell me. I want to know more. I want to know everything."

"Understood. To start with, this is our main base of operations." Lucinda continued without hesitation, astonishing Lira by providing some actual specific information. "Here we can make you strong. Give you more magical abilities. Hand you the tools you need to become the symbol for our followers to unite behind."

"And the Darkhand? Why is she so important?" Lira asked, wondering if Underground's plans for Ahrin lined up with their plans for Lira.

"She'll be an invaluable tool at your disposal, just like she has been to the Shadowcouncil." Lucinda leaned forward. "You will together bring us to victory."

"Against the Mage Council?" Lira wanted to ensure she was completely clear. It still nagged at her, wondering if they were right about the Shadowcouncil's motivations.

Lucinda sat back, crossed her legs. "Of course."

Lira studied her. That answer had been very quick. But beside her Greyson was wearing an expression of almost rapture. "Mages should be leading this world. They have the power and the skills to do it properly, like your grandfather envisioned. They'll make a better life for all of us."

Lucinda met and held her gaze. "If that's what you want too, of course."

"I want to make them all forget my grandfather and remember me instead," Lira said, keeping as close to the truth as possible. "But this is a fight for control of the mages, a better way of ruling, not a general slaughter of civilians. My grandfather let his emotions, his need for vengeance, get the better of him. It's why he lost. I won't make the same mistake."

"I agree, to a point," Greyson said. "But once we have control of the mage order, we may face resistance from the monarchs. There will be blood."

"I'm aware of that. But with our mage skills and abilities, we should be able to quell their armies with a minimum of bloodshed." Lira leaned forward. After much thought on the issue, she'd identified this as one of her grandfather's greatest errors. "Don't mistake my concern for softness. Resistance to us will lessen if people have no reason to resist. Kill innocents, and it makes people angry. It will unite them against us, like it did my grandfather."

"I'm glad you've been thinking so carefully on this, Lira," Lucinda said. "Your point is well made and something we've already considered. Be assured we will succeed where your grandfather failed."

Lira let out a breath. "Then what's next?"

Lucinda smiled, and it even held a hint of warmth. "You've had a long couple of days. Ahrin will take you to where you'll be sleeping while you're here, and she can show you where to wash and get something to eat. Rest today. Tomorrow, you can begin."

"Begin what?"

Greyson opened his mouth, saw Lucinda's look, and closed it, offering Lira a smile instead. Lira frowned, wondering what it was making Greyson seem off. But Lucinda replied before she could pursue the thought any further.

"Your training. Tell me, have you been able to consciously wield your new ability yet?"

Lira stilled.

"You'll get more of those too." Lucinda's smile turned wolfish as she read the answer in Lira's face. "You'll get everything you want with us, Lira Astor."

"Finally." Lira let a cold smile, matching Lucinda's in its ice, spread across her face. She knew it made her look like him. Knew it would reassure any doubts they held. "I can't wait to get started."

CHAPTER 31

A hrin waited outside, leaning against the rocky wall opposite the door, hands in her pockets, looking utterly relaxed. But there was a glint in her midnight blue eyes that told Lira she wasn't pleased to have been left out of the meeting.

Lira frowned. What mistake could Ahrin have made that led to the council learning of her presence at Temari? Lira could ask, but knew the response would not be forthcoming, and would likely only bring on one of the Darkhand's cold furies.

She wondered if Lucinda or the Shadowcouncil understood the twin-edged blade they had in Ahrin. More importantly, she wondered how successfully Ahrin had duped them into thinking she was a loyal follower. Unease shivered through Lira. Lucinda didn't strike her as someone who could be fooled. Not for long, anyway.

"Good chat?" Despite her discontent, the Darkhand's voice was casual as she escorted Lira back along the tunnel.

"Better than previous conversations with Lucinda. I was surprised to see Greyson here."

Ahrin glanced at her. "As was I."

Lira immediately picked up on the tone that signalled Ahrin was uneasy. "Is there something wrong?"

"For him to travel all the way here in person, his information must have been important." Her jaw hardened slightly. "Yet I have not been told what it was."

"You just got here," Lira pointed out.

"Greyson is supposed to communicate with Lucinda through me. *I* decide what is important enough for him to risk breaking cover to travel to meet her."

"They told me about Temari. They're probably just punishing you." Lira paused, decided to push at the hold Lucinda had over Ahrin, weaken it as much as possible. "Tell me, are you planning on simply waiting out your punishment like a good, well-trained attack dog?"

"Good try." Ahrin smiled in what appeared to be genuine amusement. "You just won't let go of the fact I'm the Darkhand, will you? Are you envious of the position I hold?"

"You know why I won't let go. I don't understand it," Lira said. "My reasons for being here, for joining Underground, are obvious. But you... none of this is like you."

"And you keep worrying at it like a dog with a bone. Why do you care so much?" Ahrin challenged, coming to a sudden stop.

"I..." Lira was genuinely flummoxed for a moment, not even sure *she* knew the real answer. But then it came, smooth and easy. "You're my enemy, Ahrin. And what did you always teach me about my enemies?"

"Understand them better than you understand yourself," the Darkhand murmured. "I'm only your enemy if you get in my way, Lira, and I see no reason that has to happen, especially now you're here."

"True," Lira said softly, allowing a little smile to cross her face to match Ahrin's. "Together, you said?"

"They need us more than we need them." Ahrin's gaze searched hers, as if looking for something she couldn't find.

"You confuse me with your constant switching between 'them' and 'us'," Lira murmured. "How loyal are you to the Shadowcouncil?"

"As loyal as I need to be."

Another non-answer.

"Tell me, Lira, how loyal are *you*?"

"You still doubt me?" Lira lifted an eyebrow.

Ahrin said nothing, instead turning away and beginning to walk again. Lira let out an inward sigh of relief, thoughts clearing as she was released from the intensity of the Darkhand's attention. She changed the subject. "Do the rest of the Shadowcouncil live here too?"

Ahrin glanced at her, something speculative flitting over her expression. "No."

A brief silence fell, throughout which Lira reminded herself that she had to be beyond careful where Ahrin was concerned. She had the advantage of knowing Ahrin better than Lucinda did, even with all of Lucinda's impressive abilities to read people and situations and keep everything under her control. But Ahrin knew Lira just as well, and recruiting her wasn't going to be easy.

Ahrin turned into a wider tunnel with doors set into the wall at regular intervals. It was a short tunnel, and daylight shone in from the opposite end, showing trees and a light drizzle falling. Ahrin stopped at a door halfway along. "This is you. Get some sleep. Someone will be by in the morning to show you around."

"And where will you be?"

The Darkhand glanced left and right, then lowered her voice. "They're sending me back to Alanan tonight to finish up things there. We'll talk when I get back."

"What exactly is Underground doing there?"

"You already know about the strikes and unrest." Ahrin was growing impatient. "The Shadowcouncil is taking the first steps. When I left, the Alanan city government, with the support of the Mage Council, were about to concede to our demands."

Lira lifted her eyebrows; that was the opposite of what Duneskal had told them. "Which are what, exactly?"

"Better pay and conditions for every guild."

Lira snorted. "I see how that helps those who Underground recruit for its cause, but I'm far from convinced that's what Lucinda's true motive is."

"Then you should ask *her* about it."

"All right," Lira conceded, then glanced toward the trees at the end of the tunnel. "I'm allowed to just wander around?"

"You're not a prisoner here, Lira." Ahrin's voice stayed low. "I'll send you a message when I've returned. It shouldn't be more than a few days. Come to me as soon as you get it—take a left at the fork we just passed and follow that tunnel all the way to its end. My door is the final one on the right. Make sure nobody sees you."

Lira's eyes narrowed in suspicion. Was Ahrin setting some sort of trap? "So I'm not a prisoner but I have to sneak around to—"

"Just do as I say," she said, what sounded like genuine frustration filling her voice.

Lira lifted her hands in surrender. "All right."

Ahrin walked away. Lira turned the handle on her door, pushing it open.

"Lira?"

She turned back. Ahrin had stopped several paces away, a speculative look on her face. "Yes?"

"What you said back there, that your reasons for being here, for joining Underground, are obvious?"

"What of it?"

"That's the thing. They're not obvious, not at all. Because I know you inside and out, Lira Astor. You want nothing to do with your grandfather's name. You never have. And I don't believe that changed during your time at Temari Hall."

Ahrin turned, coat swirling around her ankles, leaving without giving Lira an opportunity to respond—which was just as well, because Lira didn't have a good response to give.

A chill rippled through her, this time not so quickly displaced by the thrill of danger. Lira was abruptly glad Ahrin was leaving.

Managing the Darkhand was going to take preparation and planning.

CHAPTER 32

Lira's gaze lingered on the tunnel where Ahrin had disappeared for several long moments before she realised what she was doing and tore her attention away. The door in front of her opened soundlessly, revealing a small cave with a single bed, a lit lamp, and a chest of drawers. Next to the lamp on the chest was a tray of food and water.

It didn't take long to case the room. No windows. No other exits apart from the door.

Leaving the room untouched, she left and walked down to the end of the tunnel. It emerged onto a sloping field surrounded by thick forest. The grass was muddy and disturbed, like it had been trampled by multiple booted feet, but right now it was deserted. The light was fading rapidly as the sun sank below the horizon, and a light curtain of drizzling rain fell around her.

Nobody appeared to stop her when she walked out into the field, testing the freedom Ahrin claimed she had. Her instincts roused, telling her she should go further into the forest, identify an escape route in the event she needed one. But for now she quelled them. Testing Lucinda could wait until she was on a more solid footing with the woman.

Best to act like she was exactly where she wanted to be.

LIRA SLEPT RESTLESSLY THAT NIGHT, unwilling to truly relax in the headquarters of the enemy without any means of barricading or locking the entrance to her room. Eventually she gave up on sleep when a quick glance out the door showed early morning light at the end of the tunnel.

A knock came just as Lira finished the food she hadn't touched the night before; several slices of now-stale bread and a topping made of mushed vegetables. A tall man stood outside the door. He looked about Ahrin's age, and was clearly Shiven; broad-shouldered and muscular with white-pale skin and dark brown eyes. He was also heavily armed. Lira's roving gaze caught multiple knives and a dagger strapped to his body in addition to a large sword hanging down his back. She'd put money on there being more weapons hidden on his person.

He bowed slightly. "I've been asked to give you a tour, Lady Astor."

Lira brightened. She'd been worried, despite her words, that Lucinda planned to just leave her in this room staring at the walls. "Good. What's your name?"

"Shiasta."

"Nice to meet you, Shiasta. Shall we go?" Lira stepped out and closed the door.

Shiasta set off with long, graceful strides. This was a trained warrior, despite his young age. He wore simple breeches, shirt, and tunic in plain grey, all fitting his muscular frame perfectly. The part of Lira that had once pick-pocketed throughout Dirinan caught a glimpse of a chain around his neck, though it was hidden by a high collar, and noted it as the only accessory he wore.

There was something else too, a very faint dissonance Lira felt near him. A blurring of her senses. She blinked, shook her head, but the sensation remained. "Are you a mage, Shiasta?"

"No, Lady Astor. I'm a soldier."

And a man of few words, it seemed. "Where are we going first?"

"The Seventh has given me clear instructions. First she wishes me to show you to where the prisoner is being kept."

The Seventh. Lira had heard Lucinda addressed that way once before, by Jora back at DarkSkull during their captivity. She wondered what it meant—was Lucinda the seventh member of the Shadowcouncil? That would make sense. They'd always assumed there were eight of them to match the eight councillors on the Mage Council, after all.

"You hold prisoners here?" she asked, wanting to test how much Shiasta was allowed to tell her.

"Just one at the moment, but we are outfitted to hold several more if necessary."

By now Shiasta had taken her down a narrow set of steps that ended in an equally narrow passageway branching to her left and right. Lira had picked up the underlying scent of human waste the moment they'd started down the steps, a smell not entirely masked by fresh straw and smoke from the torches lining the tunnel.

Interestingly, the cells looked almost identical to the ones she and Tarion had seen at DarkSkull. Shiasta turned right, leading her to one at the end. All the others they passed were empty. Lira braced herself —an Underground prisoner could be anyone—and peered inside.

Then froze.

A girl sat on a pile of blankets at the back of the cell, cross-legged, busy pulling her wavy blonde hair back into a braid. Light blue eyes widened with shock at Lira's appearance.

"Athira?"

A hooded look dropped down over Athira's eyes as her gaze shifted to take in Shiasta. "Lira Astor, what a surprise."

Lira didn't hesitate, didn't show her shock—or the relief that surprisingly surged in her chest—but merely crossed her arms and gave the girl a cool stare. "So this is where they've been keeping you?"

Athira returned her look and didn't say a word.

Lira smiled slightly while Shiasta remained still and silent at her side. "The council have been looking for you."

"Is *that* why you're here, because you were looking for me and now you've found me?" Athira said, anger edging her voice. "Or is it because you're secretly a member of Underground and have been for years?"

"Clearly you already know the answer to that." Lira shrugged. "What have they told you about me?"

"*Told* me?" Athira huffed a bitter breath. "*Bragged*, more like."

Lira took in the cell. "Are you comfortable?"

"I'm a prisoner." Athira's jaw hardened. "They experiment on me. I can't control..." She took a deep breath, her icy demeanour returning. "Just leave me alone. I don't want to talk to a traitor."

Lira couldn't blame her; she'd feel the exact same way in Athira's position. It wasn't like Lira could tell her the truth with Shiasta standing right beside her. Asking him to leave so they could have a private conversation was a risk she wasn't willing to take yet. "How long have you been here?"

Athira shifted on the pile of blankets, lay down on her back, and stared up at the ceiling.

Lira sighed, looked at Shiasta. "Is she always this communicative?"

"Guards don't talk to the prisoner, Lady Astor. We have orders."

So well trained *and* highly disciplined, this young man. Lira nodded. "We can go."

Before Athira's cell was even out of sight, Lira had started thinking about how she was going to get the girl out of this place without Underground knowing Lira was responsible. It couldn't be her first priority—that had to be maintaining her cover and digging her way deeper into the group—but if an opportunity arose, Lira promised herself she would take it. She owed Athira that much. Not to mention, it was what Tarion and Garan and the others would want her to do.

And that mattered to her now.

"You said 'we' back there. No guard posted outside her cell, though?" she asked at the top of the stairs.

"No need, Lady Astor. The prisoner has no ability to break through the bars. Even if she did, there is no way for her to get off the island before one of us hunted her down."

She glanced at him sharply. "How many of you are there exactly?"

"If you would hold that thought one moment." He brought them back to the tunnel her room was in and continued all the way along till they emerged into daylight.

Lira's eyes widened at the sight before her. Whereas the previous night the clearing had been empty, now three rows of warriors, dressed identically to Shiasta, filled the space—training with real blades in an intricate drill that looked more like a dance than combat. All were Shiven, with what appeared to be a roughly even split of men and women. None looked older than their mid-twenties, the youngest appearing roughly Lira's age.

"I hope we meet with your approval, Lady Astor?" Shiasta spoke suddenly at her side.

Her eyes narrowed. "Who are they?"

"My combat unit." Shiasta stepped forward to lift a hand and call a sharp order. Instantly the pattern of the sparring fighters changed, smooth as silk, and they whirled around to face Lira's direction and salute.

But she barely noticed. Her gaze had gone straight to the inside of Shiasta's right wrist, where the sleeve of his tunic had fallen when he lifted his hand. To the black tattoo on his skin. Three jagged lines, like claw marks.

The same as Ahrin's.

Shiasta dropped his hand, turning to look at her with a question in his eyes. She quickly hid her shocked expression and gestured to the warriors. "They look well trained. Have they ever actually been in a fight?"

"Not yet. But when the time comes, we will not fail you."

"I hope not," she said coolly, trying to hide the inner chaos of her thoughts. What did that tattoo mean? Where had Underground gotten these warriors? Who had trained them? For a moment she warred with herself, finally settling on the most innocuous question she could think of. "How long have you been here, Shiasta?"

"Some years, Lady Astor. We have been preparing a long time."

"Is your unit the only one here on Shadowfall?"

"Currently, yes. But others exist."

"Was it Underground who taught you to fight like that?"

Shiasta answered as smoothly and quickly as before, like these answers had been prepared and practised by rote. "We were trained to be a deadly tool for your coming war."

"And that tattoo on your wrist? Where did you get it?"

"Many years ago, Lady Astor."

Lira nodded, repressing a sigh at another vague response. Shiasta wasn't the right person to ask those questions. "Thank you for showing me, Shiasta. Where to next?"

"The kitchen and meals area. You are welcome to eat there whenever you choose."

"When do you and your unit usually eat?"

"We eat separately from the other inhabitants of the island, so a little earlier than you might be used to for breakfast, lunch, and dinner."

"How many other inhabitants are there?" And what did they do, she wondered.

"I couldn't tell you," he said.

She narrowed her eyes, unclear whether he didn't know, or wasn't allowed to tell her. His demeanour hadn't changed at all, not even a slight shift. The wrist tattoo wasn't his only similarity to Ahrin.

"After the tour, can you take me to the Seventh? I need to speak with her."

"I am sorry, she left strict instructions not to be disturbed today." He sounded genuinely apologetic. "After our tour, I am to take you to meet the mage who will be teaching you. I will ask if the Seventh is available to see you tomorrow, if that suits?"

"Thank you, Shiasta. You have been very helpful."

SHIASTA'S TOUR took most of the morning, and after eating a brief lunch together, the hulking warrior took her along a corridor leading straight from the dining area to a large, open cavern. Several spots on the rocky walls were dark with charring and the space was clear of any furniture.

A man waited in the centre of the space, and at their entrance, his gaze shifted to Shiasta. "Leave us."

Shiasta bowed and departed without a word. Annoyed by the dismissive tone the mage had used with Shiasta, Lira nonetheless schooled her features to cool disinterest as she walked over to the man. Once she was close enough, she recognised him quickly. He was one of the mages who'd been part of their kidnapping—Lucinda had called him Jora. They hadn't been sure of his mage ability, but he'd appeared to be more involved in the experiments than the others with Lucinda, so she'd suspected he had healing magic.

The sight of him brought back the helpless fury of being held captive in that place, strapped to a table, and her hands curled into fists at her sides. "You try and touch me ever again, we're going to have a problem. Clear?"

He smiled thinly. "I will do whatever is necessary to ensure your training is successful. Those are my orders. I don't take them from you."

Her mouth tightened in contempt. "And how is a paltry healer mage going to help *me*?"

A red flush rose up his neck, but he didn't otherwise respond to her taunt. It was enough to tell Lira that her guess as to his mage ability had been right though. So she dropped the antagonism, letting out a sigh and using a brisk tone. "I want my training to be a success too. The stronger I am, the more use I'll be to the cause. If you can help me then I'll willingly accept that help," she said, then paused. "As long as we're clear on one thing."

"Which is?" He lifted an eyebrow.

"I am Shakar's heir. One day you will be taking orders from me."

"That is very clear, Lira." His smile didn't reach his eyes. "Shall we start with you telling me what your new ability is? I am told the experiments we conducted at DarkSkull were successful."

Lira took a breath and summoned her new fire magic, the violet-edged flames wreathing the fingers of her right hand.

"Good, an offensive ability. Anything else?"

She let the magic go. "Not yet. Should there be?"

"You were given three treatments. If all of them worked, you should have displayed those abilities within a matter of weeks. It's been more than two months. We'll submit you for another treatment soon."

Lira shivered. Her thirst for more magic was tempered now by witnessing what had happened to Tarion, not to mention her lingering fear over what that look of triumph on Lucinda's face had meant. Until she understood what had been done to both her and Tarion, she wouldn't be allowing any more tests. "Was that all you did at Dark-Skull? Just three injections of razak blood?"

"That was all," he said, impatience beginning to colour his voice.

"I'm given to understand that was a particularly dangerous thing to do, that I could have died?"

"In your case the risks were lower than for others, because of your existing mage powers and your bloodline." He shrugged. "We must all take risks for the greater good."

"I couldn't agree more." She smiled. "Do you know why the experiments didn't work on the others? None of them broke out with new abilities after we got back to Temari."

"Yes, our spies informed us of the same thing, but they are a different matter entirely." Jora waved a hand, dismissing the topic. "Shall we begin your training?"

Lira conceded. Best not to be suspicious by pushing too hard. "There's nothing I'd like more."

It was the first truth Lira had spoken in days.

AFTER FINISHING WITH JORA, the remnants of her magic still humming delightfully in her veins, Lira went searching for Lucinda despite Shiasta's words from earlier.

The woman was nowhere to be found. Lira asked one of the cooks in the kitchen about Greyson, and the young woman told Lira he'd left the night before. She didn't know where Lucinda was, or where the woman's quarters were. After a long, circuitous walk, Lira found the sitting room Ahrin had led her to the previous day, but the fire was out and the room empty.

Giving up on Lucinda, Lira went back to see Athira. The girl was still sitting on the pile of blankets and listlessly picking at a tray of food. Her head came up at Lira's appearance, but she said nothing.

"What are they doing to you here?" Lira asked. There had been no guard at the top of the stairway entrance, and Lira had made sure to check every cell was empty on her way through. Their conversation should be private.

"What do you care?" Athira's voice was harsh, but her eyes glistened as if she fought back tears.

Lira's fury at Underground surged unexpectedly. Athira didn't deserve this. She might be a pureblood mage, arrogant and ignorant, but torture wasn't what she deserved.

"I don't, really." Lira paused, looked around, just to make sure nobody was around before continuing. "But I am curious. Underground need me, but they're not always forthcoming."

Athira snorted. "If you think I'm going to help you in your little ego trip with Lucinda and her goons, you've got another thing coming."

"You know, their experiments worked on me." Lira lifted her hand, summoned enough flame to dance around her fingers. "Is it the same for you?"

"I'm not going to tell you anything."

"If you help me, maybe I can get you some nicer food? A walk in the fresh air? I do have some sway here, you know."

Athira's mouth tightened and she said nothing.

Frustration burned. Lira wished she could just tell Athira the truth, so that they could work together. But that was too risky. She couldn't rule out that Underground had a telepath mage here on the island, and besides, there was no guarantee Athira would believe her.

"Suit yourself." Lira shrugged. "Enjoy that cell."

Athira said nothing, so Lira turned and left, trying to push away the guilt that continued to nag at her. The girl was at least alive and appeared to be in relatively good health. And Lira being on Shadowfall meant she was closer than ever to bringing down Underground. All she had to do was keep playing her dangerous game with Lucinda and Ahrin successfully.

Athira would be fine. Lira would make sure of it.

CHAPTER 33

Lira deliberately went to the kitchens early that evening so she could join Shiasta and his warriors for dinner. The following day, she did the same at lunch and dinner.

Ahrin wasn't the only one it would be useful to recruit to her side. If Lira could win what seemed to be Underground's fighting force out from under them too, then all the better. Not to mention they were another source of potential answers.

Digging for information was mostly a frustrating endeavour, though. The Shiven warriors were unfailingly polite, deferential even, but had little to say when asked questions. While she'd learned from one of them that there were two other units based on the island—both led by female warriors—and several others based elsewhere, they couldn't or wouldn't tell her where or exactly how many. They were similarly unable or unwilling to answer questions about Lucinda, the Shadowcouncil, or what Lucinda and her mages were up to on Shadowfall Island.

After spending a handful of meals talking with them, Lira began to grow more confident they weren't hiding things—they simply didn't know the answers. Nor did they seem curious about the answers to the questions she asked them.

That was the oddest thing about them. They behaved like any other disciplined soldier—elite fighting skills aside—but there was something *other* about them. It took her a day or two to figure it out, and when she realised what it was, she started paying closer attention. They didn't get angry. Or upset. They didn't laugh, or even chuckle. Occasionally one of them smiled, when they'd defeated an opponent or perfected a particularly difficult move. When Shiasta praised them, they looked pleased and proud. But that was the extent of their emotion.

Ahrin's words came back to Lira as she watched them eating one day at lunch, quick efficient movements, but no chatter or banter. "*I don't know affection, Lira, I was never taught it. I never experienced it.*"

The tattoo on Shiasta's wrist was proof that there was a connection between these fighters and the Darkhand, and Lira would bet everything she owned it was that connection that had drawn all of them to Underground's attention.

But what was it?

A<small>HRIN RETURNED FOUR DAYS LATER.</small>

Lira had just arrived back at her room after another dinner with her warriors. Once again it had been a mostly quiet affair, Lira's attempts at conversation the only words that were spoken. They weren't annoyed by her questions—not obviously anyway—but once they'd answered her they never sought to continue the conversation.

If she was honest, they were really growing on her. She found herself missing the company of Garan and the others, their easy banter. And while these warriors were nothing like the other apprentices, she felt comfortable with them in the same way she'd grown comfortable with those she'd been kidnapped with.

Who *were* they, though, and how had they ended up with Underground? Her frustration wasn't helped by Lucinda's continued absence, and Jora's refusal to tell Lira when the woman would see her. Lira wanted to move forward, but she couldn't do that while she was sitting on this island learning nothing.

Relief flooded her when she sat on her bed and noticed the small coin under the pillow. The promised message from Ahrin. Good. Hopefully the Darkhand was back to stay, and Lira could work further on her recruitment... actually start accomplishing something.

Remembering Ahrin's insistence she not be seen, Lira cracked open the door and peered down the passage outside to ensure it was empty before slipping out and closing it behind her. She spent a moment recalling Ahrin's instructions, then set off, using the quiet step of her old criminal life, ready with an innocent explanation about being in search of a snack if she ran into anyone.

Ahrin opened the door at the first quiet knock and waved Lira in without a word. Lira stepped inside, then came to an immediate halt, her gaze taking in the four-poster bed, crackling fire, wardrobe, and table and chairs. "Why is your room so much nicer than mine?" she demanded with mock-indignance.

Ahrin ignored the joke, her expression tight as she closed and locked the door. It put Lira immediately on guard. Wariness filled her.

"Did anyone see you come here?" Ahrin asked.

"No, I was careful. You told me to be."

Ahrin came to stand before her, gaze hooded. "Good. Now, tell me what's really going on, Lira."

Lira lifted an eyebrow, kept her stance relaxed, expression slightly puzzled. "You might have to be a little more specific."

"Your friends escaped Alanan. They're fine, and safely back at Temari Hall."

Lira couldn't hide it. Not entirely. Not when Ahrin was so close, her sharp gaze watching every minute change in Lira's expression. Her relief was visible, even if only for the briefest of seconds.

"That news clearly pleases you. Explain to me why. Now." She spoke with deceptive mildness, putting Lira even more on guard. This was Ahrin at her most dangerous, the time when you either did what she told you, or you didn't escape the situation.

Lira tried to deflect anyway. "I don't know what you're—"

"Save it," she snarled, then her voice lowered. "You're working against Underground, aren't you? Spying on them. For the Mage Council, I presume?"

There was so much certainty in Ahrin's voice. How could she

know... sudden realisation ripped through Lira. Then she cursed herself for a fool for not figuring it out straight away. "You lied to Lucinda about messing up at Temari Hall."

Ahrin cocked her head, stepped closer. "I don't make mistakes, Lira, you know that better than anyone. There's only one way the council found out about me, and that's you telling them. Unless there's another explanation you'd like to give me right now?"

Lira said nothing, her thoughts rapidly working to figure out a plausible explanation that Ahrin would buy. It would have to be airtight or the Darkhand would see through it instantly. But she took too long.

"Don't," Ahrin said flatly, disgust crossing her face when the silence drew out. "I can practically see your brain trying to come up with a good lie. You told them about me. Why?"

Lira's desperate search for a plausible lie to save herself was momentarily side-tracked by puzzlement. She was in no doubt about how deeply her life was in danger—Ahrin wasn't a foe Lira could easily overcome, if at all. Yet the Darkhand was keeping her voice low, as if she didn't want anyone passing outside to hear her. And she'd lied to Underground about how she'd been caught at Temari, protecting Lira and taking Lucinda's punishment without complaint.

Lira frowned, trying to figure out Ahrin's game. What was she after? If she could figure *that* out, then she could get herself out of this. Salvage the mission.

The silence stretched out. Eventually Ahrin let out a sharp breath, turning abruptly to cross over to her fire, where she started to pace. Lira watched her, despite the danger unable to help being mesmerised by the grace of Ahrin's movements, the way her dark hair swished around her shoulders. Her coat hung by the door and she wore only a loose shirt over breeches, her feet bare on the rug.

Lira swallowed and dragged her gaze away. She needed to work out what Ahrin wanted so that she could figure out the right lie. Giving nothing away until then was better. Less for Ahrin to read into, to pick apart. She cleared her throat, ensured her voice came out relaxed but confident. "You're making a lot of incorrect assumptions."

"Am I? You really want me to list all the reasons I know I'm right, or can I save us both the tedium?" Ahrin snapped.

"It's not what you think," Lira said carefully. Ahrin was so certain. But she hadn't handed Lira over to Lucinda. Lira could work with that, surely.

"We don't lie to each other, Lira. We *never* lied to..." Ahrin stopped pacing, her dark blue eyes distant as she stared at the fire, turned mostly away so Lira couldn't see her expression. Her fingers tapped against her leg—her single tell, the one that betrayed she was unsettled.

Lira's first instinct was to laugh out loud in incredulity, but the sad note in Ahrin's voice... she'd never heard it before, and it slid right through all the walls she'd put up. It made her own misery spill out. "Our whole life was a lie, Ahrin. You made it a lie."

Thick silence fell. Lira didn't know what was going on, what to say, so she just stood there, the familiar ache filling her chest so fiercely that she unconsciously bit her lip. She had no shields, no barriers, no ability to protect herself where Ahrin was concerned, no matter how hard she tried. If anyone knew that, if *Ahrin* found out... Lira would be completely at their mercy.

When Ahrin spoke again, her voice was distant, and there was a note to it that Lira had never heard before. Melancholy? "Back in Dirinan, I got word that there were folk asking around about you. People looking for an orphan girl who was rumoured to be the last living heir of Shakar."

Lira stilled. Literally every muscle in her body froze, and it seemed as if the very breath in her lungs hung there, unable to move, not until...

"I looked into it." Ahrin shrugged. "The gangs tend to protect their own, but I knew if these people offered the right amount of money, someone would rat you out. Not least the Gutter Rats. They had it out for you bad."

"You never told me..." Lira tried to keep control of her racing thoughts, but it was like grasping at falling sand. "When *was* this?"

Ahrin took a breath and turned to look at her. Everything was wiped from her expression, the way it always was when she was truly upset, when her masks failed her. "I had some of Transk's runners check it out. Crew mages had been going missing, washing up dead on the shore, as you know, and I worried the two were connected. The runner told me the people asking about you were dangerous. Worse than dangerous. And they were offering a lot of money. I was surprised someone hadn't taken it already."

"Ahrin." Lira's throat closed over as she started to see where this was heading. As she remembered back to three years earlier, Ahrin's distraction those last few weeks before she'd abandoned the crew, how something had been bothering her but she'd refused to say what it was no matter how often Lira asked. "What did you do?"

"I knew the only place you'd be safe was Temari Hall, where you'd be surrounded by warrior mages and could learn your magic so that you could protect yourself." Frustration rippled over Ahrin's face. "But you kept refusing to go, despite how hard I pushed. And I knew you were only staying in Dirinan because of me. So I took myself out of the picture."

Lira swallowed. "Are you telling me you left because..." She couldn't finish saying the words. Her throat had closed over too fiercely at the implications, at the re-ordering of her entire world. Tears stung her eyes.

"I left because it was the only way I could think to get you to *leave*, to go to Temari Hall where you would be safe." Ahrin's face hardened. "And the day after you finally left, after watching you ride away from Dirinan in that cart, I approached Underground and offered to join them. Without you, my prospects of taking Transk's spot were poor, and I figured they were another way to get the power I wanted."

Lira lifted a trembling hand to pinch the bridge of her nose, shaking her head as if to dispel the words, make them untrue. "These are just more of your lies. You're only telling me this as another manipulation. I know you. You like being part of Underground, they gave you magic, they give you power. You *kidnapped* me. You helped them torture me."

"They're a means to an end, which I've told you from the beginning. Yes, I enjoy the power they give me. Yes, I'm using them," Ahrin said, her words sharp, incisive, cutting through everything Lira had ever believed. "I orchestrated their kidnap plan because if I didn't, they would have left me out of it. Which meant I wouldn't have been able to protect you."

"Protect me? By convincing me to hand myself over to them?" Lira practically shouted the words.

"Did I?" Ahrin asked softly. "Or did you want it the moment I told you about it, no matter how dangerous?"

She had. It was true.

"It would have happened whether I convinced you or not, and by delivering you so willingly, I gained further influence with Lucinda. I was able to argue that they should use the least dangerous approach first... because it *is* dangerous, Lira. The more frequently it's done, the more dangerous it gets."

"This can't be true." Lira whispered the words mostly to herself. It couldn't. Because she'd lived the past years utterly broken by Ahrin's abandonment, and her re-appearance with Underground had dug even deeper into that wound. She'd nursed the anger from it, used it to bury the pain. Used it to make her stronger, focused, to hold everyone else at arm's length so that she couldn't be hurt that way again.

It couldn't be that the whole time Ahrin had been trying to *protect* her.

That Ahrin had cared enough about *Lira* to give up everything she'd been working for.

Ahrin sighed, looking weary. "I wanted better for you, Lira. Better than this. Better than what I am."

The words echoed through the room, despite how softly they'd been spoken.

"Why?" Lira's voice was raspy, thick with emotion. "You wanted Transk and his patch and his money and his power more than anything else in the world, yet now you ask me to believe that you gave all that up to get me away from Underground. Why would you do all that for me?"

"You know why," Ahrin said bluntly, not an inch of softness in her voice. "You just refuse to accept it because you think it's impossible for anyone to love you."

More silence. Lira stared at her. She shook her head, still unable to believe it, too *scared* to believe it. "You said you didn't care about anything. You told me that. You said it wasn't in you."

"It isn't! It wasn't!" Agonised fury rippled through Ahrin's voice, born of frustration and confusion, and several books went flying off the table by her bed to slam against the wall. She turned back to Lira, eyes blazing. "What I feel for you is uncomfortable and unfamiliar, and it's a *weakness,* and I hate it, and I don't know what to do with it." She laughed bitterly. "More fool me. Now I know you're a spy... when you kissed me, pretended to start trusting me... it was all an act, wasn't it? You were trying to recruit me for my access into Underground. Turning my own game around on me. I should be proud."

"Ahrin..." She trailed off, unable to lie.

"You're the only person in this world who could fool me like that." She huffed a bitter breath. "The *only* one. And I let you do it."

"Yes, I was trying to recruit you," Lira said, clearing her throat. "But there was no act. You know there wasn't."

Ahrin lifted her eyes to Lira's. "Do I?"

Lira crossed the space between them in three strides, leaning up to press her mouth to Ahrin's. Ahrin's arms were instantly around her, pulling her flush against her body, turning the kiss fierce and hungry.

Lira's searching hands found the waistband of Ahrin's breeches and yanked out her shirt and then she broke the kiss so she could tug it up over her head, revealing bare skin underneath. She stared for a dizzying moment, breath catching at Ahrin's beauty, then her palms slid over her waist, her ribs, weaving higher.

"Lira—"

She cut Ahrin off with another kiss, finding her hands and drawing them to the buttons on Lira's shirt. Once they'd begun working, she continued her exploration of Ahrin's soft skin, eyes closing in delight as Ahrin pushed her shirt off her shoulders and found the same bare skin.

Ahrin's mouth moved urgently along her jaw, her ear, her breath warm, her voice husky as she said, "Come to bed."

CHAPTER 34

Ahrin stretched slowly at Lira's side, drawing her gaze like a magnet. "So what are you offering me?" the Darkhand asked lazily. "To help you destroy Underground on behalf of the Mage Council, I mean. Although I don't know why you'd want to—using Underground to take over the world is a much better idea."

Caught up in staring, not to mention processing the utter... *wonder*... of what had just happened, Lira didn't reply immediately.

Ahrin's serious look turned into a smirk. "You with me?"

"Not really." Lira leaned down to kiss her. "Sorry for the awkwardness."

"I don't remember any awkwardness," Ahrin murmured, pressing a kiss to her cheek, then her forehead. "I don't remember anything but how something I've so badly wanted for so long was much more satisfying than I could ever have imagined. And trust me, I imagined it."

Lira tried not to turn red, failed, and in an attempt to distract herself, replied to Ahrin's original question. "Trying to take over the world with Underground just makes me Shakar all over again. Helping to destroy them on behalf of the Mage Council gives me what I want."

Maybe she was foolish for stating it out loud. Maybe that had even been Ahrin's intention, to seduce her into incriminating herself, giving her more leverage. But right at this moment, Lira wasn't sure she cared. Her world had turned upside down and her head was still spinning. No matter the truth, she didn't want to play games with Ahrin anymore.

Ahrin shifted, head turning on the pillow to face Lira, one eyebrow lifting. "Which is what exactly? The love and adoration of the Mage Council to whom you have pledged your endless loyalty, or the destruction of Underground because they kidnapped and hunted you and made you mad?"

Lira hesitated, then said, "It didn't change when I got to Temari Hall, you know?"

"What didn't change?"

"The looks. The instant fear and wariness. The suspicion." She murmured the words, the little bubble of warmth between them keeping all the remembered hurt at a distance.

Ahrin was silent a moment, cold anger flashing over her face. "You agreed to spy on Underground as a way to win recognition, respect. A way to make them all stop thinking about Shakar when they look at you, and instead thinking about *you* and your achievements."

"Yes." Lira moved, shifting so that she could press a kiss to Ahrin's bare shoulder. "And after what they did to me, I personally want to see Lucinda and Underground razed to the ground."

"And then what?"

"Hmmm?" Lira moved further down Ahrin's bare back, placing kisses as she went. Ahrin's skin tasted like peaches and saltwater, a particularly wonderful flavour she didn't think she'd ever be able to forget.

Ahrin hadn't abandoned her. Ahrin had tried to protect her. The knowledge brought a dizzying rush of emotion every time she thought about it.

"Are you trying to distract me right now?" Ahrin's voice turned husky.

"Yes."

Ahrin moved, turning over and fending off Lira's wandering hands. "You bring down Underground on behalf of the council. You get showered with glory. Then what?"

"Then they forget I'm Shakar's heir. And they see me."

"That simple, huh?" Ahrin shrugged when Lira simply nodded. "You know, if you used Underground to take over the world, and you succeeded, Shakar would be forgotten. You'd have done what he twice failed to do."

Lira cocked her head. "Is that what you want me to do?"

"It seems the simpler path, is all. Why not just take what you want? Why go to so much effort to try and *earn* it?"

"You said it yourself—I have no interest in being my grandfather. I don't want to rule the world." Lira scowled. "What a tedious hassle."

An amused smile flashed over Ahrin's face. "So you don't buy into any of Underground's dogma about mages being superior, better rulers than human kings and queens?"

Lira snorted, looked her in the eye. "Do you?"

A lazy grin stretched over Ahrin's face. "You know I don't. It's ideological rubbish. All right, what do I get out of this, if I help you?"

"What do you want?" A thrill rippled through Lira, making her lips curl in a smile. She doubted Dawn would approve her negotiating on behalf of the Mage Council, but she didn't care. Here was what she'd been aiming for: working *with* Ahrin to bring down Underground. Only this would be doing it honestly, without having to lie to her. And with Ahrin at her side... well, she didn't need the Mage Council's help or approval.

The answer was quick in coming. "I want indemnity for my actions as Darkhand, and I want Underground's money."

Lira smirked. "And if I say no?"

"I won't betray you to Lucinda." Ahrin was serious, that coolness returning. "But I won't help you either. I don't do favours, Lira, you know that."

"Not even for me?" Lira lifted a teasing eyebrow. "After that very romantic declaration earlier? You even threw books around the room."

Ahrin didn't laugh, and her voice turned wintry. "Don't."

Lira sighed. Ahrin didn't like having weaknesses any more than Lira did, so she let it go. "I agree to your terms, but I can't promise you the council won't renege on any agreement I make."

"You'll hold them to it, I know you can." Ahrin stretched again. "You have yourself a deal, Lira Astor."

Lira propped herself on her elbows, curious. "What about you? What's your end goal once Underground is gone and you have all their money?"

A wicked smile spread over her face. "Getting even more money."

"Seriously, though." Lira bit her lip, eyes sliding closed as Ahrin's fingers traced a line up the outside of her leg. "Now who's distracting who?"

"I don't see you complaining." Ahrin kissed her, pushing her back down against the sheets, their limbs entwining again.

"Did you really leave to keep me safe?" Lira asked, one hand reaching up to slide along Ahrin's cheek, holding her gaze.

"Yes." Her eyes closed in memory. "If they'd never come looking, I would never have left our crew."

"Neither would I," Lira breathed, then drew her down to kiss her.

"YOU HAVE TO GO," Ahrin said briskly, sitting up and pulling the covers off her.

Lira cocked an eyebrow. She was warm, comfortable, and a pleasant contentment filled her muscles. She had no intention of going anywhere. "Excuse me?"

"If you really want to do this, you need to sneak out now before anyone knows you were here. Then we need to start pretending we don't like each other all that much. It shouldn't be hard. Lucinda is very cleverly setting us up to be competitors."

Lira didn't move, but a smile spread over her face. "You want to run a con on Lucinda."

"That's your plan, right? Me being your spy on the inside once you break Athira out of here." Ahrin was looking at her with that implacable gaze of hers, all traces of softness gone. "And don't try and tell me you weren't planning on getting Athira out if you could."

Lira studied her for a moment, then rolled off the bed with a reluctant sigh and began hunting across the floor for her clothes. "You're really going to help me?"

"You hold to your end of our deal, and I'll hold to mine."

Lira tugged on pants, started buttoning her shirt. Her head was still spinning, really, and she wasn't sure how confident she could be in Ahrin's agreement. "Just like that?"

"Yes. Now, there are no telepaths on this island, so there will be opportunities for us to talk privately, but we'll need to keep it infrequent and be extremely careful. I recommend you keep your mental shields up constantly anyway. You can never be too careful with Lucinda."

Lira nodded. She knew that already. "After we succeed, the council would probably let you into Temari Hall. You could learn your magic, become a warrior mage." Lira finished dressing, sat on the edge of the bed.

Ahrin sat up, snorting. "No thanks."

"Then what do you get out of all this? Other than the money," Lira asked quietly.

"Still don't trust me, huh?"

"Would you?"

A wicked smile flashed over Ahrin's face. "No."

Lira leaned forward, kissed her. "You're impossible."

Ahrin turned serious again. "I was born with nothing. I've been a criminal my whole life. I want to start my own enterprise. Underground is getting plenty of coin from somewhere, so when we tear them apart from the inside, I want that money. That's all, Lira."

Lira understood, remembered that hunger on Ahrin's face back in Dirinan. "You still want that bigger crew. You want Transk's place."

"Yes." Ahrin reached out to take her hand. "And I still want it with you. So after all this is done, if you decide being a warrior mage isn't for you. I'll be there."

Lira pulled her hand away and stood up, suddenly uncomfortable. "It can't ever be the way it was again. You know that, right?"

"Yes." Ahrin's jaw tightened. "You're pure mageblood. You belong in that world, in that life. I don't."

"I—" It was on the tip of her tongue to disagree, to say that she'd never felt more out of place than during her time at Temari Hall. But then she thought about her magic classes, about Tarion and Garan and

Fari and Lorin. About how part of her wanted to be just like Alyx Egalion one day. "You could belong there too."

"You know that's not true."

Lira nodded, trying not to show the sadness tearing through her, and moved to open the door.

"Lira?"

"Yes."

"Why does it bother you so much, people thinking you might be like Shakar?"

Lira swallowed, one hand on the doorknob, staring at the grains of wood in the door. "He wasn't born as the Darkmage, Ahrin. He was powerful, arrogant even, but he was just another person, really. Then the Mage Council hunted down and killed his Taliath lover. The grief and hate consumed him, and he couldn't let it go until they were all dead." She paused, the words drawn out of some deep part of her she'd never consciously acknowledged before. "It bothers me because they're right to worry. Ahrin, if anyone touched you, I'd burn down the world and not care two coppers for the consequences."

With those words torn from her, she turned the knob, opened the door and left. Running away from the truth that she'd always hidden away in the deepest parts of herself.

That they *should* be afraid of her.

CHAPTER 35

L ira made it back to her room without anyone spotting her, dousing the lamp and crawling under the covers as darkness enveloped the space.

She didn't sleep, though.

She wished she was back in her dorm at Temari, with Fari in the bed opposite, so Lira could talk to her about what had just happened with Ahrin. About the delight and the emotion of it, her worry over getting the mechanics wrong. Fari would have advice—no doubt, *plenty* of advice about what to do next time.

Worry pulsed in her chest at the thought of Fari, though Ahrin's news had eased the concern about the others that she'd been doing her best to ignore.

She let out a breath, staring through the darkness toward the cavern roof, allowing herself to think about them now she knew they were safe at Temari. Garan had seen Lira leaving with Ahrin. He wouldn't understand what Ahrin had been doing in Alanan, but given she'd appeared in the middle of an ambush, it was an easy logical leap to make that Ahrin was a member of Underground.

Garan would tell the others what he'd seen. And then when they told Caverlock, or Dawn... *they* knew Ahrin was the Darkhand.

Would they tell Garan or Tarion that Lira had been spying on Underground on the council's behalf? No, they were too careful of her safety, of the possibility of a rogue telepath mage reading it in their thoughts. Lira bit her lip—their parents wouldn't tell them, and it would seem like Lira had willingly left with Underground. The council would let them think that because it bolstered Lira's cover.

They would think Lira had betrayed them, that she'd been betraying them the whole time.

She shifted restlessly, the thought so distressing she had to push it away. It was useless to worry about it. She'd be able to explain everything to them once this was over. They would understand. She knew they would. She trusted them to.

It was a new, delicate thing, that trust. Born of what they'd been through and their persistent acceptance of her. Maybe... just maybe... it wasn't always guaranteed that trust was inevitably broken.

Another strange feeling came along with that tentative realisation: a desire to be worthy of that trust. Lying there in the dark, Lira made a decision. Ahrin and all the knowledge she possessed about Underground was on her side now—Lira would make it her first priority to find out what happened to Tarion, so that she could take that information back with her to help him. It wouldn't be easy with she and Ahrin pretending to dislike each other for Lucinda's benefit, but the first private moment Lira had to ask, she would. All her other questions could wait.

It was on that thought of trust, untangling knots so deep inside her she'd forgotten they existed, that Lira fell into true sleep.

THE NEXT MORNING she woke feeling more rested than she had in a long time. She rose and dressed in the dark, then opened the door to let in the morning sunlight coming from the tunnel opening. Ahrin appeared as Lira was lacing up her boots.

"Sleep well?" she asked, tone cold.

"What do you care how I slept?" Lira kept her attention on her laces in case others were in the hall outside. From here on out they would pretend to be wary allies and nothing more. She understood the sense in it, but she didn't love the plan. At this particular moment she'd rather grab Ahrin by the hand, drag her into the room and to her narrow bed, and lock the door.

"I don't."

"Then why are you here?" Lira finally looked at her.

"The Seventh instructed me to let you know I've returned," Ahrin said, no tell on her face or in her voice to show how she truly felt about taking orders from Lucinda. A slight pause, then she added, "I heard you've been visiting the prisoner."

It was a thinly veiled warning, Ahrin letting her know that Lira's solitary visit to Athira hadn't gone unnoticed.

"So what?" Lira shrugged. "I'm curious as to why she's here, why she didn't get returned to Temari Hall with the rest of us. It's not like you've given me an explanation and Lucinda hasn't been available to talk to since I got here. Nobody told me I couldn't see her."

"There's no rule against it." Ahrin shrugged, but her look warned Lira to be careful.

"Lucinda has certainly done her best to impress upon Athira how much of a traitor to the council I am. She refuses to talk to me." Lira sounded surly, but tried to make clear that Athira hadn't told her anything useful.

"She's been hard to manage since she arrived. Lucinda thought it would be a good idea to dispel any illusions the girl had about you, and even then she doesn't shut up when she's training with Jora... goes on and on about how the council is going to destroy us all."

Another nugget of information disguised as a retort. They let Athira out of her cell to work with Jora. Interesting. Lira nodded. "When do I get to meet the other inhabitants of the island? Shiasta told me two other fighting units like his are based here."

"Shortly. They're away from the island, but not for much longer."

"Away right when I arrive, huh?" Lira shook her head. "She still doesn't trust me at all, does she?"

"No," Ahrin said bluntly, then glanced in both directions down the tunnel before lowering her voice. "I'm surprised you're here, to be honest."

Lira frowned, dropping her voice to a murmur as well. "If she truly suspected what I was up to, I'd be dead, not hanging out here being given scraps of information."

"That's true." Ahrin didn't sound convinced.

Lira raised her voice back to normal volume, just in case anyone was listening in or passing by who might wonder at the sudden silence. "I like Shiasta very much, by the way. He's been good to me." Lira studied Ahrin for her reaction. Their alliance was new, and she didn't want to threaten it—or their new closeness—by bringing up a subject Ahrin had repeatedly warned her not to raise. The curiosity of their matching tattoos would have to wait. Besides, she'd promised herself that Tarion came first.

Ahrin looked away, another glance in both directions to make sure they were alone. Her voice was casual. "His team are good, aren't they?"

"Surprisingly so. I didn't realise Underground had a fighting capability so skilled. How well do you know them?"

"They take orders from me when I need them for missions, otherwise I don't see them."

Ahrin was hiding her true feelings very well as always, but Lira sensed something was off. For now, she changed the subject. "Are the other Shadowcouncil members as paranoid as you and Lucinda?"

"Don't know, never met them."

Lira's head shot up. "What do you mean?"

"Just what I said. I've only ever met Lucinda."

"And you don't think that's odd? You're the Darkhand."

Ahrin shrugged. "I think there are many odd things about Underground, and the other members of the Shadowcouncil being secretive and paranoid is the least of them."

"Are you sure they exist?" Lira spoke without thinking.

"I've seen correspondence from them. I've also heard Lucinda talk about them." Ahrin cocked her head. "I overheard her once say something about how they rarely travelled to speak with her because they're so far away. I get the impression she's their point person—the one who moves about and takes the most risk."

"Which makes it unlikely she's their leader," Lira murmured. That was another interesting nugget. Someone *else* was potentially pulling

Lucinda's strings, as frighteningly capable and clever as the woman seemed.

"Agreed."

"How far away are we talking? The northern tip of Zandia, the southern peninsula of Rionn?" Lira asked sceptically.

Ahrin gave her an irritated look, glanced both ways along the tunnel again, and lowered her voice. "Can these questions wait? I've lingered too long here already."

"I know, but there's one thing I need to know right away." Lira stood up and crossed the room to Ahrin, standing close enough she could feel Ahrin's warm breath on her cheek. She fought the urge to settle her hands on Ahrin's hips and pull her even closer. "What was done to Tarion?" she murmured.

Ahrin's midnight blue gaze flicked to hers. "Why, what's happened?"

"I asked first."

"He wasn't given razak blood." Ahrin barely breathed the words. Clearly this was something Lira wasn't supposed to know. "He was injected with nerik blood. It's the first time, as far as I know, that they've tried it."

"Nerik blood... is that what you call those flying things that attacked us? Were they at DarkSkull Hall too?"

A faint shake of her head. "The razak were kept there with Dasta controlling them. But they must have had a supply of nerik blood with them. The three creatures that attacked you were being transported here, presumably for more experiments."

"Where from?"

"I don't know."

Lira hesitated, terrified of the answer but needing to know. "Was I injected with nerik blood?"

"No, it was just Tarion. He was the variable." Ahrin's gaze roved her face. "What happened to him? Is that why he wasn't in Alanan with you?"

Lira stepped away, relief flooding her. "I'll explain another time. Have you got any thoughts as to where these creatures are from?"

"I asked once and was told to mind my business, so I left it alone.

I'm only here to take orders and get what I wanted in return." Ahrin flicked her fingers, a scarlet concussion ball spinning in her palm. "Power."

"You're going to have to do better than that if you want to make a good spy," Lira remarked.

"Are you giving me orders, Lira Astor?"

"Would that be so bad?" Lira smirked. "I took orders from you for years."

Ahrin snorted. "I don't take orders from anyone unless it suits me. Not even you, dearest."

"Dearest?" Lira bit her lip as a laugh threatened to spill out.

Ahrin's face darkened, but before she could respond, the sound of approaching footsteps filtered into the silence. Ahrin stepped away from the doorway and out into the hall in a single graceful movement. "What is this, an interrogation?" she snapped, voice loud enough to carry. "I didn't come here to be your repository of information. Find someone else to ask your questions of. I have more important things to do."

She strode off, leaving Lira fighting a chuckle. Her amusement sobered quickly, though—Tarion had been experimented on with nerik blood, and clearly it had different effects than the razak injections did. Hope lifted in her chest. Surely this information would improve Finn A'ndreas' chances of figuring out how to help him.

Relief was there as well. Knowing she wasn't going to randomly turn into a mindless monster was another weight off her mind. It made her energised, full of renewed determination. She needed to end this so she could get back to Karonan with the information she held.

But she needed patience too. There was no point in returning unless she held enough information about Underground to bring them down in one single move. Tarion would want her to do this properly. So would the others. And she *had* made progress. Ahrin was working with her now.

Together, Lira had no doubt they would succeed.

AFTER EATING BREAKFAST, Lira went to see Athira.

She was only halfway down the narrow steps when the sound of screaming hit her. Lira ran the rest of the way, coming to a sliding halt outside the cell, only to realise the screams were the result of a nightmare and not an attack or another experiment.

The girl was still asleep, her body thrashing on the pile of blankets. At first, all that Lira could think was that she needed to stop the horrific sounds. "Athira! Athira, wake up, you're dreaming!"

That didn't seem to work.

Lira summoned a quick burst of telekinetic magic, using it to yank the girl off the pile of blankets and onto the hard floor. "Athira! WAKE UP!"

Athira's eyes flashed open, and the depth of the horror and fear in them almost sent Lira stumbling away from the bars. But she held her ground, met that gaze and refused to look away. "Just breathe. Slowly. You're okay."

Athira's chest heaved, her breath coming in panting gasps, but she held Lira's gaze, using it as an anchor. Slowly, her breathing calmed. Her rigid body relaxed. Once Lira was certain Athira was fully awake, she lifted an eyebrow and spoke coolly. "Some nightmare."

"Memories. Not nightmares."

Lira stilled. "I will find a way to help you. I swear that to you."

There was no immediate reaction visible in Athira's cool expression, her innate haughtiness untainted by the tear streaks on her face or tangled blond hair. All she said was, "You're a prisoner here too, you know? They're using your name and manipulating your desire for power to get what they want. You do get that, don't you, Spider?"

Lira huffed a bitter laugh, sparing a glance down the tunnel to ensure they were alone. Now she knew there were no telepaths on the island, she could be a little freer with Athira. "There hasn't been one place in my life I've ever been safe. I'm no fool."

Athira's gaze studied her. "Why promise to help me? You're one of them, what do you care about my fate?"

Lira looked away. They were still alone. She looked back and shrugged. "Because you held the door."

Athira frowned, clearly confused, though the distraction of conversation seemed to be helping her to relax. "You might have to explain that one to me."

"My village kicked me out the day after my mother died. At the orphanage, the older girls tried to drown me and almost succeeded. I escaped after that. Fell in with a group of homeless kids on the streets, pickpocketing to survive. The first time the city guards caught us, the other kids in the crew ran faster than me. I was lagging behind... the kid ahead of me shut the door in my face to save himself. The guards caught me and beat me within an inch of my life. I was thirteen years old." Lira didn't mention how Ahrin had come back for her. How she'd tended all of Lira's wounds. Punished Timin for weeks for leaving Lira behind. Ahrin had *always* protected Lira. It was so clear now.

"I'm trying to figure out how that story relates to me, but I'm not getting there."

There was a touch of amusement in Athira's voice. No pity. No fear. No wariness. Lira shrugged. "At DarkSkull... I was being chased down the corridor by the razak. You held the door open until I got there, even though the monster had almost caught up to me. You could have been killed right along with me for holding that door."

"I remember." Athira shifted. "But don't paint me as a hero. You said it yourself, back when we were all there. We needed your magical strength and your ability to survive to get out. That's why I held the door."

"No, it wasn't." Because Lira had seen worry on Athira's face. The determination to stand firm no matter how scared she was. "Lorin said something to me after we got back. About how no matter where we're from, we're all mages, and that's what mages do. We look out for each other. It's the ideal that Alyx Egalion built her new mage order on. That stupid bonfire sigil on all their cloaks." Lira paused. "That's why you held the door open."

A brief silence, then Athira said, "Yes. That's why I held the door open."

"That's not why I'm going to help you, to be clear," Lira said then. "I owe you one, and I don't like owing anybody. That's why I'm going to help. I want the debt between us cleared." And Lira told herself that was the truth.

Athira barked out an amused laugh. "That actually makes me believe you, Spider."

"They sent us all back, did you know that?"

"Yes." Her jaw tightened. "I've been told repeatedly how I'm the only one who didn't get to go home." She paused, clearly wrestling with herself, but eventually caved, meeting Lira's eyes. "Are they okay?"

Lira heard the mostly-hidden fear and grief in her voice, but ignored it. "Lorin's leg was badly broken but..."

"What?"

"They are okay, I think." She relayed the recent events in Alanan. The only thing she left out was what had happened to Tarion. Instinct warned her that the results of their experiment should never get back to Lucinda and her people.

"They did that just to get you?" Suspicion returned to Athira's voice. "You must be important to them."

"I'm their symbol," Lira said. "They need me to recruit enough mages to defeat the council."

Athira accepted that with an ease that was irritating. "So they held us at DarkSkull, huh? Makes sense, in a twisted way."

Lira hesitated. She shouldn't linger. If people here were paying attention to the fact she was visiting Athira, they'd be noticing how long she spent here too. But there were things she needed to know, and the girl finally seemed willing to talk to her. "What have they been doing to you here?"

"I don't know. They've taken me twice, but I don't remember either occasion. Otherwise they have me training with Jora, using my enhancing ability." Athira swallowed. "I think they might be trying to strengthen my magic so they can turn me into a weapon. Imagine if I could boost the magic of a hundred mages at once?"

Lira shivered. That would be a power indeed, one that would give Underground a strong advantage in any fight against the council. "Have they succeeded?"

"Not yet," she said bleakly.

"Are there any others being experimented on here?"

"They really don't tell you anything, huh?" Athira scoffed. "Serves you right, Lira Astor. If you think I'm going to hand over the answers you want, you're sorely mistaken."

Conversation was clearly over for the day.

"I'll get you out, Athira." Lira stepped away. "But I need to do it in a way that they don't know I'm responsible."

"I take it that means these little visits are going to stop?"

"Yes. But I will hold to my word."

"Forgive me if I don't take the word of Shakar's granddaughter." Athira deliberately turned away from her.

Lira left without another word.

Athira would forgive her once she knew the truth. The real problem was that Lira *cared* whether Athira would forgive her. Lira didn't even like the girl.

Ugh. Lira was turning into one of them.

Maybe she did have a side, after all.

CHAPTER 36

S omething was up with Lucinda.

The woman's finger had been tapping relentlessly against her wine glass since they'd sat down, and her attention, usually incisive and entirely focused on those she was with, appeared distracted. Lira wasn't even sure Lucinda realised it.

Lira and Ahrin, along with Jora, had been invited to dine with the Shadowcouncil member, a rare honour. Lira was pleasantly tired after a day spent wrestling with her fire magic—it was far behind her telekinesis in terms of her ability to control it—but was thrilled by the opportunity for face-to-face time with Lucinda.

She had no idea what Ahrin had been doing all day. They hadn't spoken privately since that morning outside her room, their interactions limited to a few falsely tense conversations in view of others. Now, Ahrin's disdain for Lira's presence at dinner oozed from her. Even knowing the Darkhand so well, Lira wouldn't have guessed she was faking it without knowing.

Lira was similarly distant, the game they were playing flawless. It felt so good to be working with Ahrin again. Their ease together had been the thing Lira missed most after Ahrin had left their crew in Dirinan. The knowledge there was someone nearby she could lean on, trust to be there if she failed.

The feeling she wasn't alone in the world.

But even that was dangerous, a swaying rope bridge over a perilous drop, the rope fraying with every swing. A little trickle of doubt went through her. Ahrin *could* be playing her and Lira wouldn't know. It had happened before.

It didn't matter. She was fully invested with Ahrin now. There was no way out. If the Darkhand betrayed her, Lira was done. And maybe that would be fitting. Brought down by her only weakness.

The two other Shiven combat units had returned several days earlier, as had a trickle of Underground mages from across the continent. Lira had met each of them—a twenty-strong mix of council mages turned traitor and those born with mage ability who'd never gone to Temari Hall or joined the council. None were the result of humans successfully injected with razak blood, which Lira found odd. She'd thought the backbone of Underground's mage army would have been formed of those mages.

Lucinda must be keeping them away from Lira for some reason.

All the mages Lira met appeared to be fiercely loyal to the Shadow-council, and had treated her with a gratifying reverence. Unlike the coolly unemotional Shiven warriors, these men and women were a hotbed of devotion and ferocity. Far more like Greyson and his cell members in Karonan than Lucinda.

Still, Lira hadn't yet learned anything about the identities of the other Shadowcouncil members, or how far and wide Underground was spread across the continent, including where their other bases were. Nor was she certain these were all the mages and warriors they had. They were just the ones she was being allowed to see.

The Mage Council would need all those answers before being able to conduct an effective operation to wipe out Underground. Ahrin could get some of this information, of course, but Lira also needed to know more about the experiments on Tarion, as well as figure out how to get Athira free, and so she was determined to remain until then, despite how increasingly dangerous it was.

Wearing the mask of a believer was becoming easier, however, the longer she spent away from Temari Hall. She enjoyed it, the constant peril, the need to be always on her toes, always sharp around Lucinda and everyone else on the island. The knowledge she had no recourse or easy escape if she were found out.

Her glance shifted without thinking to Ahrin. Like usual, the Darkhand had been cool and aloof since Lira arrived for dinner, her body casually but deliberately turned away from her and towards Lucinda.

"Jora reports that you're doing well at your training, Lira." Lucinda finally spoke, breaking what was growing into an awkward silence. Her distraction vanished, attention once again becoming razor-like.

Lira darted a glance at Jora. The man rarely spoke for himself, and Lira got the distinct sense Jora was accustomed to not being able to speak unless explicitly given permission to do so. It made her curious. "The stronger I get, the more help I can be to you. I'm keen for that to happen as quickly as possible," she said.

"But still only one additional ability has broken out?"

"Yes." Lira didn't have to try hard to feign annoyance at that. Part of her remained horrified at what she'd allowed Underground to do to her. The other part craved more magic, more abilities, no matter what it involved.

"Perhaps we need to set you against our Darkhand in a duel." Lucinda gestured in Ahrin's direction. "See if we can't force any other abilities out."

"It's been too long. I think at this point we must assume the second and third injections didn't work," Ahrin said coolly, not even looking at Lira. "Besides, I wouldn't want to damage your precious symbol."

"Trust me, that is unlikely," Lira said flatly.

"I crushed you at DarkSkull, what has changed since then?" Ahrin lifted an eyebrow.

Real irritation surged then; Lira could tell when Ahrin was being serious. "You did nothing of the sort."

Lucinda glanced between them, a little smile playing at her mouth. "Really, the two of you should get along better than this."

"Why *is* that?" Lira asked, meeting Lucinda's eyes. "I rather thought you preferred to keep an edge of competition between us."

Lucinda's finger started tapping against the wineglass again. "I suppose I can understand your paranoia, given your life so far. But no. You two are destined to work together."

Lira almost snorted. Lucinda was not the type to believe in things like destiny; this woman made her own destiny. "And what is that supposed to mean?" Too late, Lira noticed the stillness that had descended over Ahrin. The one that meant she was severely unimpressed with this line of conversation.

Lucinda arched an eyebrow. "She hasn't told you?"

"Enough." Ahrin's voice was granite, not at all deferential, and Lucinda's gaze switched to her Darkhand quick as a striking viper. "Betray your group's secrets, if you like, but keep mine out of it. I still don't trust the girl. I don't care whose granddaughter she is."

Lira's own anger rose then, and she levelled a look between them. "Someone better tell me what's going on."

Lucinda's gaze lingered on Ahrin for a moment, a smile toying at her mouth, then she turned to Lira. "Ahrin was born to be your general, Lira. Your Hunter."

Her what? That word roused something in her memory, but her thoughts were derailed from chasing it down by the sight of Ahrin's left hand, the one resting on the table, sliding towards the knife by her plate. It was a slow, casual move, but Lira didn't fail to notice it. She was in the midst of frantically trying to decide whether to intervene if Ahrin attacked Lucinda when the door opened.

Ahrin's hand stilled, and all four gazes swung around as one of Lucinda's mages ducked in, breathing hard. "Timor is back. He's on his way up the cliff path."

Timor. Lira recognised that name from their kidnapping; he was the one she'd suspected was the cause of the mist shrouding the grounds while they were there. Whatever news he brought, Lucinda must have been desperate for it, because she rose from her chair without another word and strode for the door. Jora followed suit. Ahrin and Lira stared at each other in astonishment as it closed behind her.

"Do you know—"

"No." Ahrin shook her head. "She's been on edge for a few days. It's highly unusual. But when I asked, she said everything was fine."

"We're going to talk about what just happened later." Lira gestured to where Lucinda had been sitting. Then she jumped to her feet and ran for the door. Lucinda had already disappeared from sight along the tunnel outside, Jora and the messenger too, so after a quick glance to ensure nobody else was around, Lira set off after them.

Not once in the entire time she'd known Lucinda had the woman shown a shred of unease or anxiety. Lira needed to know what information Timor was bringing. Maybe there was a weakness the council could use.

"I certainly hope you're not planning to follow her all the way." Ahrin caught up a few seconds later, voice lowered to a murmur. "She knows how to pick a tail."

Lira levelled a look at her. Ahrin shrugged.

They followed the curving tunnel around as it began to angle upwards on its journey to ground level. The scent of salty ocean hit her senses a bit further along, but instead of following the tunnel all the way out, Lira ducked right into a narrower tunnel that led into a cavern in the cliff face open to the sea.

The roar of ocean crashing against the rocks below grew louder as she hurried along the tunnel, then crossed the floor of the cave right up to the edge. Ahrin was a silent shadow behind her.

A narrow ledge ran from the eastern side of the cavern along the cliff face. Lira, having explored this area days ago, knew that it eventually led to the path up from the jetty where it intersected with the top of the cliffs.

The path that Timor would be coming up with his news.

In the dark and with a strong wind tugging incessantly at her hair and clothes, it was a precarious journey, her back firmly pressed against the rock as she shuffled sideways along the ledge. Again, Ahrin followed without comment.

As Lira approached the top of the cliff path, she slowed her pace and pressed as far into the rock as possible to ensure she remained out of sight. Seconds later, the sound of voices drifted on the wind. Lira shot Ahrin a triumphant look, was rewarded with a slow smile, then turned her attention back to the voices.

She could just make out the dark shape of what must be Timor's back as he stood at the top of the path. She inched as close as she dared, trying to improve the quality of what she could hear. "The news isn't good," he was saying.

"Tell me." Lucinda sounded angry already, her cutting tone clear even over the wind and the crashing of the ocean far below.

Timor seemed to hesitate. "Dasta is dead."

Silence followed, nothing but whistling wind filling it. Lira frowned, wondering if they'd moved away, out of earshot. She was about to give up and turn back when Lucinda's voice came again, only now it was barely recognisable. She sounded shaken, unsettled. "Are you sure?"

"Yes."

"And the razak?"

"All dead too. Somehow Caverlock's force overwhelmed them."

"How? We planned meticulously—the size of that force should never have been able to..."

"... isn't good..." The wind gusted, screaming, cutting off Jora's words.

"Should we pull out?" Timor was saying when the wind steadied and Lira could hear again. "Without Dasta, we can't..."

"Almost there with... but we must honour..."

"I am sorry." Timor's voice sounded full of grief, deep, aching grief. "We have lost one of the..."

"A grievous loss." Lucinda actually sounded as if she meant it. "What else do we know? How was he killed?"

"It's unclear. The council are keeping secret the... not sure why they..."

"That won't matter any longer... word that... he'll be able to tell us what we need to know." Lucinda's composure seemed to have recovered, her voice turning to its usual cold edge.

"Even so, we obviously underestimated..." Timor moved out of sight, and slowly the voices vanished entirely from hearing.

Once it was clear they were gone, Ahrin began edging her way back along the ledge and Lira followed. By the time they stumbled into the cavern Lira was shivering with cold, hair and clothes damp from sea spray, but her mind was awhirl. Instinct told her that what they'd just overheard was critical to understanding Underground better. But how?

"I've never seen that woman display a shred of emotion." Ahrin seemed to be thinking along the same lines. She moved closer to Lira, keeping her voice low. The cavern was only dimly lit by faint moonlight outside, the tunnel leading to it even darker, but they couldn't rule out somebody passing by and hearing them talk. "But she wasn't faking the devastation I heard in her voice at Timor's news."

"It sounded as if the ambush they planned at DarkSkull was critical to their plans in some way, but why? I still don't understand why they did it." Lira frowned.

"It was opportunistic, at least I thought so. They knew the council would eventually figure out where we'd taken you and come sniffing around, so they set an ambush." Ahrin's head snapped up suddenly. "Wait, how do you know about the—" Ahrin cut herself off. "You were there."

Lira hesitated only a second before answering honestly. Ahrin already knew enough to destroy her, and if they were going to successfully work together, there was no point in holding back now. "Caverlock made up the story about us needing protection, and took us with him to DarkSkull in case we could help them find what they needed. I was the one who killed Dasta, and the razak. All of them."

Ahrin stepped closer. "How?" she demanded.

Lira hesitated. "My fire magic can break through the razak's immunity."

There was a moment's silence, Ahrin's pale Shiven skin turning deathly white in the silvery glow of the moon. "Lira, Lucinda can *never* know that. Do you understand me?"

"I wasn't planning on telling her." Lira frowned. "What is it?"

"That's why she wants you so badly. I don't think she cares two coppers that you're Shakar's heir." Ahrin's voice was low, intense. "They've been hoping that by running their tests on subjects with the bloodline of a mage of the higher order with Taliath immunity, they'll be able to create a mage whose magic can break through the razak's immunity to it."

It was Lira's turn to go quiet, realisation cascading through her.

334

"That's why they took me. Why they took Garan and Tarion too." They are grandsons of Temari Egalion, who, like Shakar, had been a mage of the higher order who'd absorbed their lover's Taliath immunity. Tarion had that from his mother too. And Fari... there had been a Dirsk a couple of generations back who'd been a mage of the higher order. Lorin was the only person that didn't obviously fit the category.

"Yes," Ahrin said. "Only the experiments didn't work on them. They haven't manifested any new abilities. It only worked on you."

"You're wrong, it worked on Tarion too. Why does Lucinda care so much about being able to use magic to kill the razak? She controls them."

"I don't know." Ahrin hesitated. "But it's really important to them. To Lucinda and her mages, I mean. It's almost as if..."

"As if what?"

"Nothing." Ahrin dismissed the question. "I'm serious Lira. She cannot know this about you. Or Tarion either. I don't care coppers about him, but if you truly want to bring her down, you need to keep her from getting what she wants, even if we don't understand why she wants it."

"I won't say a thing," Lira said. "But at some point she'll test my new magic to see if it works against the razak. Or subject me to more tests until she gets there."

"Then you have to be gone before that happens."

Lira let out an angry breath. Why did everything always feel so slippery with Ahrin, like she could never be on solid footing? "Why didn't you tell me this before? I asked you why she wanted me so badly."

"I haven't exactly had time since you arrived here to give you chapter and verse everything I know about Underground," Ahrin snapped. "Just like you didn't tell me about what happened at Dark-Skull. Or what happened to Tarion."

Lira took a breath. There were probably many things Ahrin hadn't told her yet. "Fine. Then we need to find the time to talk properly, or this little plan of ours isn't going to work."

Ahrin stepped away, starting to pace again. "Her mages have died before, she's even killed one or two herself for failing on a mission. Why such a reaction over Dasta?"

335

"It's odd," Lira said. "It comes back to the razak again, though, doesn't it? He was the one who could control them. When you add that to the fact she seems so keen on creating a mage who can break their immunity..." But what was so important about the razak? And what did any of it have to do with following her grandfather's legacy and overturning the Mage Council?

Ahrin nodded, glanced towards the tunnel. "She might come looking for one or both of us when she gets back. Me, most likely, if she wants anything done about what happened at DarkSkull. We should get back to our rooms."

"Right, I..." Lira's voice trailed off. They hadn't been alone together since that night in Ahrin's room, and it was maddening. And now she was so close and Lira didn't want her to be gone again.

"Don't tell me you miss me, Astor." Ahrin moved closer, pressed a slow, lingering kiss to her jaw, then her cheek.

Lira turned just enough so she could kiss her, her hands reaching up to slide into Ahrin's hair so that she could deepen the kiss. She let it go on for a few minutes, then pulled away, heart thudding, smiling. "Never."

"Liar." Ahrin's voice had turned husky, their bodies still pressed tightly together, neither willing to step away. "We really should go."

Lira shook her head. She reached down, slid her fingers around Ahrin's right wrist, then raised it between them. "Tell me about this tattoo."

Ahrin made to pull away. Lira refused to let go. "I can't have Lucinda knowing things I don't, not if we're working together against her. If she knows this about you, why can't I?"

"I can't talk about it." She'd turned utterly rigid, every muscle tensed. Lira hated that she'd caused this reaction, didn't want to prolong it, but she had to know.

"Then start with what you *can* tell me. Did your parents give it to you? Did it have something to do with how you ended up an orphan in Dirinan who'd clearly been trained to kill?"

"I was given it as a small child. I didn't have parents—they gave me over to them after I was born. They were the ones who taught me to kill, starting as soon as I could walk. I ended up in Dirinan because I ran away." As she spoke, voice oddly flat, Ahrin's gaze held Lira's almost desperately, as if she needed to hold on to something to avoid falling.

"Who was *them*?" Lira asked, as gently as she could, her hands tight on Ahrin's, holding that gaze.

"I can't, I can't say it..." Ahrin swallowed, body even more rigid now, sweat beading on her forehead. "I'm a Hunter, Lira. At least, that's what the Mage Council called us. *He* called us Magekillers. When I saw you in Dirinan, when you told me your name... it had been drilled into me since birth. Loyalty. Discipline. Obedience. Over and over and over."

"Who called you that?" Lira frowned.

"The Darkmage."

And instantly it all clicked for Lira: what Lucinda had been referring to at dinner, what the word Hunter meant. Her grandfather had had his own personal army of Shiven Hunters, carrying medallions that made them immune to mage power. Elite, skilled warriors who'd hunted and killed mages for him.

That's what Shiasta and his warriors were.

Ahrin was a Hunter.

Shock rippled through Lira, along with an insistent niggle of unease she ignored. "But he died before you were even born. Before I was born."

Ahrin shuddered. "I can't. I can't."

"Did they use magic on you?" Lira's gaze searched Ahrin's, hating that this was hurting her. "Brainwashing? Did they make it so you couldn't talk about them, about what happened?"

Ahrin swallowed. Nodded. Her breathing was coming faster.

"How does Lucinda know about you and the others then?"

"I don't know. I assume the Shadowcouncil has ties to the remains of Shakar's old network."

"I..." Lira didn't know what to say. Had no words of comfort to offer. Didn't even know how she felt about learning that Ahrin was one of her grandfather's warriors. So instead, she pulled Ahrin close. Wrapped her arms so tightly around her that she couldn't fall. Tried to soothe the Darkhand's rigid tension with her touch.

Ahrin let her, fingers digging into Lira's back, body shuddering and finally relaxing against her. "I'm sorry," Lira murmured, kissing her cheek, her jaw. "I won't bring it up again."

Ahrin said nothing, merely pressed closer, arms tight around Lira's back. Lira held her, ran her fingers in soothing strokes through the Darkhand's long hair. Too quickly Ahrin pulled away, the cool mask falling over her face so completely it was like those moments of distress—the only true distress Lira had ever seen in the girl—had never been. "We really have to go."

"I'm aware." Lira forced herself to shift away, straightened her clothes, then headed for the tunnel entrance. Ahrin's hand found hers as they walked, sliding their fingers together, and she didn't let go until they reached the main tunnel.

There, she gave Lira one of those slow smiles of hers before walking away.

Lira headed reluctantly in the opposite direction, mind awhirl.

Lucinda hadn't been wrong—it was like Ahrin had been destined for Lira. But in what way? Lira hated the thought of what had been done to Ahrin. Hated that her fierce, proud spirit had been dominated, controlled, hurt in such a way, and as a *child*.

And how many like Ahrin were out there? Underground had clearly found some of them—warriors like Shiasta and his unit.

The council needed to know. But Lira felt oddly reluctant to tell them. Instead her instinct was to protect these young men and women. They'd been trained, created, conditioned, for her grandfather. She was his heir.

They were *hers*.

CHAPTER 37

Lucinda wasn't visible at all over the next few days. In every spare moment Lira had, her thoughts dwelled on what she and Ahrin had overheard. Dasta's death had thrown the perfectly controlled Lucinda for a loop. The Shadowcouncil clearly relied on his ability, or the razak he controlled, far more than Lira had guessed.

And whatever that explanation was, Ahrin didn't know it. Which meant the information had to be a critical vulnerability for the group, so critical that not even their right hand was trusted with it. This was the key to Underground's destruction. It had to be.

At least now she knew why Lucinda had looked so triumphant when Lira had been lying on that experimenting table back at Dark-Skull. Lira had become exactly what Lucinda wanted.

It sharply increased the danger Lira was in, effectively trapped on this island with only Ahrin as an ally. How long would it take Lucinda to figure out how the razak at DarkSkull had died? And who the most likely candidate was to have done it? She would have to be gone before that happened.

Everything circled back to the razak, though Lira couldn't figure out why. The creatures were dangerous, particularly dangerous to mages given their immunity to magic, but could that be the cause for such distress over Dasta's death?

Or was it less about Dasta and more about an inability to acquire more razak for experimentation purposes? Finn A'ndreas and the council hadn't been able to establish where the creatures came from. There was no recorded instance of them in any of the countries on the continent... and it was impossible they'd gone without notice for any length of time.

Underground somehow creating the creatures—via magic?—had seemed the most logical answer. Lira wished she could discuss it with Ahrin, but didn't dare while Lucinda and everyone else on the island were so on edge. The only other possibility would be that they'd come from somewhere else, somewhere...

A sharp knock at the door started Lira from her thoughts. Lucinda herself stood there, Shiasta hovering behind her. "Lira, Jora told me you were soon to start training for the day. I was hoping you'd indulge me with a display?"

Damn. Lira lifted an eyebrow. "You don't have better things to do than watch me make fire and fling things around?"

"If you walk with me, I'll explain." She stepped aside from the doorway.

Lira shrugged and followed. Making a battle of this wasn't going to get her anywhere, though she was wary. Lira suspected this was what both she and Ahrin had known would come eventually. Lucinda was going to test her.

"The injections of razak blood we gave you were not purely an attempt to increase the number of your magical abilities." Lucinda confirmed it a second later as they started walking. "To defeat the Mage Council and its Taliath guardians, we need an advantage over them. Our most recent experiments have been focused on creating mage abilities that can break through a Taliath's immunity."

"An excellent goal, and a brilliant idea," Lira murmured, brain racing. For Lucinda to be willing to tell her this now... she must really need Lira's cooperation. Either that, or she'd become utterly confident in her ability to contain Lira. The thought sent a shiver down her spine. "Though I'm not sure what that has to do with watching me practice my magic."

"I'd like to test your fire ability against Ahrin."

"I don't—"

"Wearing her Hunter medallion," Lucinda cut over her smoothly.

Lira could have kicked herself, and if Lucinda hadn't been watching her every facial expression, she probably would have let out a loud curse.

The chain Ahrin had always worn in Dirinan hidden under her shirt.

Realisations cascaded through her mind with the speed of falling dominoes. Ahrin had *not* been wearing that chain when she'd reappeared in Lira's life, this time with mage powers. That chain was the reason Lira's magic had taken so much longer to break out than Egalion and A'ndreas had expected. Lira had unknowingly been living in close proximity to a Hunter for years. From her research into her grandfather's past, Lira knew those medallions stifled mage power... that several medallions close together could effectively repel it, cut it off entirely.

"I take it from your lack of surprise you've finally figured out what our Darkhand is?"

"I'm annoyed it took me so long," Lira said, not admitting it had been Ahrin who'd told her. "You impress me, Lucinda, with the sheer scale of your preparations over the years to build us into a force strong enough to defeat the council. Not to mention the patience it must have taken."

"Thank you. Now you must hold up your end of the bargain."

"Does your Darkhand know that there's a chance she's about to get badly burned, if not worse?"

"Ahrin knows what she needs to."

They'd reached the cavern, where Ahrin waited, expressionless. Jora was there too, along with what appeared to be Shiasta's full unit and a handful of Underground's mages, all lining the walls.

Lira *felt* the presence of the medallion as soon as she got close to Ahrin—it was the same odd, dissonant feeling she'd been getting whenever she was around Shiasta and his warriors. But so many of them together should have done more than just cause an odd feeling... it should have cut off her magic entirely. She turned to Lucinda. "Only Shiasta wears a medallion, not his unit. Why?"

"They are given them for missions only." Astonishingly, Lucinda gave her a full answer, lowering her voice so only Lira could hear. "They are highly disciplined, but even so I prefer to be cautious. You can imagine it isn't ideal to have so many warriors immune to mage powers around us at all times."

"Indeed," Lira murmured, keeping the impressed note to her voice without any effort.

The familiar glint of the silver chain flashed under Ahrin's collar. Lira once again cursed her stupidity for not figuring it out sooner.

Ahrin arched an eyebrow. "You know I'm not going to hold back, right?"

"I'd be insulted if you did."

Lira was only partly concentrating on the Darkhand, on what she'd just learned. The rest of her was frantically trying to figure out how to hide the fact that her flame ability could break through immunity.

She should have help, at least. Ahrin would have figured out what was going on, of course, even if Lucinda hadn't warned her. Rotted carcasses. Lira couldn't see a solution. She tried to stall to give herself more time. "Can you use your magic, with that medallion on?" she asked Ahrin.

"No. But we both know I don't need magic to beat you."

Lira scoffed. "We'll see about that."

"Lady Astor?" Shiasta appeared at her side, offering one of the dulled blades his warriors used in training, before giving a second to the Darkhand. A small number of lessons with Tarion in Alistriem ensured Lira knew how to hold a sword properly, but Ahrin was a master swordswoman.

Maybe this wouldn't be difficult after all. Ahrin could probably defeat her before she could even touch her magic. Sourness filled her at the thought.

Ahrin shifted into a ready stance, sword slightly lifted. Her expression challenged Lira to come at her. Lira hesitated until Lucinda's voice snapped through the cavern. "Can we start, please?"

342

Ahrin leapt at Lira before the words faded from hearing. Lira had no time to do anything but scramble backwards and lift her blade to counter. Ahrin knocked it away contemptuously, stepped in, and slammed her shoulder into Lira's chest.

Two things happened simultaneously—the air whooshed from Lira's lungs, and she figured out Ahrin's strategy: visibly overwhelm Lira, keep her constantly on the defensive, so that she could pretend not to be able to gather the focus needed to use magic.

Reluctantly, Lira conceded the utility of the plan. It wasn't going to be dignified for her, but it was something she could work with. She staggered backward before hunching over her knees, taking several gasping breaths, making herself seem more winded than she really was.

Ahrin didn't give her room to recover, launching another attack with a predatory look on her face. Lira scrambled sideways, lifted her blade to counter, but had it swatted away with insulting ease. When the next attack came, Lira lifted her free hand, making a visible attempt to use magic, but Ahrin was on her so quickly she had to drop her hand and twist away to avoid being hit.

Ahrin gave her no quarter, and what followed was several minutes of Lira desperately stumbling to avoid getting hit, while trying to visibly demonstrate she was trying to use magic without overdoing the acting.

Without magic or her staff, she was nowhere near good enough to beat Ahrin, not unless she could get close enough to use fists. But Ahrin knew that too, and deliberately didn't let Lira close on her.

And the more frustrated she got with the pretence, the more her magic tried to rise to lash out at her adversary. Holding it back while pretending to try and use it was the most exhausting thing she'd ever done.

"Enough!" Lucinda said suddenly, voice ringing through the cavern. Lira stepped away from Ahrin, panting, covered in sweat. "Lira, that was disappointing. I'd expected better from you."

"I'm sorry." Lira's chest heaved. "I haven't practiced using my fire magic while concentrating on something else. I'm trying, but I just can't summon and use it fast enough to avoid getting skewered."

It was close to the truth. Ahrin's medallion prevented her from using her telekinesis and she wasn't as skilled with her flame magic yet. It also wasn't something Jora had been training her on, so she could get away with the lie.

Lira glanced at Ahrin. Her plan had temporarily stalled Lucinda, but the woman wasn't above ordering the Darkhand to simply stand there and do nothing while Lira tried to use magic on her. They needed a better plan. Quickly.

"Vensis, this is a learning process. You will slow down, allow Lira to access and use her magic to defend herself against you."

Ahrin gave Lucinda a contemptuous look. "I have better things to do than play teacher to your pet Darkmage. She won't learn anything with me going easy on her. And if you think I'm just going to *let* her try and set me alight, you're sorely mistaken."

Lucinda's face turned cold, but just as she was opening her mouth to no doubt give the order anyway, Timor appeared at her side. He murmured something too low for Lira to hear. Lucinda's expression didn't change, but when she looked at Lira and Ahrin, her intensity had gone. "We'll do this again tomorrow. Lira, you'll spend today training with Jora on this. I expect you to be better at using your fire by tomorrow. If you want the continued information and inclusion that you demand from me, then you need to earn it."

Ahrin stalked off without another word.

Lira let out an internal sigh of relief. Ahrin had won them another day. They'd have to come up with a better plan. Doubt flickered in her chest—Lucinda was too clever. Lira doubted any plan would fool her for long... and if she and Ahrin were caught deliberately lying, the game would be over.

Maybe it was time to think about getting out.

CHAPTER 38

I t was nightfall by the time Lira had been reluctantly released from training by Jora, eaten dinner with Shiasta, then returned to her room. Once there, she tugged up her shirt to stare morosely at the blooming purple bruising on her left shoulder and across her right side. She'd have to get Ahrin back for that sometime.

She was pleasantly musing on how she might go about doing that when a single knock came at the door.

Ahrin stood there, the medallion gone from around her neck, one eyebrow lifted. "How are the bruises feeling?"

"What bruises?" Lira fought a smile. From where she stood, she couldn't tell if the tunnel outside was empty or not. Best to remain cool and aloof just in case. "Don't tell me Lucinda wants us to fight again already? If so, tell her I'm not interested."

Ahrin quickly glanced around before stepping inside and closing the door. That wicked smile Lira loved flashed over her face. "She and Jora went out to meet a ship bringing an important messenger. They'll be gone a couple of hours at least. Since I'm a spy now, I thought it was a grand opportunity to go digging around her quarters."

Excitement thrilled through Lira, but it faded as quickly as it had come. "You really think she'll keep anything important in there where anyone could stumble across it?"

"*I* wouldn't. But you never know." Ahrin shrugged. "Besides, everyone here is terrified of her. Who would dare go wandering into her private quarters?"

Lira frowned, though it was a good point. "Who did they go to meet with? And why are they travelling out to a ship—why isn't whoever it is coming ashore?"

Ahrin's gaze narrowed slightly. "She wouldn't say."

"You're uneasy."

"All of these people make me uneasy. There's something not right about them."

Lira snorted. "And you're just figuring this out now?"

Ahrin scowled.

Lira reached out, took her hand, twined their fingers together and squeezed lightly. "We're going to bring them down."

"Right." Ahrin let go of her hand and stepped away, putting some distance between them. "So you can start your perfect life as a mage warrior for the council?"

"I never said it would perfect. But it will be a life." Lira was stung by Ahrin's words, though she wasn't sure why.

"Better than the one we had back in Dirinan?"

Lira looked away, anger making her words sharp. "Too much has changed to go back to that. I'm a mage now, for better or worse. Maybe next time you won't make life choices on my behalf. You might consider talking to me instead."

Ahrin's face hardened. "You were part of my crew. I was responsible for you. I did what I had to do to make sure you were protected."

It was on the tip of Lira's tongue to ask whether that was true, or whether the real reason was that Ahrin had been so protective because of *who* Lira was. Because Ahrin was a Hunter, conditioned to serve the Darkmage. It had been worrying at the back of her mind ever since she'd found out. But she remembered how distressed Ahrin had been talking about it, and Lira couldn't do that to her again. "Without pausing for a second to consider what I wanted," she muttered mulishly instead.

It wasn't the time for this conversation, not if they wanted to take advantage of Lucinda's absence, but it had been brewing between them since Ahrin's confession, since Lira had had time to process what had really happened back then. Ahrin hadn't abandoned her because she'd didn't care. She'd done it to protect Lira... but she'd also taken away Lira's freedom of choice.

"I knew what you wanted, Lira." Annoyance rippled through Ahrin's voice. "But you were too damned stubborn to listen to anything I had to say."

"If you had told me what was going on, I—"

"You would have insisted on staying in Dirinan and dealing with Underground yourself. They would have found you, and I would have been unable to stop them taking you. I didn't have the resources or the influence to protect you from them." Her voice was cold, clipped.

"My magic broke out. If you'd waited a single day—"

"They have mages too." Ahrin was quickly transitioning from annoyance to anger. "And you were untrained. They would have taken you."

"It was still my choice to make. It was *my* life, Ahrin." Lira was angry now too. Angry at Ahrin for making the choice on her behalf, but equally angry that the Darkhand was completely right. Lira would have stayed. And Underground *would* have taken her. And what would she be now if they had? Dead from their experiments? Even more powerful? Would Lira have been strong or aware enough at fifteen to protect herself from Lucinda, or would she have fought tooth and nail to get free, to get back to Ahrin and their crew, until Lucinda was forced to kill her?

"You wouldn't have been the malleable symbol they wanted and Lucinda would have had you put down." Ahrin clearly understood what she was thinking. "You were my crew. That made you my responsibility," she said flatly. "That's how it worked. You know that."

"Yes." It was true, that was the world in which she and Ahrin had lived. "But I'm not your crew anymore. You don't make unilateral decisions for me, not ever again. Promise me."

A moment's silence held, then Ahrin gave a jerky nod. "I promise."

Lira faltered, surprised by Ahrin's capitulation, and more words came spilling out unbidden. "I know what you gave up to protect me. I was your ticket to taking out Transk and replacing him and once I was gone you had nothing. And you're right, I would have stayed even if I knew what was happening. I'm sorry, Ahrin."

For a moment Ahrin was still, then she took a single step forward and kissed Lira, hard. Just as quickly she was pulling away again. "No apology necessary." She reached for the door to open it. "Make sure there's nobody out there before we leave. Once we move, if anyone sees us, look unhappy and start complaining about having to practice again."

Fighting a smile, Lira nodded. "I can do that."

LUCINDA'S QUARTERS WERE LOCKED, but it was the work of seconds for Lira to use her telekinetic magic to pop it open. The room's only light came from a fire burning low in the hearth, casting a dim glow over everything. A bookcase with cupboards and drawers lined the far wall, and several piles of parchment were stacked with precision on a massive desk that dominated the main room. An archway in the rock to their left led through to a smaller room that seemed to contain only a bed covered in thick blankets.

"Take the desk," Ahrin instructed. "I'll look in the drawers."

Lira scowled at her, but did as ordered anyway.

She made sure to move carefully. Lucinda would notice if any of her neat piles were even the slightest bit out of order, so she fixed a picture in her head of the exact position of each one before beginning to go through them.

Supply lists made up the first stack, mostly food for the base on Shadowfall. Inventory notes made up the second. The third looked like letters, but they were written in some sort of code—one Lira didn't recognise.

"Ahrin?" she called softly. "Can you decipher these?"

Ahrin crossed the room to Lira's side, leaning over to scan the first parchment Lira pointed at. Her raven hair swung down, and with a little smile, Lira reached between them to tuck it behind her ear and out of her way. Ahrin shifted, pressing closer to her.

348

"It's a code the Shadowcouncil uses," she said after a moment, a little frown on her face as she scanned the letters. "Nothing interesting though. Smalltalk, polite reports, regurgitating the Underground dogma. The second one mentions followers being recruited, but no numbers or names." Silence fell as Ahrin continued reading through, and Lira waited patiently. "It looks to me like she's communicating with cell leaders. Greyson in Karonan, a couple of others I know across Shivasa, but also two unfamiliar individuals in Reller and Pernor."

"Those towns are in Tregaya," Lira said thoughtfully, part of her noting this was the first occasion her mind-numbingly boring Mapping lessons had been useful. "She never sent you on assignments there?"

"No, but I've always suspected I was being kept isolated from any of their activities beyond Shivasa." Ahrin kept reading. "The Tregayan groups seem smaller than the one in Karonan, but judging from these messages, their recruitment is increasing."

Parchment rustled as Ahrin continued going through the stack. "That's about all of use. No mention of any other cities, and the cell leaders are only ever referenced in code, so I can't give you names." She tapped one page. "I think this one is about the strikes, though. It's written deliberately vaguely, but it sounds familiar to what I was asked to set in motion in Alanan."

"She's so careful, keeping Underground's operations segregated even from their Darkhand," Lira murmured. "Do you think it's because they don't trust you as much as you thought?"

Ahrin considered that. "Either that, or they need me for a different purpose than what they've said."

Lira was confident the latter was correct, and that it had to do with what Ahrin was, with that tattoo on her wrist. Lira had made a point of looking for it, since seeing it on Shiasta's wrist. None of the warriors in his unit had them. Neither had any of the other warriors from the other two units she'd discreetly watched training. It was another puzzle that needed solving, but she wouldn't raise it with Ahrin until she had an answer, not wanting to cause any more pain.

"Lucinda isn't one to be fooled," Lira said softly, worried that Ahrin would get too confident in the game she was playing with the Shadow-council.

Ahrin finished reading and straightened, turning to look at her. They were bare inches apart, the space between them suddenly turning into a magnetic force until Ahrin's mouth was sliding against hers. For a moment Lira forgot all about Underground and spying and searching for important information. Ahrin's hands reached for her, pulling her impossibly closer.

"I hate this pretending thing," Ahrin breathed as their kisses turned hungry.

"You and me both." Lira got her hands under Ahrin's shirt, slid them over her hips, around her back, silently counting the knobs of her spine.

Ahrin turned them, pressing Lira hard against the bookcase behind the desk, fingers sliding down to places that—

They broke apart at the faint clicking sound.

A small panel in the back of the bookcase right beside Lira's head slid to the side, revealing a dark space beyond.

"She's got a secret hidey hole," Ahrin said, glee lighting up her beautiful face.

Lira groaned in frustration, head thumping back against the shelf as Ahrin moved away, leaving her skin flushed and heart racing. "Brilliant discovery."

"What is this now?" Ahrin reached in and drew out a small scroll—the wax seal had already been broken—and carefully unrolled it to read.

"What does it say?" Lira asked impatiently when Ahrin went silent for a long while.

"More importantly, look at the signature on the bottom." Ahrin passed it to her, pointing.

Lira froze. "That's impossible."

"I'd agree, except for the lack of any other plausible explanation for how it got there." Ahrin took it back, began scanning the contents. "Why is the Magor-lier of the Mage Council writing to a Shadow-council member?"

Lira had seen Tarrick's personal signature before, only a couple of times, but enough to remember it. "Maybe she stole one of his letters?" A shiver of dread shot through her. "Do you think they've got a spy that close to him?" If they did, it was only a matter of time before Lira was discovered as the one who'd killed all the razak at DarkSkull.

"No." Ahrin shook her head. "It's clear this is a letter from him to Lucinda, and it's in Underground's code. There are no specifics... but it reads like the Magor-lier telling her that something he was supposed to do went as planned. To be exact, the code says here 'the first phase is complete'."

"What is that?"

"It doesn't say. It's dated three weeks ago." Ahrin's expression turned thoughtful. "It was roughly two weeks ago we overheard Timor and Lucinda on the cliffs. I bet she'd gotten this just before then. It would make sense of some of what she said that night." Silence ticked over as Ahrin kept reading. "He's confirming that phase one is complete, that the package is on its way, and that he'll commence what was agreed as the next step. That's it."

"What package?" Lira asked aloud, mystified. Tarrick Tylender couldn't possibly be working for Underground. "Could that be what she and Timor are out there doing now—receiving whatever this package is?"

"Maybe. I—"

"Wait." A thought suddenly occurred to Lira. "Why did they have you at Temari? Did it have something to do with this? Some kind of coup to take over the council, maybe?"

"No. My instructions weren't to take over Temari Hall, though I'm flattered you think me capable." A brief look of amusement crossed Ahrin's face, but it faded as quickly as it had come. "They had me watching Finn A'ndreas."

"Why?" Lira asked blankly.

"Lucinda wouldn't tell me. I just had to report everything I saw and heard him do. That doesn't matter now." Ahrin quickly re-rolled the parchment and put it back in its place. A quick hunting around found the button that closed it over again. "We need to get out of here before she gets back. If she knows we've seen this, we won't get off this island alive."

Lira shook her head, mind racing. "It's worse than that. Two weeks since we overheard them—she'll have written right back to him, asking what happened at DarkSkull."

Ahrin's expression hardened. "Does the Magor-lier know you were there?"

"Yes." Lira stilled, cold fingers closing around her chest. "And he knows I'm spying for the council."

Her eyes flashed. "They might be meeting with the messenger bringing his response now—maybe that's what's so important they went out to meet the ship. You have to leave now."

Lira nodded. "And I'll have to take Athira with me. The council needs to know about this. We have no way of knowing what comes after phase one, but we can be confident it's not good."

Ahrin was already shaking her head. "The council is headed by the Magor-lier, or have you forgotten? You can't trust them with this."

"I can trust Dawn A'ndreas. And Egalion and her husband," Lira said. "I'll go straight to them, and only them."

"If Tarrick Tylender has been compromised somehow, what makes you think those three haven't?" Ahrin's voice was calm, measured, but she kept glancing between Lira and the door. "They're all close friends."

"I know Dawn. She would never be compromised by Underground, and neither would Egalion or her husband, not after everything they went through with my grandfather." If nothing else, Lira trusted that. *But neither would Tarrick Tylender.* Lira pushed away the nagging voice of doubt at the back of her head. She just needed to get this news to Dawn. They'd help her figure out what it meant.

"Even if you're right, do you really think they'll believe you? The granddaughter of Shakar telling them the Magor-lier, a man they love and trust, is in league with Underground?" Ahrin's voice was sharp, cutting, making too much sense for Lira's comfort.

"Ahrin, stop!" Lira took a step back. "I understand where you're coming from, but you don't know them like I do. Dawn A'ndreas was the one who trusted me enough to send me to spy for the council. And this is why she did it, so I could bring her the information they need to bring the Shadowcouncil down."

A brief silence, then Ahrin nodded. "Fine. Then think about this. If you escape now, especially if you break out with Athira, there'll be no way of hiding it, and they'll assume someone helped you. I'll be under suspicion like everyone else here. It will take me time to regain their trust."

Lira hesitated, fear spiking deep at the thought of anything happening to Ahrin. She couldn't risk her life. She *wouldn't*. Not for the Mage Council, not for anyone or anything. "Okay. We'll figure something else out."

Ahrin gave a huff of irritation. "That's not what I meant. I can protect myself if you go, I'm just saying it will be a while before I can re-establish enough trust to start feeding information to you like we agreed." Ahrin hesitated. "You'll be completely done, Lira. There will be no way of talking yourself back in."

Lira smiled, stepping closer so she could lift a hand to Ahrin's cheek. "But I'll have you. I'll take what I've learned to Dawn, then you can help us fill in any gaps. Until they're all gone."

"And I walk off into the sunset with their money." Ahrin smiled slightly, but it was half-hearted.

"That's the plan, right?"

Ahrin nodded, letting out a sigh. "Now is probably a good time to move anyway, given Lucinda's not here. If you and Athira are gone by the time she gets back, she can't use that blasted magic of hers on you."

"Exactly."

Ahrin was still a long moment, clearly thinking everything through. Eventually she shifted. "All right. There's something you should have, just in case it all goes to hell." Ahrin rummaged in the waste basket beside the desk and pulled out a torn piece of parchment. With quick strokes of Lucinda's quill, she wrote down an address in Karonan and passed it to Lira. "I don't know if it will still be there, but once you're back in Karonan, go check it out. Be careful. They might have guards."

"Why—"

"No time for explanations. But it's something you might need." Ahrin straightened and moved around the desk, heading for the door. "Go now, get Athira and head out the way we first came in. Move as fast as you can across the island. They'll expect you to go for the boats here, but the fishing villages to the south have them too. I'll do what I can here to keep them from realising that's the direction you've gone in."

"Ahrin, we—"

"Once you've got a boat, head west. That's the shortest distance to the Shiven coastline. Don't stop and don't slow down, no matter how tired you get. They will come after you."

"Ahrin!" Lira slid her hand over Ahrin's before she could turn the doorknob, catching her gaze. "I don't want to leave you either."

She scowled, irritated. "Don't be sappy. You know I hate that."

"Don't risk yourself to cover my escape. Promise me. I can do this without you protecting me." Lira searched her face.

"Don't worry, I wouldn't want you burning down the world on my behalf," Ahrin murmured. "I'll be fine. I always am."

Lira grinned. "Remember the spot where I keep my change of clothes hidden for Underground meetings? Once you've won their trust back, leave a message for me there. I'll keep checking."

"I'll come as soon as I can." Ahrin's blue eyes held hers.

Lira leaned up to kiss her. Hard. "You'd better."

Ahrin held her close, her hands on Lira's hips almost bruising with how tightly they held on. Lira pressed her forehead into Ahrin's shoulder, took a deep breath.

Then she pulled away, opened the door and ran.

It felt like she was leaving her entire world behind.

CHAPTER 39

Moving swiftly as she could, Lira made it down to the tunnel holding the cells without anyone seeing her. To her credit, Athira didn't hesitate when Lira appeared, threw open the cell door, and told her they were leaving. She rolled off the blankets and joined Lira without a word.

They headed straight up the steps, Lira pausing at the top to check the tunnel beyond was empty before waving Athira after her.

"Why now?" Athira asked in an undertone.

"I just found out that Lucinda and one of her mages are away from the base, meeting someone."

"Your girlfriend tell you that?"

Lira fought not to roll her eyes. "It doesn't matter who told me. They're not here. Therefore it's the perfect time to go."

"It *does* matter. She's beautiful, your girl, but she's dangerous. How do you know she isn't manipulating you into an ambush?"

"Because I know. Do you want out or not?" Lira held her gaze. "This base is full of trained Shiven warriors, even if Lucinda and her paralysis magic are away, so if we're doing this, you need to be focused."

Athira didn't push it any further. "What's the plan?"

"Go out the back way, hike across the island, steal a fishing boat, row for all we're worth."

"Row? All the way to the Shiven coast?"

"Or sail. I'm not entirely sure how to sail a fishing boat, but it can't be too hard with magic."

Confusion flickered over Athira's face. "So you're not just getting me out. You're coming with me?"

"Yes."

Athira was silent for a moment as they reached a turn into another tunnel, and Lira peered around to make sure it was empty before continuing around it. Once they were walking again, the girl murmured, "Something else has happened. You look unsettled. I've never seen Spider look uneasy before. You're always in control, no matter what happens. And it makes no sense that you're coming with me if you're one of them."

Lira hesitated, then answered, "I found something unsettling in Lucinda's office."

"You were spying in her office?" Athira stopped in her tracks, the confusion in her expression slowly changing into realisation. "Wait. Why would you do that? What's really going on here? Have you been spying on *them*?"

"Not the time to have that discussion." Lira kept moving. "I promised I'd get you out and I'm holding to it. We can talk about everything else later."

"No, now is the time for discussion." Athira's arms crossed stubbornly over her chest.

Lira almost left her right there, had even taken a step away... but she stopped. She'd made a promise to herself that she would do right by Garan and Tarion and the others. Even if that risked her own survival. So she took a breath, spoke quickly and quietly. "Fine. Yes, you're right. I've been spying this whole time for the council because they asked me to."

Athira wavered, glancing back the way they'd come. "Then you shouldn't take me with you. I should stay."

Lira blinked in surprise. Athira wasn't even questioning the truth of Lira's claims. "What?"

"I've been paying attention while they do their little tests on me. I've got a lot I can tell the council about them, but not enough to figure out what's going on, not yet. If I stay, I can feed information to your girlfriend. I assume you're working together? And the more I can learn, the sooner Underground gets destroyed, yes?"

"If you stay, you risk those experiments killing you before the council can come for you. Or Lucinda killing you when she figures out what you're doing."

"I'm willing to take that risk."

Lira stared at her. "I don't understand."

"I know you don't, but I'm a mage, Lira. I can help bring Underground down. I can help stop them from doing this to anyone else. So I'll stay." She stood with her arms crossed, expression pale but determined.

"I can't linger here to argue the point with you, Athira."

"I know. Just go. Make sure you get out so that one day I can get out." Athira's haughty features lit up with a smile.

"I... you're a crazy person," Lira muttered, at a complete loss.

"Takes one to know one."

Lira's breath escaped in a half laugh. "That's fair. Stay, then, if that's what you want. I'll come back for you as soon as I can."

"Make sure you do."

Athira turned and ran before Lira could say anything else.

IT WAS A CLOUDY NIGHT OUTSIDE, keeping light to a minimum. Fortunately, just enough of the stars were visible that Lira could orient herself to the east.

She ran for an hour, eventually slowing to a quick walk when her lungs started burning and legs began trembling. Being out in the dark and open relaxed her, made her feel comfortable and in control again. Despite that, she cast frequent glances behind her, but the night remained quiet and still. There was no indication her escape had been discovered. All going well, nobody would realise she was gone until the next morning.

Unless Lucinda sent for Lira when she returned from whatever she was doing on that ship.

Moonlight lit the ocean in a silvery glow as she emerged from the forest and approached the southern shore of the island. Huts dotted the landscape, home to the fisherfolk that made their living here. She oriented towards the closest village, the area quiet and empty—the village fishermen wouldn't be up until much closer to dawn.

She was jogging along a dirt trail leading toward the village when her instincts began to prickle along the back of her neck. Coming to a halt, she stilled, senses straining.

Nothing *seemed* out of place, but there was something wrong. Her survival instinct knew it. Rotted bastards. They'd planned an ambush. But how had they known...?

It was her own fault. She should have known, should have thought it through better before leaving. Ahrin had been right to be cautious. At the very least, Lucinda likely had contingencies in place for if Lira or one of the others tried to leave while she was away from the island. At worst, she'd left the island tonight as a test. To see what Lira would do.

If it was a test, she'd failed miserably.

Still, she could salvage the situation. It didn't matter anymore that she'd blown her cover with Underground. She still had Ahrin, and now Athira too, inside. What mattered was getting her information to Dawn and Alyx Egalion. Lira tried to quell the rush of worry for Ahrin —what if Lucinda knew she'd helped Lira?—and tried to focus on what to do next.

Lira glanced around. It was dark, and she was far enough away from the village that she hadn't tripped the ambush yet. But if she lingered much longer, they'd know she'd sniffed them out. If Lucinda was there, she was done for. Lira couldn't counter her paralysing magic.

They would have seen her by now, so turning and going back the way she'd come wasn't an option—they'd simply chase her down. Playing hide and seek on an island Lucinda's warriors knew far better than she did wasn't a good recipe for survival.

She shrugged. She'd just have to spring the trap and fight her way out of it.

Lira started moving, trying to appear watchful but not alarmed, not wanting the ambushers to know she was prepared for them. The sense of danger increased, sending little thrills of excitement through her blood, as she hit the outskirts of the village and began cutting through the homes towards the jetty. The muscles along the back of her neck tightened to almost painful levels.

She spotted the ambush point before reaching it—the village centre, surrounded by buildings, but a nice open space within which to contain her. She made it easy for them, slowing her pace as she reached it, losing some of her apparent watchfulness while internally readying to fight.

They waited until she was halfway across the square before springing the trap. Darkly-clad figures emerged from the shadows where they'd been hiding, in perfect position to ensure she was surrounded.

She spared a brief thought for the villagers that owned these homes —had Underground done something to them? Surely not, or they would be revealing their presence on the island. Quickly, though, all her focus shifted to figuring out how to escape the trap.

None of those surrounding her were Hunters, a realisation that gave her brief pause, but which she instantly filed away for later consideration. There were six of them, all individuals she recognised as Lucinda's trained, experienced, mages.

Lucinda wasn't amongst them. A brief moment of relief flooded her, but it didn't last long. These weren't raw mages still learning their newly-acquired magic. These were older men and women, confident and armed.

One of them stepped forward. It was Timor, Lucinda's most senior mage, the one she trusted most.

"We don't have to fight," she said to him, shifting from foot to foot so she could explode into movement if necessary. "If you try and stop me, we might wake up a few villagers, and then people might start asking questions about who you are and what you're doing here."

"No, we don't have to fight." Timor stepped forward. "Come with us now, and you won't be harmed."

"Sure. Right up until Lucinda kills me." Lira shook her head. "No thanks."

"You can't beat all of us. You're not strong enough." Timor took a step forward. "We've been training you, remember, so we know what you can do. You can't even fight and use your new ability at the same time."

"You planning on defeating me with that terrifying mist of yours?" Lira threw out the taunt to buy time to think, glancing to the east, the direction she'd come from.

Timor caught the look and smiled. "She knows, Lira. What you've been doing on behalf of the Mage Council. She's known for quite some time. She knew you'd try and escape tonight and she sent us here to wait for you. She doesn't want your death, you know that already, you're too useful to us. But if you resist... well, our leader does enjoy causing pain." He cocked his head. "You don't need to be fully functional to be the symbol we need."

"Your leader?" Her eyes narrowed. "I thought you followed the Shadowcouncil, not Lucinda."

A brief silence.

Lira's mind raced. How long had Lucinda known she was a spy? Frustration surged in her. The woman was always one step ahead. Lira was a fool to think she'd convinced Lucinda of anything.

Ahrin.

She forced thoughts of her aside. Ahrin was a master at this game. She would be fine. But the worry closed over her anyway. Worry and fear. If anything happened to Ahrin... Lira closed her eyes, took a deep breath. Began drawing on her magic, readying it to save herself. And the more she drew on, the more invincible she felt.

Timor was wrong, she *was* going to survive this. No quarter. No mercy. Only survival. A lesson she'd learned well at the Darkhand's side.

"She should have come herself. She's the only one who can stop me," she said, meeting Timor's gaze, hers holding only a challenge. "You can all try, but you'll fail."

He smiled, part of his smile admiring, the rest resigned. At a single gesture from Timor, they closed on her together, staffs drawn. No magic yet—she wondered if it was true that Lucinda truly did want to keep her alive?

Whatever the reason, it was a calamitous mistake.

Lira allowed her building magic to explode. She shaped it as it burst from her, wrapping her fire around the nearest mage and pushing more power to bring it flaring to life. He screamed as violet-edged white flame lit him up. The screams tore through the night, stark and raw, and scraping against her senses. She deliberately pushed away her stomach-turning response to it.

The mage beside him faltered, her expression going wide with shock and horror, but before she could turn, Lira pushed out more magic and lit her up too. Her screams soon joined her companion's.

Lira could have used telekinesis instead. Could have disabled rather than killed.

But not six mages at once, not when she was unarmed and had nothing to combat their staffs. And she couldn't afford to give them time to use their magic on her.

Survival was her only priority. So she killed them as quickly as she could.

By the time she lit up the third mage—in a matter of seconds since the fight had started—her power was beginning to drain, and she could feel the strain on her body, magic burning through blood and muscle.

She let go of the magic momentarily, a fourth mage too close now for her to do anything but duck under his swinging staff, scrambling backwards before sending another burst of flame magic to light up his robes. He screamed as he burned.

Gasping, sweat pouring off her, Lira switched to telekinesis, robbing the fifth mage of his staff and sending it flying into the night sky. His hands moved. A second later the weapon stopped mid-air, his own telekinesis working against hers. Lira gasped with the effort, but poured more power into what she was doing.

Abruptly, before he could react, she switched direction, going *with* the flow of his magic and bringing the staff slamming into his head. He dropped soundlessly to the ground, mouth open in shock.

Then only Timor was left standing. He was backing away in fear now, all his calm assuredness of earlier gone.

361

"You didn't expect me to be so ruthless, did you?" She moved towards him, voice harsh, cold, rigid with the anger and determination sweeping through her. "That was a mistake. She does like to underestimate me, your leader."

There wasn't much magic left in her now, but adrenalin still fired through her blood, keeping her strong and alert. "I'm not going to give you a chance either, Timor."

His chest heaved, face white with terror. Desperation edged his voice when he bellowed, "Warriors! Attack now!"

With a click of her fingers she lit him up.

As he burned, her gaze ran over the bodies scattered around her. Mostly just piles of ash now. Her fire burned far hotter than normal flame.

She'd killed them all. Six mages in under a minute. And she hadn't hesitated, hadn't let the screams stop her, hadn't let the terror in Timor's voice make her merciful.

Some objective part of her wondered—was this what Shakar had thought as he'd murdered innocents? That he'd had to do it for his own survival? Was that how he'd justified it to himself?

These mages weren't innocent though. They were loyal to Underground. And they'd have killed her if she hadn't acted first.

Still—

Movement in the shadows around her snapped her from her spiralling thoughts. Shiven warriors closed in from the cordon position they must have been holding a distance away.

Lucinda had not intended Lira to leave alive.

That knowledge shuddering through her, Lira turned and ran for the jetty, ignoring weariness that was beginning to weigh down her body. The remains of her magic were rapidly draining away. They closed in on her quickly, too quickly, taller and fresher and faster.

Her chest burning, legs slowing, she forced herself along the jetty to the nearest fishing boat. She glanced over her shoulder, fingers untying mooring rope as Shiasta and his warriors came closer and closer. They reached the jetty, boots thumping on wood, swords drawn.

Lira got the rope unmoored, half-jumped, half-fell into the boat, and pushed away from the jetty. The closest Shiven leapt after her, but she used a touch of magic to jerk her boat sideways so that he landed with a splash in the water.

Shiasta snapped a crisp order and his team spread out, making for the other boats tied up nearby. Lira took a deep, shuddering breath, summoned every drop of magic she had left and sent her telekinesis ability roaring out of her. The other boats tied up at the jetty lurched hard, tearing their mooring ropes and surging into the water before her magic failed and they stopped, adrift.

Too far out for the Shiven to reach them, even if they swam.

She sagged in exhaustion, gave herself a moment, then forced herself up. It took almost a half hour to figure out how to raise the sail, and even once she did it was a clumsy job. But the night breeze caught it well enough, and she slumped in exhaustion at the tiller, steering west.

Once the boat was properly moving, she lasted only three breaths before the reality of what she'd just done crashed over her and she had to lunge to empty her heaving stomach over the side, retching until there was nothing left.

"Enough," she told herself aloud.

She stared dazedly at the ocean around her, hoping she was heading in the right direction. But it was a cloudy night and she couldn't see far across the dark expanse of water.

She was free of Underground.

Better, she had crucial information to foil whatever they were planning next, and the Darkhand was still inside the organisation willing to feed her information. She had done everything she'd set out to do for the Mage Council. It didn't matter that she'd had to kill her way through six mages. That she'd had to leave Ahrin behind.

But if Lucinda had known that Lira was spying for the council, then it was entirely possible she knew Ahrin was—

No. Lira cut that thought off. Ahrin was beyond careful.

All Lira had to do now was make it back to Temari Hall, and she would be safe.

CHAPTER 40

Two days passed. When the wind died off, Lira rowed clumsily until her palms bled and her arms burned with fatigue. Her steering was rough at best, though she kept to a westerly heading as much as she could.

Constantly she looked behind her for the pursuit she knew would be coming. All she saw each time was unending grey ocean.

The boat almost capsized twice on the second night when she reached a particularly rough patch of ocean, and the sail tore as she tried to reel it in. Lira wrapped her arms around the mast and held on for dear life until the swells lessened, the weather cleared, and the sea settled again.

By then she feared she might have blown so far south as to miss the southern tip of Shivasa. The night stars had been concealed by clouds, even if she had been able to do anything to steer during the storm. But she kept going anyway—there was little else she *could* do. A chest on the boat revealed a half-full flagon of stale water and dry rations, probably saving her life.

When her boat eventually washed up somewhere along the west coast of Shivasa, Lira merely put down the oars, slumped over in the boat, and slept.

. . .

IT WAS MORNING when she woke, dawn rays sliding over her face and waking her from a deep, exhausted sleep. Her skin was cracked and dry, her clothes filthy, her hair encrusted with salt.

She was bone-tired despite the rest, no doubt a lingering consequence of using so much magic escaping Shadowfall Island. She wished she could just curl up and go back to sleep.

But she'd made it.

All she had to do now was get to Karonan and Temari Hall, tell either Dawn or Egalion she had her own spy inside who could give them enough to bring down the group entirely and figure out what was going on with the Magor-lier.

And it would be done. She could finish at Temari Hall, take her trials, begin moving up the ranks of the mages. Gain a seat on the Mage Council. Be Magor-lier one day. Have their respect instead of their wariness. Their loyalty rather than their fear. The life she'd been building for herself ever since taking her first step out of Dirinan three years earlier. Everything that had been so complicated would become simple. Finally.

But she had to make it first. And Lucinda would have sent her warriors after Lira. She'd probably also sent word ahead to the mainland for Underground members to try and intercept her. It was bright daylight and her boat was too visible on the beach.

That realisation gave Lira enough strength to clamber wearily out of the boat, finish the final drops of water in the flagon, and begin walking inland.

AN HOUR INTO HER WALK, Lira came across a road. Her strides quickened despite her weariness, and she headed west along it, arriving at a bustling town not long before midday.

The town wasn't large, but it was sizeable enough that she didn't get too many strange looks as she entered it. She wandered the busy market in the centre of town until she'd pick-pocketed enough coin for new clothes, a room at an inn with a hot bath, and a large meal. Her thieving skills were a little rusty, but sound, and she had enough coin for all those things after an hour or so of working the crowd.

Once the meal and hot bath were dispensed with, she sank into the delightfully comfortable feather bed and slept for a couple of hours. This time when she woke she felt fresh and full of energy.

After dressing in her new clothes, she knelt to dig through the pile of ragged clothing she'd dropped on the floor before her earlier bath. The note Ahrin had written, an address in Karonan, was a little smeared, but had survived the journey.

Lira committed the address to memory, then stood and tossed the note into the fire. Intrigued as she was about what Underground were keeping at that location, she had more immediate priorities.

She was clear of pursuit for the moment—even if warriors from the island found her boat washed up on the shoreline, they would have no way of knowing which way she'd gone. Now she had to get herself to Temari and figure out the best way to approach Alyx Egalion when she got there... it was probably too much to hope for that Dawn would happen to be visiting.

First things first. Lira finished lacing her boots and left the inn.

A short time later, she'd spent a good chunk of her stolen coin on a carriage service heading for Karonan first thing the next morning. From there she further depleted her money paying for one of the fastest birds in the town's messenger's mews to carry a message to Temari Hall.

She addressed the message to Alyx Egalion, telling the councillor that Lira was on her way back, travelling via the southern road, and had urgent news. Her quill hovered over the final sentence—she didn't dare ask Egalion not to show the message to Tarrick Tylender, so she'd just have to hope he wasn't at Temari Hall. It was unlikely given he was permanently based in Carhall.

In the end she simply scrawled her name and sealed the note, lingering to watch as the handler attached it to the bird's leg before letting her fly.

Satisfied that she'd done all she could for the moment, Lira returned to the inn to enjoy a steaming lamb pie and tall glass of mead for dinner.

Lucinda had to be panicking over Lira's escape. The thought of the normally perfectly composed woman losing that iron control caused a smile to curl at Lira's mouth. There was nothing Lucinda could do now... everything she'd revealed to Lira on Shadowfall Island would soon be passed on to the Mage Council. Worse, her Darkhand had turned traitor and she didn't even know it.

The Shadowcouncil wouldn't live much longer.

Lira couldn't wait.

THE FIVE-DAY JOURNEY north was interminable, stuck inside a stuffy carriage with other travellers who looked askance at her non-Shiven features. A few times she was tempted to introduce herself as Shakar's heir, just to see the horror ripple over their faces, but held herself back.

She didn't want to play on that anymore. She didn't need to. She had won her place in the mage world—or at least she soon would. It was time to forget about her grandfather completely. He'd had enough of a hold over her life so far.

A few miles before reaching the southern causeway into Karonan, Lira hopped out of the carriage to walk the remaining distance. Old survival instincts warned that Lucinda would expect Lira to make for Temari Hall, and if the woman had managed to get a message off the island quickly enough, it was possible Underground members were waiting to intercept her.

Better to approach on foot, cautiously, where she could read the lay of the land before going into the city.

Stretching her legs after being in the cramped carriage so long was a pleasure, especially given the sunny morning. Farms spread out into the distance on either side of the main road, green and tilled, the warmth in the air presaging summer's approach.

Nothing about the quiet, peaceful morning tripped her instincts.

Her steps quickened at the thought of seeing Garan and Fari and the others. Would Tarion be back at Temari? Surely by now they'd figured out a way to manage his new... ability. She found herself looking forward to seeing them again. Talking to Fari about Ahrin, despite how crazy it all was. Seeing how Lorin was progressing in his training and whether his leg was getting stronger.

Maybe it was time to agree to forming that combat patrol.

But when she rounded a bend in the road to see the lake surrounding Karonan in the distance, some of the peace of the morning faded. The familiar pressure began to inexorably tighten in her chest. Doubts swirled through her. Since fleeing Shadowfall Island, she'd kept herself going by focusing on getting back to Temari, but now she was almost there, and fast approaching was the reality of trying to explain to Alyx Egalion what she'd learned. Her confidence wavered.

She was no doubt in for a long briefing session with Egalion, maybe Finn A'ndreas too. She had a lot to tell them, and she needed to make sure they used it.

If they believed her.

Lira winced, Ahrin's doubts—so far ignored in the interests of simply getting back—returned to plague her. A crazy-sounding claim that the Magor-lier was working with Underground wasn't going to be an easy thing for anyone to accept, let alone his closest friends. Especially when that claim came from Lira Astor.

More, she was going to have to convince them to uphold the deal she'd made with Ahrin—immunity and all money recovered from Underground in return for helping the council.

That was all right; Lira could understand their wariness. Maybe it might be smarter to talk to Tarion first if he was back at Temari. She could trust him. He could come with her to talk to his mother. Maybe even Garan too. They would help her.

And she had Ahrin, who should be able to dig up further proof for Lira to show them. Lira would just have to be patient and careful.

The thought of Ahrin helping her bring down Underground made Lira smile. She knew it would probably be a while before they saw each other, and that suspicion would fall on every member of Underground after Lira's escape. But Ahrin would worm her way back in, and then she would come to Lira.

The Darkhand was a survivor, and Lira trusted that more than anything else in the world.

They would succeed. Together. A smile flickered over her face. Maybe after all this was over, she'd be able to ask for a mage assignment wherever Ahrin decided to go. They would figure it out. Because after everything, after learning the truth, Lira had only one certainty in her life, and that was the knowledge that Ahrin was hers, and she was Ahrin's. Council mage, criminal, whatever Lira ended up doing, it didn't matter. She had no interest in a life that didn't include Ahrin Vensis.

The sight of the causeway ahead, backdropped by the walls of Karonan, drew Lira from her whimsical thoughts. She shook them off, straightened her shoulders. Right now she needed to focus. Dreaming of a fragile happiness could come later.

The causeway was busy with traffic moving in both directions, the lake unfrozen since the last time Lira had seen it, a deep green colour on such a still afternoon. There was nothing out of place, no indication that anyone was paying undue attention to her. No sign of Underground members waiting to intercept her.

Even so, Lira walked swiftly across the causeway, weaving between the carts, horses, and others on foot.

It wasn't until she was halfway across that she realised what all the traffic meant—the strikes and protests must be over. The general vibe was too calm, and too many heavily-laden wagons, carts, and merchants were travelling, for them still to be going on. It felt like a normal day for the city.

Had Underground called the protests off for some reason? Lira frowned. Maybe the council and Shiven authorities had successfully dealt with them in Lira's absence.

The gates stood open as always, but two blue-cloaked mages approached Lira as soon as she passed through them, clearly having been waiting for her. Egalion must have gotten her message and wanted an escort to ensure she was safe. But as Lira lifted a hand in greeting and headed over to meet them, movement in her peripheral vision had her turning on instinct.

Three Taliath had moved into the space behind her.

She froze, eyes narrowing. She didn't recognise any of them—they weren't from Temari Hall's usual guard detail. "What's going on?" she asked the mages.

"Apprentice Astor, we're here to escort you." One of the mages stepped forward. She was an older woman, of average height, her dark hair drawn back in a neat braid. She had an assured, competent air about her that instinctively set Lira at ease, even though her street instincts warned her not to relax.

"Who are you?" Lira asked, too aware of the Taliath at her back, the three mages arrayed in front of her, of what now felt more like an ambush than a greeting.

"I'm Warrior Jayn. This is Warrior Manser." She gestured to the second mage. He had an aloof expression, pale Shiven skin, and dark hair. "Will you come with us?"

Lira's gaze flicked between them, cataloguing. She didn't recognise those names, so she had no way to tell what their mage ability was. "Escort me where?"

"We can explain on the way. It's not safe to linger out here." Jayn gestured to a carriage waiting nearby. The Taliath behind Lira remained silent, but she could feel their watchful gazes on the back of her neck.

It didn't feel right. Without thinking, Lira began cataloguing potential escape routes. When she didn't move to follow them, Jayn took a step closer. "I can deploy a shield that will block anything you try and throw at us, and I've faced down worse than you in my time, Lira, so I don't recommend refusing to obey our instructions."

"I'll freeze you before you take a step." Manser added. "And I can freeze that fire of yours too."

Lira's breath stilled in her lungs, fear beginning to creep through her with icy tendrils.

They knew about her fire ability. Which meant Garan or one of the others had told the council about it. Danger thrilled through her so profoundly that for a moment she froze. Then she took a breath, allowing the rush of it to keep her relaxed, keep the fear at bay, using it rather than letting it use her. "I'm a mage apprentice, I'm not trying to hurt anyone." Lira glanced between them. "I was just on my way to Temari Hall with important information for Councillor Egalion."

"If you come with us, you can present that information," Jayn said, still calm. "Alyx will get it, I promise you."

Alyx. Lira quickly put the pieces together. These were older mages, around Egalion's age. And nobody called the most powerful mage in the world by her first name, not unless they were a close friend. Some instinct told Lira these two were known and trusted by Egalion. Which meant they'd been part of the fight against her grandfather.

In the end, it was that assessment that had Lira complying with their instructions, even though every instinct she had was telling her something was off. If they were trusted by Egalion, then Lira should trust them too. Maybe Egalion truly did just want to make sure Lira got to Temari safely after everything that had happened.

"All right, I'm coming." She lifted her hands in the air to show she was no threat and walked to the carriage, climbed up and stepped inside. Jayn closed the door behind Lira without getting in, and the carriage rocked as she then climbed up to sit by the driver. Manser followed suit. Lira craned her neck out the window to see the three Taliath mounting horses that had been tethered a short distance away.

Then the door on the other side of her carriage opened and a third mage climbed in. He looked to be the same age as the others, handsome, with blonde curls and a friendly smile.

"Where did you come from?" she asked suspiciously.

"Hello, Lira." The smile widened. His voice was like honey, smooth and warm and making her want to listen to it all day. "My name is Brynn."

"Hello," she said faintly, trying to maintain her suspicion and wariness but struggling for some strange reason.

"Here, are you thirsty?" He pulled a flask from inside his cloak and passed it to her. "You look like you're really thirsty. Have a drink."

She took the flask without even thinking about it, but then hesitated. Something wasn't right. Her instincts were screaming at her. But she couldn't quite grip them, hold on enough to pay attention to them. They were oddly distant. Like frantic knocking on a door too far away.

"You look really thirsty." Brynn spoke again, that voice drawing and holding her. All Lira's doubts faded as if they'd never been. "Have a drink, it will take the edge right off."

"Okay." She took a sip—it was water—then drank several mouthfuls. She *was* thirsty.

Under her, the carriage lurched into movement. Lira turned towards the window, frowning. The carriage was heading out through the gates onto the causeway rather than into the city in the direction of Temari Hall.

She spun back around in her seat to look at Brynn. "Where are we..." She swallowed, tried to shake away the sudden heaviness in her head. "Where... are..."

The mage gave her a genuinely apologetic look. "I'm sorry, Lira. But this was the only way to do it without anyone getting hurt."

Brynn took the flask from her as she slumped over on the seat of the carriage. The last thing she saw before her eyes slid inexorably closed was the look of fear on his face as he watched her pass out.

CHAPTER 41

The sharp clang of a steel door slamming shut jolted Lira awake.

Her eyes flew open and she rolled off the surface she was lying on, scrambling to her feet before her brain was even properly alert.

Her feet were bare. That was the first thing she noticed. The second was the loose blue pants and tunic she wore. And the dim light that came from somewhere behind her.

Then the bars of the cell she was in directly before her.

Her heart thudded, her throat turning dry. She spun, gaze taking in every inch of the space in which she found herself. A large, arched window letting in afternoon light filled much of the back wall. Thick bars were embedded in the window frame on the outside of the glass. The floor under her feet was cold, rough stone, and a narrow bed with a single blanket filled the left wall. A tiny desk, a chair, and a bucket for waste sat directly opposite.

Lira went straight to the window and stared out of it, eyes drinking in every detail as she tried to work out where she'd been taken. She saw roofs, streets, all packed in narrowly, becoming progressively less clean and well-off the further away they were, running all the way to high stone walls.

They weren't the city walls of Karonan though. They were too high. Too thick.

Her heart thudded as realisation clicked into place.

She must be in Carhall. The capital of Tregaya. Seat of the Tregayan king.

Headquarters of the Mage Council.

She'd been unconscious for days, more than a week, if they'd brought her this far. Fear slid through her belly—it could have been even longer. Why? Why would they take her away, hold her prisoner? It made no sense.

Her thoughts, still groggy from whatever drug they'd given her, careened through her head. They had to know about Tarrick, about Underground. Had Egalion not gotten her message? A chill slid through Lira at the thought that maybe it had been intercepted. But even so, why drug her and drag her to Carhall?

Something else was going on.

And underlying her fear and confusion was a simmering anger, at being drugged and taken somewhere against her will *again*, and this time by those she counted as allies. Those she was supposed to be able to trust. Her nails dug into the soft skin of her palms as she tried to stop the well of tears that wanted to fall.

The clanging sound came again—a door opening this time—and bootsteps approached, at least three or four pairs.

Wary, Lira moved away from the bars, fists clenching and unclenching at her sides. She reached for magic, found it there waiting for her, and was reassured. A tall man strode into sight, stepping straight up to the bars, displaying no fear or unease. Tall, broad-shouldered, Zandian. Assured power radiating from him. Shock flared and Lira took another instinctive step back.

It was Tarrick Tylender, Magor-lier of the Mage Council.

Dread began creeping in tiny, unerring tendrils all through her body, worming deeper and deeper into her bones as Lira began to wonder just how thoroughly everything had gone wrong.

"Magor-lier," she said calmly, burying her fear. She would be calm and respectful until she figured out exactly what was going on. "What am I doing here?"

He cocked his head, frowning a little. "It surprises you that a traitor to the council would be locked away?"

"A traitor to the..." Her words trailed off, and she forced away the spike of panic that wanted to consume her. "What are you talking about?"

"There's no need for denials, no matter how convincing. We know everything, Lira."

Lira had to fight down the sudden, overwhelming urge to flee, fight her way out, do whatever she needed to get free. Her glance flicked beyond Tarrick to the two Taliath standing protectively along the wall behind him. Another blue-cloaked mage hovered a short distance off. Lira's eyes widened when she recognised Dawn A'ndreas. The lord-mage looked upset, pale.

Was *Dawn* a part of this too? Lira glanced away from her, back to the Taliath, hands near the hilts of their magnificent swords. No doubt they'd have them drawn in a blink if necessary.

Fear thudded through her and she was hard pressed not to simply let her magic explode, blow her way out. Only a massive effort of will held it back. Logic helped force it down. Her flame might have the ability to harm a Taliath, but she would never come back from killing two Taliath in the eyes of the council.

"What is it that you think you know?" Lira's gaze swung back to Tarrick, still aiming for calm.

"That you joined Underground several years ago, back when you were in Dirinan. That you were already a member of the group when Lord-Mage A'ndreas approached you last year to request that you spy on them for us. That you've been working with them to bring down the Mage Council." Tarrick paused. "Should I go on?"

Lira looked at Dawn, then back at Tarrick, trying desperately to figure out what was going on. "None of that is true. I've been working *for* you, to take Underground down. To destroy them."

"Oh, Underground is most certainly destroyed." Satisfaction shone from Tarrick's dark eyes. "And now we have you, the final piece. It's finally all over. The last remnants of Shakar, gone forever."

What?

Lira swallowed, looked straight at Dawn. "What is he talking about?"

Dawn said nothing. Abruptly, Lira checked her mental shields, reinforced them, realising Dawn was probably trying to read her thoughts while Tarrick spoke.

"We arrested the Karonan cell leader two weeks ago, Greyson. He told us everything—every single detail of where the Underground cells were located, how many members each one had, their names." Tarrick's dark Zandian gaze held hers. "Most of his cell were killed trying to escape us. Few survived our searches, and those that did are secured away like you. Including him. It's interesting how much he knew about the group and its workings, yet you never reported any of it to the council, despite attending his meetings every week."

How was that possible? Greyson captured? He must have only just arrived back from his trip to visit Lucinda on Shadowfall...

Lira's thoughts raced, trying to figure it out. Despite the setback in DarkSkull, Underground had been in control, with strikes across multiple cities, a secret army of mages and Hunters training on Shadowfall, the Magor-lier in their pocket... Lira couldn't make sense of what was happening here. She looked at Dawn again. "Lucinda? The Shadowcouncil?"

"Lucinda was nothing more than a bit player." Tarrick shrugged. "We'll find her eventually. And the Shadowcouncil no longer has any teeth. They'll fade away into obscurity."

Dawn spoke for the first time then, sounding exhausted. "Lira, as good as that look of confusion is on your face, there's no point keeping up with the lies. We know everything."

Silence yawned between them as Lira tried to process what Tarrick had said while simultaneously working to figure out what to say to get herself out of this. She swallowed, thought back to when Dawn first spoke to her about Underground. "No, you don't know everything. I don't know who's been telling you all this, but... you read my mind when we first met. You know that I wasn't a member of Underground then. I only joined because *you* asked me to."

"But you can hide from me, can't you?"

"Only after you taught me how!" Lira said in exasperation. "Not back then. And you know better than anyone that mental shielding isn't completely infallible."

"No, you can do more than hide, you can make me see things in your thoughts that aren't true." Dawn was angry now, her mouth in a firm line, all the friendliness and warmth gone from her beautiful face. "That's how you convinced me."

"That's not true!" Lira shouted, then swore inwardly. She had to stay calm, rational, or they'd never believe her. But that was hard. The bitterness and frustration were rising in a tide, wanting to explode out of her. They weren't even listening to her.

"Greyson told us they gave you extra magical abilities. Abilities that you hid from us. I saw the truth in his thoughts. Is that a lie too?" Dawn asked.

Lira stilled. "I know Garan and the others saw my ability with fire, but that happened because they experimented on us at DarkSkull Hall when we were taken. I only hid it from you because I was worried about how you'd react because of who I am." Heavy despair climbed through her. Not this again. Not again. "Because of how *everyone* reacts when they learn who I am."

"But they didn't kidnap you. You were willing, weren't you, you *wanted* them to give you more abilities? And it's not just fire," Dawn pressed.

"Who told you that?" Lira demanded. "Greyson? I never chose to be kidnapped and tortured!"

Dawn shook her head. "Does it matter who told us? I can see the truth on your face. I don't even need to read your thoughts to see it. You wanted what they gave you."

Lira closed her eyes briefly, trying desperately to hold down her combined fury and terror. Losing control in front of these two would only make her situation worse, confirm their suspicions about her. "I am no traitor. I was experimented on just like the others. I didn't tell you because I know how wary you all are of me, even when you're pretending not to be. I wanted Underground gone after what they did to all of us and I feared you'd take me off the assignment if you knew. I wanted them destroyed. I still do. That is the truth."

"That's one version of it. You put my son and my nephew in significant danger, Lira." Dawn was back to sounding weary. Tarrick glanced between them, seemingly content to remain quiet. "More than once. They could easily have died. Not to mention Fari and Lorin."

"I *saved* Lorin's life," Lira snarled, all composure vanishing in the face of their accusations. "I risked my own life to do it. And I saved your precious nephew's life too when I burned all the razak on that roof. If I hadn't done that he'd have bled out and died."

"*Saving* their lives? Is that what you call arranging an attack on them in Alanan and then walking off to safety while they watched?" Tarrick asked mildly.

"Are they..." Lira's fury came to an abrupt halt. Had Ahrin been wrong? "They're not... are they okay?"

"That concern almost sounds genuine," he said. "You're certainly not a bad actor. I suppose that's how you carried on for so long without us realising."

"They *are* okay." Lira glanced between them, her thoughts catching up. "If you know about my fire it's because one of them told you." The sharp sting of betrayal hit her then.

"How we learned of it is none of your concern."

A thick silence fell. Wretchedness crept through Lira. For everything they had an answer, a twist on the truth. This had been planned for, prepared. Perfectly. And she'd played right into the trap by keeping secrets. If only she'd told them the truth all along.

Tarrick spoke softly. "Ahrin Vensis. Tell us about her, Lira."

Lira said nothing. Realisation sunk through her, far too slow in coming. They had her. Underground had clearly told them everything, only with a nice twist that put Lira in the frame for all of it. They'd gotten to the council before Lira could. Had taken her out before Lira could take *them* out.

She was no match for Lucinda. She'd known that and she'd been arrogant enough to go at her anyway, to think she could outmanoeuvre her.

Lira's mouth curled in a silent snarl. This wasn't the end. She refused to let it be the end.

"Is it a lie that you've known her since childhood? That you've been working with her since then?" Dawn asked, face drawn.

"I knew her in Dirinan, I told you that. I left to come to Temari Hall and didn't see her again until she showed up with Underground while we were at DarkSkull."

"You know she killed all the guards at Temari Hall that night, she killed Master Alias, too?" Dawn said, and Lira couldn't lie. "You knew all that and you never told us."

"You *knew* her in Dirinan." Tarrick sneered. "It was much more than a passing acquaintance, though, wasn't it? Was she already the Darkhand when you left? I'm assuming you planned your infiltration of Temari Hall together very carefully."

Lira said nothing. The fight had gone out of her at the realisation of how thoroughly she'd been outplayed. She needed a moment, space to figure a way out of this, but they weren't going to give it to her.

"You're close, aren't you?" Tarrick asked curiously, as if he didn't already know.

Lira swallowed, forced herself to look them both in the eye. "You're really choosing to believe Underground over me? A criminal organisation who has been trying to destroy you, who kidnapped your children? Who kidnapped me too, by the way."

"An organisation *you* worked for, Lira. You and Ahrin Vensis together," Tarrick said just as quietly.

Dawn stepped forward. "If what you say is true, then let me read your mind, see everything. Lower your shields to me."

Anger bubbled up in Lira then, hot and cleansing. It dispelled her fear, but it also made her reckless. "If you think I am letting you anywhere near my head right now, you are sorely mistaken, Lord-Mage. I don't trust you not to lie about what you see, not anymore."

"A traitor's answer," Tarrick said.

Lira gave them a scornful glance. "Two minutes ago you stood there and said you couldn't believe what you read in my thoughts because of my apparent ability to alter what you saw there. Now you say reading my thoughts will absolve me. Which is it?"

They shared a glance. Another silence fell.

"Your lies are starting to trip over each other," she said scathingly, directing this at Tarrick. "Do you truly think me guilty of being a traitor, or are you just keen to get rid of me for some reason?"

Nothing.

Lira's gaze shifted to Dawn. She couldn't manage to believe that Dawn had been drawn into whatever Tarrick was doing with Underground. She was not only the most powerful telepath alive, but a fundamentally good person. She didn't have the edge that Egalion or Caverlock had. She must genuinely think Lira was a traitor, which meant there was room to convince her otherwise.

But not while Tarrick was around.

"I'm not the traitor here." Lira stepped up to the bars, curling her hands around the metal, keeping her voice cool and confident as she stared at Tarrick. "I know you were writing to Underground, to Lucinda, Magor-lier. Planning something. I saw the letter myself. What was it?"

Tarrick didn't even blink, a little smile curling at his mouth. "You'll try anything to get yourself out of this, won't you?"

"You better believe it." She locked her gaze on his, the words coming out as a snarl. "How *dare* you lock me away in here. You're one of them, and you call *me* traitor."

They stared each other down. Lira allowed a hint of her magic out, enough that a violet flow lit up her hands where they were clenched around the bars, an implicit threat. She refused to look away.

Eventually Tarrick did. He glanced back at Dawn, then at Lira. "There's no point in talking to you any further, you're clearly not willing to admit to anything or help us hunt down what remains of the Shadowcouncil."

Her eyes narrowed. "Is that why you're here? To try and find out what I know before you kill me? Make sure I haven't told others your secrets?" She hesitated on her next words, knowing if she spoke them they would never cease hunting Ahrin, or leave her alive if she'd been caught... but Lira knew her, believed in her so fiercely. "Like Ahrin Vensis, perhaps?"

Tarrick flinched, and triumph flared in Lira's chest. She'd landed a hit. Whatever had happened, Ahrin was free. She couldn't stop that triumph from showing on her face. "Who do you think her ultimate loyalty is to, Magor-lier?"

Tarrick stepped away from the bars. "We're not here to kill you. But you have thrown your life away, Lira. I hope you enjoy the rest of it in prison."

All Lira's momentary triumph died, and cold began creeping through her. "I'm owed a trial in front of the council before you can lock me away forever."

"The evidence is overwhelming. They've already tried and convicted you." He glanced around. "This prison was constructed to hold mages, powerful ones, so I wouldn't recommend trying to escape. You won't succeed."

Tarrick turned on his heel and strode away before Lira could figure out a response to that—tried and convicted already, without a chance to speak for herself—but Dawn lingered, waiting for the Taliath to peel away and follow the Magor-lier.

Lira simply stared through the bars at the wall opposite, head hanging. She was done. There was no way out of this.

"I know what most people think of you, and why." Dawn's soft voice sounded. "I know it's unfair. I know it gave you few options if you wanted to survive."

"You know *nothing* about survival." Lira whipped her head up, the anger surging again, making the words come out in a snarl. "So don't you dare stand there and talk to me about it."

Matching anger filled Dawn's face then, the first time Lira had ever seen the woman look like that. It was terrifying. "I fought your grandfather. I fought him and his Shiven army for years. I lost friends I loved. I watched Cario Duneskal die on the floor in a pool of blood in front of me. I was there that night when the Darkmage brought the roof of DarkSkull down over Alyx's head, and it was only my voice in her mind that kept her focused, alive, using her draining magic long enough to save them all." Despite her anger, Dawn's voice was calm, steady, and all the more cutting for it. "I saw the hatred on his face. The anger. I saw his power, his arrogance."

Lira's hands curled more tightly around the bars, the bitter frustration so powerful it made her skin feel too tight. "And now you think I'm like him too. I've never even *met* him."

"But you look like him. You sound like him. You have the same arrogance, that same anger, on your face right now. The same ruthlessness. Do the reasons for it really matter, in the end?" Dawn's words hit like a hammer blow. "Even if the circumstances were out of your control, you've still ended up too much like him for me to trust you anymore."

Something cracked inside Lira, and she let out a gasping breath, her head hanging. "I tried. Despite all of it, I tried to help you. I did what you asked. I risked my life working with Underground. I wanted to be one of you... I trusted you to do the right thing when trusting was the hardest thing I've ever done after the life I've had." Hot, silent tears slid down her face. "And you do this to me."

A thick silence weighed.

"If only I could believe you," Dawn said. "But I don't. Goodbye, Lira."

"Is that what you want?" Lira screamed after her, anger scouring away the despair. "To back me into a corner until you turn me into him? Has that been what all this was for?"

Dawn stopped, turned, that sad look back on her face. "We all make our own choices. I can't force you to be anything you don't already want to be."

The door at the far end of the corridor clanged shut. Silence fell.

Lira sank to the ground, curled in a ball, scrubbed at the tears on her wet cheeks.

She'd lost. Underground had thoroughly outplayed and outwitted her. She faced the rest of her life in this cell.

Tarion, Garan, Fari, Lorin, they would believe her a traitor now too. Dawn had turned on her. The head of the mage order had a vested interest in keeping Lira locked up. Ahrin would come to meet her in Karonan and Lira would simply never show up. Lira had no way of getting a message to her.

She had nobody who would help her.

It was over. Her hopes were ashes.

Her thoughts shifted then. Maybe it had been wrong to spend her life running from who her grandfather had been. Maybe that had been her mistake all along.

At once, in the blink of an eye, the thread inside her snapped. The one that had held her tethered to Temari and the council and everything she'd wanted to be in an effort to erase him. The one that had strengthened because of Tarion and Garan and Fari and Lorin. The one that had made fitting herself inside that constricting box easier. The thread that had her seriously contemplating joining a combat patrol. The one that had allowed her to pretend a different Lira had never existed.

The real Lira.

The one who'd grown up on the streets of Dirinan and learned to love the danger and the thrill, especially when it had hidden that void inside her. The one who prioritised survival above all else. Who didn't care much about right or wrong, just about the rush of her magic and the strength it gave her.

The one who, she'd always known deep down, was too much like her grandfather.

The thread snapped, and Lira stopped pretending. She stopped pushing bits of herself away. And she closed her eyes at the flood of relief that swept through her as she came back to herself.

Then she scrubbed at her tears, sat up straight, and studied the four walls around her speculatively.

What would the Darkmage have done to get out of this?

To be continued

Consider a review?

'Your words are as important to an author as an author's words are to you'
Hello,

I'm really hoping you enjoyed this story. If you did (or even if not), I would be humbled if you would consider taking the time to leave an honest review on GoodReads and Amazon (it doesn't have to be long –

a few words or a single sentence is absolutely fine). Reviews are the lifeblood of any book, especially for indie authors like me. Not to mention a review can absolutely make my day!

Thank you so much for reading this book,

Lisa

Want to delve further into the world of *Heir to the Darkmage*? By signing up to Lisa's monthly newsletter, *The Dock City Chronicle, you'll get* exclusive access to advance cover reveals, book updates, and special content just for subscribers, including:

• An exclusive forward from the beginning of *Heir to the Darkmage*

• A short ebook with a collection of short stories from *The Mage Chronicles* universe;

• A pronunciation guide;

• Exclusive content from Lisa's other fantasy series;

Sign up for The Chronicle and enter the adventure...

If you haven't read Lisa's *Mage Chronicles* series yet, then you can read all about Alyx Egalion's war against Lira's grandfather - the Darkmage - by diving into *DarkSkull Hall* now!

ALSO BY LISA CASSIDY

The Mage Chronicles

DarkSkull Hall

Taliath

Darkmage

Heartfire

A Tale of Stars and Shadow

A Tale of Stars and Shadow

A Prince of Song and Shade

A King of Masks and Magic

A Duet of Sword and Song

Heir to the Darkmage

Heir to the Darkmage

Mark of the Huntress

ABOUT THE AUTHOR

Lisa is a self-published fantasy author by day and book nerd in every other spare moment she has. She's a self-confessed coffee snob (don't try coming near her with any of that instant coffee rubbish) but is willing to accept all other hot drink aficionados, even tea drinkers.

She lives in Australia's capital city, Canberra, and like all Australians, is pretty much in constant danger from highly poisonous spiders, crocodiles, sharks, and drop bears, to name a few. As you can see, she is also pro-Oxford comma.

A 2019 SPFBO finalist, and finalist for the 2020 ACT Writers Fiction award, Lisa is the author of the young adult fantasy series *The Mage Chronicles,* and epic fantasy series *A Tale of Stars and Shadow.* The first book in her latest series, *Heir to the Darkmage,* released in April 2021. She has also partnered up with One Girl, an Australian charity working to build a world where all girls have access to quality education. A world where all girls — no matter where they are born or how much money they have — enjoy the same rights and opportunities as boys. A percentage of all Lisa's royalties go to One Girl.

You can follow Lisa on Instagram and Facebook where she loves to interact with her readers. Lisa also has a Facebook group - The Writing Cave - where you can jump in and talk about anything and everything relating to her books (or any books really).

You can check out Lisa's website - lisacassidyauthor.com

Printed in Great Britain
by Amazon